Return to Quag Keep

Also by Andre Norton

Quag Keep
Three Hands for Scorpio
Beast Master's Planet

Also by Jean Rabe

The Finest Creation
The Finest Choice

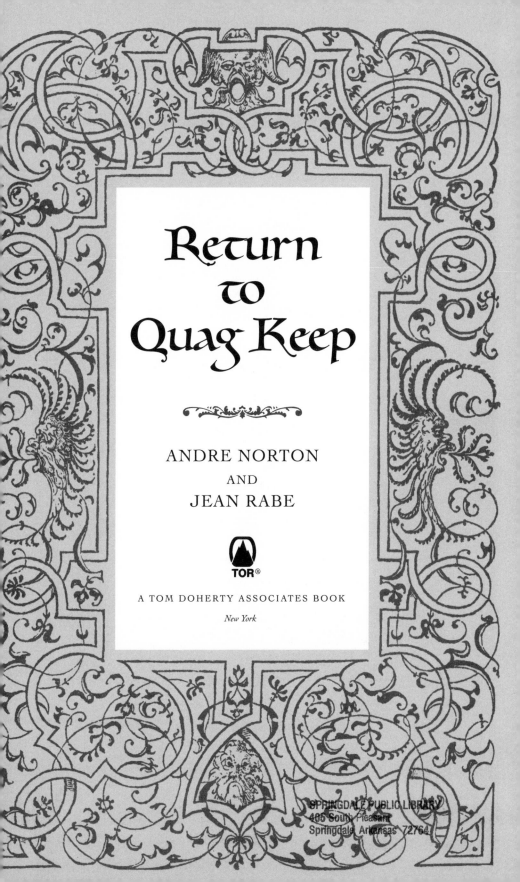

Return to Quag Keep

ANDRE NORTON

AND

JEAN RABE

TOR®

A TOM DOHERTY ASSOCIATES BOOK

New York

This is a work of fiction. All the characters and events portrayed in this novel are either fictitious or are used fictitiously.

RETURN TO QUAG KEEP

This book is printed on acid-free paper.

Edited by Brian Thomsen

A Tor Book
Published by Tom Doherty Associates, LLC
175 Fifth Avenue
New York, NY 10010

www.tor.com

Tor® is a registered trademark of Tom Doherty Associates, LLC.

Library of Congress Cataloging-in-Publication Data

Norton, Andre.
    Return to Quag Keep / Andre Norton and Jean Rabe. — 1st ed.
        p. cm.
    "A Tom Doherty Associates book."
    ISBN 0-765-31298-0 (acid-free paper)
    EAN 978-0-765-31298-3
    1. Adventure and adventurers — Fiction. 2. Quests (Expeditions) — Fiction. 3. Role playing — Fiction. I. Rabe, Jean. II. Title.
    PS3527.O632R48 2006
    813'.52 — dc22

                                                    2005016797

First Edition: January 2006

Printed in the United States of America

0 9 8 7 6 5 4 3 2 1

For Don and Linda

Acknowledgments

Thanks to—

Bill Fawcett and Jody Lynn Nye for brainstorming sessions over delightful dinners—your company and comments were even better than the strawberry lemonade.

Beth Vaughan, African Violet slayer, for your fine recommendations about some of the foliage that appears in this book.

Bruce Rabe, for your late-night dramatic readings of the original *Quag Keep*.

Brian Thomsen, my editor—your suggestions proved invaluable in coloring Milo, Naile, and the rest of the merry band.

Introduction

Quag Keep was the first novel based on D&D (Dungeons & Dragons). Andre approached me about her writing a book about the game, and I said sure. I think it was back in 1978. We were going to Gen Con South, and we took a side trip to visit with Andre in Maitland, Florida. I met her and all her kitty cats.

We went out into a little conservatory room. It had a tile floor and lots of windows, and that's where I ran a game. Andre said she wanted to see how an adventure went, and I was happy to oblige. The players? That was a long while back. I don't remember who of my children were with me on the trip, but I suspect it was probably Heidi and Luke. And Andre, of course.

The adventure was fairly typical. I think we did some outdoor exploring, and then I had them discover an entrance to an underground labyrinth. It was the usual mix of searching and fighting and finding treasure.

We rolled up a character for Andre so she would get the sense of how the game went. I made sure no characters were killed. I wanted everyone to have a good time.

Introduction

I still have *Quag Keep* somewhere around here. Like a piece of trea-
sure, it's lost in the thousands of books I have spread from attic to
basement. I was pleased, certainly, with the novel. It was a fun read.
It wasn't heavily D&D, but I thought it was an excellent adventure.
And I'm all for having a sequel. Books and gaming are a good mix.
Books require imagination, and that's what D&D is all about.

> *E. Gary Gygax*
> *Dungeons & Dragons Creator*

How did *Quag Keep* come about? Well, in a sense it started with Sputnik. Once there were very few book-length tales of fantasy fiction,
save those which appeared in the serials of pulp magazines. Jules
Verne and H. G. Wells scratched at the barriers, and the highly imag-
inative art that loomed gaudy-bright on drugstore magazine racks
caught the eyes of readers hungry for fantastic plots and unending
action.

When Sputnik went into orbit, science fiction and fantasy became
more respectable. Readers wanted books about wonders, about damsels
with streaming hair racing across a Martian landscape and seven-foot-
tall land-based lobsters. Gaming and game-related books became a part
of that.

Then miniatures came on the scene. There have always been those
who, from childhood on, craved miniatures — houses, ships, castles,
towns for the more ambitious and deep of pocket. Wood, wax, paper,
clay. And for the gamers, metal.

One of my very good memories is the coming of Dungeons &
Dragons. Unable to attend many of the conventions, I listened with
keen interest to tales of the games. Then, unexpectedly, I was granted
the honor of watching a master game run by the first and foremost in
the field. Gary Gygax himself! Further, I had the chance to view the
gems of Donald Woolheim, his prized military miniatures.

One could just imagine what would happen if someone, desiring to

Introduction

role-play, could become the mage or the swordswoman represented by the miniature one held in one's hand.

And what if you were trapped within a dragon-world in that form? Rules to be followed, yes. An element of luck, yes. Need the proper weapon for a duel? Toss and roll and see if the dice bring you what you need the most.

What if and if.

And what if a roll of the dice would make that all so?

Andre Norton

I learned to play the game in November of 1974. It was in the con suite of the first WindyCon in downtown Chicago. The game master was wearing a rug for a cape, a pair of red shorts, and a beanie-propeller hat. He'd just come from the costume competition . . . and I don't think he won. I remember that our little adventuring party was attacked by wild boars, and that I'd managed to slay one. I didn't understand the game much, but I had a good time. And I didn't have the opportunity to play again until nearly three years later, in college. I was hooked, and I found it much more fun than going to "happy hour" with many of the girls from the wing of my dorm.

I've played the game ever since—that's a lot of years—and I suspect I'll keep on playing. Through some of those years I worked for TSR, Inc., running their RPGA (Role-Playing Game Association) Network, writing and editing game material. I even penned novels in their Forgotten Realms and Dragonlance lines. When I was interviewed this fall for a Fort Wayne, Indiana, news program, the reporter asked if I considered myself a gaming geek. "Yeah," I told him. "And proud of it."

My husband—whom I met gaming—introduced me to *Quag Keep* and recently re-read it to me over the course of several evenings. I was honored when Andre invited me to work on the sequel. I run a game every three or four weeks, often trying out plot elements that

Introduction

find their way into my various novels, including this one. Oh . . . the things I've inflicted on my players' hapless characters.

I'm convinced that adventuring around the dining room table is good for stirring one's imagination. And it's good for the soul.

Jean Rabe

Return to Quag Keep

ONE

Separate Ways

Gulth poked his snout out of the alley, quickly looked down the street, then snarled and drew back into the shadows.

"The sun has set, priest, and there's no sign of them." He hissed and dug the ball of a clawed foot into the ground. "The light is leaving, and I should be leaving with it. I'll not wait much longer." Much softer: "I can't afford to."

The early autumn wind that whipped down the street and found its way into the alley was chill and carried with it the promise that the coming winter would be harsh. It spun the dust around Gulth's feet and nudged the debris discarded at the back door of an inn halfway down the alley, stirring up the scents of rotten cabbage, spoiled curds, and strong, bitter ale. He made a gagging sound when the wind gusted more strongly and uncomfortably settled all those scents on his tongue. He spat, which did nothing to help matters, and wrapped his cloak tightly about his bulky frame.

"I do not like this city, priest. Any city. The growing darkness makes this place slightly more palatable. But the dark only hides the sins and ugliness. It can do nothing about the stench of men and their greed and—"

"Patience, Gulth, I'm certain our friends will be here soon. Let's give them a little more time." The speaker stood near the inn's back door, illuminated by a lantern that hung from the jamb swinging slightly in the wind, causing the shadows to dance as if they were living things. He was a tall man, dressed in white, though the dust had turned his robes the color of sand and streaked his long face. "An hour, perhaps two if need be, Gulth, and—"

"One hour. Two. Three. Time. You know I don't have a lot of that, priest . . . Deav Dyne."

The man nodded. "I know, Gulth."

Gulth shuffled away from the street and toward the priest, the cloak billowing behind him flapping loudly. The lantern light showed him to be a lizardman, covered with coin-shaped scales so dense they looked like armor. Once, in the recent past, the scales had been as vibrant green as forest moss, supple and snake-smooth. Now they were drab and tinged with gray, cracked and curled in places like thick, chipped paint. He had the shape of a man, but his hands ended in talons, and his limbs were muscular, as was his tail, which twitched nervously, tracing and erasing patterns in the dirt. Though his shoulders were broad, they were hunched, a near-defeated posture.

"Deav Dyne, we've seen nothing of them since we came to this wretched, hell-darkened place a week past."

"And promptly went our separate ways."

"Yes."

"You've not seen them because you've kept to the alleys, Gulth."

"Necessary, priest, especially now. Look at me! I don't understand why they wanted to come here."

"It's the largest city around, Gulth, so it makes a certain amount of sense to—"

"Cities make no sense to me, priest . . . Deav Dyne. Too many people. All the crowds with their schemes, blood, filth." Again he dug at the ground with his foot. "Easy to get lost in a city this big."

Return to Quag Keep

Deav Dyne shrugged. "I found Yevele easily enough to arrange this meeting."

"But will they find us in this alley *easily enough?*"

"Patience," Deav Dyne repeated. "Patience, Gulth. They will come."

The lizardman cocked his head quizzically. "Will they? Or perhaps they've forgotten about this meeting and found some grand adventure to pursue instead. Certainly something more interesting than talking with us." A pause. "With me. You call them friends, Deav Dyne. I doubt any of them would call me that."

"Patience," Deav Dyne suggested once more. This time the word was a drawn out purr that made the lizardman relax slightly. "They'll come, Gulth, that I promise you."

The priest stepped away from the lantern's glare so he couldn't be seen by anyone who might open the inn's back door. Gulth stamped through the dirt to hunch at the mouth of the alley, occasionally poking his snout out for a quick glance at the street beyond. "Patience. Patience. Patience," he hissed.

Night had thoroughly claimed the city by the time three figures did close on the alley. The tallest was a woman, nearly six feet and clad in a worn leather surcoat. The crude and battered armor was too big for her frame, but not too bulky to conceal all of her curves. A long sword in a battered scabbard hung from her waist, and a sheathed dagger was strapped to her right leg. Thick auburn curls spilled out from beneath a bowl-like metal helmet and were harshly teased by the chill wind. She blinked when an errant strand whipped at her eyes.

"Yevele," the lizardman growled at her.

She stepped past him and into the alley, nodded, and offered him a weak smile. Her gaze met his for a brief moment, then wandered over him and narrowed when she picked through the shadows and noted his condition.

"Gulth, when we parted a week ago you did not look quite so . . ." Yevele left the thought unfinished.

Andre Norton and Jean Rabe

Behind her were two young men, one an elf in dark green leggings and a tunic, the clothes so soiled from the road and time that they looked nearly black. The elf glided gracefully and silently past Yevele and the lizardman and headed toward the inn's back door and Deav Dyne.

Her other companion was colorfully dressed in far better clothes. (Gulth suspected he stole the outfit.) His face and hands were as dirty as his fellows' and he looked every bit as tired. He adjusted a lute slung over his back and reached out, trying to shake Gulth's hand. Instead, the lizardman turned and withdrew farther down the alley to join the elf and the priest.

"We're late, I know," Yevele said as she followed the lizardman. "I offer no apology for that, Gulth, as we've been looking for work these past few days. That's why all of us came here, you know."

"And we finally have a line on something." This from the elf.

"Ingrge," the lizardman said in acknowledgment. The elf's name sounded like a growl. "Ingrge, you are—"

"Filthy. Aye, the lot of us are as dirty as any urchin. It hasn't rained in all these days, and our surroundings have been. . . . Well, let's just say a good downpour would make us all a little more presentable and less . . . pungent."

Gulth wrinkled his nose in agreement and looked over his shoulder at the colorfully dressed man. "Wymarc. Good of you to come, even if you are late."

The light spilling from the lantern confirmed Gulth's suspicion about the bard's clothes. The leggings were too short and tight, not something the man would have purchased by choice. And the tunic was tight across the shoulders, seams threatening to give at the next movement. Perhaps a tall boy's outfit that had been washed, hung out to dry, and subsequently "borrowed" by Wymarc. Gulth remembered that the bard's previous change of clothes fit better, but had more holes than fabric.

A door slammed somewhere out on the street, and two men laughed. One of them was stomping across a wooden walkway that connected the businesses in this part of the city and kept the citizens from slogging through mud when it rained. The other man shuffled, sounding as if he dragged one foot. From their irregular steps and loud guffaws, it was likely that they'd come from one of the many taverns in this neighborhood and were drunk. They paused at the end of the alley, staring at the gathering, then after a few moments they laughed again and moved along.

"Milo and Naile . . . where are they?" The lizardman directed this to the elf. "They were to meet us here, too."

"That line on employment I mentioned," Ingrge began. "They're following it as we speak. We've learned of a place where mercenaries are hired. Not just anyone would hire the lot of us, you know. Not so many of us all in one place. And working in a stables or smithy won't pay enough to suit us."

"And isn't at all challenging," Yevele added softly. "That kind of work is beneath us, Gulth."

"Boring, she means," Wymarc said. "And none of us know how to do it."

"Mercenaries," Gulth said. "So you're mercenaries now."

"*We're* mercenaries, Gulth. You're one of us." Ingrge pointed to a bracelet on the lizardman's wrist. It was copper, and gems of varying cuts and colors dangled from it. The lizardman's bracelet matched Ingrge's, matched Yevele's, matched. . . . They each had one. "We'll all be mercenaries, Gulth, if that's what it takes . . ."

". . . to get a decent amount of money," Yevele finished. "Our last coin was spent two days ago. We don't have a single copper for a kettle of soup, never mind coins for a room or decent boots or . . ." She tucked her chin into her neck and sniffed, wrinkling her nose. ". . . a hot bath, something new to wear." She met the lizardman's gaze again. "But you know all of that, Gulth. As Ingrge said, you're one of us. You're in the same sorry boat we're —"

"A worse boat, I'm afraid." All heads turned to the priest. "Gulth is dying, Yevele."

"Dying? I'll admit he looks rough, worsened a bit during this week. But you're a healer, can't you —"

"Yes, I'm a healer, but I haven't a clue to his malady. Nothing I've tried has worked. The shops I've visited, the other healers I've talked to, they have nothing to help. I spent all of my coins trying. I don't know what's—"

"It's this city," the lizardman cut in. "It's this man's hole. That's what's killing me. The crowds and noise and filth. So dry. Too cold. No rain and . . ." His voice trailed off to a rasping whisper, and he looked past the assembly and to the dark street beyond the alley, watching another drunken man stumble along. "I need to go home, Yevele, Ingrge. Wymarc, you understand."

The bard's face grew pale. "Dying? Gulth? You're truly dying?" Wymarc tentatively touched one of the lizardman's larger scales, scowling when an edge broke off. "You did not look so bad a week ago. We shouldn't have tugged you here with us. We should have left you out in the woods, came to get you after we'd found work and got some money, and—"

"Home," Yevele interrupted. "That would be Toledo, right Gulth? Ohio?"

The lizardman stared at a ceramic shard embedded in the alley dirt. "Used to be," he said after a moment. "In another lifetime. When we played the game around my Aunt Beth's dining room table. But that was before we were spirited away here for some unknown reason. We thought there was some grand purpose to our coming here. We fought our way across a desert, lived through meeting a dragon, made our way to Quag Keep. But we still have these bracelets, and we still have these forms. And we're still here. And if there was a grand purpose to it all, we missed finding it somewhere along the way."

"You can't give up," Yevele stressed. "We'll all get home. Somehow."

"But Toledo's not home now. And I'm no longer that person who played the game at Aunt Beth's."

The priest cleared his throat. "We're going south to the swamp, Yevele. His people . . . other lizardmen . . . are there. I pray they can help him. Maybe just being in the swamp will help. Gulth seems to think that's the key. Being away from the city. Being someplace warm and humid and thoroughly sodden."

"And you're going with him?" Yevele gave the priest a disapproving glare. "We need you, Deav Dyne."

"For what? Why do you possibly need me?"

The priest's question was met with silence and blank faces.

"None of us know how to get home . . . to our real homes," Deav Dyne finally said. "We're stuck in this place, as far as I'm concerned. You see that, too, Yevele. Otherwise, you wouldn't be looking for mercenary work. And so Gulth and I are simply marking time here."

She shook her head, her eyes flashing angrily. "We'll find a way home, Deav Dyne. Maybe find a clue in this very city. But first we need work so we can get some money and . . ."

"And those things will not help Gulth." Deav Dyne cupped her chin with his hands. "Yevele, you don't need me. None of you need me, at least not at the moment. But Gulth needs someone with him. So I'm going with him to the swamp. Then, when I know he's safe and healing, I'll come back here and look for you."

She shook off his hands and sucked in a deep breath. "We might not be here when you get back. Who knows where the fates will take us! Maybe home . . . to our real homes. Maybe we'll find the way home while you're trudging through the swamp."

"Maybe," the priest returned. His tone sounded skeptical. "I hope you do. And so, if you're not here when I return, I will look for my own way home. Or I will make my own way in this backward, medieval world." He nodded to Yevele, Ingrge, and Wymarc. "Tell Milo and Naile we wish them well. And we hope they find a good mercenary contract for the lot of you."

"Priest . . . Deav Dyne." Gulth gestured to the opposite end of the alley, where a road led to the edge of town. "Time to leave."

"Then there is no more to say, save good-bye." Yevele made a fist and brought it forward, meeting Gulth's fist. "Good luck to you." She turned and retraced her steps, the wind whipping her hair and fluttering her threadbare cloak. She waited at the end of the alley.

Ingrge took one of Gulth's hands in both of his and bowed. "May you find what you need in the swamp." To the priest: "And if the fates are kind, may we meet again in this city." Then he headed toward Yevele.

Wymarc was the last to leave. He shifted his weight from one foot to the other. "I don't like this, splitting the company. Not a good idea."

"Company?" Gulth raised what amounted to an eyebrow. "You accepted me, bard, but you never considered me a . . ."

". . . friend? Probably not," he admitted. "Prejudice is thick even in this world." He thrust his fingers into a narrow pocket and pulled out two copper coins. He cupped them close to his chest. "Look, be quiet about this, 'kay?" He pushed the coins at Deav Dyne, careful to keep his body turned so his fellows couldn't see the glint of the money. "It's all I have. Came with the outfit. Maybe you can buy something to eat along the way." Then Wymarc turned and bounded toward his companions. He looked once over his shoulder before he reached the end of the alley.

Gulth and Deav Dyne were already gone.

"Let's go tell Milo and Naile that we're down two," Wymarc said.

Yevele brushed the hair away from her eyes. "And let's hope they've found a way to earn some money or we'll be down more. Starved to death, all of us. We haven't a single coin for a loaf of stale bread."

TWO

Pain and Ale

The ale tasted faintly of oats and warmed Milo's throat. But it went down too quickly, and he found himself staring morosely at the bottom of an empty mug. Wrapping his long fingers around the base, he thumped it soundly against the table, a signal for a refill.

Though Milo thumped the mug again and again, the sound didn't carry far enough through the noise of the packed Golden Tankard. No empty seats tonight, as patrons crowded shoulder-to-shoulder at the bar. Conversations were a rough buzz . . . politics, wives, lame horses, the weather.

The patrons were a sampling of this part of the city. This tavern was one of the most popular, Milo had heard, because the music was good. But what music? he wondered. He and Naile had been here a while, and there was only the infernal roar of chatter, the clank of mugs and plates, and the occasional outburst of laughter.

There were common laborers, who likely came here before going home to their families, the grime of the day thick on their hands. Merchantmen, some of whom Milo recognized during his week in the city, clustered together and discussed business. A few men had the look of miners, with coal-dust smeared on their cheeks. A handful of what Milo would consider men of a higher class sat around the largest table, out of place and pointedly trying to avoid their lower-class neighbors. There were two priests in a corner, hunched over sheets of parchment and sharing a bottle of dark wine. Near them sat a black-robed man, at a table by himself. The cowl pulled over the man's head, Milo couldn't see his face, and thereby was instantly suspicious of him.

The only other patron who sat alone was dressed in clothes the shade of cold ashes, cloak pulled close despite the heat from the fireplace and the crowded bodies, hood partially concealing a narrow face. Milo couldn't see the patron's eyes, but from the nose down, the skin was pale and smooth, indicating a young man . . . or perhaps a woman. Milo couldn't tell who or what either of the cloaked strangers was looking at, though he suspected himself and Naile were as likely candidates as any.

"I'm still thirsty," Milo told his companion. "Can't get any service here." He thought about going to the bar, but he'd drunk the first two ales much too quickly—on an empty stomach, and he knew his feet would be unsteady. So he tried another tact, waving the mug in his sword-calloused fist. At the same time, he strained to pick through the conversations to hear a lanky skald who had just perched himself on a makeshift stage. "Ah, finally the music this place is known for." A pause: "Some music." The skald was singing something about castles and courtly dancers, neither of which was appealing to this crowd or to Milo.

Finally, Milo got the attention of one of the tavern wenches. The stout young woman nodded and awkwardly threaded her way toward him. She was saying something as she squeezed between the seats, but he couldn't hear her and didn't know if she was talking to him anyway.

The skald sensibly ended the first song and started another, this one louder and livelier, about a king who hunted goblins. The conversations hushed a bit, and a few of the patrons joined in, evidence the song was a well-known favorite.

"Hic. Now, *that's* music," Milo observed. He started tapping his foot.

And his axe dripped dark with the scaly ones' blood
The moon rose full and pearly, pearly white
King Kale dropped another goblin in the mud
And the moon gleamed high and pearly, pearly bright

Milo breathed deep, taking in the scents of the place. Ale, mostly, was thick in the air, heady and pleasant and helping to mask the odors of sweat-stained clothes and men who'd been too long without baths. Some kind of meat was roasting over a spit in the fireplace a few yards away. A cow, probably. His belly growled, and when the wench poured ale from a large jug, he ordered a slab of the meat—and some bread and cheese for good measure.

"And you, sir?" The woman turned to Milo's companion. "Aren't you hungry?" Her expression said: *you certainly look hungry.*

Naile Fangtooth didn't reply, but he held out his mug.

Though Milo Jagon was a big man, at six feet with wide shoulders and thickly muscled arms and legs, Naile dwarfed him. He was a head taller and was easily the largest man in the tavern. His neck was thick and short like the stump of a tree, the roots thick veins that disappeared into the neckline of his tunic. He was massive without being fat, with a barrel-like chest and a broad, haggard-looking face, eyes so black one could not discern his pupils. Naile was by no means handsome, which Milo bordered on, but he had a presence. And where Milo was dressed in a city man's jerkin and breeches, with hair reasonably short and combed, Naile looked as if he had been dragged in from some forest. He wore animal skins—wolf and fox pelts, boar, bear, and deer hide, all crudely stitched together into a tunic, trousers, and cloak. His metal helmet was pitted, and boar's tusks curved up and away from the sides, resembling horns. The hair that spilled out was a tangled red-brown mass that matched a bushy beard that hung to his waist.

Most of the patrons had taken turns ogling the mismatched pair, with most of them paying more attention to Naile and giving him as wide a berth as possible in the jammed confines. However, the server edged closer, thinking Naile hadn't heard her.

"Sir? Aren't you hungry? Shall I bring a plate for you, too?"

Naile shook his head and made a noise in his throat that sounded like the growl of a wild animal. His dark eyes, crinkled with faint lines at the edges, absorbed the light from the fireplace and, glowing, held her gaze for a moment.

"You must be thirsty," she said, unable to take her eyes from his face. But then he blinked, and she quickly filled his mug, then she moved to another table.

Milo watched her, wondering how long it would take her to bring the food. In this world there wasn't as much to choose from, no long menu to peruse while you sat in a comfortable padded chair and sipped from a glass of ice water. He'd taken so many things for granted back home; money in the pockets of his favorite jeans, his own apartment (though a small one-bedroom place, he didn't have to share it), a car (albeit a rusty one with too many miles which he'd been intending to replace), an impressive collection of comic books and science-fiction and fantasy paperbacks, and an assortment of movies and tapes. What he wouldn't do to be home right now. He made a fist and squeezed, his fingers digging so tight he could feel the pulse in them.

Taking another gulp of ale, he managed to shake off those thoughts and returned his attention to the serving wench, wondering if she might speed up her route to the beef. At the same time, he listened to the skald continue his song.

> The goblin army came with the first spring flood
> The moon shone full, this pearly, pearly night
> King Kale dropped their general in the mud
> And the moon spilled down on the bloody, bloody sight

"Over all of this noise . . . hic . . . I can hear your stomach rumble, Naile." Milo was still looking away from his companion, his eyes following the wench, who had a platter in her hand, piled with bread and cheese. She sliced a piece of meat off the spit, then worked her way back toward the pair, grabbing up another jug on her way. Milo glanced at the black-cloaked figure, swearing to himself that the cowl was aimed right at him. Was the ale making him suspicious of strangers? Then Milo looked for the patron in the ash-colored clothes. "Gone," he said. "Hic."

"I *am* hungry, Milo," Naile admitted. He drained his second mug. "But it's bad enough that I'm drinking this ale. It's not right, me drinking this."

When the server arrived, she dropped the platter in front of Milo. She filled Naile's mug without his asking, topped Milo's off and announced she would bring their bill soon.

"That jug," Milo said. "Leave it."

She nodded then hurried to a nearby table, where a quartet of obvious farmers were waving for her and singing along with the skald. Milo speared the piece of meat and began to devour it without pausing to inhale. Naile stared at the blood dripping from the slice and unconsciously licked his lips.

"It's not right, you eating that," Naile said when the last piece of meat was gone. But the words lacked conviction.

Milo shrugged and stuffed a hunk of cheese in his mouth. He followed it with a long pull from the mug of ale. The drink was beginning to mar his speech. "Wa's . . . what's . . . not right? We'll be good for—"

"It's not right," Naile continued. "We don't have a single coin to pay for the ale, let alone the meal you're shoveling down your throat. When that waitress—"

"*Waitress?* Wench," Milo corrected, finishing the mug, then pouring more, wagging a finger at Naile when he was finished. Milo's gesture was clumsy, and his red-rimmed eyes blinked when he tried to lock onto Naile's stare. "Don't you know that around shere . . . here . . . in this time and place, they're called serving wenches. Hic."

"Fine. When that serving girl comes back later and finds out we can't pay for what we've been drinking . . ."

"When that *wench* finds out . . ." Milo paused, hiccuped, and finished the cheese. He shook his head as if to clear it, and blinked furiously. "Well, I'm certain by then we'll have the coins to pray . . . pay." He took another gulp of the ale. "We'll have found us some work by the evening's bend . . . end. That guy we talked to, the one who told us about this tavern . . . he said they hire mercenaries shere. And he shaid he knew someone coming by tonight looking for folks."

"Wonder if they hire drunk ones?" Naile said too softly for Milo to hear.

"And the guy who shires us . . . hires us . . . you know he'll give us some sort of advance. We'll use that to pay for the ale and food. 'Sides, Naile, we had to order shomething. Can't come into a tavern and not order shomething. "It wouldn't be proper."

"But you ordered too much," Naile said. He finished his ale and poured the last bit from the pitcher. "And you're drinking far more than I am. And too quickly. You're drunk. Very." This he said loud enough for Milo to hear.

"Like you can talk. 'Sides, I got plenty to drink about." Milo wiped at the ale that had dribbled down his chin. "Stuck in this world, like shomething out of our game. Drawn here . . . these bracelets." He let his jangle against the table. It was the same as Naile's, copper links with gems of varying cuts and colors dangling from it. "Dice is what they are," he said of the gems. "Like in the game we splayed . . . played. 'Cept this isn't a game, this world. We could've been skilled . . . killed . . . by a dragon, Naile. A friggin' dragon! Fought swamp creatures. Found our way to Quag Keep. None of sit . . . none of it . . . took us home. So I don't know about you, but I got plenty to drink about."

Milo waved his hand, and the serving wench brushed by him, lingering for a moment and pressing against his back when she refilled his mug and set a full jug on the table, taking the empty one away. He stared at his reflection in the ale for a moment, then drained half the mug in one gulp. "But I shtink I am a little too drunk, my friend. And I shtink I better start sobering up if I want to get hired."

Naile raised a hairy eyebrow. "When's this guy coming by anyway? The one doing the . . . hiring?" Naile was having a little trouble with his words, too. They were coming out slightly slurred, and they were thick, to match the feel of his teeth. He picked up his mug, inspected it, then drained nearly all the contents in one gulp.

"What guy?" For a moment Milo seemed oblivious. "Oh. Yeah. The guy hiring mermermercen. . . ." He couldn't quite wrap his tongue around the word. "Hiring men. Don't know. But I wouldn't shtink it should be much longer. I shtink—"

The door flew open and three men staggered in. The dust from the streets was heavy on their clothes and faces, and their hair was streaked with gray, making them older than most of the patrons. The one in the lead looked to Milo and Naile's table and headed toward it, pointing and posturing at Naile as he stumbled along.

"S'gots me seat," he said. "Some big, hairy, ugly cuss's gots me seat."

Naile made a move to rise to accommodate the stranger, but Milo put a hand on his forearm. "We were here, first, Naile. And 'sides, they're drunk. And 'sides, they ain't the ones who're hiring mermermercen . . . men."

"We're drunk, too," Naile said. "At leash I am a little bit, and you are more than quite a bit."

Milo shrugged and ate a hunk of bread. He kept his voice to a whisper so he wouldn't interfere with the hushed conversations and the skald's lengthy ballad. "Y'know what I mish most about home?" He didn't wait for Naile to answer. "Going to the movies on Sunday afternoon. But not in the fall and winter, that's when I swatched football. Go Pack, y'know? Me being from Wisconsin. Rooting against Da Bears. But I mish movies and buttered popcorn the most." He paused and took another pull from the mug: "But this meat's not bad . . . whatever it is." After another moment: "Better than popcorn. I wonder what it is? This meat?"

"I miss Alfreeta," Naile said flatly. He watched the three men stop a few feet away, the one in the lead shaking his finger and mouthing *me seat.*

The skald raised his voice in an effort to be heard over a burst of laughter that had erupted at the bar over an obnoxious bad joke.

> The goblins fell hard in a spreading pool of blood
> The stars gleamed hot, so pearly, pearly white

Andre Norton and Jean Rabe

King Kale's axe came down with a thud
And the moonlight shone on the ugly, ugly fight

"S'my seat you gots," the lead man said.

Naile ignored him. "I miss her a lot, Milo. I miss Alfreeta."

Milo finished the mug, stuffed another piece of bread in his mouth, and poured some more from the pitcher. "Alfreeta? That little flying lizard of yours?"

Naile nodded and stared at the ale. "Ish not like a boy an' his dog, Milo. Ish more than that." He waved a hand in front of his face, as if to brush away a cobweb, then he drank some more.

"S'my seat you gots." The lead man spoke louder and poked Naile in the shoulder.

"Quiet, all of you," a nearby patron snapped. "I want to hear the end of the song."

"I really do miss her, Milo, my little Alfreeta. She disappeared right before we came into this town. She was handy in a fight." He took another drink from his mug and turned so his back was to the trio. "She wash . . . was . . . my friend. And did I tell you she wash handy in a fight? Must've wanted to be with her own kind. Jush flitted away, she did. Jush flitted away."

"I had a dog once," Milo offered. "One of them little schnittzle-wiener fellas." He frowned at the memory. "I was a kid. Got hit by a car, the dog. And my folks didn't let me get another one." His eyes filled with tears and he made a sniffling sound. "Now why'd you make me go and shtink about that dog?"

"Alfreeta's more than a dog, I tell you again," Naile said. "And she was handy in a fight. Hey, maybe we should let them three sit here. The skinny one looks upset. Did I tell you she was handy in a fight?"

"S'my seat, I say. S'my seat."

Milo sternly shook his head. "We was here firsht."

The trio moved around to the other side of the table, the lead man standing in front of Naile now. He bent over and belched in Naile's face. "I said, ugly man, that you's gots me seat. And if you don't give me that seat—"

Return to Quag Keep

Before Naile could reply or the man could finish the threat, the tavern door banged open again, and a portly gentleman strode in. He was dressed in a fine brocade tunic that hung to his knees. A heavy, burgundy wool cloak trimmed in rabbit fur swirled around his booted feet. He looked of money, as did the younger and significantly smaller man at his side, and they drew the attention of nearly every patron. The room quieted.

> King Kale's axe came down with a thud
> And the moonlight shone on the bloody, bloody fight

"That's got to be the man doing the shiring," Milo said. He blinked to clear his foggy vision. "Lesh go talk to him."

Milo pushed away from the table and shakily stood, Naile doing the same and accidentally knocking the man over who was shaking his finger.

"First you takes me seat, and then you hits me. Hits me! He hits me!"

His two grizzly companions helped him up, at the same time shouting that Naile had started a fight.

Naile took a step back and spread his hands in a peaceful gesture, and he tried to apologize. But his tongue was thick from the ale, his head woozy from drinking on a long-empty stomach.

> King Kale's axe came down with a thud
> And the moonlight shone on the ugly, ugly fight

And suddenly there was so much noise in the tavern that Naile couldn't be heard no matter how loud he talked. There were the sounds of glass breaking and something heavy hitting the floor. There was the sound of knuckles breaking, when one of the three men punched Naile squarely in the chest. There were moans—from that man and from others who were suddenly being pummeled by people they'd been dining with. Unintelligible shouts filled the air—a shriek from one of the serving wenches; Milo thumping his empty mug on top of a stranger's head; that same stranger jabbing a fork into Milo's stomach and cheering when Milo doubled over; the skald yelling out the lines to his song, then suddenly stopping in mid-word and howling.

Naile glanced to the makeshift stage and saw the skald holding his broken jaw, blood spilling down from his broken nose.

Pandemonium ruled.

A chair was splintered against Naile's broad back.

"I felt that," Naile growled. A bench was leveled against the back of his legs—this bringing him to his knees and coaxing a snarl of pain from his lips. The grizzled trio surrounded Naile and begin pounding on him with fists, mugs they'd acquired from somewhere, and a platter that shattered against his helmet.

Naile retaliated, though he tried at first to pull his punches. One swing took down the man in front of him, the one who'd wagged his finger so vehemently. Another took down one of the man's companions. A head-butt sent the last to the tavern floor.

At the same time, Milo was flailing away at a pair of miners, who were using chair legs as clubs. Milo reached a hand to his side, intending to pull his sword. But then he remembered he'd had to "check" it at the door.

"The door! The guy doing the shiring . . . hiring," Milo cried. He turned and searched for the portly merchant through the press of swinging, battering, ramming, pummeling, pounding fists and legs. Everything was a blur of color, splashed red from blood flying in arcs from shattered noses, cut lips, and worse. There was a small cloud of black, the mysterious cloaked man, making his way toward the door. The aristocrats were trying to leave as well.

"The guy doing the shiring!" Milo called again.

But there was no sign of the merchant and the younger man with him—the pair he was certain was hiring mercenaries. There was only the press of fighting bodies. Milo gagged on the scents of spilled ale, sweat, and blood. He was jostled by bodies shoving against bodies, people pressing closer, jabbed by elbows. He hit back, swinging now at anyone, accidentally connecting with Naile's arm when the big man got too close.

"Shorry."

Naile seemed not to notice. He was punching everyone who came within reach of his fists, too. "Milo . . . Milo!"

"What?"

"Milo, the door! Lesh . . . let's . . . get out of here!"

"Thash . . . thash . . . that's . . . one way to avoid paying a bill with coins we don't have." Milo threw all his efforts into parting the bodies in front of him.

Naile simply picked up those blocking his way and tossed them.

The pair staggered and fought their way to the door.

"Hear something?" Naile called.

"Yeah, thish fight," Milo returned.

"And a whishle . . . whistle."

"Yeah, Naile, it's coming from outside."

THREE

Picking Up Some Pieces

Yevele had taken the lead, Wymarc walking directly behind her and pushing to keep up with her quick, long strides. Ingrge was back nearly a city block, keeping close to the edges of buildings. It wasn't that the elf disliked the company of the other two, or that he couldn't match their pace—he could have passed them by if he so chose, and with very little effort. He was just overly cautious. Ingrge preferred either to scout ahead for danger, or—as was the case this night—trail back and keep to the shadows to make sure no one was following.

Deep down, the elf knew his tactics were unnecessary in this city, as no one knew them here or cared about their comings and goings. But skulking was a practice Ingrge hadn't been able to shake since coming to this "backward, medieval world," as Deav Dyne had called it. The elf figured it was better to be unduly deliberate than to be dead.

Ingrge studied the other people he saw out this evening. Nearly all of them were walking to or from taverns—drinking and gambling being the main time-passers in this neighborhood. Only a few people seemed to have other destinations, these being to rented rooms on the second floors of the various businesses that lined the street. Most of the people in this part of the city would be considered "commoners," Ingrge decided, with passable clothes, likely a few copper coins in their pockets, and reasonably clean hands and faces. The elf had learned early on that the cleaner a person was, and the better he smelled, the richer he tended to be. At the moment, he considered himself and his companions squarely in the lower class.

They were all humans out this night. During the mornings and afternoons of the past week, Ingrge had noted a scattering of elves, dwarves, and gnomes—larger cities seemed to attract a variety of races. But in the evenings, those folk kept to themselves and stayed in the city's "foreign district," leaving the streets to the predominant population. Ingrge smiled thinly—in another time and place he'd been human, too, a disc jockey at an oldies country western station, playing Loretta Lynn and Willie Nelson late into the night.

"Whiskey River," he said, recalling the "handle" he used in place of his real name—James Ritchie. The sadness of fond recollections passed across his narrow, angular face, and he felt a pang in his stomach, an ache not for food, but for home. "James Ritchie, lastly of Daytona Beach. Forty-two steps to the sand from my back door. Fifty-seven to the ocean. What I wouldn't give for a swim right now."

The buildings he passed were adequately kept up, a mix of one- and two-story weathered structures that were made of logs and sawed planks, mudded and nailed together and decorated with shutters, trim, and with painted window boxes that held the dried remains of the past summer's flowers. The buildings were neither large, nor impressive, nor were they particularly well made, Ingrge noted. The ones in the merchant's district and the wealthier part of the city were more impressive, many of them made of stone with scalloped slate roofs. Ingrge, Yevele, and Wymarc had spent little time in those quarters, as in their current dress and with their current lack of funds, they were woefully out of place.

So Ingrge told himself that this section of the city suited them better anyway, and that the people—though they dressed plainly and in drab tones—were actually more colorful here. The sounds of this neighborhood were certainly more interesting, and concentrating on them helped him shake off his thoughts of Florida. His keen elven ears picked up Wymarc trying to talk to Yevele, who at the moment was saying nothing.

"Yevele, do you think Deav Dyne's right? That we may well be stuck here?" Wymarc shook his head and let out an exasperated sigh. "Some part of me always thought it would be great fun to live in this time, in a place like this. High fantasy, dragons and damsels and dungeons. But that part didn't know how dangerous this would be. And how . . . broke . . . we'd be here. How truly rotten living conditions would be. The filth and stink. Do you think we're stuck?"

Yevele made a noncommittal grunt.

"All of us played the game, you know. Not all together, though. None of us from the same city, none of us knowing each other before we came here. But it was something about the game that brought us." The bard jangled his gem-dice bracelet for effect. "I know it was those special figures my game master got that last night. So fine, they were. Who knew that . . ."

"I don't know if we'll be stuck here," Yevele finally said. "I don't know if we'll be here for a day, for a year, for the rest of our lives. I don't know. And you know that I don't know. So stop prattling about it."

"Where are you from?"

She didn't answer him.

"You never told us. I'm from North Carolina, High Point. Originally from Chapel Hill. Name was Lloyd back there." Wymarc sounded wistful. "Lloyd Collins. I was an actuary. *Am* an actuary. Had a wife . . . *have* a wife, two boys, girl from a previous marriage, a big gray cat. My wife played the game sometimes, too. But she wasn't there the night we had the new miniatures. She took the kids to the carnival. Lucky for her. It's all still a little fuzzy, like a dream, and—"

"You've told me this before."

"Yeah, I know. But where are you from? You never told us. We didn't get our memories back until we were at that keep."

"Quag Keep."

"Yep, and to think I didn't know who I really was until then. To think I believed that I was this bard named Wymarc."

"You are a bard named Wymarc. Here anyway."

"Yes, Yevele, but—"

She stopped for a moment, and Wymarc nearly slammed into her. She turned and looked over her shoulder. "Canberra," she said. "If it's that important to you. Susan Spencer. A curator at the war museum there."

"Canberra?"

"Australia. Where I'm from."

"Oh. You don't have an accent like you're from Australia."

The air hissed out from between her clenched teeth. "And you don't have an accent like you're an American, a twang like I figure someone would have from North Carolina. We sound like the people here." She paused: "Because we *are* people here." Yevele started walking again.

"And I bet you wouldn't be upset if we were stuck here," Wymarc said. The words were whispered, but Ingrge managed to hear them. "I think you like it here, Susan Spencer. War museum, huh? No wonder you're good with weapons."

"I handled the World War I exhibits, Gallipoli, the Royal Flying Corps."

"Oh. Hey, *Mad Max* was filmed in . . ."

Susan glared, obviously not a Mel Gibson fan. Much softer: "You didn't leave a family behind, did you, Susan? Bet you didn't leave anybody."

Ingrge mused that Yevele still hadn't revealed much about herself, perhaps wanting to retain some secrets. He heard the sharp intake of her breath as she picked up her pace. Then the elf heard music coming from above and behind him, dissonant and unrhythmic, as if someone was just learning to play an instrument. A woman's soft laughter was spilling out a nearby window; this Ingrge found considerably more pleasing. He tried to imagine what the woman might look like, and what she was finding amusing.

Return to Quag Keep

Suddenly the angry tromp of heavy boots and a door slamming drew the elf's attention. He stepped away from the side of a building and toward the middle of the street so he could better see who was making the noise. For an instant he thought it might be Naile, as the man had some size to him. The man was stomping down a wooden walkway on the opposite side of the street, swinging his arms and muttering about a ruined evening. When the man stepped under a lantern, the elf saw it wasn't Naile after all, it was a shorter and thinner fellow, and one who had the slight stagger of being drunk. The man glanced across the street at Yevele and Wymarc, glanced at the elf, then clumsily ducked into the next tavern he came to. Conversations buzzed out the door of the place.

A handful of minutes later, Yevele and Wymarc stepped into a tavern, too. This one was a little farther down the street and called the Golden Tankard. Ingrge studied the street outside briefly, wondered at the lack of raucous noise coming from the Tankard, and then after a few more moments joined his companions inside.

It looked like a war had been fought in the one-room tavern. Broken tables, benches, and chairs; smashed mugs and plates; spilled dinners; pools of ale and blood—all of it littered the floor. A stout serving girl was on her hands and knees, picking up shards of pottery and tossing them in a metal pail, cursing with every gesture. Another girl was inspecting broken chair legs, and putting pieces beyond repair in the fireplace. A third was sweeping up around the bar, behind which stood a balding man who was wiping blood off his careworn face.

Yevele walked to the center of the room, the hard soles of her boots crunching pieces of plates into the floor. The stout girl scowled at her, but said nothing. Yevele turned slowly, taking everything in, then she locked eyes with the barkeep.

"What . . ."

". . . happened here?" He set a bloody towel on the bar and shook his head. "What do you think happened here, woman? A fight. The likes of which I haven't seen since . . . well, the likes of which I've never seen. And in my place." He slammed his hand down hard on the bar. "My place!"

Yevele set her fists against her hips. Her eyes flashed a mix of ire and exasperation. "We were to meet two men here tonight."

He slapped his hand on the bar again before she could continue. "There were plenty of men here tonight. And all of them ended up fighting."

The woman sorting through the chair legs cleared her throat. "Except the few lucky ones who scampered out the door before things got real bad."

"Got real bad, real fast." This from the girl on the floor.

"Ruined my place," the barkeep added. "Just ruined it."

"Awwww, you'll be open again tomorrow night," said the girl sorting chair legs. "Most folks'll just have to stand is all. Have to get you a new singer. One without a broken jaw and busted ribs."

"Ruined my place."

"The two men we intended to meet," Yevele persisted.

"I know where they are." This came from the tavern entrance.

Yevele, Wymarc, and Ingrge spun to see a man standing just inside the doorway. He was dressed all in black, and the fire that crackled and lanterns that burned around the room only made his clothes seemed darker, as if they were absorbing all the light that touched them.

Ingrge dropped his hand to a dagger sheathed at his side, fingers wrapping around the pommel, but not tugging it free. "I'd like to see who we're talking to," the elf said.

The figure nodded. "Fair enough." Thin, elegant hands edged out from the ends of the impossibly black sleeves, reached up and pushed back a hood.

Wymarc gasped at the sight, but Yevele and Ingrge managed to keep their faces as stoic as masks.

The man had a moon-shaped face and large, dark green eyes that were set under a heavy brow that shadowed them. His nose was hawkish, his lips overly thin and tinged blue. His most striking feature was his shaved head, which was tattooed with a myriad of colorful sigils and runes. The designs spread down the sides of his neck and disappeared into the black tunic that hung on his thin frame. A few small ones were on the backs of his hands.

He swept into the room, impossibly black cloak billowing around him, and he stopped directly in front of Ingrge.

"Unusual to see an elf in this part of the city at night. I wonder what brings one of your kind—"

"Our friends," Yevele interrupted. "You claim to know the whereabouts of the two men we seek."

"And just who are you?" Wymarc cut in.

"Fisk Lockwood," the black-garbed man quickly returned with a slight bow. "I am a humble priest of Glothorio the Coin Gatherer."

"And how does a humble priest know who we look for?" Ingrge asked.

"Two men, as you mentioned," the bald man said. "Both impressive-looking scoundrels. one civilized, the other wild and with a long beard."

"Milo and Naile," Wymarc supplied with a nod.

"Them two!" This came from the barkeep. "They're what started the fight. That one with the beard, the regulars said he was the one that threw the first punch!"

The bald priest looked to Yevele now.

"So, Fisk Lockwood, where are they, our friends?" she asked. Her eyes glimmered with impatience.

"That information is going to cost you," he returned.

The barkeep shuffled over. "Cost them two ruffians, as well. Like I said, they started the fight. They ruined my place. And they're going to have to pay for all the damages."

FOUR

Pain and Jail

Milo groaned, the mournful sound echoed by Naile, who lay curled against him.

"Where are we?" Milo tried to sit up. Instead, he managed to roll over and bump painfully into the wall. He grabbed his aching head, searched through the shadows, and decided the surroundings were too awful to look at. Closing his eyes, he groaned again.

"We're in jail," Naile answered loudly, adding to the pain thumping above Milo's eyes. "We're in hell. Truly no place could be worse than this. Can't sleep, all the noise, the stench, and that double-damned torch in the hall doesn't ever go out. Hell. Don't you remember getting tossed in here?"

"Don't want to remember. Just want my head to stop pounding. Hell, huh?" Milo wasn't going to argue that notion. Some part of him thought he'd went straight there that night he picked up the enchanted miniature and was spirited away from the game and sent to . . . to . . . here.

Wherever this medieval realm was. There were none of the amenities civilization should have.

No running water.

He swallowed hard, finding his tongue swollen and his throat parched, the inside of his mouth tasting like spiced ale, a taste he now loathed.

So thirsty.

He craved something so simple and beautiful as water running — when you turned the tap, cupping your hands under it, splashing your face, taking a steaming bubble bath and wrapping a big beach towel around your waist as you shuffled to the bedroom to get dressed.

Cold water, hot water.

Clean, wonderful water.

So very, very much he'd taken for granted . . . and all of that had been taken from him. That small one-bedroom apartment where he kept all his stuff and retreated to every night — that was heaven. And this was hell all right, Milo decided. Whatever had he done to deserve this?

He'd been no saint, certainly, but he'd done nothing to hurt anyone or anything, never stolen or . . . and at the tavern he'd broken bones and ruined furniture, and all because he didn't want Naile to give up his seat. His other self — *his real self* — wouldn't have punched someone, wouldn't have even been in such a place and wouldn't have gulped down so much of the now-horrid-tasting ale. His other self might have led a boring life in comparison to this, but he wanted to be that man again — not as strong as his Milo-self, not as handsome, but better, happy, and for the most part satisfied — driving the rusted car to the cineplex.

He wanted the blessed, simple, incredible life. The seats were theater-style there, so you could see the screen unobstructed. They rocked a little, and the backs were just high enough so you could tip your head up or down without hurting your neck. The place was run-down just a bit, but in better repair than absolutely anything he'd seen in this world, the gum-covered, soda-covered floor that pulled at the soles of his tennis shoes more sanitary than any stretch of ground he'd walked across in this city. It was a good life he had in Wisconsin, and he was missing it with a passion he hadn't known himself capable of. Milo felt tears forming at the corners of his eyes, so fiercely he was longing for his old self . . . his *real* life. He brushed the tears away with the back of his hand. Could it be possible this was all some nightmare, and that he really was back in Wisconsin? His body anyway. Had he been in a car accident, hooked up to tubes in a hospital? Was he dreaming all of this?

Please, God, let me be dreaming, he prayed.

Naile had been talking, but Milo missed some of it. He focused through the pounding in his temples and decided no dream would feel this real.

"If Alfreeta was here, she'd get us out of this." Naile struggled to sit up, crossed his legs and let his back slam against a cold stone wall. Under them, the floor was likewise stone, but it was coated with a grime of grease so thick it felt as if they sprawled on a soggy carpet. No stools nor beds, they were forced to sit in the muck. Naile judged the cell was roughly five feet square, with a ceiling that stretched up only a little more than that. Naile knew that neither he nor Milo could stand upright in it.

Shadows were everywhere, the faint light that filtered in through a half-barred door kept them at bay only in the center of the room. The light helped make it hell, Naile explained . . . not letting you see everything, but forcing you to see just enough. "And not letting it get dark enough to sleep, not that you'd want to sleep here."

The place stank—of the two men who had been too long without a bath and a change of clothes; of urine and worse; of rats, living and dead; and of fuzzy clumps near the door that Naile suspected were meals the former occupants, and the rats, had passed over. There were no windows to the outside, so no fresh air wafted in. The only openings were the spaces between the iron bars on the door. The faint, oily scent of fat-soaked torches drifted in—plainly thickened with the stench seeping out of other similar cells and from their inhabitants.

Naile's stomach churned from all the horrid odors, and from too much ale he'd drank on an empty stomach. Last night? Was it last night he and Milo had been pulled from the Golden Tankard by the city watch? Or was this still the same night? No outside window, he couldn't see the sky to guess.

His head pounded fiercely, and he ached from hunger—neither of those things would help him mark the passage of time. He did not at all feel rested.

"Any idea. . . ."

". . . what time it is?" Milo finished for him. "Not a clue. Ugh, but this place stinks. I've never smelled anything so awful. So utterly disgusting and awful." He made a gagging sound and pushed himself up on his elbows. "Ugh, what's on the floor?"

"I don't want to know," Naile returned. "And you don't want to know, either."

Milo sat against the opposite wall, bent over with his head resting on his hands. "I feel . . . awful. Just awful."

"It was the ale."

"And the fight." Milo's words were muffled in his hands. "We should have beat them, you know. All of them. We were stronger and bigger."

"There were too many of them."

"Still . . . all you had to do was—"

"I'd thought about it," Naile said. "But then I heard the whistle, and the city watch came. Thought about fighting the watch, too, but only for a moment."

"There were a lot of them, the city watch. If I remember right."

"And they had swords. We had to leave ours at the door of the tavern." Naile paused. "I wonder if we'll get them back?"

Milo let out a clipped laugh. "I wonder if we'll get out of here. I don't suppose they have lawyers here. Or due process. Bail." Another laugh. "Bail. Now that's a sorry thought. We didn't have any coins to pay our way at the Golden Tankard. Wonder how we'll pay our way out of this?"

Naile growled.

"Don't worry, Naile, we will get out of this. We have to."

Milo stood and let out a sharp cry when his head cracked against the ceiling. He promptly sat down again. "Now this is torture. Sticking us in this stink box. Can't stand up. Can't hardly breathe. Don't know what time it is, how long we've been here." He looked to the small window. "Hey! Anybody out there! Yoooo hooooooo!"

"Shaddup! Some of us 're trying to sleep!"

"Yeah, Shaddup! Shaddup! Shaddup!"

"Still night, I guess," Milo dropped his voice to a whisper. "Is it the same night? Wonder how many others they grabbed in from the Tankard?"

"Does it matter?"

Milo peered through the shadows and studied Naile. The big man was a mass of tangled hair, cuts, and bruises. His right eye looked swollen shut. "You okay, Naile?"

"Does it matter?"

"We're going to get out of here," Milo repeated.

Naile leaned forward and gave him a cynical look.

"I figure Yevele is looking for us. We told her to meet us at the Tankard. So she'll eventually find us here and bail us out."

"With what?"

Milo was silent for several minutes.

Sounds crept into the cell from the hallway beyond. At least two men were snoring. There was a steady drip of something, rhythmic and annoying. A chittering signaled rats prowling just beyond the cell, and scratching showed they were trying to get inside. After a few moments they gave up and their chittering faded.

"Maybe they do have lawyers somewhere in this city. And maybe we won't have to pay for one. They had lawyers a long time ago. Shakespeare mentioned them. Medieval people weren't so backward, you know. And, yes, I know this isn't a real medieval place. Not a historical one, but—"

Naile growled louder.

"What?"

"Milo, I *am* a lawyer."

Milo sputtered in surprise.

"You? A lawyer?"

"In Brooklyn. Maxwell Stein, Max to my friends. Graduated law school two years back, Harvard no less, and got a job with a good firm in Brooklyn."

"A lawyer."

"Specialize in copyright laws, infringements. That sort of stuff."

"A lawyer. From Brooklyn. You don't sound like you're from New York."

"Well, you don't sound like you're from Wisconsin." When Naile said Wisconsin, it came out "Wis-kaaaaahn-sen," the nasally way he'd heard a tourist from Milwaukee say it once.

"A lawyer."

"Well, copyright law isn't going to help us here. Besides, I don't know anything about the local laws. What's legal and illegal. What they can and can't do with prisoners." He made a huffing sound and tugged at a clump of something in his beard. "No idea what we're charged with. But I'd guess destruction of property at the very least."

"A lawyer, playing the game."

"Learned to play in college. Still played on the weekends with a couple of clerks from the firm. I was always the fighter. Always. Had no desire to dig through the books and figure out how the wizard spells worked, the duration, effects, stuff like that. Did enough reading with my work."

Milo slapped his leg. "I never would have figured you for a lawyer."

"Yeah, well how about you? What did you do before you picked up one of those enchanted miniatures and ended up here? I picked up one that looked just like this." Naile pointed to himself, then he jangled the bracelet for emphasis. "What did you do?"

Milo glared at him.

"Well, what did you do?" Naile prodded. "Other than eat buttered popcorn at the cineplex and root for the Packers?"

Milo stood again, this time careful to hunch over so he didn't hit the low ceiling. He shuffled to the small window and looked out, then he tested the door. "It's none of your business what I did, Naile."

"But I told you I was a lawyer."

"That was your choice to spill your guts." He set his legs shoulder-distance apart, crouched, and bunched his muscles. The door budged, but only a little. "I don't care what any of us did before we landed here. Our past is just that—past. Besides, who knows if we'll ever get back home. Right now I only care about getting out of this hell-hole." He strained again, then let the breath hiss out between his teeth. "I'll tell you what, Naile. I'll tell you what I *didn't* do before I got here. I didn't drink. Not like I did at that tavern. I didn't drink myself stupid. Never, ever. And I didn't get into fistfights, and I didn't ever spend a day in jail. I just . . . I don't know . . . I just let myself get depressed last night. I just gave in and drank and drank and ate and figured what's the difference. I figured we were going to get some work and would be able to pay for everything we ate at the tavern, and then get out of this town. Get some money, new clothes. Lord, a bath! Use some of the money to spread around . . . maybe get a clue to find our way home. Find out if we can get home." He paused. "Back to Wis-kaaaahn-sen."

"Door won't give," Naile said after a moment. "I tried it while you were . . . sleeping."

"Maybe together then."

Naile grudgingly got up, crouching to avoid the ceiling. He rubbed the palms of his hands on his tunic, scowling to note that very little of the filth from the floor came off. He set his shoulder to the door, and Milo did the same. Together they strained against it. The wood gave a little, the splinters biting into the men's arms.

"If we do manage to get this door down," Naile said as he continued to press. "What then?"

Milo eased back from the door, and Naile waited.

"We get it down, we get out of here," Milo said simply.

"We don't know if we're underground, in the belly of some lord's castle. We don't know if there are guards, and if there are guards . . . how many and how are they armed. We don't know what will happen if we get caught again. Maybe they hang prisoners who try to escape. We don't—"

"You think too much like a lawyer, Naile. I need you to think like a burly berserker, not Perry Mason. We're heroes now. In this world, we're bold men with . . ."

Naile shook his head, his wild mane of hair whipping at Milo. "We're not heroes, Milo. Maybe in the game we played, we were heroes. Sitting around a table, rolling dice and writing notes on scraps of paper, righting some great imaginary wrong and rescuing the princess. But here . . . well, heroes don't get drunk in taverns on ale they can't pay for. They don't break the arms of strangers in a brawl. And they don't end up in a foul, stinking cell waiting for . . . waiting for what? For Yevele to come bail us out with money she doesn't have?"

It was Milo's turn to growl. "All right. So we're not heroes." He scratched at his head. "We're adventurers then."

Naile nodded. "I'll settle for that."

They set their shoulders against the door again, and Milo made a gagging sound when he realized he stepped in one of the fuzzy clumps.

"On the count of three," Milo said, after he scraped the muck off his boot. "Ready? And one . . . two—"

"Visitors!" called a voice from down the hall. "Visitors!"

"Shaddup," someone from another cell shouted. "Trying to sleep. Shaddup!"

Milo and Naile stepped back from the door as boot heels click-clacked against the stone floor. Three or four men walking, someone stopping in front of their cell and looking in through the small window. From the narrowed eyes, the pair guessed it was a guard.

"Got visitors for you two," the guard announced. "So you step back a little more. That's it. Back."

Milo was the first to comply. Naile followed after he offered the guard a sneer.

The guard worked the bolt, and then rammed his side against the door to set it back properly on its hinges. Naile and Milo had been close to knocking it free. The guard finally yanked it open, and more light spilled into the small cell.

"Their fine's pretty steep," the guard announced to someone be-hind him. His eyes sparkled merrily now. "A big sack of coins. They're in here for breaking up a tavern. Put more than one man out, they did. A lot of damage to bodies and furniture. The owner wanted their heads lopped off. But they didn't kill anyone, so all we could do was lock 'em up for a year or two."

Milo swallowed hard at that last comment.

"Of course, you can have 'em if you pay the fine."

"Already paid, my good fellow." The voice was unfamiliar, cer-tainly not belonging to Yevele, Wymarc, Deav Dyne, or Ingrge. It had none of the sibilant hiss of Gulth's voice. "Here is the lord's letter to release them." There was the sound of paper unfolding and folding and being stuffed into a pocket. "So let's see what I've bought."

The man who stepped into the cell's doorway filled the frame and blotted out the torchlight.

FIVE

Ludlow Jade

The man who filled the doorway took a step back as the guard brought a torch to hold into the room. The light was so the man could see the two prisoners he'd just arranged bail for. But the light also served to reveal the man.

He was portly and dressed in a heavy brocade tunic that hung to just above his knees. It was green, set off with shiny burgundy thread embroidered to resemble oak leaves, and it was trimmed around the collar, sleeves, and hem with scalloped strips of matching green silk. His leggings were a shade darker green, the hue of wet elm leaves, and they disappeared into calf-high black leather boots that were so reflective they had to be new. He had a thin woolen cloak, the burgundy of the leaves, trimmed in rabbit fur and hanging precisely to the top of his boots. His hat was of the same burgundy material, big and floppy and slouching over his left eye. Despite the damp and the cold, sweat leaked out from his hatband and ran down the right side of his face and neck.

His face was smooth, cherubic like a child's, unlined and unmarred. But Milo and Naile could tell he was not a young man. Rings of fat hung from his dimpled chin and made it impossible to button the collar of his tunic. The hair that poked out from beneath his hat, and the thick, carefully trimmed eyebrow that could be seen was a wiry salt-and-pepper mix. So at the same time the man looked child-like and distinguished . . . and from the cut and fabric of his clothes considerably well-to-do.

His hands were large, the fingers thick and stubby and adorned with gold rings, some of them set with rubies and emeralds. The nails were manicured, and the skin smooth and the color of ripening peaches. He smelled subtly of musk, difficult to notice with all the offensive odors that permeated the place.

"Yes, those are the two," he pronounced. Even his voice sounded rich, deep and melodious and echoing off the back wall of the small cell. "Just as they were described to me. Big, strong men."

"I was told it took a dozen guards to lay the hairy one down and tie him. A dozen more to get both of them in here," the guard said.

"Yes, strong men. I think they'll do nicely."

"I want to see." This voice was thinner, but it had the same musical quality belonging to the portly man. This speaker was a study in contrasts. He was easily half the other's age, thin and almost emaciated looking the way his cheekbones, knees, and elbows protruded. He wore no hat, his hair a black curly mass that spilled onto his narrow shoulders. There were similarities between the two, as the young man was dressed in a tunic of like style, though the brocade fabric was a deep blue rather than a green, and the boots were made of the same black leather, though they rose to just above his ankles.

"Father, they reek," the young man continued, his nose wriggling. "They're filthy, and they're — "

The portly man cleared his throat, the sound commanding silence. "They'll clean up well enough."

"Excuse me?" Milo set his balled fists against his waist. He stood hunched over, but his head grazed the ceiling. "Who are you, and what does 'they'll do nicely' mean?"

The portly man beamed, and in that instant Naile and Milo recognized him. He was the merchant who came into the Golden Tankard right before the fight broke out.

"I am Ludlow Jade," he said. "And this is my son Zechial. I've just hired the two of you as guards for my wagons. The caravan is leaving within the hour, so you'd best hurry and get yourselves cleaned up. I'll not have you looking . . ." He drew his lips forward until they looked puckered. ". . . or smelling like that while you're in my employ."

Naile bristled and stepped in front of Milo. "Your employ?" It was true they were looking for work, and now it seemed like work had found them. But Naile had wanted the work to be his idea. "How much does this work pay?"

Ludlow Jade threw back his head and laughed, the sound loud and bouncing off the stone and drawing calls and jeers from the prisoners in other cells. He held his stomach and continued to laugh, then he finally came up for air.

"Pay? Why, the wage is your freedom. I paid your fine, which was rather exorbitant. Almost too exorbitant, but I was looking for muscle. And so now you're indebted to me."

Milo came closer to the man, careful not to get next to the torch and risk setting his hair on fire. "I thank you for bailing us out . . . Ludlow Jade. But not getting coins for work, that isn't sitting right. We need money. And we don't know enough about this work you're *hiring* us for, where it's going to take us, how long it's going to be for. We have things to do and. . . ."

Ludlow Jade laughed again, this time deeply. There was a mix of amusement and a threat in it. "As I said, your wage is your freedom. You can work for me, to work off that debt, or you can rot in this wretched cell for a year or two, and I'll go to the lord and get my coins returned. The latter might not be such a bad idea, as I could use the gold for other things. But it's your choice. Just choose quickly, the caravan is leaving soon."

Naile brushed past Milo, raising his arm to move the torch and force the guard back. "Pleased to meet you, Mr. Jade," Naile said. "I'm happy to be in your employ. If you've a place for me to . . . clean up. . . ."

"There's a bathhouse down the street," the merchant said. "I've made arrangements for you to clean up there."

Milo waited a moment, then followed Naile. He scrutinized the merchant. "You mentioned guarding your wagons."

Ludlow Jade beamed again and nodded.

"Our weapons—"

"Are with my other guards. I made arrangements. Now, about the bathhouse."

Naile could have passed for another man. He was clean-shaven, his square-set jaw feeling cold without the thick beard covering it. His hair was shorter, too, cut to just below his shoulders and tied at the back of his neck with a leather thong. His furs and skins were gone, as was his pitted helmet. In their place he wore gray woolen trousers belted at the waist with a green sash that matched the color of his wool cap. The dark gray tunic they'd given him was so short it served as a shirt, and this he tucked into the trousers. He wore a green vest over this, too tight to button, and a green wool cloak that dropped to the back of his knees. His boots were the ones he'd been wearing, though they'd been cleaned. One of the merchant's servants had tried to fit Naile with new black leather boots, but none were large enough. Naile's two hand axes had been cleaned and oiled and were hanging on a new weapon's belt. His bone sword was gone, someone having stolen it from the Tankard.

"Acceptable," Naile pronounced everything. However, it was clear by the gleam in his eyes that it was more than that.

Milo, too, looked different. His dark hair had been cut short, grazing the back of his corded neck and the tops of his ears. His gray woolen trousers matched Naile's, as did his cloak—evidence they were wearing a uniform of sorts. But Milo had a chainmail shirt instead of a tunic, the links shimmering in the mid-morning sun. It was expensive armor, from the look of it, and it felt heavy. Milo knew it would take some getting used to.

Return to Quag Keep

The two were led by Ludlow's son, Zechial, out the city gates and to a collection of large wagons.

"Need to leave word for Yevele," Milo said. "Have to find a way to do that."

"That won't be necessary," Naile answered. He tapped Milo on the shoulder and pointed to the largest wagon. Yevele was standing next to it, in a uniform similar to theirs. She, too, wore a chainmail shirt, but it looked like she'd been poured into it, the armor fitting that well. "Looks much better on her."

Ingrge was there, too, though only the green woolen cape marked him as in Ludlow Jade's employ. The elf wore dark green leggings and a charcoal gray tunic. He had on leather slippers, rather than boots, and his hair was tied back like Naile's. He had a quiver on his back, filled with arrows, and a long bow slung over his shoulder. A thin-bladed sword hung from a scabbard on his hip.

"This Jade spares no expense," Milo mused. "He even provided two changes of clothes for each of us."

Naile increased his pace and was the first to reach the wagons.

Ludlow Jade was waiting for them. He waved his hand to indicate four wagons. They were the most impressive of the two dozen that stretched to the north. Large and covered, one with sides and a roof of wood planks, his wagon had painted green trim and bronze nuggets pounded into the wheel spokes for decoration. Four massive horses, easily fifteen to sixteen hands high, pulled each wagon, their tack of the same shiny black leather as Ludlow's boots. There were no words on the wagons to indicate Ludlow owned them or what was inside.

"Three times a year," Ludlow began, "we take a caravan to the northern villages. It's a lucrative venture, but dangerous, and that's why I need guards. There are bound to be bandits. Always are. Somehow they know the route, paying informants to tell them when the caravan leaves the city. So we've been forced to hire more and better men. And this last trip of the year . . . well, you look formidable enough. There'll be bandits for sure this last trip. Maybe your appearance will keep them at bay. Weather's starting to cool. Last chance for us . . . and for the bandits . . . to make a good turn of coin."

Naile looked at the other wagons. Many were open, with crates and barrels piled high. Only a few were plank-covered and boxy, like Ludlow Jade's largest. One of these had "Korey's Excellent Elixirs" painted garishly on the side. He shivered at the thought of what the mixtures might be made of.

"What do you sell?" Naile asked. "What's so valuable that you need the likes of us to protect it?"

Ludlow Jade spread his hands and smiled, his eyes sparkling with pride. "Rugs and blankets, cloaks, and quilts. All the finest kind, and all the warmest you'll find anywhere. My goods are known throughout the country, and I command the best prices. And at this time of the year, with winter around the corner, I'll sell out before we reach the last village." He paused. "Of course, I'll pick up some things along the way, herbs. Those I can resell at a profit when I get back here. Maybe some beads and necklaces that the northern women make. None of it worth as much as my blankets, but I might as well bring something back with me to sell here. Profit all the way around."

"Father is quite the merchant." This came from Zechial, who was wedging a bundle into the back of the largest wagon.

"Zechial's quite the merchant, too," a proud Ludlow Jade added. "A quick learner, my son is. Now, if you'll excuse me." He headed toward a wagon that was open on the sides, but had a tarp stretched on a frame over the top, reminiscent of awnings at outdoor cafés. A half-dozen robed men milled near it, one of them clad entirely in black.

"Fisk Lockwood," Yevele told him.

"He was in the Tankard," Milo said, remembering the man he considered suspicious. "Didn't like the looks of him there."

"You better like him," Yevele returned. "He told us where to find you. And in turn he told Ludlow Jade about all of us. You might still be in jail if it weren't for him."

Naile raised an eyebrow and continued to watch Ludlow Jade.

Return to Quag Keep

Five of the robed men stepped away as the merchant approached. The black-cloaked man pulled back his hood displaying the sigils on his skin.

"What's wrong with his head?" Milo asked.

"Tattoos," Ingrge said. "Fisk Lockwood's a priest of Glothorio, and I understand all of the priests cover themselves with tattoos."

Milo shuddered. "Didn't like the looks of him at the Tankard. Don't like the looks of him here."

Naile snorted. "Jade's paying him. Look."

The portly merchant dropped a small pouch of what likely contained coins into Fisk's hand, then turned and waddled back to his own wagons. Fisk looked inside the pouch, nodded, and dropped the pouch in a pocket. Then Fisk headed away from the caravan and toward the city gate.

"What was that about?" Milo asked as the merchant came near. "Paying that priest?"

"He found you for me," Ludlow Jade answered. "I paid him a finder's fee."

"Since when do holy men care about money?" This came from Naile.

"He's a priest of the second rank of Glothorio the Coin Gatherer," Ludlow Jade said. "My wife was a member of the faith, bless her long-departed spirit. I still have ties to the temple, and so I turn to them sometimes to help find mercenaries and buyers for my rugs. I always pay them for their work. Everyone has to make a living. And those priests, even the ones of the second rank . . . they gather coins."

Ludlow Jade busied himself with the horses, then climbed up onto the lead wagon. "Time to leave," he said. "Yevele, you ride on the last wagon. You can handle a team, right?"

She nodded.

"Milo, Naile . . . those are your names right? You'll walk by the wagons for a time, with my other two guards—Sam and Willum. They've been with me a few years. Ride for a rest when your feet get tired." He paused and pointed to the elf.

"Ingrge."

"Yes, Ing. . . ." Ludlow Jade had too much trouble with the elven name. "You said you're a scout."

The elf nodded and jogged to the front of the caravan.

"Wait a minute." Milo spun to face Yevele. "Where's Deav Dyne?"

She quickly explained about Gulth and the trip to the swamp.

"And Wymarc?" Milo watched her rush toward the last of Ludlow's wagons.

"He's paying off the rest of your debt," she called over her shoulder. "Your bill for busting up the Tankard."

Then the wagons lined up, the lead man shouted to move, and the procession headed north.

No one saw a figure in clothes the shade of cold ashes—the other stranger who had watched Naile and Milo in the Golden Tankard. The figure stood in the shadow of the city wall, hood pulled low so only a narrow mouth could be seen. The figure watched the caravan stretch out, then after a moment followed the last wagon.

SIX

The Swan's Song

Down in the garden where the red roses grow
Oh my, I long to go
Pluck me like a flower, cuddle me an hour
Lovie, let me learn that Red Rose Rag.
Red leaves are fallin' in a rosy romance
Bees hum. Come. Now's your chance;
Don't go huntin' possums; mingle with the blossoms
In that flowery, bowery dance.

Wymarc was aware the patrons didn't know what a musical "rag" was, and it really didn't matter. The men sitting at the table closest to the stage were tapping their feet to the beat, and two of them were trying futilely to sing along.

Pick a pinky petal for your papa's pride.
Beg a burnin' blossom for your budding bride.
Woo me with that wonderful wiggle wag
Tip to toes to tease me, and to tickle, too,

Andre Norton and Jean Rabe

Do the dainty dance like dandy doodle doo
Ring your rosie round that Red Rose Rag!

Wymarc's voice grew louder with the last line, and the apprecia-
tive audience applauded. A tall man in the back stood and whistled
and yelled: "wiggle wag and tickle, too!"

"A drink for the skald! On me!" another man called to a serving
wench. "Anything he wants!"

Wymarc nodded his thanks to the man and found himself looking
forward to the free ale, which would soothe his throat and help relax
him. He had a nervous edge, performing in front of so many people.
He noticed that the crowd was a little larger tonight, that each night
more of the folks from the neighborhood came to hear him sing.

The Golden Tankard was noted for having good music, one of the
serving wenches told him last night, and she claimed he was the best
she'd heard in quite some time. "Truly the best," she had said at closing before she kissed his cheek and hurried off down the street. He
vowed to tell her at the first opportunity that he was a married man.

Married . . . he wondered what his wife was doing, the kids, too.
Wondered how long he'd been gone from North Carolina, and if time
moved differently here than home. Did they even know yet that he
was missing? Or had he been gone so long they thought him dead?
He had to get home, tell the kids about this adventure, every grand
and lousy minute of it, tell his wife about the crowd listening to him
so attentively, like he was some pop star.

Wymarc was still wearing the tight outfit he'd pilfered the first
day he'd come to this city. But at least it was presentable, as he'd
been washing it every other night in a rain barrel that was on the
porch of the filthy hovel he'd been calling home. He probably could
afford slightly cleaner accommodations now, given the coins he was
tipped by the better-off patrons. But he had to pay for his meals,
and he was saving money for clothes and for more lute strings. Two
or three more nights, he guessed, and he would be able to buy
something that fit him properly and that would not be identified by
a previous owner. Nicer clothes, an improved image, he might make

even more coins. He wasn't going to risk stealing another set of clothes . . . not after he'd heard from Fisk Lockwood about the cell Milo and Naile had been thrown in.

He wasn't earning a wage from the barkeep for packing the tavern. But that had been the agreement. Wymarc would sing until he paid off the damages Milo and Naile were saddled with. It was going to take several weeks, he figured, to work off the sizeable debt. Only one table and a bench had been salvaged after the fight, and so the barkeep decided to replace everything. Newly-made tables, chairs, benches, and stools filled the one-room tavern. There were new mugs and plates, too, and new shutters on the windows—though the old ones had not been damaged in the fight. Wymarc had overheard the barkeep order a new and larger sign for out front, too, and he wondered if that was being rolled into Milo and Naile's debt. The barkeep had also accounted for lost business for going three days with crates and barrels in place of tables and chairs.

"Another!" yelled a farmer who was one of the Tankard's regulars. "Sing us another one, skald."

"Aye, the one of the poet William Joel," called one of the few female patrons. "The one you sang last night."

Wymarc smiled and began "She's Always a Woman to Me." It was one of his wife's favorite songs, and he pretended now that he was singing it to her. Wymarc wished she could hear him—in this world his voice was at the same time crisp and mellow, with just a hint of sadness to it. A beautiful tenor voice, he knew, one his real-world persona didn't possess. Fortunately, however, that persona knew an endless supply of songs of various eras, memorized through years of attending concerts and listening to CDs and to old vinyl records that had been part of his father's extensive collection. He wondered what Ingrge would think of the selections he sang—not a single old country western ballad in the mix.

The song he'd opened with tonight, the "Red Rose Rag," dated back to 1911, the words by Edward Madden. Wymarc's father had been a jazz and blues buff, and used to play the scratching and popping recordings all the time, often among them was Madden's material. Wymarc told the audience that he'd written the "Red Rose Rag," lied to them that he'd written most everything he sang. But he didn't lie about his wife's favorite song.

Wymarc was flawless on the lute, a fact that amazed him, as his real-world persona couldn't play a note on any instrument. All right, "Chopsticks." He could handle "Chopsticks" on his youngest son's toy piano.

With all the tunes in his head, and with some he'd begun to pen himself, he knew he could perform in this city for quite some time . . . if he had to. He'd rather be home with his family, singing off-key and working overtime, admiring his new two-story saltbox. He prayed Yevele and the others would find a way to get them back home. It would be so easy to be morose about this, he knew. But it was in his nature to find the best in a bad situation. And the best thing he could do now was sing and work off Milo and Naile's debt, and try not to think too much about his family.

Tomorrow he planned to do a mix of Dylan and Springsteen, closing with Sachmo's "What a Wonderful World," and altering the lyrics where necessary to fit this medieval society. The evening after that would be toned-downed and slowed-down Zeppelin and The Who. And after that . . . well, he knew a lot of Queen and liked the Red Hot Chili Peppers.

Ah, if only his wife could hear him. The kids, too, though they were so young they wouldn't wholly appreciate the caliber of his wonderful voice. It took on a haunting quality now, as he thought of his family despite his admonition not to, the emotion dripping so thick in Joel's lyrics that all conversations ceased and the serving wenches stood still, caught up in the music and the power of his voice.

He wished Yevele and Ingrge could hear him, too, and he wondered what they were doing. A part of him envied them—guarding a merchant caravan and getting out of this city. Sleeping on the ground in the open might be preferable to his rat-infested hovel. But a larger part of him relished the accolades of this crowd. And that part thought he got the better end of the arrangement. Paying off this element of Milo and Naile's drunken folly wasn't terribly bad. Still, when he saw Milo and Naile next, he would make sure they appreciated his sacrifice, and he would tell them about the rats under his bed.

He sang several more tunes. Bread's *If* seeming to be the most popular among the bunch. The audience didn't quite catch on to "Goodbye Yellow Brick Road."

Wymarc scanned the crowd. Most were commoners, as they lived in this section of the city, and the Golden Tankard's prices were affordable by the lower class. But there were some merchants in the mix, and two aristocrats who were slumming just for the music. And there was Fisk Lockwood. Wymarc was pleased to see the priest of Glothorio the Coin Gatherer. The priest had not been to the Tankard since the night of Wymarc's first performance. That was early last week. Eight days ago.

Eight days he'd been doing this! How much longer? Three or four weeks, he suspected. The barkeep liked his singing and would try to drag it out. He finished a Peter, Paul, and Mary tune and bowed, then took a deep pull from an ale tankard set beside him.

"Another!" the tall man in the back called.

Fisk Lockwood stood and brushed his hood back. The light from the lanterns and the fireplace reflected on his bald head and made the tattoos appear to move. "Yes, please sing another," the priest said. "The sad one about the boy and the pipes!"

"All right," Wymarc agreed. He settled back on his stool, took a sip of ale, and began:

> Oh, Danny Boy, the pipes, the pipes are calling
> From glen to glen, and down the mountain side,
> The summer's gone, and all the roses falling
> It's you, it's you must go, and I must bide
> But come ye back when summer's in the meadow,
> Or when the valley's hushed and white with snow.
> I'll be here in sunshine or in shadow,
> Oh, Danny Boy, oh Danny Boy, I love you so!

Andre Norton and Jean Rabe

Wymarc was definitely looking forward to doing some Dylan and Springsteen tomorrow, a break from some of the sappy, overly pleasant stuff he'd been crooning for the past eight days. Give the patrons something a little edgier and see how they'd react. Maybe if the barkeep didn't like it, Milo and Naile's debt might get paid off faster. Of course, Wymarc knew he was going to have to stay in the city anyway, and likely in this neighborhood, until the caravan came back. Two months. He cringed at the thought. Yevele said the caravan would spend a month traveling north, and then a month coming back. Did time pass here as it was passing in North Carolina?

The song finished, he stood and bowed, scooped up the ale tankard and a few coins that had been tossed near it—one of them gold, from an aristocrat—that made his heart leap. Then he stepped off the stage. He slung the lute across his back and in a half-dozen steps was at the bar.

"Done for the evening," he pronounced. Wymarc had performed the required dozen songs and wasn't in the mood this evening to go beyond that—though he usually did. He wanted to spend one of the copper coins at the bathhouse, which might still be open, then fold himself into what passed for his bed. Tomorrow he might finish one of those songs he'd started to write himself, and then see if—with that treasured gold coin—he had enough money for a new tunic, trousers, and a warm cloak.

"Beautiful," the barkeep said. "One of the best to sing here, Wymarc, my friend. Unusual songs, you know. But I tell you that every night." He wiped his hands on a towel and gestured to the door that led to the kitchen.

Wymarc followed him, hoping the barkeep might offer up something to eat.

"Tomorrow night, skald, you do that song again by that poet William Joel. The folks expect it now."

Wymarc mumbled his agreement.

"I understand you've been living above Rumpul's place."

Return to Quag Keep

"I can't afford anything else," Wymarc was a little too quick to say. "You aren't paying me, remember?"

The barkeep nodded and reached into his pocket. "I'm still not paying you." He pulled out a key and pressed it into Wymarc's palm. "That's to the room above. You go out back and up the stairs. It's yours to use while you sing here. A little dusty 'cause I haven't cleaned it since my last tenant left. But it's much better than Rumpul's pit."

Wymarc stared at the key.

"And about wages," the barkeep continued. "I figure once you finish paying for your friends' damages—oh, five weeks should do it, I figure—I'd be happy if you stayed on. I'd give you a fair wage then, all based on the number of folks you draw in."

Wymarc put the key in his pocket. "Thank you for the place to stay. And. . . ."

"And don't you be telling anyone I'm setting you up with a room. Wouldn't be good for my image. Understand?"

Wymarc's lips edged up in a slight smile. "I understand. And as for your offer . . . I will think it over."

"Good coin I'll pay you."

Wymarc edged past him and out the back of the Tankard. He suspected he'd stay here until Yevele and the others returned, and any coins he earned after the debt was worked off . . . well, that would be *his* money. He wondered if they found a way back home if the coins might come along. And might his wonderful singing voice come, too?

It was dark behind the Tankard, there being no lanterns because the barkeep was careful with expenses. But just enough starlight filtered down that Wymarc could see to make his way around the crates filled with garbage near the back door. He looked around . . . ah, the stairs were at the edge of the building, a rickety set that led up to a sound-looking door. Whatever the room looked like, it had to be better than "Rumpul's pit," he decided. No need to go to the pit first. He had nothing there. Everything Wymarc owned in this world was on his back and in his pocket.

He started toward the stairs, then stopped when a figure stepped out of the shadows. For a moment, Wymarc's heart pounded, fearful it was a cutpurse intending to rob him of his precious coins. Then he relaxed.

> Don't go huntin' possums, mingle with the blossoms
> In that flowery, bowery dance.

"I don't understand all those words, Wymarc. But it is a lovely song."

"Fisk."

The priest nodded. "I enjoyed your performance this evening, and the song about the woman 'throwing shadows at you.' An interesting picture, it conjures. But I particularly like the song about the boy and the pipes."

"Danny Boy."

"Yes, that's the song."

"It's an old, old song," Wymarc said. In truth it was. "Danny Boy" had been adapted in the early 1900s from "The Londonderry Aire," a piece that was likely more than three hundred years old at that time. Not that anyone in this world would know that, he realized.

"A pretty song, but sorrowful," Fisk said.

"I'm glad you came out to talk to me. I was wondering about the caravan, my friends Yevele and Ingrge."

"The elf and the warrior-woman," Fisk said. "And the two big men who caused so much trouble for you."

"Yes, them. Milo Jagon and Naile Fangtooth."

"I've heard nothing about the caravan and your comrades. But I will be leaving in the morning to learn its progress, and to perhaps converse with the Glothorio priests in their midst."

The surprise on Wymarc's face was evident even in the darkness. "They've an eight-day lead."

"I travel rather quickly." Fisk stepped closer and reached into the folds of his robe. "Before I go, Wymarc, I'd like to hear the second verse again, of that song about the boy named Danny."

Wymarc shook his head. "I'm done singing tonight." For a moment he brightened, thinking to offer up the song in exchange for some money. Priests of Glothorio the Coin Gatherer likely had money in their pockets. But before he could propose the notion, he saw Fisk draw a wavy bladed knife from a fold in the black robes.

"What?"

"I said, sing about the boy," Fisk repeated.

"Sing," Wymarc said nervously, his breath catching in his throat. A priest with a knife? "Sure, I'll sing. No need to threaten me. Put the knife away, Fisk, and I'll sing for you."

Fisk came closer still, and made no move to replace the knife. He smiled, the faint starlight showing a row of perfect teeth.

Wymarc took a step back, and then another, intending to retrace his path and go inside the kitchen, where only the cook wielded a knife. Then suddenly he stumbled over a low crate of garbage. He fell backward, the handle snapping off his lute. Before he could get to his feet, Fisk was on him, moving surprisingly fast and silent.

The priest held the wavy blade to Wymarc's neck. "Sing for me," he hissed.

Wymarc swallowed hard, finding that his throat was tight, his mouth becoming dry as sand. "I . . ."

"Sing, skald. That verse from the Danny song."

Wymarc closed his eyes and worked up some saliva.

"I'll not tell you again, skald. Sing."

Wymarc's fingers twitched nervously, clawing at the alley ground. His chest heaved with fear.

But when ye come, and all the flowers are dying,

The words caught a little, and his perfect voice sounded less-than-perfect now, a frightened tremor to it.

If I am dead, as dead I well may be,
Ye'll come and find the place where I am lying,
And kneel and say an Ave there for me,

Wymarc stopped, but Fisk pressed the blade against his throat, and he felt a hotness, knew he'd been cut.

"Go on."

> And I shall hear, though soft you tread above me,
> And all my grave will warmer, sweeter be,
> For you will bend and tell me that you love me,
> And I shall sleep in peace until you come to me!

Fisk leaned back, and Wymarc made a move to rise, thinking he'd satisfied the priest. Thoughts flashed through the bard's mind. This was a holy man! A priest! How could a holy man threaten him? Unless he wasn't a holy man. And if he wasn't . . . what about Yevele, Ingrge, Milo, and Naile?

"Who are you?" Wymarc demanded.

"Fisk Lockwood," came the reply. Then the priest, who seemed impossibly strong for his size, shoved Wymarc hard against the ground, splintering the rest of the lute, the wood biting into the bard's back. In one fast motion, the priest drew the blade across Wymarc's throat.

Fisk stood and looked around, making sure the noise of the song and his deed had not attracted attention. But the alley was dark and empty, and so he was satisfied.

"Pity," he said in a hush. "Your voice was remarkable. But it was not worth as much as the coins I was paid to silence it."

Fisk cleaned the blade on Wymarc's tight tunic, and took the coins from the dead skald's pocket. Then he kicked Wymarc's corpse, and, humming "Danny Boy," melted into the shadows.

SEVEN

Ingrge's Unease

Ingrge cherished the time alone. It gave him time to think, mostly to remember his life in Florida. He'd been alone there, no steady girl, no relatives within four hundred miles to visit or to be visited by, no neighbors he was especially fond of. It wasn't that he was a loner, he certainly enjoyed the company of Yevele, Naile, and Milo, but in Florida he often was on the air at night, and he slept well into the day. His schedule hadn't allowed him the luxury of close friends. Just the luxury of enjoying the beach.

The elf scouted nearly a mile ahead of the caravan this early morning, the ninth day of the journey. Frost was heavy on the tall grass that lined the trail, and his breath puffed away from his face and mingled with the misty air. The weather was too cold for him, the chill breeze seeping through the material in his leggings and stinging his skin.

By God, he missed Daytona Beach, where it occasionally frosted and threatened the citrus crop. But those frigid days were few, sometimes years apart. He'd moved to Daytona Beach to escape the Midwest winters; his scant relatives, cousins and uncles and aunts, clung to the cool climes of Illinois and Indiana. Brrrrrrr. And until this venture, he'd managed to avoid truly cold weather in this medieval world. They'd traveled through a swamp, across a desert, up the side of a mountain—where it was cold. But he didn't remember it being *this* cold, and certainly not for this many days in a row. And now they were traveling farther north, at a time when the temperature would be doing nothing but dropping. Brrrrrrr indeed.

"Good thing Gulth went south to the swamp," Ingrge mused. "He'd not tolerate this well. And it's going to get worse. I can feel it." The elf could tell an early winter was coming, as last night before falling asleep, he saw a few flakes of snow. They didn't stick long, but it was enough to make him yearn for walking forty-two steps to the beach, fifty-seven until his toes teased the sea. He suddenly and very desperately tried to push Florida to the back of his mind. Florida didn't exist here, and there were no beaches in his immediate future, only this bleak land. Worse, there was no promise he'd ever get back home. Whiskey River might never sign on for another evening shift. He might never hear another late-night request for Little Jimmy Dickens or Dolly Parton, might never hear the soulful sound of a steel guitar. Forty-two steps. Fifty-seven to the sea.

Did his relatives know he was gone? Was the landlord banging on his door for rent? The bosses at the station, had they replaced him? Was he a missing person? Were the cops looking for him? Or had no one noticed he was gone? How long had he been gone? Forty-two steps.

Again he tried not to picture Florida. But his efforts were unsuccessful. The sky would be a clear, brilliant blue, the air hot. The humidity would be so high that the sweat would run down his face in streams as thick as night crawlers. There might be a few clouds, low on the horizon and touching an ocean that would be glimmering and dark and electric with motion. There would be gentle swells with foam the color of eggshells, and gulls dipping low looking for food. The sound of the waves and the gulls, the feel of the sand beneath his feet was heavenly. Everything was so warm and nearly perfect.

Everything here was so cold.

Return to Quag Keep

"I have friends here. Make the best of this," he said. "Find the good in this place."

For a while, that hadn't been too hard. This medieval land was fresh and unpolluted and incredible to take in. Just when they'd arrived at the city, a little more than two weeks ago, the colors on the trees were amazing, more brilliant than anything Ingrge had seen at home—even when he had lived for a time in St. Louis. Vibrant reds and oranges, yellows so bright they practically glowed, rich velvety browns. Late-blooming wildflowers scented the air, and a swollen, fast-moving stream gurgled pleasantly. The elf's senses were teased and treated, and he found himself lingering along the road then, forcing his companions to adopt a much slower pace so he could relish his surroundings.

How fast the countryside and the trees had changed in this short time!

Now most of the trees were bare, and the damp, fallen leaves were filling the air with a fusty, moldering scent. Not a single bloom from a wildflower remained, and the only sounds were the infrequent caws of crows and the faint clicking the branches made as the wind nudged them together. The oaks had retained their leaves, of course, but they were curled and dusty-brown, everything looking dismal. The sun hadn't appeared yesterday, the sky cloudy-gray like this morning. Likely Ingrge wouldn't see the sun today either.

"No." Ingrge swore he saw a flake floating down. His tunic was wool and warm, but not warm enough as far as he was concerned. He rattled off a string of curse words in the elvish tongue and watched another flake drift in the slight breeze, held his hands under his armpits. Odd that he knew the complex, lyrical elven language, that he knew all these nature skills. Odd that he could shoot an arrow more than five hundred feet with an astounding degree of accuracy. Odd that he knew how to use the thin-bladed sword at his side. But he did know all of those things—and more.

His elven form could see and hear this world far better than his human senses could have managed. His old, Florida eyes likely wouldn't have spotted the snowflakes high against the pale sky, and they wouldn't have noticed details like a red-tailed hawk toward the top of a big oak and all but invisible because of concealing clumps of leaves. They wouldn't have detected a slight motion in a patch of dead weeds beneath that tree. A mouse or a ground squirrel, as the breeze was not responsible for the erratic movement. A moment more and the hawk dove from his perch, feathered lightning streaking down to grab a ground squirrel in his talons and then race to the sky.

The caravan left its fifth village yesterday afternoon, Ludlow Jade not faring so well there, as it was a particularly poor community, and only one family bought a blanket. However, the merchant purchased a dozen casks of mulled wine the villagers produced, and he seemed pleased on that account.

The wagons would reach the next stop before nightfall, if the map Ingrge got a look at was accurate. So far it had proven reasonably true. The trail they were following was wide and relatively even, though there were depressions from wagon wheels. It would wend its way through a section of light woods, then would dip into a valley. The breeze would be cut there, Ingrge hoped. There were places where the grass was tamped down, leading away from the main trail; these looked like lesser-used paths, perhaps leading to farms.

He knelt on the trail. The earth was hard for the most part, but it was loose at the edges against the grass, and this is where he concentrated. It was not yet frozen, though that would be starting soon, and so his keen elven eyes noted recent depressions. A boot heel? There wasn't a full impression of a foot, but that's what it looked like. Ingrge's fingers brushed at the dirt and felt the bottom of the depression, the grains of dirt registering against his sensitive skin.

Definitely a boot heel, made by a slight man with a narrow foot. Another a short distance away, the same man. Apparently the man walked back and forth across the trail, and apparently he worked to cover his tracks. Why?

Ingrge moved off the trail, with considerable scrutiny finding another track, and then another. The ones around them had been covered up, expertly so, only a few missed. A woodsman, perhaps. Whoever it was, they didn't want their presence known, and that raised the hairs on the back of Ingrge's neck. The tracks weren't made this morning, but they were likely made last night. Was someone searching for something? The caravan? He ranged a little farther on both sides of the trail, but found no other tracks.

Bothered by the prints, but unable to do anything about it, Ingrge jogged back to the caravan.

Yevele drove the fourth of Ludlow Jade's wagons, which was near the end of the caravan. Only two wagons were behind her, these belonging to a cheesemaker, who had hired two guards, these being retired soldiers on the far side of middle age. She got along with them well enough, admired their long swords and crossbows, and she occasionally glanced around the side of her wagon, looking to the other wagons and the guards, waving to them, and studying the trail behind them when it curved and she could catch a glimpse of it. There'd been no hint of bandits, for which she was grateful. There was only the trail, stopping in villages, and sitting on this uncomfortable wooden bench-seat. She was bored.

She looked ahead and to the right, where Naile walked alongside the third of Ludlow Jade's wagons, which was driven by one of the merchant's long-time guards. Milo was to the left and near the second wagon, the one with the canvas roof. Another guard was assigned the first wagon, the largest of the merchant's, and no doubt carrying the most valuable merchandise.

Yevele speculated that Ludlow Jade was brokering something other than blankets and rugs . . . why else make arrangements for a half-dozen sellswords to protect the goods. Seemed to her that the protection, including Milo and Naile's bail, was more costly than what he professed to be selling. But whatever that other something might be was not her business, she decided.

"I'd give you a copper piece for your thoughts . . . if I had one." Naile had drifted back and was looking up at her. "You're staring at something far beyond the back of that wagon." Naile gestured to Ludlow Jade's third wagon.

Yevele shrugged. "Just thinking."

"I'm a good listener."

Her eyes simmered with ire, and something dark passed across her face.

"Yevele, something on your mind?" Naile's voice was deep and not unpleasant. Neither was he unpleasant to look at this morning. His swollen eye had almost completely healed now, the last trace of his cuts and bruises were gone, and he was keeping his face clean-shaven and his hair tied at the back of his head.

"Yes," she said after a moment. "All of this is on my mind." She held the reins with one hand and gestured to her wagon, the wagon in front of her, to Naile, and to Milo, who was walking slower and drifting back to overhear the conversation.

Naile waited for her to continue, but she didn't. He had to prod her. "Guarding a blanket peddler? This is bothering you?"

Her eyes narrowed. "This world, our predicament. That's what is bothering me. The fight you and Milo started . . . that *you* started. You threw the first punch."

"I sort of did." Naile cast his eyes to the ground, then looked up at her. Yevele's face was hard, her jaw clenched. He noticed that the knuckles of the hand that gripped the reins were white, she was squeezing her fist so tight. "You've been stewing about the fight."

"I suppose you could call it that." She let a breath whistle out between her teeth. "You brought all of this upon us, Naile. It's going to be harder for us to look for a way home now, since we've been shackled to this caravan. A month there, a month back to the city to find Wymarc, and hopefully Deav Dyne . . . two months if we're lucky and there are no complications. Two months out of our medieval lives." She sucked in the chill air, her face reddening from her irritation and her boredom. "And we're working for nothing because you and Milo caused so much damage. A fight you started, Naile, by throwing the first drunken punch."

He thought to argue with her for a moment, as he truly hadn't punched that man in the Golden Tankard tavern, just accidentally knocked him down. But he stayed silent and continued to stare at her face. It had softened just a little, and her eyes had brightened almost imperceptibly. His own face relaxed.

"We've not a coin," she continued. "We're fed by Ludlow Jade, clothed by Ludlow Jade, at the mercy of Ludlow Jade. At least Wymarc has been spared this. He's warm and safe in the city, and singing. Doing something he enjoys."

Milo was indeed eavesdropping, hoping Yevele and Naile either wouldn't notice or wouldn't care. He glanced over his shoulder and stopped, just so he could watch them. Then he started walking at the caravan's pace again.

He hadn't liked what he'd seen. Sure, Naile and Yevele were arguing—or to be precise Yevele was uttering all the angry words. But her expression no longer matched those words, and that concerned him. He'd seen her watching Naile on and off these past many days, and Naile returning the looks.

Milo, himself, had fancied the warrior-woman, but had kept his distance and instead concentrated on whatever matter was at hand . . . crossing the swamp, the desert, climbing into the mountains, delving into Quag Keep . . . trying to get home.

"It's wrong," he said, thinking that something might be developing between the two. "He's not human. Not wholly. Even though he looks that way." Milo considered Naile confrontational and quick to lose his temper. Certainly not good-looking. "And he's a lawyer." Milo shuddered at his thoughts. "It's just wrong."

He glanced down at the bracelet on his wrist, wondering why the dice hadn't spun, and why the whole affair hadn't tugged him to a new destination. It had tugged him and the others before—across a stretch of swamp, to a dragon's lair, to Quag Keep. Maybe the bracelet was broken. He tried to snap the links again, and found them as strong as ever. Then he studied his rings. He wore two, neither of which would come off, and both of which he knew to be enchanted. The one, set with a large dark stone, some sort of gray crystal, had served as a map of sorts, when they were trying to reach

Quag Keep. It was dull and blank now. The other? It was an oblong filmy green stone, across which in no discernable pattern ran red veins and dots. He hadn't a clue what it did. And neither of the rings were doing anything to make Yevele give him the looks she was giving Naile.

"Wrong."

Milo picked up his pace and returned to his station at the side of the second wagon. He scanned the countryside to the west, and looked up to the bench seat, where Zechial was perched. The merchant's son nodded to Milo, then Milo looked east again. He saw Ingrge jog past, the elf not acknowledging his wave and continuing south.

"Wrong," Milo repeated.

Ingrge decided to scout behind the caravan for a few hours, giving up on the mysterious tracks ahead. He was trying to convince himself that the tracks were nothing, and that the wind and blowing clumps of weeds had been responsible for covering them. But he wasn't being convinced enough.

"Perhaps I want to be bothered by something," he said. Ingrge stood in the center of the trail and watched the caravan continue north. He let it get about a mile ahead, then followed off the side of the trail.

Morning drifted into late afternoon, and Ingrge started thinking of Florida again, wondering about his job at the station . . . if it would still be there for him if he managed to find a way out of this medieval nightmare.

But was it such a nightmare? When he dabbled in the role-playing game with his friends, most often at local science-fiction conventions, he imagined what it might be like to live in a world such as this. It was primitive by the standards he was used to. No radio stations or television sets with attached DVD players, no flush toilets or refrigerators dispensing chilled water and ice through the door. No Disneyworld, to which he'd bought a season pass and managed to visit more often than he thought he should.

But it was not . . . dreadful. His elven senses appreciated how clean this place was, how untouched from car exhaust and smoke from factories, from the chatter of people who were everywhere. So very many people. This world was not as populated. It was simpler. Maybe better.

Would it be so bad if he couldn't make it home for a while? And would he forget his Florida self if they tarried here too long? Would James Ritchie cease to exist and only Ingrge remain? Would it be so bad?

He knew it would be better in one respect—that being if he was earning some coins and working at something other than paying off Milo and Naile's debt.

"It would be. . . ." He stared at a spot on the horizon south of the caravan. Near a clump of willow birches, he thought he saw something moving. A deer was his first guess, but after he focused on it, he could tell the shape was wrong. Too far away to make it out for certain, and still bothered by the tracks to the north, Ingrge skirted off the trail and dropped to a crouch, expecting trouble.

Hidden by the tall grass, he made his way toward the shape. He moved silently, avoiding stepping on dry twigs that could snap and give him away. The elf carefully brushed aside the branches of bushes and reed stalks, not making a sound as he continued south and closed in on what he now knew was two-legged quarry.

So someone was following the caravan. Perhaps several someones, and the elf had managed to only catch a glimpse of this one. Breathing shallowly and practically crawling as he closed the distance, Ingrge circled the figure and then came up behind it.

The figure was moving away from the willow birches now and straight down the trail. The caravan ahead had become a speck, and so the figure was not risking being seen by any caravan guards.

A spy? Ingrge thought. But for whom and why? Did one of the merchants have an enemy? The elf waited in the foliage, looking around and making sure the spy had no other companions. When Ingrge was satisfied the spy was alone, the elf crept up.

The figure was dressed in clothes the shade of cold ashes, nearly matching the color of the sky. It was on the small side, as thin as the elf and not quite as tall. A boy or a woman maybe, but the figure carried itself like a man by the roll of the hips and the way the arms swung. When the wind gusted, the figure's cloak billowed away, revealing more of the ash-gray clothes, and a strap filled with daggers that ran along his back from his right shoulder to the left side of his waist. Likely more daggers were sheathed on the front side. The pommels were wrapped with gray leather twine, as were the pommels of the daggers strapped to the man's thighs and calves.

The elf had no way of knowing that the figure had watched Milo and Naile in the Golden Tankard many days past, and that he'd managed to slip out as the fight began.

"A walking arsenal, with all those knives," Ingrge whispered. "And certainly up to no good."

The elf reached for the pommel of his thin-blade, then changed his mind and drew a dagger of his own. Easier to run with a shorter weapon, he knew. He moved onto the center of the trail, sprang forward into a fast gait, and a moment later slammed into the back of the ash-gray man.

Ingrge knocked the wind from the man, and the elf held him on the ground, right knee in the small of his back, dagger trained at the back of his neck. With his free hand, Ingrge began pulling daggers from the leather band and tossing them to the side of the trail. Then the elf jammed his other knee on the man's left hand, which was reaching down to grab at a dagger strapped to his thigh.

"I will kill you," Ingrge hissed, "if you make a move to draw a weapon." In the back of his mind, the elf knew that James Ritchie of Daytona Beach would be horrified at the notion of taking a life. But James wasn't here, Ingrge was. And the elf had no compunctions about killing this man.

The slight man tried to nod and say something, but he only gagged, his face pressed in the dirt now by Ingrge's other hand.

"I'm going to roll you over," Ingrge continued. "And you're not going to make a move." The elf paused, then did just that, transferring his right knee to the man's stomach, his left to the man's right arm. One hand still held a dagger at the stranger's throat, the other began pulling more knives from the leather band and throwing these off the trail.

It was difficult to guess the man's age. At first Ingrge thought he was human, and placed him in his late twenties. He had wheat-blond hair and gray eyes, no hint of age lines around them or his near-colorless lips. But then the elf noticed how thin the face was, that there was no trace of a beard, and that the stranger's ears had the faintest of points to them. Elvish blood ran in the stranger's veins, not strongly, as he would pass for human in most cities. But it was there, and that stayed Ingrge's hand—the elf had intended to kill him.

"Who are you?"

"A friend," was the reply.

Ingrge sniffed. The man was not quite so dirty as the guards in the caravan or the various city folk he'd been around. Cleaner, though he still wore some dirt of the road. Common people in this part of the world took baths, but not often. It was a luxury, one this fellow had indulged in recently. Ingrge snarled and pressed the dagger against the stranger's throat.

"No *friend* follows the caravan as a spy would. Tell me . . . were you well in front of the caravan before? Last night?" The elf looked to the man's boots, seeing they were gray leather slippers and could not have made the heel impressions he'd noted earlier.

The stranger paled, and despite the cold weather, beads of sweat appeared on his forehead. "T-t-truly," he stammered. "I am a friend. I'm not following the caravan to hurt you, but to help you. I'm trying to save our world."

EIGHT

Dead Men

The sun was edging toward the horizon when the caravan was called to a stop. The next village was only a handful of miles ahead, and they would reach it before sunset. But first the merchants wanted to make themselves look presentable, rub down their horses, and do any necessary sprucing up to the wagons—in the event they had shoppers who didn't want to wait for the morning.

It was a practice the merchants had adopted since the beginning of this venture—wanting to look their best, believing it would bring them more customers and ultimately more money. Yevele found the preening all tedious and unnecessary. She was telling Naile just that, Milo watching the two of them from a few yards away.

"Wrong," Milo said, "him thinking he has a chance with her. He ain't even human." Then he turned his attention to Ludlow Jade, helping the merchant down from his wagon. "And he's a lawyer."

"Such good fortune we've had so far," the merchant told Milo. "Perhaps it is your impressive presence that has kept the bandits away. Or perhaps for once they simply didn't discover when we were leaving the city." He sighed. "I consider that latter possibility unlikely."

Milo watched Ludlow Jade inspect the horses attached to his first wagon. The merchant retrieved a brush and started working on their manes. Milo decided to help and took a damp rag to the few mud spots on the horses' legs.

"I should sell more blankets in this next village," Ludlow Jade said. "Wheaton Dale, it's called. The place has several wealthy farmers, was named after the grandfather of one of them. And there is a large orchard that stretches farther than you can see." He brightened. "There should still be plenty of sweet yellow apples, I think. I will have to buy some for us . . . and for the horses. You like apples, don't you Milo? I think everyone likes—"

A scream cut through the air, coming from the front of the caravan.

Milo spun away from Ludlow Jade and took off running, drawing his sword and hollering for Naile and Yevele. His feet pounded across the trail, then suddenly he was flying face forward and landing hard on his stomach. Something had grabbed his ankle, and in his surprise, the sword flew from his fingers.

Something still held his ankle, and Milo pulled against it, at the same time trying to sit up. He had a knife in a scabbard on his thigh, and he drew this, thinking he'd caught his foot somehow in an exposed root.

"Holy—" Milo's jaw dropped open when he saw what held him. It wasn't a root, it was a skeletal hand, and the bony fingers were digging deep into his flesh. Before Milo could react, a second hand erupted from the ground, and the rest of the body began to unearth itself.

"Undead!" Milo hollered. It was a cry that was repeated from someone toward the front of the caravan. He threw himself forward, leading with the knife and striking at the wrist of the hand that held him. All his strength behind the blow, Milo severed the skeletal hand and scampered free. He jumped to his feet and in a few strides was at his dropped sword. He made a move to grab it, just as another hand rose from the earth, fingers groping about and finding the blade. "No you don't," he cautioned.

Return to Quag Keep

Milo stepped on the fingers, hearing them crunch. Then he bent and retrieved the sword. Knife in one hand, sword in the other, he put his back to a wagon and quickly took in what was becoming a hellish scene.

Along the length of the caravan undead were bursting from the ground, at the point where the trail met the tall, dead grass. Milo imagined the undead were on both sides of the wagons, judging by the panicked screams of the merchants and the sounds of things scrabbling in the hard-packed dirt.

There were skeletons, reaching out with their hands, fingers bony needles. Others Milo labeled zombies, having rotting flesh hanging from arms and legs, vestiges of clothes clinging to their shoulders and ribs. A few that Milo could see looked freshly dead, their bodies intact, but the skin gray and mottled. One of the recent dead had no eyes, another had a broken neck, and its head hung limp against its breastbone. There were dozens on this side of the caravan, and all of them exuded a stench that had Milo, and the other guards that he could see, gagging.

Milo fought to keep from retching as he held his breath and surged forward, thrusting with his knife while he swept his sword in a wide arc to keep the undead from closing in.

The knife sunk into the chest of a recently dead man, cutting through a yellow linen tunic and into a heart that wasn't beating. The wound didn't stop the creature, and it began clawing at Milo's arm, its fingers breaking against the chainmail sleeve.

Yevele and Naile were fighting on the other side of the caravan, alongside the cheesemaker's guards.

"Bandits?" she cried. "You feared bandits, Ludlow Jade? These men might have been bandits in life! They certainly aren't bandits now!" She didn't look for the merchant, expected him to be hiding in his box-like wagon, his son quivering behind him.

She saw one of the cheesemaker's guards trembling, and watched his face bead with sweat. Then she saw only the undead, as she waded forward, sweeping her long sword in front of her and cutting through the chests and waists of skeletons and zombies, bringing her sword lower and slicing through thighs and breaking leg bones. She wasn't killing them, she knew, some other force had already done that. But she was crippling several to the point they weren't a significant threat. They lay on the ground, twitching and clawing, trying to crawl forward, as they could no longer walk. The cheesemaker's guards came up behind her and starting bashing in the zombies' skulls.

There was a sparkle in her eyes, and she worked to keep from smiling. Though the stench was nearly overwhelming, and the creatures' appearance utterly repulsive, Yevele's spirit soared. Too long she'd been idle, driving a team of horses while her sword arm grew sluggish and her muscles soft. She felt the warm, welcome rush of adrenaline and swore she could hear her heart pounding in her ears.

She brought her sword down hard on a zombie that stumbled toward her, lopping off its right arm, then spinning, ducking beneath the swipe of its remaining arm, jumping up and cutting off its head. The creature still shuffled forward aimlessly, arm flailing about and trying to connect with something living. Coming up behind it, she grabbed the pommel of her sword with both hands and swung hard, cutting the creature in half.

"Finish it," she yelled to the cheesemaker's guards. Then she was rushing forward again to meet the charge of a recent-dead, a once-warrior who'd been buried in boiled leather armor. The dead man wielded a mace, and was using part of a coffin lid for a shield. "Finish that one, then follow me!"

Naile hurried toward the front of the caravan, where it looked like the concentration of undead were swarming the guards and horses. A wave of skeletons had clawed apart the horses pulling the first two wagons, effectively keeping the caravan from moving forward and escaping.

As he ran, Naile threw his vest and cloak on the ground, and then

Return to Quag Keep

kicked off his boots. He concentrated on something deep inside him, and managed to tug his shirt off before he felt the change begin. What would the partners at the law firm think if they saw him? Impressed and frightened, he suspected, and ordering some secretary to write him a suitable severance check. He could kiss his legal career in New York good-bye.

He'd considered changing that night in the Golden Tankard, turning himself into the beast that lurked in the shadowy part of his soul. He'd overheard Milo call him "not human." He wasn't wholly, he had to admit. He was a werecreature, a man who could, with focus and effort and pain, turn himself into a rampaging wild boar. His twitching fingers fumbled with his belt. A moment, and the belt and the hand axes were on the ground, too. A moment more, and he was clutching at his belly and dropping to his knees, trembling as fire raced through his veins.

His skin rippled and his muscles bunched. Coarse brown-black hair sprouted in clumps then spread like melting butter to cover every inch of him. The bones in his face popped and cracked and grew, his mouth becoming an elongated snout, tusks growing up near a wet, quivering snout. His ears grew long and pointed, twitched and pointed forward as he ran on all fours now.

Naile had become a massive boar, red eyes glowering, hooves tearing up the cold earth as he headed toward the closest skeleton. The wereboar hit the skeleton hard, shattering its calves and knocking it backward. He trampled the undead and rooted through the remains, tossing rib bones into the air and then knocking its head away with a shove from his snout.

The wereboar squealed in victory and moved to another skeleton, then splintering it, moved on to one more. Naile was making short work of the undead in his path, inflicting much more carnage than he could have with his hand axes. There was incredible strength and fury in this form, but he assumed it only when he felt there was no other recourse. Because with that strength came a detachment, it was as if Naile was relegated to a dark corner of the boar's mind and had to watch what transpired. He had a reasonable amount of control of the creature he'd become, choosing his foes and attacking with a blind rage. But he wasn't the same "Naile," he didn't think as rationally. He acted on emotion and impulse. Logic and reason became foreign concepts, and he had difficulty stopping a rampage once he started it.

He slammed into a zombie, then trampled it, hooked his tusks into its side and tossed it into the air before he trampled it again. The creature tried futilely to rise, before Naile charged it one last time and separated its head from its shoulders. He cast his gaze about, seeing skeletons circling him, reaching out with needle-fingers. He couldn't see the caravan for all the bony legs, but he could hear the merchants and guards, all of them shouting and screaming. He could hear the harsh whinnies of horses that he knew were being cut down by the dead men. And he could hear Yevele shouting orders to guards.

With a snort, he plowed forward and broke the leg bones of another skeleton.

Milo had edged toward the middle of the caravan, where a wave of zombies was converging on the wagon belonging to the priests of Glothorio the Coin Gatherer. Milo thought that the priests might need aid; he was confident Yevele and the cheesemaker's guards could tackle the fewer numbers of undead that were at the rear of the caravan.

But the priests didn't need help, and Milo was momentarily caught motionless, in awe. Two of the five Glothorio priests were on this side of the caravan. Their backs were against their wagon, and their hoods were thrown back and sleeves pushed up, revealing the myriad of tattoos. The eldest of the two closed his eyes and began humming. He rocked back and forth on the balls of his feet, and his fingers danced up and down his arms. In response, the artful sigils on the priest's left forearm began to writhe like snakes. A red swirl detached itself from the priest's skin and hovered, faintly glowing, above his dancing fingers. Then, like a cracking whip, it lashed out at an approaching zombie. The tip of the sigil flashed when it struck the undead's chest.

Return to Quag Keep

The zombie howled, a sound Milo knew he would never forget, then it exploded in a burst of reeking ashes. More sigils were unwinding from the elder priest's arms, some of these acted like the first, enchanted whips that turned the undead to ashes and dust. But two sigils were different, these rising above the priest's head and turning into plate-sized discs that flew unerringly toward the recent-dead, and then decapitated them.

The younger priest was formidable, too. Brother Reed, his name was.

Milo watched as a midnight-black sigil that looked like a curling elm leaf floated free of the priest's shaved head and lightened to a charcoal gray. At the same time it doubled in size, then tripled. Then it floated toward the rear of the mass of undead that was pressing forward. The gray shape continued to stretch, and when it was the size of a blanket it dropped down over a half-dozen zombies and skeletons, smothering them and driving them back into the earth. In the passing of a few heartbeats the gray shape and the undead it touched were gone.

The priests were still facing more than two dozen undead, but Milo had no doubt that their tattoos would take care of the threat. So he slipped between wagons and to the other side of the caravan. His breath caught when he saw the carnage.

Naile was more than sixty yards east of the trail, his boar-form rending zombies and shattering skeletons. Guards hired by chandlers, shoemakers, tanners, silversmiths, carpenters, potters, and more were slashing at what had become an undead army. The ground that stretched east of the trail looked chewed up, where all of the bodies had dug themselves free.

At the edge of his vision, Milo saw still more undead creatures clawing themselves out of the ground. Most of the men had been dead quite some time, as evidenced by the strips of cloth and flesh that clung to them, and most had been adults. But there were a few smaller undead, what likely had been children. Naile had just trampled a pair of slight zombies, obviously elves. And there was a squat, thick-boned skeleton missing half its skull that was making its way to the front . . . the remains of a dwarf. Milo took a deep breath of the stinking air and trudged forward, bringing his sword down hard on the skull of the dwarf, splintering the bone and hacking at the thing again and again until it was dead a final time.

Ingrge ran toward the caravan, the stranger lingering behind on the trail to gather all of his daggers. The elf grabbed his side, as he was winded from the run and from struggling with the gray-cloaked man. When he was about five hundred feet away, he stopped and drew his bow, began notching one arrow after the next and firing at the ghoulish attackers.

Each one of the elf's arrows found their marks, he was that expert of a shot. But the arrows did nothing to slow the undead. Snarling, Ingrge slung the bow over his back and continued to run, drawing his thin-blade with one hand, and his dagger with the other.

"Hurry, you," Ingrge called over his shoulder to the gray-cloaked man. "If you say you are a friend, now is the time to prove it."

The stranger sheathed the last of the daggers and jogged after Ingrge. "By the braids of my sister Sherrie," he said, running after the elf, then coming to a stop. "What manner of evil could spawn this?" From this distance it looked like a war was being waged, with the undead forces multiplying and closing in on the hapless caravan. Even from this distance the stench of the undead was oppressive, giving the stranger pause.

"Don't want to die," he said, as he continued to take in the fight. "I hadn't intended to be a hero, not really. Not here." He watched a moment more, then looked back over his shoulder, where the sun was turning the trunks of the willow birches a molten orange. The woods looked safe and inviting. "Not really a hero," he repeated. "But certainly a fool." With that, he ran as fast as he could toward the caravan, pulling two daggers free as he went.

Within a few minutes, the stranger and Ingrge were fighting a force of undead that had sprouted at the rear of the caravan.

Return to Quag Keep

More and more skeletons grew like weeds from the ground, and as Milo watched another dozen scramble out, he decided that he was going to die. Everyone died, he knew. But his time was coming any moment now.

"Never going to see Wisconsin again," he muttered. "No more buttered popcorn." He wondered if when he died his body would show up in his apartment. Or if he died here would he be alive back home. "I'd rather not find out. Better change my attitude fast."

The bones from skeletons he'd slain were broken all around his feet, a detached hand had its fingers wrapped stubbornly around his scabbard. Still, he wouldn't quit. His sword arm felt on fire, the muscles burning with fatigue as he drove the blade down on one undead after the next. When the fallen bodies became too thick around him, he climbed them and pushed forward into another mass.

He could see Naile, the wereboar, continuing his frenzied assault. And toward the back of the caravan, he could see Yevele. She was several yards away from the wagons, whirling and slashing with her long sword and a dagger. He couldn't see her face clearly, but he imagined it was determined. Perhaps she was smiling, as she seemed to live for battle. Was Yevele different than Susan Spencer?

Ludlow Jade and his son were fighting, too, back to back near the largest of their wagons. The merchant was using a large, curved sword that Milo had not seen him carry. It was an impressive weapon, and Ludlow Jade used it with some amount of skill.

Still, despite the guards and the merchants, and despite the fact that they fought with courage and deftness, they were too outnumbered. The undead were clumsy and practically mindless, but they were relentless and difficult to stop, and more and more and more of them were appearing.

"So much for my change in attitude. We really are all going to die," Milo breathed. "But I'll take as many with me as the fates allow." Somehow he managed to redouble his efforts, and he cleaved through the corpse of a young man in a military uniform. The insignia on the tabard was nothing Milo was familiar with, and so he guessed this body was from somewhere distant.

It was clear to him that the undead hadn't come from the same graveyard. From the tattered remnants of clothes, Milo could see that some had been commoners and laborers; others had been aristocrats and warriors; and there were elves and dwarves in the mix—not likely they'd all be buried together. And what single graveyard could have held all these corpses? Some might have died . . . for the first time . . . as recently as yesterday, their flesh not yet foggy gray. Others had bones so yellow and not a trace of flesh anywhere; they might be centuries dead.

"Why?" Milo screamed, as his sword lodged in the chest of a particularly thick-chested zombie. He struggled to pull it free, wincing when the creature clawed at his face. Then he managed to tug the sword out and swing it again, cutting through the thing's spine and a heartbeat later cutting it in two. "Why is this happening?"

Ludlow Jade had told them to expect bandits. The merchant likely hadn't expected this. None of them had, Milo knew. Why would an army of undead strike at a merchant caravan? Certainly something controlled them. And what did that "something" hope to gain by this assault? All their deaths?

"Why? Why in the name of all that's holy?" Milo screamed then, feeling an intense pain shooting up his leg. He glanced down, a skeleton . . . or rather the remains of a skeleton from its shattered chest on up . . . had drug itself on top of a pile of bones and had thrust the needle-like fingers of both its hands deep into Milo's right thigh.

He brought his leg up, tugging the half-skeleton with it, and tried to beat it off with the pommel of his sword. Distracted, he didn't see another skeleton come up from behind him and do the same thing to the back of his left leg.

This time Milo clenched his teeth and fought from crying out. He dropped his sword and used his hands to pull the skeleton in front loose, then to pitch it high over the heads of more undead. He turned his attention to the one behind him, ripping its arms loose and tossing them aside, cursing to note the finger bones were still lodged in his leg. He brought his heel down hard on the offending skeleton's head, then he retrieved his sword and paced in a tight circle to access the battlefield.

The three Glothorio priests on this side of the caravan were working in concert now, and the chandler's two guards were keeping the undead back so the priests could work uninterrupted. Milo fought his way toward them to help.

The center priest was singing, a high-pitched dissonant tune that added to Milo's pain. As he neared, he felt the air change. It was still cold and filled with the horrid scent of decay, but now it crackled with energy that caused his hair to stand up. His fingers tingled, and it became an effort to hold onto his sword. Milo managed to draw nearer and fought to keep a grip on the pommel. He thrust his blade into the belly of one zombie, raising his leg and kicking out at another.

"Help us!" one of the chandler's guards called. He motioned to Milo with his free hand and jabbed futilely at a skeleton with his sword.

"I'm trying," Milo returned between clenched teeth. He worked to shove the pain to the back of his mind—it hurt with every step he took on his injured legs. He tried to focus on clearing out the undead around the priests. "I'm—"

The priest's song rose to a hurtful crescendo, and the other two priests joined in. At the moment that they held a shrill high note, several tattoos broke free from their heads and necks and whirled in the air high above them. The center priest raised his hands like a conductor, then gestured, and one by one the tattoos glowed darkly. Tiny motes of light appeared on the sigils, winking bright, then disappearing. When the glow faded, the priest gestured again, and the tattoos became arrows that raced earthward, piercing the ground.

The earth trembled in response, and Milo watched as the black arrow-sigils melted and spread over the trail, then stretched outward like a growing pool of oil and into the grass and churned-up earth where the undead had erupted. Where the magical oil touched the undead, there were puffs of ash and hollow cries.

"They're consecrating the ground," one of the chandler's guards explained. "At least, I think that's what they're doing."

The blackness continued to spread across the earth, leaving in its wake piles of ash where zombies and skeletons once stood. It even reduced to ash the severed limbs of the fallen creatures, and it spilled into cracks in the earth where more undead were trying to claw their way up.

"You," the center priest croaked. His voice was a harsh whisper, and his eyes were dull and lifeless. There were no tattoos remaining on him, and his fellows had only a few on their necks and the back of their hands. He pointed to Milo. "You, man. Unhook the dead horses, and take fit horses from other wagons. Then get the people and this caravan moving."

"This ground is foul, enspelled," another Glothorio priest said. "Much of our holy magic is spent, and we need to rest."

"To get away from here," the third priest said. "Hurry, man."

Milo headed to the front of the caravan and started unhitching the slaughtered horses. With Naile's help—he'd changed back from his wereboar form—they and some guards managed to tug the dead animals off the trail. Yevele, Ingrge, and the gray-cloaked stranger worked to divide the healthy horses between the wagons and get the caravan on its way.

Then Naile turned to retrieving his dropped clothes and hand axes, avoiding the gazes of surprised merchants and refusing to answer questions about how he could turn into a wild animal.

"Who are you?" Milo gestured to the gray-cloaked stranger. He remembered seeing him many days ago in the Golden Tankard, and remembered that the figure had managed to slip out before the fight spread to all corners of the room. "Well?"

Milo leaned against Yevele for support, his wounded legs throbbing painfully. He railed against a wave of dizziness that threatened to spill him to the ground. Between his efforts at fighting the undead and moving the dead horses, he'd opened up the gouges and gotten dirt in the wounds. It was becoming difficult for him to walk, and fiery jolts shot up from where the finger bones were still embedded. "I say again, who are you?"

The stranger drew back his hood. His eyes were clear and determined, and his face did not betray even a hint of fear. "You may call me Berthold of the Green. As I told Ingrge the elf, I am here to help you."

NINE

Berthold of the Green

Milo stretched out on a cot in the common room of Wheaton Dale's inn. It was the first time in quite a few weeks he'd had a place to sleep indoors, but this was only because of his wounds. Zechial had cut off Milo's leggings and worked the finger bones out of his legs, then he cleaned the wounds with brandy, and said he'd visit him later and would arrange for more care.

A dozen other caravan guards occupied cots, too, all of them injured from the fight with the undead. An equal number of guards had been killed, along with the shoemaker, and all of them were being buried in a mass grave just south of the city.

"One of those Glothorio priests is tending to the burial," Naile said. He was sitting on a stool next to Milo's cot, the stool creaking in protest under the big man's weight. "The priests are worried that if some spells aren't cast and the ground isn't consecrated, the dead guards might rise up and come after us."

"A cheery thought." Milo propped himself up on his elbows and looked to the far end of the common room. The inn had been turned into an infirmary, and it smelled of camphor and other sharp things he couldn't put names to. Lanterns burned low throughout the room, showing two Glothorio priests ministering to the potter's guard, who was in danger of losing an arm.

"They'll come tend you, too," Naile said. "I saw Ludlow Jade's son pay them."

Milo shook his head. "I'm surprised the priests didn't charge for casting spells against the undead back on the road."

Naile dropped his gaze to the tips of his boots. "Milo, they did. The merchants pooled some money, enough to satisfy the Coin Gatherers, I guess. The head priest said the tattoos cost them, and all of his would have to be replaced."

Milo eased back down on the cot. "Do any of the priests have the vaguest idea why the—"

"Undead attacked us? No. And I asked Ludlow Jade about it, too. He just paled and talked about taking up a different route next year. Said he wouldn't be taking his wagons this way again. I got the impression he'd hightail it back to the city come morning, but he said the towns north were expecting this caravan." Naile eased off the stool and walked to a window next to Milo's cot. He opened one of the shutters. "He thought he should keep his promise."

"Figures they need his blankets and rugs, huh?"

"And that he needs their money, I suspect."

"Where's Yevele?"

Naile raised his gaze to the moon. "And the moon rose full and pearly, pearly bright," he whispered, recalling the line from a song at the Golden Tankard.

"Yevele."

Naile closed the shutter. "Helping bury the dead, like I should be doing. Just wanted to check on you first. We'll come back later, all of us. Later tonight. In the meantime, I'll make sure someone brings you something to eat." He made a move to leave, then stopped. "Milo, what did you do . . . in Wisconsin? What did you do before you came here?"

Milo pretended he was sleeping.

Return to Quag Keep

Milo guessed "later" was close to midnight. The priests had worked their magic on his legs, taking quite some time with the left one, as they said it was gravely infected. He hadn't liked the use of the word "gravely," and when they muttered in a language he couldn't understand, he worried that he might lose his leg. But one of the priests cast some sort of healing enchantment that required the use of a swirling black tattoo. Minutes later, the ache was gone from Milo's legs and he could flex them.

They'd told him to rest for the evening, and so he was doing just that, appreciating a roof over his head, a full belly, and a somewhat comfortable straw mattress beneath him. He wondered if Ludlow Jade would tack on some additional service to his debt to pay for this, and for the healing from the Glothorio priests.

"Probably," he said.

"Probably what?" Naile was sitting on the stool, the shadows cast from a low-burning lantern giving the big man a haunted look.

"Just thinking," Milo said. "I've been doing a lot of thinking, just laying here."

"Thinking about home?"

"And about here. About the undead and our bracelets, my rings. About this world. About a lot of things. Yevele coming?"

"Soon. Last I knew she was looking for Ingrge and the guy with all the daggers. It seems they. . . ." Naile glanced at the doorway, where the trio was entering and trying to be quiet. Several of the wounded men were soundly sleeping, but a few were awake, their eyes following Yevele.

She knelt next to the cot, opposite Naile, and brushed the hair off Milo's forehead. "You've a fever," she whispered.

"Not so warm as he was a couple of hours ago," Naile supplied.

Milo propped himself up on his elbows. "I want to know who he is." He gestured with his head to the foot of the cot, where Ingrge stood next to the stranger.

"Berthold of the Green, I told you." The man had his hood back, and his cloak was off his shoulders. He was displaying the slightness of his frame to them, and at the same time showing off the arsenal of daggers that stuck from sheathes everywhere.

"Well, Berthold of the Green, that's not good enough." This came from Naile, who leaned forward on the protesting stool.

Berthold let out a deep sigh and crept close to Yevele. He kneeled silently on the floor. "Look, I explained all of this to Ingrge."

"Explain it to us," Milo said a little too loud.

Berthold drew his face together until it looked pinched. He put a finger to his lips in an effort to keep Milo quiet. "Listen," he said so softly they had to strain to hear. "I'm like you. I'm not from around here."

It was clear he had their attention. "Several months ago, probably a year. I've sort of lost track of time. My game master back home brought out these incredible miniatures he'd received in the mail. As usual, I got last pick, and so I got stuck with the thief, as always, I might add." He paused, apparently lost in some memory. Yevele nudged him to continue. "So I picked up the miniature, was looking at the detail. And then . . . poof . . . all of a sudden I wasn't in an imagined medieval city, one like our characters were adventuring in during the game. I was in a real one. And when I looked in a pool and saw my reflection, I found out I looked just like the thief miniature."

Milo swung his legs over the edge of the cot and brought his head down so he could better hear Berthold.

"There were five in my group in this place, all strangers to me, and all on this road headed . . . somewhere. I didn't know I was anybody other than Berthold—scoundrel, rogue, thief supreme."

"Just like what happened to us," Naile whispered.

"We stopped in a tavern, the five of us. We were drawn there. Some magical force, some . . . I don't know . . . something tugged us there. We sat in the corner and tried to figure out how we all came to be on that road. None of us could recall our 'real selves' at that point. Didn't get very far with the talk before this mysterious messenger—more like a ghost—appeared before us and beckoned us to the dungeons of Quag Keep. The image . . . ghost . . . whatever it was . . .

explained that a wizard was held in the deepest part of the dungeon in the keep and had magically brought us here to save our home world . . . and possibly save him and this realm in the process. That's when our memories came flooding back, our real selves." He paused: "Well, our selves in our real world. I'm not sure what is real. Anyway, the image was pretty weak, just like the wizard who spawned it apparently, and it was in mid-sentence when it quit. Curious, and having nothing better to do, we set out for Quag Keep. We knew if we wanted to get home, we were going to have to free the wizard."

"We were there, too, in Quag Keep," Yevele said. "But we didn't see a dungeon or a wizard."

"We didn't even make it to the Keep," Berthold explained. "Keth got sucked down into a stretch of swamp water and drowned. Matthew and Marc had their faces eaten off by some weird flying monsters on the other side of the marsh. And Roland . . . I woke up one morning and he was gone. So I ran back to the city hoping to find some other folks from home. And I did. I found you."

"How?" Naile looked skeptical.

"I saw you wearing these." Berthold pulled a bracelet out of his pocket. Its links were broken, but it looked like the ones on their wrists.

"How'd you get that off?" Milo asked.

"It wasn't easy. But maybe I can break your bracelets, too. There's some risk involved, though. Keth got burned real bad when I managed to get his off."

Milo stared at his bracelet and toyed with one of the gem dice.

"Oh, I bet they came in handy for a while, those bracelets," Berthold said. "Tugging you here and there, warning you about danger." He gave a clipped laugh. "Danger. Yeah, the bracelets are what's dangerous. Before Roland disappeared on me, he figured out someone was using the bracelets to track us—someone who wanted to keep the wizard in the dungeon, and who wanted to stop us from reaching him. Someone wants to keep that wizard held captive for a reason I've no clue to."

"The undead," Ingrge said. "Maybe that someone sent the undead after us."

"Maybe," Berthold cut back. "To keep us from going after the wizard."

Naile didn't buy that. "We weren't going after the wizard. We didn't know about any wizard. Not until you told us."

"But maybe that 'someone' didn't know that," the thief said.

Milo tapped Berthold on the shoulder. "We were never contacted by a . . . ghost or magic spell . . . and were never told to find a wizard in a dungeon. I'll admit we were drawn to Quag Keep, and we explored most of the tower. But Yevele's right. We didn't find a wizard."

"So you're doubting me. You've a right, I guess. But I bet the wizard ran out of energy to contact all of you . . . and maybe he wasn't able to contact whoever else got pulled into this place. But I also bet the wizard was able to tug you to the Keep nonetheless. And so you explored the tower, but not the dungeons under it. You didn't know to look for a wizard *below* the tower, but you have to help me find him now, or we'll never get home. Perhaps, never save our home. We can help each other."

"To save our world?" Milo asked. His expression said he still wasn't wholly convinced. "I'd like to believe this might be a way to get home," he added after a few moments. "You did have a bracelet, after all."

"So we can help each other?" Berthold looked hopeful.

Milo nodded. "I'm willing to give it a try."

"Great!" Berthold's voice carried to the nearby cots, and he quickly brought it back to a hush. "It's still dark, so we can sneak away from the caravan and head toward Quag Keep now."

"No." Yevele stood and put her hand on Milo's shoulder. "No journey for Milo and Naile." Her eyes were smoldering. "Milo needs rest. And the merchants need protection—look how many guards they've lost. Sure, they'll hire some sellswords in this village, but probably not enough to replace the ones who were killed. What if the bandits attack? Or what if more dead men rise up from the ground? Milo and Naile need to stay."

Recurn to Quag Keep

Milo shook his head. "We've got ourselves to think about, Yevele. Getting home." He jangled his bracelet and pointed to his rings. "We should be worrying about us."

"I don't disagree with that," Yevele said. "But you and Naile are sworn to work for Ludlow Jade, since he bailed you out of jail. You promised him. And on your honor, you owe him."

"But what about Quag Keep?" Berthold gave her an incredulous look. "I can't go there alone. I don't want to go alone."

"You won't be alone." This came from Ingrge, who moved to crouch next to Naile. "Yevele and I will go with you."

Naile growled, but the elf cut him off.

"We'll meet up with Naile and Milo in the city, after the caravan returns there." The elf's face was as stern as any of them had seen it. "With luck, we'll have this wizard freed and our dilemma solved before the caravan returns home."

"Then let's get going," Berthold advised. "I'd like to be well away from this caravan before the sun comes up. This Ludlow Jade fellow might not be so amenable to letting any of you go. No reason to cause a scene."

Ingrge, Yevele, and Berthold of the Green slipped silently from the room.

Naile continued to growl softly and shake his head. "He could've taken off these bracelets before he left." He gave a futile tug on the links, then growled again. "I should've asked him about doing it."

"I don't like this," Milo said. "Any of this. It was always a bad idea in the game to split the party. And that's what we're about to do."

TEN

Cross Country

They slipped out of Wheaton Dale and headed south down the trail. After a few miles, Berthold stopped and looked east. Pale rosy pink and yellow lights played above the rim of distant trees.

"Beautiful. I've never seen fireworks so beautiful." Berthold stood in awe.

"They call that the Celestial Dance," Ingrge said. "Those sky ribbons appear this time of year, and again in the early spring, when the sky is clear and the air is cold enough. Our people of the Seneval Pass believe the lights are an omen, that this time of year they signal an unforgiving winter coming to slay many of their brethren. However, such displays mean good hunting and a fine growing season, long and well-yielding." He paused and scratched his head. "I don't know why I know that. I never saw the Dance before." Much softer: "I don't know why I know a lot of things. I remember things I couldn't have experienced."

The elf continued to watch the lights. At times the sky looked like a watercolor painting, where too much water had been used and the colors smeared down to touch the horizon. In places the stars winked through. Moments later the colors brightened and undulated, like parade streamers blown by a strong wind. They were hypnotizing, and Ingrge's eyes followed the swirls as his breath caught.

Berthold pointed to a constellation directly overhead and nudged the elf. "Ingrge, that would be the Dog King, wouldn't it?"

The elf struggled to take his gaze away from the ribbons and tipped his head up. "Yes, the Dog King. Named for a squat, ugly king long centuries past who was said to have ascended to godhood after dying in a great battle to retake stolen lands. Only the dwarves from the Rhinehold Mountains still worship him. They believe he was this world's first dwarf. Other races call him the faded god."

"So, we follow where its snout points, right?" Berthold was looking at the constellation, then dropped his gaze a little so he could watch the flash of the Celestial Dance. "I said I never made it to Quag Keep, but we were headed this way. I know it lies in this direction. Somehow I can just feel it."

"Aye," Yevele said, losing interest in the sky show and striking east off the trail. "The damnable place is indeed this way." She sniffed audibly. "You wanted to be long absent from that town before the caravan roused, Berthold, so let's move. I'm good for more than a few hours. Until noon at least. I'm sure Ingrge is, too." She let out a clipped laugh. "Not that any in the caravan would take the time to do so, but none will be able to track us . . . Ingrge was their only scout."

"Wait." Berthold hurried to catch up to her. "Your bracelet, Yevele. I can remove it. Why don't I see to that now?"

She held out her arm and let out a deep sigh.

"You said there was a risk." This from Ingrge, as he joined the two.

"Slight, I should think. I had practice removing my own bracelet, and my former comrades'." He tugged a small leather pouch from his pocket and unfolded it. Inside, silvery picks glinted in the starlight. "It shouldn't be so hard for me this go 'round." He selected a thin pick, resembling a dentist's probe, to set about working on one of the links.

"Don't you need more light for that?" Ingrge peered intently over the small man's shoulder.

Berthold shook his head. "Thief supreme, remember? Thieves are used to working in the dark."

"Well, thief, just don't get the idea to turn any tricks on us," Ingrge cautioned.

Yevele cut him a cross look. "We have nothing to steal. In fact, we—ouch!" There was a flash at her wrist, and Berthold jumped back, slamming into Ingrge, almost knocking the elf down as the broken bracelet fell to the ground.

Berthold shook his hand and blew on his fingers. "Told you there was a little risk. Nothing major. Not near so bad as what happened when I got Keth's off." He looked up at her. "You're not hurt, are you?"

She was rubbing her wrist. "No."

"What happened to Keth?"

Berthold looked across at the elf. "Burned two fingers so bad they were useless. Curled and black they were. Not that it mattered, really. He drowned in the swamp a day or so later." He frowned and cast his head down, as if he were silently praying. Then he raised his head. "Next?" Berthold gazed straight at the elf.

Ingrge shook his head and pressed his hand tight against his chest until he caught Yevele's questioning stare. "Sure." But he did not hasten to pull up his sleeve and extend his wrist. "Take care of the fingers, mind you. I need them to use my bow."

It was several minutes later, and the use of several different picks before this bracelet came off. The flash was just as bright, and a burn around the elf's wrist showed clearly on fair skin. Though the elf regarded that with surprise, he said nothing. The elf's eyes were watery, silver in the night and looking as if they held mysteries and pain.

The bracelet fell to the ground, joining Yevele's, and Berthold dropped his, too. Then the thief jammed the heel of his slipper on them for good measure.

"C'mon," Ingrge urged.

Yevele had already started eastward once more—quick, long, long strides that even trained company would have trouble matching. Berthold let out a soft groan and started jogging.

Three days later, they were clear of the forest and were starting across a stretch of low hills. Heading southeast, the weather was still unseasonably cold, and the sky was fog-gray and cut by low-hanging threatening clouds.

"Not cold enough to snow," Ingrge observed happily. "But still could rain."

It did so in the late morning, starting with a soft misty drizzle that at the same time chilled and invigorated them. For the first time since they'd left Wheaton Dale, Berthold had been able to keep up with Yevele without huffing. But the drizzle turned into a steady rain, and then a cruel driving storm that hammered at them relentlessly and finally sent them searching for cover.

It was nearing mid-afternoon when Ingrge found a cave which he suspected had been abandoned by a large cat. It smelled musty inside, the air heavy but tolerable. And it was relatively small. They huddled in it and listened to the rain rat-a-tat-tatting against the rocks. Occasionally the wind gusted, sending a lance of rain against their already wet cloaks and freshening the air.

Yevele was studying Berthold, glumly plastered against the rock wall opposite her.

"What?" he demanded at last. "What are you looking at?"

"This wizard," she began, "the one that we are supposed to rescue. . . ."

"Yes?" He shivered. "Can't seem to get warm enough. My clothes, soaked. Brrrrr." He pushed away a fold of his cloak, shook it, and scowled when the wind blew it close again.

"How is finding and freeing this wizard going to save *our* world? And which world? This one we find ourselves in now? Or the one we left behind?"

Berthold pursed his lips. "Well . . . a world. Our world. I'm not sure. But it's what the message said. It seems to be worth pursuing. Better than floundering around with no leads at all."

"And just how will freeing the wizard save . . . our world?"

Berthold held a pensive look for a long moment before he jerked off his sopping cloak and shoved it to the back of the cave. "Yevele, that message faded out in mid-sentence. Remember? The message . . . well, it never really explained anything."

She ground her teeth and turned her head to stare at the rain.

The silence dragged on between them, becoming a palpable thing that made the thief increasingly uneasy. He watched the rain, which appeared never ending, its rat-a-tat-tatting tune never changing, save for brief intervals when the wind gusted stronger or changed direction and made the rain louder or softer. But that happened only briefly.

Hours might have passed, judging by the darkening of the sky. They had dozed on and off, Ingrge fitfully. It had to be sunset, perhaps a little later, the sky a dark gray now, the rain continuing relentlessly.

"This isn't unlike a medieval house," Berthold said. He felt the need to talk about something.

"I'm wondering." Yevele was still watching the rain, a solid sheet of cold water continuing to wash away stunted grass and pockets of soil outside the cave mouth. "What a local house must be like."

"This cave," he responded sourly. "If you weren't upper class, you typically lived in a house about this size. Damp and dark, frequently cold. It was usually nicer outside the house, lighter and warmer at least. There were only a few windows, and they were small and had shutters, stretched animal skin for panels. So you could see out when you wanted to, but it was difficult for others to see in."

"And you know this because as a thief you've broken into these houses?" For the first time in hours Ingrge spoke.

Berthold shook his head. "I used to read a lot about history, kings and famous knights, especially the Hospitalers and the Templars, and about how bad things were for the common folks. Playing the game got me interested in it." He paused. "You know, in a true medieval society, women had little power. They certainly weren't warriors. You're lucky this is some sort of fantasized version of a medieval world."

Yevele looked away from the rain and studied Berthold again. His face and features were obscured by the shadows. "And what did you do, Berthold of the Green, before coming here?"

"Traveled with those folks I told you about. Keth and Marc and—"

She poked him in the shoulder. "No. Before you came *here*."

"Oh." Berthold studied a spot on his gray leggings. He could barely make out his knee because of the thickening shadows.

"Answer her," Ingrge said sharply.

Berthold sucked in a breath but did not turn his gaze from outside. "I was a cop in Bowling Green."

"A cop. A policeman? Where is Bowling Green?" Yevele persisted.

"Kentucky." Berthold let out a deep breath. "Bowling Green, Kentucky. I wasn't always a cop, though. I started as a security guard for the Corvette plant there, right out of high school. The plant was something, so huge, and up front they had a couple of the first Corvettes that ever came off a line. The plant let employees drive the new cars, not that you could put many miles on them, but you could sign one out at night."

Yevele seemed uninterested in this particular bit of information.

"But the police force had openings, and they paid better. And without a college degree, I knew I'd never get into management at the Corvette plant. So I took some tests, and on my second time around, they hired me. At twenty-two. I was passed over the first time in favor of some guys who were coming out of the Army and had served as MPs. Funny, I'd went back to the Corvette plant the Tuesday before . . . before the miniatures arrived. I put in an order for a black one. It was going to stretch me to the very limits of my paycheck. But I wanted one of those cars real bad."

"Berthold of the Green," Ingrge mused.

"Priorities change. I couldn't care less about a damn car now. My real name was Bertrum Wiggins. Never liked it. But Berthold of Bowling Green . . . Berthold of the Green . . . has a nice ring to it. Patrolman Wiggins. Traffic sometimes, riding around catching speeders. Got to work a robbery a few times."

"And the game . . ." Yevele pressed.

"Started playing it in high school. Same group to this very day.

Well, right up until the day I was bamfed here. I was always the thief."

Ingrge snorted. "All the game conventions I went to, the cops, sheriff deputies, whatever, they all played thieves. Probably figured they knew how to get away with things better than the real criminals."

Berthold shrugged. "I know how to use all these tools. I know how to cut the strings of someone's purse, how to pick their pocket, open practically any locked door."

Ingrge's eyes narrowed.

"And, yeah, I've stolen from some people in this world. Not a lot. Three or four times. I was hungry, like I am now. Had to eat."

"We ate this morning, the hare I killed." Ingrge crossed his arms in front of his chest. "I'll find something else tomorrow morning. I'll not hunt in this rain. Too difficult."

Berthold nodded. "Should've thought to take something from the caravan before we left, a few supplies."

"Stealing," Ingrge tsked. "Like you're used to stealing."

"I needed clothes. Broke into one of those little homes only once. For clothes. You do what you have to, you know."

"To survive," Yevele said. "You do anything to survive." She was looking out the cave mouth again, her eyes following small dark shapes that were moving slowly across a swath of mud, illuminated by a lantern that must have been shielded from the rain somehow.

"Goblins," Ingrge whispered. "A hunting party caught in this weather."

"Hopefully," Yevele said. She kept her voice low, too. "Hopefully hunting food and not hunting us. Looks like maybe two dozen."

Berthold tapped his fingers on his knee. "I can't think why goblins would hunt us. No reason."

"I can't think why undead would spring up out of the ground and go after the caravan," Yevele returned. Her eyes were daggers, aimed at the line of goblins. Her hand was on the pommel of her sword.

"You had bracelets on then," Berthold continued. "Whatever force wants to stop us from freeing the wizard . . . I know in my heart something is trying to stop us . . . could track you by the bracelets.

I'm certain it tracked Keth and I and the others. Maybe that's why the undead came, because of your bracelets. But without the bracelets—"

Ingrge made a hissing sound. "But Naile still has a bracelet. Milo too."

Berthold shrugged. "So? They won't be going near Quag Keep, and won't tip anyone off that we're getting close to the wizard."

"So this force can track them, you claim. Naile and Milo?"

Another shrug.

Yevele continued to watch the goblins, their forms growing smaller as they moved away, the deepening shadows swallowing them. "You do what you have to. Isn't that right Bert? To survive?" She slipped out the cave entrance, and headed off through the downpour, mindless of the weather and the darkness.

Ingrge's eyes were narrow slits. "A diversion? A distraction? Is that what Milo and Naile are to you? Let the . . . whatever it is, whoever it is . . . track them by their bracelets while we venture safely to Quag Keep?"

Berthold followed Yevele, slipping and sliding on the wet rocks and falling. "They're not a diversion, they're caravan guards," he replied, as he got to his feet and tried to wipe the mud from his leggings. "I simply forgot to take their bracelets off. An oversight."

The elf's voice was laced with anger: "We could go back to the caravan, and have you remove those bracelets. But we're three days to the southeast, and they're three days to the north. A week to catch up, if we're lucky. And if something is after them, tracking them with the bracelets, we could be too late. Our trip wasted."

"They're strong men, those two," Berthold said. "They could well defeat whatever the fates throw at them." He paused: "I really did forget to pry loose their bracelets."

"Yeah, I'm sure you forgot." Ingrge let Yevele and Berthold get a few dozen yards ahead, then he started after them, trying to peer through the rain and find a trace of the goblins or any other threat. "I'm sure you did."

ELEVEN

Dark Men

Pick a pinky petal for your papa's pride.
Beg a burning blossom for your budding bride.
But when ye come, and all the flowers are dying,
If I am dead, as dead I well may be,
Ye'll come and find the place where I am lying. . . .

The cold didn't bother Fisk Lockwood. He barely registered the night's icy breeze against his face as he softly sang. His hood was back, sleeves pulled up above his elbows, cloak billowing behind him as he sat astride a big mare of blackest black. The horse snorted, her gray breath fanning up from her nostrils like smoke seeping from a dying fire.

"Ah, sweet Keesh," Fisk said, as he stroked the horse's neck. "The pipes, the pipes are calling. From glen to glen, and down this very mountainside." He slipped from the horse's back and glided to a rocky ledge and looked down.

They were on a tall hill north of the city. From his lofty vantage, Fisk could see the small farms that spread across the plains below, and in the distance on a riverbank, marked by the flickering lights of torches and lanterns, he spotted a tiny village of fishermen. He knew the name of the place once, but it was an inconsequential piece of information, and so he'd discarded it.

It was early evening, and Fisk imagined that families were finishing meals and chores and preparing for bed: a droll existence. Women might be singing to their helpless, parasitic babes. Men might be trying unsuccessfully to scrub the dirt of the fields out of the cracks in their fingertips.

He looked west, to the forest, where the wolves were reported to hunt in large packs. Maybe he had more in common with them than with the people below. He was cunning like them, vicious when he needed to be, and, yes, he did prey upon the weak and slow. Now he held his head high to listen, hoping to hear the howl of a wolf, instead picking up only the wind rustling the tall dead grass around the mare's hooves. It sounded mournful enough though, and so he found it pleasing.

He closed his eyes, imagining, for just a few moments, that he was running with the wolves. A couple of times he had done so in his younger days. Now Fisk pretended to feel the drying fall grass against the soles of his feet, the touch of the branches against his chest and arms as he dashed through the woods. Scents became more intense to him then, his senses had not been dulled by the time spent in cities . . . with all their people and business, cookstoves belching out the odors of cooked meat and vegetables. The blacksmith's shop adding acrid things to the once clean air. Fisk missed those days for the simple things. But these days he relished because he had more to do, certainly more important things than running through the woods. Still, he let his mind drift there once more.

Then, humming Joel's "woman" song, Fisk returned to the horse and waited.

The stars began peppering the sky by the time he had company. Fisk hadn't heard anyone approach, but he smelled a harsh, sour scent that made his eyes water.

Return to Quag Keep

"Master," Fisk said, going down on one knee. "I came at your summons."

A rattling sound, like a large snake might make, was followed by a belch of air filled with sulfur.

"I understand, Master," Fisk bowed his head a fraction.

There was more rattling and a sibilant hiss. "Displeasssed, Fisssk." The words came breathy and low, and the harsh, sour scent intensified. "Very displeasssed." The rattling resumed.

"My apologies, Master. No, I have not slain the full company of adventurers, as you bade me. But I will. I have never failed you, not in all these years." Fisk cocked his head, listening to the rattling, and then at length replying. "I caused the deaths of four of the previous company, two meeting most beautiful, grisly ends. The thief escaped their midst, Berthold of the Green he calls himself. But his escape is actually fortuitous, Master. He has broken the present company I am after."

The rattling grew louder and faster. "Explain, Fisssk."

"He lured two of them away, the woman and the elf. He's taking them somewhere. I haven't determined their location yet. I suspect it matters not where they go, Master. I will follow them through the gems they wear. The company broken, fewer to deal with, they are easier to slay. Divide them and kill them."

Fisk bent forward, splaying his fingers on the ground and inhaling the sour scent deep into his lungs. He lowered his head and listened to the odd rattling tongue.

"Disssapointed, Fisssk."

He trembled at the repeated pronouncement. "Master, I know the undead blooms did not slay the company. But I had not expected them to. The company is strong, when it is together. The two large men are especially formidable, one of them can become a rampaging beast. I used the undead blooms to study them, to learn their strengths and frailties and fears. I used the blooms to weaken the caravan they guard, and to make the ones around them afraid. I will admit, Master, that I thought the undead might slay one or two of the company. But I had not anticipated the spells of the Glothorio priests."

"Priestsss. 'The Coin Gatherersss.' Hate the priestsss."

"Yes, they were ... threatening ... to the undead blooms. But they used so many of their spells. I watched the magical tattoos fly from their heads and arms. They have little magic remaining, Master. The undead weakened them."

The darkness at the top of the hill moved, and a patch as black as the mare came close to Fisk.

"Your intentionsss, Fisssk?"

The assassin touched his lips to the ground.

"Everything is as I planned, Master. The company split, the two men travel with the doomed caravan. The blood of the woman and the elf will be easier to spill. The ground will drink up their life, Master."

"Sssoon."

"The true threat to the caravan lies in wait farther to the north. I have set that in motion, Master. A coiled cobra leaning back and ready to spring. Days from now that trap will be sprung."

"So you mussst see to the woman and the elf first, Fisssk."

The rattling grew louder still, settling uncomfortably in the assassin's ears. Fisk clenched his teeth and closed his eyes, waiting for the sound to pass.

"Yes, Master, the woman and the elf first, and the thief from the previous company who travels with them."

"All of the otherworlders mussst die."

"Yes, Master."

The rattling faded, but the black shadow remained. The breeze rustled the dead grass and Fisk's cloak. The assassin raised his face from the ground and stared into the heart of the shadow.

"All of the otherworlders?"

"The lizard-thing and the priessst, too. Where are they, Fisssk?"

The assassin moved his thumbs in circles on the ground and rocked back and forth on his knees. Though he was still looking into the shadow, he was seeing a place to the south, picturing Deav Dyne and Gulth. "I see them, Master. They travel to the swamp."

The rattling started again, soft this time. "I favor the swamp, Fisssk."

"Yes, Master."

"You will go there, Fisssk, when you are done with the others. And you will kill the lizard-thing and the priessst. All of the other-worlders mussst die."

"Yes, Master. I have never failed you." The assassin rose, eyes still on the heart of the shadow. He listened to the soft rattling, then when it stopped, he returned to his horse. The black mare whinnied anxiously, and Fisk stroked her neck. "We ride, Keesh, to find the elf and the woman first, the little thief who leads them."

The horse reared back, and flames licked from her front hooves. Gray breath puffed from her nostrils now, appearing as plumes of smoke that twisted into the sky. Her nostrils glowed red like embers, even as her eyes seemed to shoot forth flames.

"We ride, Keesh."

The horse plunged forward, racing over the rocky ledge and down the steep side of the hill, hooves barely touching the ground, yet sounding like thunder, mane whipping cruelly at Fisk's face as he held on with all his strength.

When the thunder was so muted that the breeze hissed at the dead grass, the heart of the shadow crept toward the rocky ledge. It was a pool of black, wet and glistening and reflecting the stars. It breathed, like any living creature would, expanding and contracting, and making the reflected stars wink and shimmer.

"The otherworlders mussst die," the black pool hissed. "Soon and mossst horribly." Rattling softly, the pool poured itself over the rocky ledge and found a crevice to disappear into.

Fisk Lockwood's fingers were tightly entwined in the mare's mane. The air around him was colder because of the horse's speed. It seemed to race impossibly fast, faster than any natural animal of this world. Since Fisk found the pace exhilarating, he didn't mind the chill. In truth, hot and cold barely registered, and only in the sense that the temperature had changed. He found the cold neither comfortable nor uncomfortable, and the breeze a bother only in that it caused his cloak to flap loudly behind him.

He closed his eyes and listened to the thunder of the mare's hooves, and her powerful snorts, inhaled the scent of brimstone that spewed from her nostrils. He pictured the fields she dashed over, rotted cornstalks and shriveled bean plants, ruts from plows. The humble homes she sped beyond, the people inside nursing their parasites and never realizing their dreams. Everything a dismal, pathetic blur.

Then the mare was thundering down the trail the caravan had taken, and shortly before dawn was stopping. Fisk slid from her back and stepped off the trail, traveling east a few yards and stopping. He glanced down and saw three copper bracelets festooned with gem dice.

"The elf," he snarled. "The woman and the thief." He slammed his fist against his hip. "Their time will come. I will not fail the Master." Then he was on the horse, which was lightening, as the sky was lightening, turning a dappled gray before his eyes.

A moment later they were heading north.

"The two men first, then," Fisk said, "the man and the man-beast."

TWELVE

Sandlings

"Stop. Just for a little while." Berthold held his side and huffed. "Let a guy catch his breath."

"You're always catching your breath." Yevele looked over her shoulder and shook her head. "I want to reach Quag Keep as fast as possible. I'll not wait for . . ." She frowned and balled her fists, set them against her hips.

Berthold sagged to his knees, still huffing. A moment more and he sat, reaching for the waterskin that dangled from his belt. He pulled the cork and took a long drink. "Just for a little while," he repeated. He took another drink, recorked the waterskin, shook it and scowled.

"You're stopping too often. And you're drinking too much," Yevele said flatly. "We're nearly to the desert now, and your skin is nearly flat. Ingrge and I will not share with you later, be sure of that."

Berthold rested back on his arms and swallowed as he eyed her. She was pacing in a tight circle. "You don't relax, do you? Always moving. Except when you're sleeping. And from what I can tell, you don't sleep much."

Andre Norton and Jean Rabe

Ingrge sat beside Berthold, closed his eyes and tipped his head up to the early morning sun. The elf was listening intently, but not to the words of either Berthold or Yevele.

"I know how to relax, thief." Yevele stopped pacing. "But now is not a time to take it easy."

"I have to rest. I can't keep up with you. Look at my legs."

"It is not my fault that you're short."

Berthold rubbed his legs sullenly.

"And it is not my fault that you haven't my energy either." She turned her back on the man, fists still resting on her hips, staring east. The land that stretched away was dry, flat earth spotted with scrubby patches of crabgrass and thistles. "Ingrge has no trouble with the pace."

"Ingrge's an elf, and his legs are longer than mine. Look, Yevele, I didn't ask to be small. I've the body of a jockey. I'm not in bad shape." He gave a last pat to his knees. "This isn't the real me, either. In Bowling Green, I'm six-two. Six-two! I work out in the gym three nights a week. I box in the department program. In the summer I play in a city softball league." He paused: "Wherever you're from . . . what are you like there? I'll wager you're not like you are here. You're probably fat and dumpy."

She stood like a statue, studying the horizon, waiting, apparently refusing to hear him.

"I'm sorry, Yevele. I didn't mean that. It's just that this is hard, you know. This life we have here . . . it's real. We have a past, even if it's only in our heads. We know about the land and the towns, some of the legends. The elf knows all about the constellations and the Dance and fading dwarven gods. But we have another life, too. For me, it's the police force. So it's like we're not complete people. We're here, but only part of us . . . I'm afraid I'm going to lose Bert Wiggins, you know. I'm afraid if we don't do something, I'm going to be Berthold of the Green forever. And I like Bert Wiggins, better than I like Berthold of the Green."

No response.

After several minutes, Berthold got to his feet and wiped his hands for the last time on his leggings. "I'm ready, but I want to walk for a while, Yevele. A reasonable pace. No more of this running. We've been traveling almost a week, and not on any one of those days have I been able to match you. My legs are burning."

She started walking across the scrub land, slower than before. "You are necessary, thief, Ingrge tells me. I'll try to make it easier on you. And you can try a little harder."

Still, she stayed ahead of him. Ingrge fell back for a time, often looking over his shoulder. When they reached the desert, however, he caught up to Berthold.

"What's with her?" Berthold asked the elf. "The past few days she's been as testy as all get-out. I haven't done anything to—"

"She worries over Naile and Milo. She wonders if we did the right thing by not backtracking and having you remove the bracelets. She will hold herself accountable if something happens to them." Ingrge whispered the last: "It is just her way. I think she fancies herself the leader of our little adventuring band."

"Well, I could be wrong, Ingrge, about those bracelets. Maybe no one's homing in on them."

Ingrge jogged past Berthold, came even with Yevele, then passed her. The elf began the swing-ahead pace of a scout.

Here the air was still and dry. He was thankful it was warmer than along the merchant trail and in the scrub lands. But it was certainly not warm enough to shed either his wool tunic or cloak. When he'd been through the desert before, the heat was intense, but not unbearable.

The sand made a shushing sound when his boots struck it. He ran in time with the beat of his heart, breathing deep. He could smell Yevele and Berthold, and himself, all of them in need of a good scrubbing and a change of clothing. Still, he could smell the sand itself, earthy and flecked with the husks of scorpions, laced with the skins and bones of long-dead lizards and snakes. He could also smell a trace of water in the air. Perhaps it might rain even in this dry place.

No plants to be seen, just the never-ending sea of sand and rocks, rising in places to arch as waves on water. It made him think of

Florida again, and the forty-two steps to the beach he'd trot after waking up in the afternoon. He liked to swim out to a sandbar, get a little exercise in before going in for the evening shift. A good swim worked up his appetite. Sometimes he'd bring a lunch with him, sprawl on the sand and eat two cold chicken sandwiches, plenty of mayo and pickles, wash it down with a diet soda. He'd sit back and think about the evening's stint and if there were any special promotions he had to highlight, concert tickets to give away. If he was featuring an artist, he'd run over the trivia in his head, when the singer moved to Nashville, what was the first song he or she managed to get air play. Now he was having trouble remembering any of the minutiae about even his favorite stars. How old was Willie Nelson? How much money did he owe the government in taxes? What was the first line in "Whiskey River?"

"Forty-two steps to the beach, fifty-seven to the sea," he said, repeating it like a mantra. Then he mumbled his telephone number, stumbling a bit, then getting it right. "Address. Birthdate." He bit down on his lip and repeated everything, not wanting to lose his real self to this world. "Forty-two steps."

In the distance there was a dune, and he made his way toward it, intending to climb it for a better look at the land, as he continued to recite the numbers. A glance over his shoulder revealed that Yevele was a few hundred yards behind him, Berthold a little farther back. He motioned to her, then pointed to the dune, angled toward it and ran faster.

Ingrge focused on the dune, the smells and sounds of the desert, the play of the still air against his face as he rushed across the sand, not cold like along the merchant trail, but not quite warm. Certainly it was pleasant compared to the weather of the past many days. He closed his eyes for the briefest of moments, allowing himself to savor the desert. Then his eyes snapped open—there was no mistaking that he was being pulled into the sand.

"Yevele!" he managed to shout before he was sucked down, trapped up to his waist. He struggled to pull himself out, hands flailing to find a purchase, fingers closing on a rocky outcropping and grabbing tight. He was steady for the moment, listening to his ragged breath and the pounding of Yevele and Berthold's feet across the sand. The tip of her shadow stretched out and touched him, then he was yanked completely under.

"Did you see him?" Yevele spun this way and that, hand cupped over her eyes and searching the desert for any sign of Ingrge. "I could've sworn he was here. He motioned me toward the dune. That dune." She gestured with the tip of her sword. She'd drawn the weapon the moment she lost sight of him.

"I wasn't looking for him," Berthold admitted. "I was watching you, following you." The thief pulled his hood back, as if unshading his eyes might help him find the elf. "Ingrge!" He hollered louder: "Ingrge! Where are you?"

They were quiet for a moment, looking this way and that.

"I heard him before," Yevele said. "I heard him yell."

"Well, I don't hear anything." There was worry in the thief's voice, and he drew one of his daggers, dropping his attention to the sand. "I see his tracks." The thief started following them, slowly and carefully, looking to his sides as he went. "He came this way. See?"

Yevele followed him for a change. "But they stop. His footprints just . . . stop."

Berthold knelt at the last footprint and started moving the sand around with a dagger. "There's a depression here." He started digging with the dagger, after a moment finding that futile. He sheathed it and started digging with cupped hands. "A little help would be useful."

Yevele refused to sheath her sword. Instead, she kicked the sand away. Berthold sputtered when he got a face full of it.

"A little less help would be even better," he said. "Why don't you just stand guard?"

She ignored him, continuing to kick at the sand. He closed his eyes and kept digging, spitting the sand out of his mouth.

"Gotta find him," he whispered. "God, don't let me be stuck in the desert with this woman." A pause: "Ingrge! Yevele, I think he's under the sand. I think I hear something."

She kicked away harder, and he dug faster, then suddenly he went head-first into the sand, swallowed up by it.

She disappeared a moment later.

They landed on a mound of sand in an underground cavern. It was as dark as night, the shadows so thick they could make out only vague shapes. The cavern was heavy with a foul scent neither of them could identify.

Berthold was spitting sand out of his mouth and furiously wiping at his face. On his hands and knees, his fingers danced across the sand until they found Yevele. She slapped his hand away.

"Ingrge!" Yevele was on her feet, trying to make out more detail. She looked up, seeing a pale spot on the ceiling above her. It was a small hole they'd fallen through, and the sand had filled it back in. But a little light shone through the sand covering. "Ingrge!"

"Ingrge!" Her shout was close to a scream.

"Here." That was his voice.

"Heeeeeere," parroted the dragon that had him pinned beneath a claw. The beast opened his eyes, and the yellow glow from them faintly helped to illuminate the chamber. "Heeeeeere."

The dragon was not near as large as the gold one Yevele had encountered the first time she traveled to Quag Keep. It was as long as two war-horses nose to tail, and had a snout that was faintly equine. The glowing scales were the size of pebbles, a dull brown, practically the color of the sand overhead, and it had stubby horns that stuck out from above leathery ears. Its shining eyes were its most striking feature . . . those and the blood-red claws that threatened to puncture Ingrge's chest.

"Heeeeeere," the dragon repeated. Its eyes bore into Yevele's.

"You make a move," the thief cautioned Yevele, "and that beast is going to skewer your friend."

The battlemaid hissed, but held still. Her fingers turned bone-white in the punishing grip she kept locked on her sword pommel.

"Are you all right?" she risked as she managed to pry her eyes from the dragon's and look to Ingrge.

The elf offered her a weak smile. She couldn't see him clearly, shadowed by the dragon's body, the shadows from the cavern's wall stretching out. But he seemed intact, and she didn't see any blood.

"It pulled me under," he explained. His voice was weak since the dragon's claw was pressing against his chest and making it difficult for him to talk. "My fault. I wasn't careful enough. For once I wasn't paying attention. And look where it got us."

"Heeeeeere," the dragon said. "Heeeeeere. Heeeeeere. Heeeeeere. Heee—"

"Enough!" Yevele barked. "Can't you say anything else, beast?"

The dragon cocked its head, curls of steam rising from its nostrils. Even in this gloom, the air shimmered around its face, the way the air shimmers over the sand on a hot day. "Beeeeeeast," it pronounced slowly. "Beeeeeast heeeeeere. Beast here." Its eyes brightened, seemingly pleased that it had mastered two human words. "Beast here," it repeated. "Beast here. Beast here."

"Lovely," Yevele growled. "Yes, the beast is here, right in front of me. But what to do about it?" She still hadn't made any attempt to free the elf. Her gaze moved between Ingrge and the dragon's eyes. "Got to do something. You have any ideas, Bert?"

"Berrrrrt." The word sounded like a purr coming from the dragon. The dragon repeated it—over and over, and louder. It sent a tremor through the cavern. Sand filtered through the hole in the ceiling, pouring down on Yevele until the sand was above her knees. The tremor continued, the dragon still repeating the word. No more sand filtered down, however, and the hole was clear to the sky.

Yevele spit sand from her mouth and shook her head, sand flying from her hair and catching the light that came in through the hole. She could see much better now, with the added light, and she could tell that the cavern was huge. The source of the foul odor became immediately apparent. There were piles of dragon dung here and there.

"Berthold?"

"I see them, Yevele."

Andre Norton and Jean Rabe

There were also two other dragons. These were not quite as large as the one that continued to pin Ingrge, but they were close. They'd been against one of the far walls, but were now slinking nearer, making a sound that was similar to sand being blown by a strong wind.

"Yevele, I don't think we're going to reach Quag Keep anytime soon."

"Not in this lifetime," she answered. Then she swallowed hard and redoubled the grip on her sword's pommel. She was trembling all over, and sweat was beading on her forehead. "None of us will make it there in this lifetime."

"Berrrrrrt," the first dragon pronounced. "Bert. Here, Bert." It crooked a talon from its free claw and motioned the thief to come closer. The steam rose in thicker spirals from its nostrils.

THIRTEEN

The Village Hart

The merchant caravan was angling its way north, the trail running parallel to a slow, wide river called the Amber Serpent. Milo walked on the riverside, alert for the most part, but occasionally letting his gaze drift to the water. He watched a string of "insect boats," cupped leaves that were carrying beetles and carpenter ants south. And he wondered if the insects had accidentally been swept up, or if they had enough intelligence to know to look for easy passage to a clime where they might not end up frozen to the foliage.

Milo knew he wouldn't mind a nice, lazy boat ride now. Back in Wisconsin, living so close to a lake, he used to take rides on the big paddlewheels. The older he got, the fewer rides he took, and last year he'd been out only once—and this only because he'd found a coupon for a half-price dinner cruise discarded on the sidewalk. Now he wished he hadn't considered the boat trips "old hat" and that he hadn't taken the lake for granted. It would be gorgeous this time of year, the trees ringing it so bright with fall colors, all of it reflecting on a glass surface—the stuff of postcards and jigsaw puzzles.

His feet were sore, that's what made him think about the paddlewheels and home, he told himself. It would be heaven to sit down on a padded deck chair and watch the trees and the last of the tourists go by in their expensive sailboats. His town was better in the fall, the stunted streets no longer bumper-to-bumper with cars bearing Illinois plates. Oh, the "flatlanders" were still in evidence, there just weren't so many of them. Their numbers started to thin after Labor Day. He remembered liking the smell in the fall, less gasoline fumes, the breeze off the lake bringing the not-unpleasant scents of dying leaves. If he made it back home, he'd spend more time at the lake, he decided. More boat rides, more loaves of bread to feed the geese.

Milo was in excellent physical shape, strong and no longer aching from the wounds in his legs—all that were left were scabs where the skeletal fingers had dug in, souvenirs of his ordeal with the undead. But, oh, how his feet ached from walking so many days, his feet sliding back and forth in these leather boots Ludlow Jade had provided. Calluses and blisters.

Milo had been sparring with Naile at night, both of them deciding they needed some practice to keep their fighting skills up. The two were pretty equally matched, Milo with his sword and Naile with the twin hand axes, and both were holding back just a little. Milo wondered which of them would win if the fight was for real. There'd be no sparring tonight, he decided. There'd be only sleep, and maybe ointment for his blisters if he could talk the "elixir" peddler out of something in exchange for brushing down some horses.

Milo watched the last of the insect boats slip from sight and spotted a section of the river that looked shallow because of a rise in the rocky bed.

"I'll catch up," he hollered to Ludlow Jade. "I'm going to refill my skins." Then he stepped between a pair of spindly river birches and trundled down the slope, kneeling at the bank and pulling two waterskins from his belt. He drank what little was left in one of the skins, then he refilled it. Then he dumped the old water out of the second skin and filled it to the brim.

Another insect boat went past.

Milo stared at the water and at his reflection distorted by ripples.

Return to Quag Keep

He'd not shaved in the past few days, and so an uneven stubble was growing on his face. Neither had he combed his hair, and so he looked scruffy. Dark circles ringed his eyes, evidence he hadn't slept well since the incident with the undead. He used to sleep deeply, even in Wisconsin—where sometimes he didn't hear the alarm go off and ended up late to work. But not anymore. Every little creak from one of the wagons, a snort from one of the horses, someone talking in their dreams . . . any noise seemed to wake him and send him reaching for his sword. He had nightmares about the undead, and sometimes he became one of them.

As he stared at the water, he imagined himself with gray flesh and hollow eyes. A shiver raced down his spine.

"Get a grip," he told himself. Then he splashed some water on his face and neck, pushed himself away from the bank, and hurried to catch up to Ludlow Jade's wagons. He was more wary as he resumed his post, thinking about the undead and wondering why they had attacked the caravan. Then he found himself thinking about Yevele. Was Naile thinking about the battlemaid, too? Was she safe? Did her feet ache as bad as his?

Ludlow Jade had been upset to discover Yevele and Ingrge gone from the caravan. The merchant especially fumed over the absence of the elf, who'd been serving as the caravan's scout and who occasionally hunted and provided fresh venison. Naile and Milo didn't volunteer any information about their missing friends, claiming not to know where they were. It was the truth, Milo thought. He didn't know where they were. He simply knew where they were going.

In the first few days since the pair had vanished, Ludlow Jade took it out on Milo and Naile. He didn't work them harder, but gone was the pleasant demeanor and kind words he'd been treating them to. Instead, he gave them a cold shoulder, talked to them only about which wagons they would walk next to and when they could ride. And he shared none of the apples from the bushels he bought in Wheaton Dale.

They reached the village called Hart early in the afternoon. It was larger than the previous stop, and it was mostly a collection of farmers and miners. Milo had overheard a couple of the merchants talking earlier. There was a copper mine at the western edge of the village, and though it had been mined for well more than a decade, it was still providing enough copper to keep the village going. The mine belonged to the country's Council of Lords, who had it minted into the "coin of realm." The miners were paid well, and a share was held back by the village, which was fashioned into jewelry, tools, and cookware. Some of the merchants in the caravan had plans to buy the copper goods and resell them when they returned to the city. However, Ludlow Jade did not seem interested in copper.

Only a few of the village homes could be considered shabby, and these were on the south end where the caravan entered. They were weather-beaten woodplank with thatch roofs, and it looked like a strong wind might topple them.

"The old ones," Zechial explained. "Old folks who haven't coins for better places, some of them squandering their earnings from the mine in their earlier years. The village elders make sure they have roofs over their heads, and they live off charity."

Milo mused that he wouldn't mind sleeping in one of those shacks, having tired of sleeping under the second of Ludlow Jade's wagons.

The rest of the residences were in far better shape, most of them being made of stone, mudded tightly together in spacious round affairs with wood and tile roofs. The doors and shutters were painted shades of greens and browns, and the larger homes had family crests painted high on the doors.

The caravan settled on the east quarter of the city, near a large pond where white ducks swam. Ludlow Jade dismissed his guards for the remainder of the afternoon, directing Naile and Milo to come back by sunset for dinner. His other two guards were spending the night in the village inn with coins the merchant had paid them.

There was a bakery, and Naile and Milo stopped in front of it first. The scents of bread baking, cinnamon, apples, and vanilla wafted out and set their mouths to watering.

"I'd buy every last thing in there. Every loaf of bread, every pie, every everything. If I had money. I'm a lawyer, Milo. In Brooklyn,

Return to Quag Keep

I'd stop by Chayhana on Thirteenth most Wednesdays for lunch with some of the associates or with a client. Evenings, sometimes I'd go to Mezzanote or La Tra Torria, or even Michael's if I felt like dressing up or if I had a date. Maybe carry-out from Short Ribs on Eighty-Sixth Street, not too far from my apartment. For two weeks now we've been eating dried beef and beans, and those rock-crackers."

"Hardtack, I think they call it."

"Tooth-busters is a better name." Naile looked in the window and his eyes watered, too. "I might go out tonight, foraging. See if I can dig something up better than that hardtack."

"Rooting, you mean. As a boar."

"I suppose you could call it that. I prefer to call it filling my belly."

Milo stared at an apple pie that was placed in the window by a pasty-faced man with flour on his arms and face. "I'd like to fill my belly with that pie."

"You'd have to fight me for it. C'mon, let's get out of here before I do something I'll regret much later."

"You go on," Milo said. "I'm going to watch the window for just a little while longer."

"Well, don't drool all over yourself." Naile made a grunting sound and strode past a few more shops, one a tailor's where a thin man visible through an open door was fitting Zechial with a heavy dark blue tunic. He looked into the doorway of a dry goods shop, nodding a greeting to a man measuring powders behind a counter. He passed a blacksmith's, then stopped at a two-story tack shop, where an old man on a ladder was replacing shingles. The old man had broad shoulders, but the rest of him was slim, the flesh hanging loose on his arms. His hair was white and wispy like cobwebs, and it was teased by a slight breeze. When he turned slightly, displaying a small chin and a hawkish nose, Naile thought that the man reminded him a little bit of a maître d' at Michael's in Brooklyn, so he watched for a few moments.

The old man was not so neat-handed as the maître d', and he fumbled with the tiles. One slid and fell, nearly striking Naile and splitting in two when it hit the ground. The man leaned back on the ladder, looking to see where the lost shingle landed, and in that moment he lost his grip on the top rung. His arms beat circles in the air, as he and the ladder teetered backward.

Naile reacted quickly, stepping forward and slamming the ladder back against the building. The man continued his fall, but Naile got under him. He spread his arms and awkwardly caught the old man, cradling him like a baby. Miraculously, the man wasn't badly hurt. Naile gently set him on his feet.

"You all right?"

The man's hands shook, his lips trembling as he tried unsuccessfully to thank Naile. He rubbed at his shoulder.

"Let's get you inside," Naile said. When the old man didn't protest, Nail escorted him in the tack shop and sat him in the only chair he saw, in the back corner next to an open window. The sunlight spilled in on the man's age-spotted face. His fingers continued to twitch, and his mouth worked. Naile kneeled in front of him and tried to get a good look at the man's eyes, wanting to make sure he was all right. They were clear and dark, not rheumy like a lot of old people's.

After a few moments, he managed to talk. "Gertha, she told me not to go up there on that roof. To hire that done. Said I don't listen to her." He swallowed and gripped the arms of the chair. "She's right. I don't. And I'd be dead if it weren't for you." He raised his wiry white eyebrows.

"Naile Fangtooth."

"Thank you, Naile Fangtooth." He leaned forward and touched Naile's arm. "Jake. Name's Jake Droans. I haven't seen you in Hart before. Come with them merchants?"

Naile nodded.

"Never liked them merchants stopping here. Always thought they cut into some of our business. But after today, I'm thinking you folks can come through anytime."

Naile rose and made a move to leave.

"Wait. Wait, young man. What do you sell? What wagon is yours? I'll be needing to stop and buy some of your wares. Least I can do."

Naile tipped his head. "I'm not selling anything, Jake. I'm just a

guard. And I've some time on my hands this afternoon. How about I
fix your roof while you sit there and catch your breath?"

The old man beamed, the smile reminding Naile again of the maitre
d' at his favorite fancy restaurant. "Only if you let me pay you."

"You don't need to pay me. I'm happy to help."

"I insist, young man."

It was Naile's turn to smile. "Well, I wouldn't want to insult you."

The coins in Naile's pocket didn't last long, but they were well
spent. His first stop was a bathhouse, where he indulged himself in
the hot water for nearly an hour. It was even better than the bath
Ludlow Jade had arranged after their brief stint in jail. For the first
time, Naile felt wholly human. Then he stopped by the inn, for steaming stew and fresh bread, followed by an entire apple pie for desert
that he'd bought at the bakery. He put himself up for the evening at
the inn, sinking into a soft bed, pulling a quilt over his head, and
quickly falling asleep on a feather pillow. He dreamed of the law firm,
of a case he'd been working about a movie production company bor-
rowing too many elements from a short story about vampires and
werewolves. The case was one of those proverbial slam-dunks; it was
just a matter of how much money the short story author . . . and
thereby the law firm . . . was going to walk away with. He dreamed
of other cases, too, and of the clerks he played the game with. He
woke up wondering what his fellow players were doing, and if they'd
seen him disappear when he picked up the miniature. Had they disappeared, too? Vanished to someplace else in this medieval world?
Or were they all safe and warm in their apartments, riding the sub-
way and reporting to work each day and speculating on what happened to him?

He made it back to the caravan just in time to refuse Ludlow
Jade's hardtack breakfast; he'd eaten eggs and ham at the inn,
washed down with three glasses of apple cider.

Milo's eyes were venomous slits. "Zechial told me where you've
been."

"Yeah, I saw him at dinner at the inn last night."

"Said you had money."

Naile shrugged.

Milo drew his lips into a thin line and waited for Naile to explain his good fortune but before Milo could press the matter, Naile was past him and headed toward the wagon belonging to the priests of Glothorio the Coin Gatherer. After a moment, Milo stormed after him.

The priests were brushing the horses, one of them obviously a skilled farrier working on the lead horse's hooves. The priest who had spent all of his tattoos during the fight with the undead had acquired three new ones somewhere in the village. Two were on the top of his head, both black, one resembling a bird with outstretched wings, the other a snake-like squiggle. The third was on his right forearm and looked like a letter from a foreign alphabet.

"I heard someone say you can divine things." Naile was talking to this latter priest.

The priest stepped away from the horse he was grooming and brushed his hands on a cloth tucked into the belt of his robe. "What knowledge do you seek? Naile Fangtooth, correct?"

"Quite a bit of knowledge, actually." This came from Milo, who moved up to Naile's shoulder. "We'd like to find out how two friends of ours are doing . . . Yevele and Ingrge . . . a battlemaid and an elf."

"Ludlow Jade's two absent guards," the priest said.

"And we want to know about the undead that attacked the caravan. If someone sent them and why," Naile cut in.

"And about a place named Quag Keep," Milo continued.

The latter brought no hint of recognition from the priest.

"Divining magic is my specialty," the priest said. "I can unravel many mysteries for you." He closed his eyes and held his hands in front of Naile's face. "The answers are near, and they are important for your future."

"Great!" Naile reached into his pocket.

"But it will cost you," the priest said.

"Yeah, I figured that." Naile held out the four coins he had remaining—two silver pieces and two coppers.

The priest shook his head. "You will need to gather more coins than that. Our magic is not inexpensive."

Return to Quag Keep

"Hope you had a good time last night, Naile." Milo dug at the dirt with his heel, turned and returned to Ludlow Jade's second wagon.

Naile clenched his hands, angry at himself for spending nearly all the money, angry at the priests for wanting coins for every act. He glanced over his shoulder at the small, tidy business district. He had just enough coins for another night in the inn, and since the caravan was staying another day, he'd see if that same, wonderful room was still available.

FOURTEEN

A Living Darkness

The darkness was absolute and palpable in the cell deep in the bowels of Quag Keep. Torchlight hadn't struck the walls in quite a few years, of this the prisoner was certain. He hadn't seen anything but utter black since he'd been brought here. And that, he suspected, was long, long months ago. In the first few weeks, he'd carefully noted the passage of time, this based on visits by what passed for prison guards . . . all of them unseen and unhuman . . . when he woke and slept and felt hungry, when he guessed it was morning above and outside.

But after a few weeks the rhythm of the guard visits and his sleeping patterns altered, and so he could no longer tell one day from the next. He suspected that many months had passed because his beard stretched practically to his waist now. His fingernails had also grown long, and initially he kept them this way, intending to use them as claws against a guard or his captor. But no one came close enough, and so he finally filed them against the wall.

The wizard had given up on trying to make out any features of his prison. He was chained, and so he couldn't quite reach the cell doors, and the way his hands were bound, he couldn't make the knitting gestures necessary to cast the simplest of spells. Even if he could move his fingers with any degree of accuracy, he hadn't the energy to summon a spark of magic. Not anymore. He was fed little and a few days apart—by a creature he couldn't see and could only guess was large by the loud rasping sound of its breathing. His lips were cracked from lack of water, and his throat was parched. His last meal had been purposely salty.

The scents of the place offered him little means to discern what was going on around him. He could smell human waste, the rankness of his robes, the mortar between the ancient stones. He could hear footsteps above him once in a while, these loud and sometimes shuffling, giving his imagination rise to what could be making them. He could taste the staleness in the air and the coppery spike of blood— one of his teeth was infected and rotting, the pain from it annoying.

He passed the time by dreaming, by mentally reciting the words to spells that he'd personally written in beloved, thick tomes that were far beyond his reach, and by remembering better days and other worlds. Often he thought about death, wondering what it would be like, and occasionally praying for it to claim him soon and end this miserable existence. But on those occasions he scolded himself; he'd never been one to entirely give up hope.

The wizard was talking to himself at the moment, listing the ingredients for a potion he'd been working on some time ago to help vegetable plants resist cold weather and produce into the beginning of winter. He knew it was getting cold outside, as the stone beneath his bare feet and against the one wall he could reach was getting cooler and the dampness was clinging. He stopped talking when he heard a rattling sound, like the flicking tail of a snake. He smelled sulfur.

"Pobe," the wizard said.

The rattling continued, growing louder, then fading. "Yesss, Jalafar-rula. I have come to visssit you again. Have you been longing for another chat? It has been quite a while since I stopped here."

The wizard said nothing and closed his eyes. Jalafar-rula's jailer was utter blackness, no use looking for something that matched the dark of his surroundings.

"Or do you prefer the sssilence of your cell and wish for me to go?" The rattling began again, irregular this time. "No answer? Then I will leave you to your loneliness."

There was the sound of something gliding across the stone floor and a faint gurgling.

"Wait." The wizard stepped forward, as far as his chains would reach. "Do not leave yet, Pobe."

The rattling became soft and even, like a cat's purr. "You want to talk, Jalafar-rula?"

The wizard tried to moisten his mouth so his voice wouldn't crack and he wouldn't appear so hopeless. "Tell me . . ." He hesitated, not wanting to make a request. Any request would be considered begging and would make his captor superior.

"Yes, Jalafar-rula?"

"Tell me what is happening," he said finally. This was the first time he'd asked for news of the outside, and the wizard imagined that his captor was smiling at this small victory.

"Your pawnsss, Jalafar-rula, they are not long for this world you've brought them to. Five are dead, four from your first company, and the singer from the second. That last assignment brought Fisk no joy, my old friend. He told me that he rather fancied the music."

"I don't believe you."

There was an odd sound, like parchment being crumpled. The wizard realized it was his captor laughing.

"Yesss, you believe me, Jalafar-rula. I've no reason to lie to you. Not here, and not now. Not when I am winning."

A silence settled heavily between the two, and for many minutes the only sound was the wizard's shallow breathing.

"Jalafar-rula, my puppet Fisk will be successful in killing all of them. He has never failed me in all these yearsss. He goes after the elf and the woman now. Your battlemaid has such fire in her heart. Pity that Fisk will soon extinguish her flames. Oh, and the thief, too, the one from the first company that slipped between my puppet's fingers. Fisk has promised that the thief's death will be especially slow. I look forward to hearing his report."

There was a sharp intake of breath. And in response more of the crumpling sound.

"Leave them be, Pobe," the wizard pleaded. "They can't hurt you, and they can't stop you. I wasn't able to reach them before—"

"Before I brought you here to be my honored and only guessst?"

"They don't know how important they are."

"They are wormsss, Jalafar-rula."

"Then why aren't you dealing with them? Why do you rely on minions?"

"You know I don't like to be long from this place or the woods, that I prefer now to have minions see to the lesser tasks. Slaying those other-worlders is necessary, but can be managed by my puppet. It gives him sssomething to do. It lets him be useful."

"They don't know what rests on their shoulders. They can't hurt you, I say again. And they can't win. They don't even know why they are here. They don't know I brought them. Why not let them live out their lives in this world? Why not let them be?"

The rattling started again, harsher and louder than before. When it quit, the wizard held his breath, listening. Overhead, something large clumped across the floor.

"Jalafar-rula, you think me a fool! While they live, you have hope, and they have hope. And while they walk the face of this world, there is a chance they can foil my plansss. They might stumble upon their usefulness. They might try to be heroes. There will be no rescue for you, or for their earthen realm. They must die."

"Pobe!" The wizard managed to raise his voice, and he tugged on the chains with what little strength he had. "I will find others and bring them here. My magic will not elude me forever."

"Your magic will elude you long enough, Jalafar-rula. Fisk will slay them all, your company. But you . . . I will keep you alive . . . so we can have these pleasant chatsss."

The wizard spat. "Pobe, you keep me alive only because I am a conduit between their world and ours. Because I am a link to the varied planes. You need me because you need that link open."

"Yesss, Jalafar-rula. I need you for that reason."

The wizard heard something gliding across the stone. The rattling that accompanied it was soft, almost soothing now. A moment more, and there was silence. The wizard knew Pobe was gone.

FIFTEEN

An Ill-mannered Awakening

It was the hour just before dawn, the sky a pale blue-gray that lightened as it neared the horizon. But the horizon couldn't be seen because of a foggy silver-gray mist that hovered above the pond and blanketed the ground, obscuring the trees to the east and the town to the west, even though it was a mere sixty yards away. The mist lent a peaceful atmosphere to the land where the caravan slumbered, looking like a weathered oil painting and making everything seem hushed. There was the muted cry of a hawk, answered in the distance by its hunting mate. There was the faint rustle of canvas and tarp the chill breeze stirred. A chorus of snores was the loudest sound, this coming from caravan guards sleeping under wagons, and even it seemed soft this morning.

The merchants had done well in Hart, selling more than expected, and in turn buying some goods to sell farther north and back in the city. A few of the merchants slept in their wagons, protective of their wares. Most slept in the inn, as did a handful of guards. But they would be rising soon and heading to the next village.

Hart was peaceful and small, and so there being little threat, only two guards were on duty in the hour before the sun came up. One was an employee of the cheesemaker, the other was a disgruntled Milo.

Milo was thinking less and less of Wisconsin and the lake, the paddlewheel boat he took rides on. Instead, he was thinking about this land and his weapons, his work with the caravan and what might be ahead on the trail. This place was seeming more like home, and sometimes he had to concentrate to remember his real name — Martin Jefferson. He dug his fingernails into the palm of his sword hand and tried to rattle off the titles of his treasured hardcover fantasy novels, the ones on the top shelf in his bedroom. *The Knight, Return of the King, The Two Towers* . . . he didn't have that many, why couldn't he remember more? He tried to recite them again, as he took in all the soft sounds of the campsite, at the same time scanning to the east.

He was being diligent in his task as caravan guard, partly to fulfil his responsibility to Ludlow Jade, but also to relieve his boredom . . . and to keep his mind off Yevele, wherever she was, and Naile, who was sleeping on a soft mattress in a warm room.

"Damn Naile," Milo cursed. "Those coins could have been put to better use. They could have paid those priests to use some of their magic to answer our questions. Better use than filling his belly and putting his head on a feather pillow. Jealous, maybe I am a little, but — "

"Shhhhhh!" The cheesemaker's guard had his finger to his lips. "Milo, I think I heard something."

Milo squinted and cocked his head. All he could hear was the gentle flapping of canvas and tarps, and the soft snoring of guards sleeping under the wagons.

"*The Two Towers, Return of the King.* . . . I don't hear . . . wait."

Then he did hear something. He couldn't quite tell what it was, but it was out of place. The sound of fabric rustling, perhaps. The shushing sound that pantlegs make when they are rubbing together. Then a new sound intruded, a gentle "thwup," followed by another and another, followed by a scream.

"Arrows!" the cheesemaker's guard hollered. "Everyone awake! Awake! We're being attacked!"

Shouts instantly filled the air, including Milo's. He yelled for

Zechial to stay in the wagon, called out the names of the guards he knew. He dropped to a crouch and drew his sword, cast his head back and forth looking for the bowmen and seeing vague shapes in the mist, east of the pond, then seeing one of the Glothorio priests on the ground with two arrows protruding from his chest.

"Seven of them," Milo called. "Seven that I can make out in that mist. Can't clearly see anything with all this fog."

But obviously the enemy bowmen could see. More arrows rained down on the caravan, and another Glothorio priest fell. The arrows were concentrated on the priests' wagon, and Milo cautiously started in that direction. He wanted to help the priests, but not become a pin-cushion in the process.

"Have we any bows?" Milo risked in a hushed voice. "We can re-turn their volley." He didn't want the enemy to know that informa-tion, but he wanted to know. He'd not taken stock of the caravan's weapons, and he cursed himself for being so complacent and foolish, of thinking too much about Wisconsin at the time. No one used ar-rows against the undead—but that would have been folly. He only knew that all the guardsmen carried swords or flails. He could shoot a bow, but he'd only seen Ingrge with one.

"No," came a quick reply. "The elf was our bowman. Our only bowman."

Milo grimaced. He knew he should have objected when Ingrge an-nounced he was leaving with Yevele and the thief, should have said the caravan needed to keep its scout, keep the party together.

"I've a crossbow." This came from the shoemaker's guard. He was a wagon away from Milo and was aiming it into the fog. "Arlo does, too. He's on the other side." A moment more and he was firing, but there was no sound of impact. He busied himself with reloading an-other bolt.

Arrows "thwupped" from behind Milo, some striking caravan wagons, others—by the soft sound of impact—finding their marks in bodies. He wondered who was hit, but didn't waste the time trying to find out.

Two wagons to Milo's left, the three remaining Glothorio priests were crouched over the bodies of their brethren. The tallest, the one with the three new tattoos, mouthed a fleeting prayer then turned his attention to the figures in the fog. The priest's voice rose, and Milo could make out some of the words interspersed in a string of archaic syllables. Bright. Clear. Light.

Suddenly the two tattoos rose from the priest's head and floated, shimmering, into the fog. At the same time another volley of arrows came from all around the caravan. The bowmen had the merchant wagons surrounded, some of the brigands obviously having slipped into Hart and firing from the street.

How could they see through the mist? To fire so accurately? "Have to do something," Milo said. "Can't just stand here." Then he edged forward. "Good thing Naile's in his feather bed. He might live out the day." He slipped right and left, avoiding running in a straight line and making an easy target, crouching every few steps. Within moments the mist swirled around him, feeling cold and damp, the tendrils wrapping around his legs and trying to hold him in place.

"Magic." Milo uttered the word as a curse. "The mist is a wizard thing."

A shadow loomed to his right, and he instinctively swung at it, connecting. Blood arced through the mist and hit Milo in the face. His target howled and drew his own blade, and Milo wiped at his eyes with his free hand.

"So you can bleed, and so you're men. You're not part of the fog or some spell. And since you bleed, you can die."

He kept swinging and moving, tugging against the cool tendrils that were wrapping tighter and tighter, some snaking up to grab at his arms, and one was twisting around the blade and trying to tug it down. They were slowing him, but not stopping him. And he managed to swing on the closest archer again, dropping the man this time and cutting through foggy tendrils in the process.

"They're just men!" Milo hollered to the caravan.

Then suddenly the fog was thinning, and Milo could see his foes easier. The Glothorio priest—he was thankfully responsible for this clearing air, Milo realized. His tattoos and spells, they were chasing away this foul foggy magic. For the second time, the priests might save the caravan.

Milo spotted one of the archers taking aim and drawing back on the bowstring. He couldn't see who the archer was aiming at but it didn't matter. Milo surged against the weakened misty tendrils, breaking free and racing across ground that was slick with the mist. He nearly lost his balance, but he stayed on his feet, bringing his sword up and then down on the archer's arm, cutting through the bone and lopping the man's hand off. The bow fell to the ground and Milo continued his attack, driving his blade into the man's chest, tugging it free and continuing on to the next archer.

More arrows were fired; Milo could hear the "thwup" of bow strings and a strangled cry from someone in the caravan. It was a high-pitched voice, so Milo guessed one of the merchants had been hit. There were shouts from the guards, who were better organizing themselves and rushing into the fading mist, where up close they might not fall prey to the arrows. There were louder "thwups" coming from the caravan, and Milo guessed these were from the crossbows. One bolt had obviously found its mark, as an archer a few yards away grabbed his stomach and crumpled.

Yevele and Ingrge should be here, he thought. The battlemaid would be in her element, and the elf could have taken some of these men down with his arrows. Milo charged another man, who had dropped his bow and drawn a heavy, curved-bladed sword. The weapons clanged against each other.

Milo could see this man better, the mist ephemeral now and continuing to fade. He was dressed in a tight-fitting charcoal tunic and pale gray leggings, no baggy fabric to hinder him, and likely designed to blend in with the fog. He was young, Milo guessed him to be no more than twenty, with a scar running down the left side of a heart-shaped face.

They locked eyes and began circling, the man feinting with his sword and Milo parrying. The dance was not unlike his sparring with Naile, but no one pulled punches now.

"Why are you after us?" Milo asked.

His foe's eyes flashed, and he sneered, showing a line of uneven yellow teeth.

"Why?" Milo shouted.

"Orders." Then he stepped back and drove his blade forward.

Milo leapt to the side just in time. The heavy blade skidded off his chainmail shirt, slicing a few links and piercing his cloak. The curved sword tangled there for an instant, Milo stepped in close and shoved his sword through the man's chest.

"Damn your orders," Milo hissed, as he pulled his sword free, stepped over the man, and moved onto another.

They appeared to be all dressed in dark, tight-fitting clothes. Some had coal-dust smeared on their faces, and their hair was either short or pulled back tight. And though most of them were young, a few little more than boys, there were a couple of older men in the mix. Milo noticed that these were cagier and obviously more experienced, keeping behind the younger men and relying on their bows. Three dozen all total, he guessed, on this side of the caravan. He wondered if there were a similar number on the other side. Perhaps these were the bandits Ludlow Jade had worried about. But the merchant had said the bandits always struck on the road, between villages. These men were not so hard to kill as the undead army, but they were more formidable because of their weapons, and therefore far more of a threat.

Another volley was loosened.

And then another.

More cries from the direction of the caravan . . . Someone shouted that Zechial was hit . . . Milo cut down a fourth man and was moving toward one of the older archers. Perhaps the man had some rank among them, and slaying him could disrupt the morale of those around him, Milo thought. Was Zechial badly hurt?

"Surrender!" the cry was booming and husky and cut through the air.

"Never," Milo said, as he set his sights on one of the older archers.

The mist was gone now, and Milo took a quick glance at the field. Only eight enemy archers were down, and most of those due to him.

Recurn to Quag Keep

Half of the foes remaining still relied on their bows, the rest had swords and daggers, one a barbed whip that cracked angrily. Perched on a rock on the far side of the pond was a familiar figure. Dressed all in black, hood pulled back showing his tattooed head, Fisk Lockwood smiled cruelly.

"Surrender!" Fisk hollered again. "Surrender now or die!"

Milo snarled and shot toward his intended target, raised his sword and felt as if he'd been punched hard in the stomach when he heard:

"We surrender! Stop your attack! We yield!"

"You heard him," the older enemy archer said to Milo. "Lower your sword, or they'll cut down the rest of your caravan. The blood will be on your hands."

Milo took a step back, kept his sword raised, and looked toward the caravan. The scene sickened him. Only three guards were on their feet on this side of the wagons. He counted seven guards down to arrows, and three of the Glothorio priests. He saw Zechial slumped against the wheel of the largest wagon, an arrow protruding from his throat. Ludlow Jade stood over his son.

"We surrender!" Ludlow Jade repeated. "Damn you, we yield!"

Milo looked between the merchant and the older archer, tightened his grip on his sword, then shook his head and lowered it.

"Drop the blade," the archer said. "Now."

Milo resisted for a moment, listening to thuds the guards and merchants' weapons made hitting the ground. Then he closed his eyes and released his grip on the sword. The archer slung the bow over his back and came to Milo, undoing the swordbelt, taking the dagger.

"Move. Over to those wagons you've been guarding. Move!"

The brigands herded the merchants and surviving guards like sheep, directing them to the north bank of the pond and stripping them of all their armor and weapons. One of the brigands ripped off Milo's shirt, to make sure he had no concealed daggers. A row of archers kept their bows trained toward the town to keep at bay the nosy citizens poking their heads around buildings. One fired an arrow at a miner's feet as a warning.

A half-dozen brigands watched the merchants and guards, swords and bows ready if one of them should move. Fisk paced back and forth in front of the captured assembly, twirling a dagger as he went, stopping in front of a sobbing Ludlow Jade. He flipped the dagger around and poked the merchant in the stomach with the pommel.

"Jade."

The merchant met Fisk's gaze, reddened eyes narrowing.

"Those guards I arranged for your wagons, fat man. I'll take them off your pudgy hands."

To the west of the pond, a handful of Fisk's men started looting the wagons. The merchants whispered protests, which brought a crooked smile to Fisk's face. The shoemaker's wagon was faring the worst at the moment, as tools and sheets of leather were tossed out the back. Shoes and boots for women and children joined the mess, but men's boots were gathered, put in canvas sacks the brigands had brought, and deposited on the ground. The sound of baked clay shattering came from the potter's wagon.

"Easy in there!" one of the brigands called. "The small pots, pad them and take them. Mugs, too."

"Fisk, I don't understand," Ludlow Jade said. "You're with the bandits? And my son. You killed my son."

"An unfortunate incident," Fisk said smoothly. "My condolences." He made a show of shaking his head, but there was no genuine sadness in the gesture.

"Why? You're a priest? Three of your own were killed. We follow the Coin Gatherer. How? Why?"

"Why? Because you have something I want, fat man. Your guards. I want two of them. But I see only one." Fisk gestured to Milo, who was to Ludlow Jade's right.

"Hearth glow wine!" Came a shout from Ludlow Jade's largest wagon. A brigand poked his head out the back and waved to get the attention of one of the older archers. "He's got a false floor in this one. There's bottles and bottles of hearth glow wine. A fortune."

Whoops went up from the brigands, and Fisk's eyes took on a shine.

Milo hadn't a clue why this find seemed important to the brigands, or what hearth glow wine was. But he heard a few of the merchants whisper:

"He deals in forbidden goods!"

"He brings this down upon us."

"No wonder he cares not how his rugs sell. Hearth glow wine is the Dead God's folly."

"Dwarven wine. Illegal goods, he deals in."

"This is why the bandits came!"

The brigands concentrated on Ludlow Jade's wagons now, finding nothing else interesting, save his considerable coin box.

"We'll take these wagons," one of the older brigands instructed. He pointed to the wagon where they'd discovered the hearth glow wine, and the one belonging to the Glothorio priests.

Must have found a lot of coins in the priests' wagon, Milo thought.

Fisk seemed uninterested in the loot. He poked Ludlow Jade again. "I see only one of your guards. Where is the other?"

The merchant gestured with his head to the two men standing on his left, his longtime employees, Sam and Willum.

"Not those guards," he hissed. "The war-woman and the elf, I know they left your caravan. But the big man. I want him and that one," he gestured to Milo. "The guards I arranged for you to hire."

Ludlow Jade was pale and trembling, and Milo guessed he was suffering from shock.

"Leave Jade alone," Milo tried. "Take the wine and leave us all alone."

Fisk spun the dagger around and touched its point to Ludlow Jade's stomach. "Where, fat man? That other guard. And tell me . . . where did the woman and the elf go, and the little thief?"

"Not here." The merchant glanced toward his wagons, his gaze resting on his son's body. "The woman and the elf left days ago. They slipped away in the night. I don't know where they went. That's the truth, *priest*."

Fisk spit in the merchant's face. "And the big man?"

"He left with them," Milo cut in.

Ludlow Jade did not contest the statement.

Fisk turned his attention to Milo now, taking a step back to stay just out of reach of the long, muscular arms. "So you must know where they went, your friends. Yevele, with fire in her eyes. She's always a woman to me. Tell me where I can find your friends."

"Companions," Milo corrected. He shook his head. "I've no idea—"

Fisk gestured, and one of the brigands who'd been watching the captives stepped forward and rammed his sword straight into the shoemaker's heart.

"No!" Milo made a move forward, but Fisk was fast, bringing his leg up and kicking Milo in the stomach, forcing him back into the potter. Fisk was slight, but there was considerable power in his kick.

"Try something once more, and I'll have the fat man killed next. I'll kill them all, one by one, if I have to."

When Fisk moved on to the Glothorio priests, the potter whispered to Milo: "You realize they're going to kill us all no matter what. No witnesses. Probably kill the townsfolk watching. That hearth glow wine has sealed our fate."

"Not the wine," Milo whispered. "Me. My companions and me."

Ludlow nudged Milo. "Why does he want you? What have you brought upon us?"

"I don't know," was all Milo could manage. "I truly do not know."

Fisk ordered the two surviving Glothorio priests bound and gagged, "so they cannot use their vile magic."

"I believe Teege is right," Ludlow Jade said of the potter. "I believe they will kill us all."

"You hired me as a guard, let's see if I can do something to protect you." Milo stepped forward. "Fisk!"

The bald man whirled, black cloak whipping around. He gestured to the cheesemaker, ordering his death next.

"No! Leave him be. I'm not trying anything. I want to talk."

Fisk glared at Milo from a few yards away. "So talk. I can hear you." Another gesture, and an archer aimed an arrow at Milo.

"What do you want me for? I've done nothing to you."

Return to Quag Keep

Fisk stood motionless and turned his head slightly. It was as if he was listening to someone, but no one near him was talking.

There was the sound of more pottery breaking, and things were being carried out of wagons and placed in the two wagons the brigands were taking. The thieves had an eye for what was valuable, taking first the most expensive of the merchants' goods, then adding more things if there was room. The best horses were being hitched to those wagons. The rest of the horses were slapped on the rumps and were sent running.

"They will kill us," the potter repeated. He started mumbling a prayer.

"What do you want with me?" Milo repeated.

"Not just you," Fisk finally returned. "I told you, I want the big man, the elf, and the war-woman, too. The thief. I arranged for you to be with this caravan, so I could find and slay the lot of you . . . together."

"Why?"

Fisk stiffly walked toward Milo and, oddly, started singing:

> Oh, Danny Boy, the pipes, the pipes are calling
> From glen to glen, and down the mountain side,
> The summer's gone, and all the roses falling
> It's you, it's you must go, and I must bide.

"What? Why!" Milo shouted. "Why do you want me?"

Fisk scowled to have his song interrupted. "Not your concern."

"Not my—"

Over the breaking pottery and the sounds of men unloading and reloading wagons, there was a thundering, followed by a gurgled cry.

SIXTEEN

Naile's Stand

Naile woke later than he'd intended. He'd drawn the shades, and so no light spilled into his warm and comfortable room. Reluctantly throwing back the quilt, he extracted himself from the bed. His back ached a little, from sleeping so long in the same position. But it was a welcome pain. He suspected he hadn't moved an inch since laying down last night. Stretching and working a kink out of his neck, he frowned at the thought of hardtack and beans for breakfast. He hadn't money for breakfast at the inn.

"It was good yesterday, though," he muttered. Even the memory would carry him through the day. And if he couldn't stomach another piece of hardtack or another bowl of beans, he could go rooting in the woods when the caravan paused to water the horses.

"Wouldn't mind a couple of aspirins right now."

He padded to the window and nudged the shade aside, looked out onto the street and heard the sounds of battle.

"A fight? In the village?" For a moment he thought that he might be dreaming. Then he thought he might be hearing sounds from the mine. He stuck his head out the window and saw a boy running by on the street. "You there!"

The boy slowed, but didn't stop.

"What's going on?"

"Bandits," the boy shouted. "Thieves! They're after the merchants."

Naile didn't bother with his clothes. He ran from the room naked, taking the stairs two at a time and willing the transformation to begin. His bones were snapping, popping, growing longer and thicker before he touched the last step. A massive boar thundered out of the inn's front doors and raced down the main street. The beast paused only for an instant, then dashed between the blacksmith's and the tack shop so he could come upon the caravan from outside the village. He sped up, his hooves slicing into the hard earth and throwing clumps of dirt up in his wake.

Milo saw what was causing the ruckus—a huge boar had skewered one of the brigands on his tusks, shook him loose, and went after another one. The brigands near the wagons dropped their sacks and drew their swords. But the boar had gored three of them before the first man had his weapon out.

"It's the big man!" Fisk yelled. "The animal is the big guard!" He was waving to the archers who'd been keeping watch on the town. "Shoot him! Kill the beast!" He whirled to the handful of brigands watching the captives. "Kill them all, but save that one." He pointed to Milo. "That one must know where the elf and the war-woman is. He'll tell us." Then Fisk was running toward Naile, a wavy-bladed dagger appearing in each hand. "Kill the merchants!"

Milo knocked Ludlow Jade to the ground, saving the merchant from a brigand's arrow. "All of you, down!" Then he vaulted over a few prone forms and started untying one of the Glothorio priests. The man dropped to his knees, tugged free his gag and started reciting a spell, while at the same time he untied his fellow's hands. Both priests were working magic now, the arcane words flying furiously, tattoos breaking away from their heads and arms to streak toward the archers. In midair as they flew, the tattoos enlarged then shattered, dozens of black darts striking down archers and splintering bows.

Milo dove into a brigand who was about to kill the cheesemaker. He pounded his fists into the man's head until blood gushed from a broken nose and the brigand stopped moving. Other guards were fighting with their fists, too, as well as some of the merchants. The priests continued to chant, more tattoos arcing toward the brigands, one of the tattoos lancing into Fisk.

Milo grabbed a downed brigand's sword. It was one of the heavy curved-blade weapons, and it felt awkward in his grip. He dropped it and scooped up a dagger instead.

"False brother!" one of the priests cried. "Glothorio will send you to the dark nether-realm! Fisk Lockwood, you are not one of ours!"

Fisk's face proved the priest true. The tattoos on his head had become smudged. Paint or ink, Milo guessed, as he raced toward Fisk, shoulder down and striking Fisk. The false priest fell, and Milo pulled back an arm, slamming his fist into Fisk's jaw. The bone cracked and Fisk's eyes rolled up. Then, with a rattled groan, the slight man went limp.

Milo jumped off him and ran toward one of the brigands who was aiming at the merchants.

Some of the villagers joined the battle, most of them miners, and they were wielding picks and shovels as weapons. A farmer was using a pitchfork with quite a degree of success, having speared one of the youngest brigands on the twines. Two old women were helping, throwing rocks from behind the cover of one of the village wells.

Naile continued to wreak the most havoc, hooves pounding over the grass, lowering his broad head to get under a brigand, then tossing him into the air. Once the brigand fell to the ground, Naile trampled him, and moved on to the next. An arrow protruded from the wereboar's side, and a broken shaft stuck out of his back right leg. But the wounds didn't slow the beast down.

"Run!" This came from the eldest surviving bandit. He was near Ludlow Jade's wagon and was unhitching a large horse. "Run, you all!" Then he was on the horse and kicking it in the sides, urging it to gallop away from the village.

Another brigand, a canvas sack of loot over his shoulder, grabbed one of the horses and joined him. None of the other men were able to get to the horses. Milo saw to that. His breath was coming in ragged gulps from the exertion of the fight. A few of the wounds on his legs, the ones where the finger bones went in the deepest, had opened up and were bleeding. He kept his weight on his left leg, as it was the strongest, and he shifted the borrowed dagger to his left hand, picking up part of a crate with his right to use as a shield.

Two brigands were rushing him, one of them limping badly from a gash on his leg. Blood had soaked the man's gray leggings, turning them black, and he gasped with each step.

"Drop the swords, the both of you," Milo offered. "I'm tired of killing."

The wounded man complied, but his companion only moved faster, leading with the sword and reaching behind his back. Milo suspected he was going for a dagger, or something else to throw. He wasn't going to give him the chance. Milo darted forward, makeshift shield out and bashing the man's face, sweeping the dagger under the shield and slicing through the tight tunic. The brigand fell, dead.

"I yield." The wounded man was on his knees, hands pressed to the gash in his thigh.

Milo grabbed up the man's sword, a long thin-blade that felt balanced. He pulled the bow and quiver from the wounded man's back and tossed them away. A quick glance at the field to make sure the brigands were being routed, then he pressed the tip of the sword to the man's throat.

"Who sent you?"

The man continued to press at his wound, the blood pooling up between his fingers. Milo sucked in his lower lip, guessing that an artery had been cut. The man's skin was white, and there was a fine sheen of sweat on his face.

"I said, who sent you?" Milo pulled back the sword as if he was an executioner readying a swing. He needed the man to talk quickly.

"Fisk." He sat now, tugging off his tunic and wrapping this around his leg. His hands were shaking, and he looked to Milo for help. It didn't come.

"Are you going to keep talking?" Milo persisted. "Or do I have to help you bleed out a little faster."

The man didn't look up. He tied the sleeves of his tunic tighter around his leg. It seemed to help only a little. "We go after merchants using the trail, usually not after caravans so big as this one. Too many guards this trip. But Fisk came to us, brought some men with him. All the young ones."

Milo raised an eyebrow.

"The young men must be from another band. Didn't matter to us. Fisk was paying well enough." He paused. "At the time it seemed like good coin."

"Go on."

"Fisk said on top of the coins whatever was in the wagons was ours. Said all he wanted was the fat merchant's guards."

"Why did he want the guards? What did he tell you?"

The man shrugged and looked up. His skin was shiny white, his lips tinged blue. "Didn't ask. Didn't—" He fell back, breathing faintly. Milo stepped over him and ran to where he'd left Fisk.

The false priest wasn't there. But the earth was churned up all around where he fell, from the hooves of a large horse. And there was a trace of brimstone in the air.

The wereboar was charging away from the caravan, pursuing a trio of brigands running east. He overtook the first, rearing up, tusks raking against the man's back. Then he trampled him and went after another.

Milo leaned over, hands on his knees, steadying himself, catching his breath. Dead brigands and caravan guards littered the ground near the pond. Dead merchants, too. Zechial, the shoemaker, three Glothorio priests, and Korey the elixir brewer.

"So much death," Milo said. "And for what? Why?"

Steadied, he retrieved his own sword, then went to Ludlow Jade's wagon and found his tunic and chainmail shirt. He put these on, watching the merchant hover over his dead son.

"I'm sorry," Milo said. He stepped toward the merchant, but Ludlow Jade waved him away. So Milo started prowling the field. It was something his characters had done in the game—take the coin purses of the fallen. Dead men didn't need money, and Milo figured if he didn't take it, the merchants or villagers would. He stuffed his treasures in a brigand's pack and slung it over his shoulder.

Milo didn't touch the bodies of the guards, just the brigands, tugging loose a coin pouch here and there, taking a couple of exceptionally fine-looking daggers and sticking them in his weapons belt. One of the archers had a cloak, the only brigand who had one. This, too, he took, guessing it might come in handy.

Several of the men had small brands on the backs of their hands. He made a mental note to ask Ludlow Jade about this later.

When he was finished with the bodies, he stood by the pond, listening to the ducks softly quacking, as if nothing untoward had happened here. A fish splashed in the middle, and the songs of birds began to intrude. The voices were growing, villagers coming out of the town, chattering amongst themselves and asking questions of the remaining guards and merchants. The merchants were talking, too, crying over the losses of their friends and guards, the losses of their merchandise. The guards had organized themselves into a clean-up detail and were wrapping bodies in Ludlow Jade's blankets, giving preferential treatment to Zechial, the shoemaker, and Korey.

Ludlow Jade draped the new blue tunic Zechial had bought in town over the top. The two Glothorio priests prayed with him, then they moved on to tend to their dead brethren. Some of the villagers were helping with the dead merchants and guards were offering water and bandages to the wounded. A local healer moved among the caravan, separating the most seriously injured and nursing them first.

It looked like a war had been fought here, Milo thought. And all because Fisk Lockwood wanted him and Naile, Ingrge and Yevele dead. "Why?" And what of Deav Dyne, Wymarc, and the lizardman Gulth? Were they safe because they were elsewhere? "Wymarc." Milo pictured the bard's face, recalled that Fisk Lockwood was singing a tune that had sounded somewhat familiar, something that certainly didn't belong in this world. "'Danny Boy.' He was singing 'Danny Boy.'" Milo's heart sank. He recalled Wymarc singing that tune, and several others, when they were camping at night in the Hollow Woods. "Fisk got Wymarc." He was certain the false priest had slain Wymarc first, maybe before the caravan had even left the city.

He remembered seeing Fisk in the Golden Tankard, and not liking the looks of him then. He wondered if Fisk had intended to go after him and Naile that very night. Maybe the city watch had thwarted any such plans by throwing Milo and Naile in the jail.

"So he arranged for Ludlow Jade to bail us out. So he could get us that way. And take us away from the city. Safer for him." Milo clenched and unclenched his fists, his fingernails digging into his palms. He continued to watch the guards, merchants, and villagers pick up the pieces. The dead brigands would be dealt with last, he knew. "Why does someone want us dead?"

"I don't know. But I'd like to find out."

Milo whirled. On the far side of the pond, Naile was sitting in the dead grass, working the broken arrow out of his thigh.

"Damn, that hurt." Naile saw Milo watching him and motioned him over. "I saw Fisk hightail it out of here on a black horse that moved like the wind and was as quiet as a whisper. Beautiful animal, but I could've sworn I saw flames coming out of its mouth. Ouch!" He started working on the arrow in his side.

"Stop. Let me help you with that." Milo handed the bandit's cloak to Naile.

"Thanks. My clothes are in my room. Ouch!"

Milo had the arrow free and started dabbing at the wound. "Doesn't look serious."

"It's not. It just hurts is all."

"Good thing you were in that room, I suppose. The cavalry to the rescue and all that."

Andre Norton and Jean Rabe

Naile snorted and got to his feet, wrapped the cloak around him like it was a bath towel. "I better go get my clothes and axes."

"And I better go get some answers about all of this." Milo headed straight toward the Glothorio priests, who were administering rites to their fallen brethren. He waited until they were done with the ceremony and offered his sympathy.

Then he fumbled about in the borrowed satchel and pulled out two coin purses, dropping them at the tall priest's feet. "You said your divine magic costs. Well, now I can pay you."

SEVENTEEN

Sand and Scales

"Here, Bert." The sand dragon crooked its talon, beckoning to the thief. "Here. Here. Here." The words became a rumble that chased through the cavern floor, causing more sand to sift down from the hole.

Berthold of the Green shook his head and backed up a step. "Now, that wouldn't be a prudent idea on my part, would it? Might as well just march right into your ugly toothy mouth and—"

Under him the ground heaved and Berthold fell. Yevele might have joined him, but Ingrge was there to steady her. The elf seemed to have no trouble keeping his balance.

"I hope that's not its stomach growling," Yevele whispered.

Ingrge shook his head and tugged Yevele back toward the hole in the cavern's ceiling. "No," he said, his voice so soft she barely heard him. "It's something much worse. Now, I'm going to boost you up."

"I'll not leave you or the thief," she said, no longer bothering to keep her voice down.

"If you don't get out of here right now," the elf cautioned. "There'll be no one to rescue this supposed wizard."

"He's right, you know," Berthold said. "Much as I agree with you, he's speaking some sense. I think we should—"

The rumbling deepened. This time Yevele was pitched to the ground. The three dragons, heads swinging, looked to the darkest part of the cavern, where the shadows were thickest and where the rumbling was the loudest. Then one crept forward and lowered its snout, sniffing at Yevele and Ingrge.

"Here, Bert," it purred. "Here. Here. Here."

"I'm Bert!" the thief called, trying to lure the dragon toward him, as he moved toward a far side of the cave. "I'm Bert. Berthold of the Green."

"Here, Bert," the second dragon persisted. It flicked a tongue out and touched the elf's face.

"Get behind me," Ingrge told Yevele.

Despite the closeness of the dragon, she bristled. "You should stay behind me, *elf*." She had sword in hand now as she got to her feet, bending at the knees and keeping her balance, though the floor continued to tremble. "I don't need your chivalry." Then she swept her blade up, intending to bring it down on the dragon's snout.

"Stop!" The word was like a clap of thunder, deafening in the cavern and bouncing off the stone walls.

Yevele staggered again, but she kept her grip on her weapon.

"You will not threaten my children!" One tremor after another raced through the cavern, and spiderweb cracks danced along the walls. Stone dust drifted down. A massive head followed the voice out of the darkest part of the chamber.

They couldn't see all of this dragon, but its head alone was as large as the three other dragons in the cavern put together. The eyes were wide and slitted like a cat's, and they cast a hellish yellow glow across the stone floor. From its open maw the stench of something burning escaped. Brutal and overpowering, Yevele, Berthold, and Ingrge choked and fought against a rising aura of fear which pulsed from the beast.

More of the dragon snaked out, the neck thicker than the biggest of trees and covered with dull brown fire-edged scales the size of shields. It stretched a muscular leg forward, talons screeching across the stone, the noise painful and blotting out all other sounds. Then it raised a talon to the head of the dragon near Yevele and Ingrge, deadly sharp looking and shaped like a scimitar. With an extraordinary gentleness, it brushed at the side of the young dragon's snout. The smaller creature sighed happily.

"You will not hurt my children," the dragon repeated. "I will slay you first."

"N-n-no. You don't need to do that." Berthold crawled forward, not attempting to get to his feet, as the cavern still rumbled in response to the great dragon's breathing. The thief was sweating profusely and sand had stuck to his face and the backs of his hands. He trembled all over, even though he told himself to be brave. A glance at Ingrge and Yevele revealed that they were likewise affected by being in the presence of the creature. "Y-y-you don't need to kill us."

"Here, Bert," the young dragon purred again. "Here. Here. Here."

"W-w-we weren't going to hurt your children. We just fell in here. An accident."

"Were pulled in here," Ingrge added. "Just walking across the desert, and—"

"Here, Bert."

". . . and something grabbed my leg. One of your children pulled me in here. My friends came down trying to help me."

"Here, Bert."

"Heeeeeere," one of the other young dragons said. "Berrrrrrt."

"We meant no harm," Yevele said. She sheathed her sword and stood.

The rumbling lessened, but it did not stop.

"You could slay us easily," she continued.

The great dragon blinked, and the air shimmered above its cavelike nostrils.

"You could swallow us whole," Yevele said. "We could do nothing to stop you. We ask your mercy."

"Yes," Berthold said. "We ask that you let us leave this place. We'll tell no one about you and your children. "We'll leave your desert and—"

"Here, Bert."

The great dragon let out a sigh that added to the burning smell. "I have no desire to swallow men. I do not eat the flesh of animals. My children do not eat the flesh of animals."

"Then you'll let us go?" This from Ingrge. The elf was on his feet, too, hands spread at his side, eyes fixed on the ridge above the dragon's glowing eyes.

"My children, it seems, desire you as pets," the dragon said. A smile played at the corner of her massive sand-colored lip. "They have not had a plaything in some time."

Yevele shook her head. "We can't. You can't let them. Please. We have too much to do. Important work. We're going to Quag Keep to—"

The ridge rose above the dragon's eyes and she growled, the sound causing the stone floor to tremble more fiercely than before. Again Yevele fell. Agile Ingrge threw all his effort into keeping his balance. Stone dust spilled down and into the elf's face. He shielded his eyes from it and spat the dust and sand out of his mouth.

"You know of Quag Keep?" Ingrge asked. "It is beyond the desert."

The dragon snarled and flicked her barbed tongue. "I know of the Keep."

"Then you'll let us go?" Yevele was determined. She stood once more and brushed at the sand stuck to her face.

"What do you know of that place?" the elf pressed.

"It was not always beyond the desert," the dragon said. She lowered her voice, and the tremors subsided.

Berthold was finally able to stand. The thief kept an eye on the young dragons, particularly the one that kept beckoning him close.

"It was in the heart of the desert a lifetime past. Standing above the dunes, it cast shadows to mark the time of day. The very bricks of its walls are made of the desert, hardened by wizards, shaped and strengthened. Ever taller, ever deeper. A place of great goodness when it marked the time of day."

"A lifetime ago?" Yevele was no longer trembling. She'd mastered her fear of the dragon. "In our years?"

"In mine. Centuries for you." The dragon raised her head and slowly shook it. Barbels that hung from below her jaw brushed ruts in the sand on the floor.

"What happened?" Yevele risked a step closer to the great dragon. The battlemaid was reflected now in the beast's glowing eyes.

"A darkness grew in the labyrinth beneath the tower. Deeper the levels went than higher the walls reached. Taller and deeper, and in the depths of the earth, where the sun cannot shine, came a power. Something evil stirred and found its way inside Quag Keep."

"A man?" Berthold asked. "Like us? A wizard?"

Again the dragon shook her head. She captured also the interest of the young dragons now, and they were no longer paying attention to Berthold and his companions. Her eyes searched Yevele's face, as if the great dragon were trying to gauge her intelligence and find simple words to explain the darkness.

"Not a man," she said after a moment of staring at them. She flicked her tongue and licked at her teeth. "Not a wizard. Not a dragon, nor any other creature that had walked on the earth. A collection of evil, a pool of corruptness, the badness in men and dead wizards slain by the eating of their own powers. Given life by the magic that pulsed through Quag Keep. Given strength by the wizards who lived in the tower and who were oblivious to its presence. Nurtured by their hidden thoughts, by things they dreamed about but would not do, by the dark parts of their minds."

Yevele's face had gone white, her eyes wide at the image the dragon conjured. "And what happened to this . . . darkness?"

"Years and years and years it festered and grew in the bowels of the wizard's tower," the dragon continued. "And when they had no more to give it, the Darkness rose and slew them . . . most of them . . . those who foolishly thought they could kill what they had unwittingly given strength and life. And then it took the tower for its own. And it drove back the desert."

"So the tower never moved." Yevele was an arm's length from the dragon's snout. The heat from the dragon's breath had drawn the life from her curls and the moisture from her skin.

"No, it never moved. The tower drove back the desert."

"And you were here? When it happened?"

"Smaller than my smallest child. A hatchling. Almost too young to understand."

It was Ingrge's turn: "And no one fought this Darkness?"

The dragon cocked her head. "The wizards who fled did not understand what they had unleashed. But they told others to stay away from the tower."

"We've been to the tower," Yevele said. "We saw no . . . Darkness."

"Then the Darkness was not there when you visited," the dragon returned. "It slithers from the tower from time to time. It was not there, else you would not be here."

"Why haven't you done something?" The thief's tone was politely demanding. "As powerful as you are, why haven't you gone after the darkness?

"Because I am also wise. The Darkness leaves me alone, and I give it no cause to further push away my precious desert."

"But it's evil. You said it's evil," the thief persisted.

"But it does not trouble me."

The thief shook his head. "I don't understand."

"Because you have not the capacity to understand."

"You can't expect a dragon to have human morals and values," Yevele commented.

The dragon's eyes widened, shedding more light into the cavern. "So then a woman such as you might have the capacity?"

Yevele faced the dragon again. "You'll let us leave . . . so we can go to Quag Keep?"

The dragon nodded, her barbels creating a pattern in the sand. "Seek death if you will," she said. "If you go to Quag Keep and meet the Darkness, it will kill you."

Return to Quag Keep

Yevele, Ingrge, and Berthold climbed out of the hole, boosted by one of the young dragons. "Here, Bert," it said as they started across the desert. "Here. Here. Here."

The thief made an exaggerated sigh. "I thought we were dragon food for certain. I'm going to need to wash my clothes." He walked several yards before looking back at the depression. "She said they don't eat animal flesh."

"Yes, she considered us animals," Yevele said. "And I suppose, to her, we are."

"Well, if she doesn't eat animals, what does she eat? What could possibly sustain a body that large?"

Ingrge passed the thief and battlemaid by, deciding to scout ahead again. "I believe," he said over his shoulder, "that sand dragons exist on the faint drops of dew that collect on cactus needles in the evening and the heat that rises from the sand." He stopped. "But I don't know how I know that."

He was moving ahead again, with deft, long strides. Berthold grabbed Yevele's shoulder and pointed to the ground. The elf was leaving practically no tracks.

It was well into the afternoon. The trio had spent more time in the dragon cavern than they'd realized. Tired, they nevertheless pressed on, Berthold complaining only occasionally, then sighing loudly and pointing when the edge of the desert loomed into view at sunset. There was no gradual change in the landscape, from the desert to the wooded lands beyond. It was as if an artist had painted a desert, then abruptly started painting trees.

"I don't remember it being like this when we were here before." Yevele knelt with one leg in the desert, the other in the woods. Her fingers danced from the sand to the grass, marveling at the abrupt change in texture and drop in temperature.

"We didn't come this way before." Ingrge had silently moved up, spooking Yevele and Berthold. He held his bow in his right hand, an arrow notched loosely. "I've scouted ahead, and it's pretty quiet, but not unnaturally so. I think we should keep going, along a game trail I spotted. I'd prefer to be well under the cover of trees by nightfall."

The thief rolled his shoulders, sat down and pulled off his well-worn slippers. He rubbed his right foot, then his left. "Don't you ever quit?"

"Elves require little rest."

"Don't you care about us humans?" Berthold put his slippers back on, stood, and brushed the last of the sand off his tunic. "Weren't you human back in —"

"Florida." *Forty-two steps from the beach,* he mouthed. *How many to the ocean? His telephone number . . . what was it?*

Yevele had taken off her chainmail shirt and was shaking it, sand pouring out of the armor. She put it back on and tugged her sword free and inspected it, kept it out and got to her feet.

"I'm ready," she announced.

"Isn't it dangerous to go through the woods at night?"

"Berthold, it was dangerous to go through the desert in the daylight," Yevele said, her tone condescending. "This world is dangerous. Ingrge, not too far ahead this time. All right?"

Nodding in answer, the elf directed them to the game trail. Above, the sky was still light but the land about them turned darker the deeper they went into the woods. The canopy of branches overhead was dense, birds nested on the highest limbs. A pair of owls waiting for hunting dark watched them with some interest.

Scents here were more agreeable. There were predominantly oaks, maples, and evergreen trees, some of these reaching more than eighty feet high. The evergreens filled the air with a heady pine fragrance and chased away the last of the dragon's sulfur smell. As they advanced, the odor of wood rotting from downed trees arose, and from somewhere nearby a fresher scent brought them to a brook.

They drank until they feared their stomachs would burst, then they filled their skins, and while Ingrge retrieved handfuls of late-berries, Berthold bathed.

"We should spend the night here," the thief suggested. He'd washed his clothes, too, and then had put them on wet. Though he shivered in the chill fall air, he didn't complain. "Fresh water, a nice clearing."

Ingrge pointed to a patch of earth between low-spreading ferns. "Wolf tracks. I would think they come here at night."

"Well, I'm ready to go," Berthold announced.

The elf guessed it was midnight when they reached end of the woods.

In a scrubby, circular clearing, highlighted by a three-quarter moon, Quag Keep loomed like a mountain.

EIGHTEEN

Return to Quag Keep

"Wow." Berthold had not been to Quag Keep before, and so he was awestruck by the tower. It rose from the scrubland like a crooked arm, its stone blocks brushed by the moonlight.

Remembering the dragon's story, the three stared at it from just inside the forest, hunkered down behind a small pine. They could tell, now, that the tower's stones were indeed made of sand, as they were the same color as the desert and grains sparkled here and there. The tower was nearly round, being a little distorted, though perhaps that was by design. It looked to be many levels tall, but just how many the night concealed. There were few windows on this side, all of them dark because of heavy tapestries or shutters, all of them barred.

"I don't think they had bars on them when we were last here," Yevele said. "And I don't think that was there either." She pointed to three gargoyles three-quarters the way up, carved from some dark gray stone that seemed to absorb the moonlight. They protruded from the tower from their waists, wings extended and misshapen arms stretched out, as if they'd been caught trying to flee the place.

Their features were so exaggerated, the three still sheltered by the forest could make out the details. One had its mouth open, revealing fangs made of black shards. Another's mouth was set in grim determination. The last was the most unsettling, with overlarge eyes and a snout that looked like a crocodile's. Something appeared to be dripping from its mouth, frozen in stone.

"Cheery place, that."

"You urged us here, thief." Yevele started toward the tower, but Berthold pulled her back. "And now you don't want to go?"

"Wait," he cautioned. "I just want a longer look." He continued to study the tower.

The three windows on this side were ovals rimmed by raised, curved bricks. Also they varied in size, and a faintest flicker of light appeared in the one toward the top. Though at first sight the stones of the tower, pale in the moonlight, initially appeared to be visibly cracked with age, the longer Berthold stared, the more he was certain there was a pattern to the cracks. He pointed this out to the elf.

"I'd not noticed that before," Ingrge admitted. "But it looks like writing. A language I'm not familiar with."

"Runes, no doubt," Yevele decided. "The dragon spoke of magic protecting the tower. Perhaps those are some sort of spell."

Berthold nodded. "It would make sense. If the tower is as old as the dragon claims, it would certainly need some sort of magic to keep it so well preserved."

He studied the very top now. It was crenelated, but the scalloped stones looked like inverted teeth, the edges glistening in the moonlight like they were knife-sharp. He shuddered. There were more of the cracks in their surfaces, and these definitely looked like letters or runes. Too, there was a large shape that moved between the gaps in the teeth.

"There is a patrol," he said. "And I don't think the sentry is human."

Ingrge stared at the shape. "A troll. That's not good news."

"At least there's only one of them," the thief returned.

"That we can see." This came from Yevele. She had her sword out, and she was staring at the lowest gargoyle. Its head had moved since she'd looked at it last. Not much, but enough for her to notice. And its eyes were wider. "I think the gargoyles . . ."

"Are alive," Berthold said. "Or, if not technically alive, they're . . ." He searched for a word. "Operational." The thief concentrated on the gargoyles now. "They don't breathe."

"Neither did the undead that attacked us," Ingrge said.

"But they do move. All of them. I don't think they've seen us. I think they're watching the ground just outside the tower. But the one on top is looking to the sky."

"Maybe looking for dragons." Yevele moved deeper into the forest and motioned the men to join her. "I want to look at the tower from all the angles."

"Wise woman," the thief said. He edged past her, moving silently and blending with the shadows of the woods. He paused to make sure she and Ingrge were following. He went a quarter-turn around the tower, and they stopped.

There was another gargoyle here, about twenty feet above the ground, larger than the others, possessing three arms and bat-shaped wings seeming far too small to support aloft something of its size. The eyes were round like an owl's, and for a moment the thing seemed to stare straight at them. Then its gaze moved elsewhere, and they hurried another quarter-turn around.

"The front. That's the way we went in." Yevele pointed to the tower's door. "That's the only door."

"That we can see," Berthold corrected. It was difficult to make out the features of the door from where they hunkered. Being set back into the tower a few feet, it was thickly shadowed despite the moonlight. It looked, he decided, like an unpleasantly open mouth of a beast. There were no cracks in the stones that ringed the entrance, they looked as if they'd just been poured or chiseled, the edges flat, as if no time had passed to weather them. The stones just beyond them, though, had more of the runic cracks, as did the stones around the lone window set high on this side.

"How could you live in a place, in rooms that have no windows? Dark. No fresh air," Berthold muttered.

Ingrge was viewing the lone window, too. "I cannot understand wizards, as I could not understand the sand dragon. But I suspect windows are only a distraction, like a child distracted in grade school. No distractions, more time to concentrate on their magic. Besides, fewer windows makes the place more defensible, don't you think?"

"There is a pattern," Berthold said, "to the way the gargoyles move their heads and eyes. And there is a routine the troll on the roof follows. You say these things were not here when you visited?"

Ingrge and Yevele shook their heads.

"Then perhaps they are here as a result of your visit. Perhaps the place is not so impregnable, and perhaps the occupants have grown lax."

"I see the pattern you mean," the elf said after a moment. "I believe we can reach the door unseen." Without further word, he dashed forward, low to the ground and heading like an arrow straight for the tower.

Berthold shook his head and held an arm across Yevele's stomach, urging her to stay put. "I would have liked to go all the way around the tower first," he said, disappointment heavy in his voice. "I'm a police officer . . . and a thief . . . I know what to look for, and he didn't give me a chance to—"

Then Yevele slapped his arm away to follow the elf's path.

"It's just like in the game," Berthold grumbled to himself. "The fighters always impetuous, never waiting for the thief to thoroughly check things out. Springing traps, getting themselves maimed or killed. Good thing Milo and the berserker are with the caravan. They would've had all the stone gargoyles' attention. The troll's, too." When he was done fuming, he waited for the gargoyle's head to again look away, then he raced to the tower.

Ingrge had his ear pressed against a door made of blackened wood, that was bound with iron. Yevele leaned against the stone entranceway, waiting for the elf's report. Berthold nudged the elf aside and put his own ear to the spot where the door met the frame.

"I'm the thief, remember?" he whispered. "This is my job."

"You may have some elven blood in your veins, Berthold, but my ears are more sensitive."

"He's an elf?" Yevele looked surprised.

"Half," Berthold said. "Be quiet. I think I hear something."

They stood there for an unmeasured time, shielded in the entry-way. An owl hooted in the woods beyond, and a wolf howled. A moment later another wolf answered, then another, but they were distant and of no concern to the trio. The breeze was slight, felt not at all next to the door, but it rustled clumps of dead grass and knocked together the smallest branches of the tall evergreens. The scrubland darkened for a moment, as clouds scudded across the face of the moon. Then everything was bright again, and Berthold pulled back from the door.

"I hear footsteps. Heavy, certainly not human."

"I could have told you that, thief," Ingrge said. "A troll, from the sounds of it."

The thief raised an eyebrow. "Well, he's gone now. He was near the door, though, as I heard him breathing."

"I could have told you that, too."

"Just open the door, Bert." Yevele tapped her foot impatiently.

"It's locked," Ingrge said. "I already tried the knob."

"Lovely," Berthold said. He nudged the elf a little farther away and knelt at the latch, exploring it with his fingers, as the moonlight didn't reach far enough into the entryway. There was a keyhole beneath a knob that was in the shape of an animal's head, a wolf or a dog from the feel of it, something set in the animal's eyes. Worked gems perhaps, or polished stones. "Don't like this." It felt as if the stones could depress. "Not at all."

Yevele tried to see through the shadows to figure out what he was doing. She didn't say anything, but her foot kept tapping. Ingrge risked sticking his head out of the entranceway and looking up. More clouds drifted past the moon, and the silhouette of a large bird cut across. He pulled his head back in when Yevele tugged on him.

Berthold extracted the largest of his picks and set to work on the keyhole. At the same time, he pressed his ear to the crack in the door, listening for the heavy footfalls. Having heard the tumblers in the lock click one by one, he was certain he'd defeated it, so he replaced the pick and put the pouch of tools back in his pocket. With one hand he pressed in the eyes of the doorknob and turned the handle. Then he held his breath and opened the door an inch.

He was listening again when the elf nudged the door open wider. "I don't hear anything," he whispered. Ingrge slid inside, followed by Yevele. Berthold followed uneasily.

They stood in a grand round room lit by torches that gave off light, but no smoke. The wood seemed not to char away, and each torch's flames flickered in unison. On the center of the floor was a round rug, blood red and shot through with thick shiny black threads that on first inspection had no pattern to them.

"Do not step on the rug," Berthold cautioned. "There's something not quite right about it."

"Something not right about all of this place," Ingrge quietly returned. "Didn't like it the first time I was here. The rug wasn't here then, at least . . . not this rug."

Berthold crept carefully into the room and stood at the edge of the disputed rug. He stared at it, seeing the black threads twist and turn almost imperceptibly. "Snakes," he whispered. "Someone's trapped snakes inside it. Just don't step on it. Whatever you do." He stared at the elf when he said this, not looking away until Ingrge nodded.

Then Berthold carefully studied the rest of the room. It stretched above the torchlight, and so he couldn't see the ceiling. A narrow staircase spiraled up, and two doors were across from the stairway, the same black wood as the entry. The air smelled of cinnamon and something chemical that reminded Berthold of an autopsy room he'd been in during a case back in Bowling Green. The torches didn't seem to give off an odor, so he wondered where the other smells were coming from. He walked around the outside of the carpet, noting that the thick black threads quivered and seemed to follow his course.

"We'd only went up when we were here." Ingrge surveyed the staircase. "Never bothered to look inside those doors here. One must lead down."

"Lovely place this is," Berthold whispered. "I think—" He held a finger to his lips and cocked his head. A "throoming" sound came from overhead, a troll or something equally as big walking. He motioned to the nearest door, put his ear to it, and gently turned the knob when he didn't hear anything on the other side.

The three of them went through, just as the "throoming" came down the stairs. Berthold quietly closed the door behind them and remained there, ear pressed to the crack, breath held.

"Can't see anything in here," Ingrge whispered. "But I smell . . ."

"Lots of things," Yevele answered. "It stinks in here. As bad as that dragon's cave."

In addition to scents of cinnamon and a chemical that might have been embalming fluid or a strong antiseptic, there was the musky scent of burrowing animals.

The "throoming" grew louder, regular like a guardsman's pace. It stopped once, and they guessed the troll was at the front door. Then it stopped twice more, likely at each of the other inner doors. A few minutes more and the footsteps boomed up the steps and faded to nothingness. Suddenly a soft light came on, and Berthold saw that Ingrge had lit a candle.

"By all that's holy," the elf breathed.

The room contained a menagerie. Cages stacked four high lined the walls, each one filled with a creature, and each creature eerily silent. There were squirrels and rabbits, cat-like things and possums, all looking just a little . . . wrong. One rabbit had a small horn protruding from its head. A possum had four eyes, set on its head so that looking at the creature made the observer dizzy. There was a constrictor with two heads and three tails, and a lizard with furry patches on its leathery hide. A black and white wingless bird had an orange circular mark on its neck that looked like a miniature sunburst. A bulldog had saggy jowls, and lines of olive-green drool spilled from them. And in the top cage nearest the door was a small dragon-like creature with green and purple mottled scales.

"Alfreeta," Ingrge cried.

The creature came to the front of its cage, eyes that were once dull sparkling with recognition.

"That's Naile's friend," Ingrge told Berthold. "Naile thought she'd flittered away to be with her own kind."

"The creatures in here aren't anyone or anything's 'kind,' " the thief returned. "This is like a . . ."

"Wizard's laboratory," Yevele supplied.

"A mad one." This burst hotly from the elf. He started talking to Alfreeta, in the musical elven tongue.

Alfreeta's mouth moved in reply, her tongue snaking out and dancing in the air, the air shimmering around it. But no sound came out.

"She's magic," the elf said. "She bonded herself to Naile, a relationship similar to a dog and a boy, but much more. Something held her here, some enchantment that also keeps all these creatures dumb. Else she'd be well away from this tower and perched on Naile's shoulder."

"How'd she get caught?" Berthold was standing in front of the cage, neck craned so he could get a better look at Alfreeta.

Ingrge shrugged. "She was with us all the way through the woods and on the road to the city. We stopped for the night, just a few miles out, and in the morning she was gone."

"So something lured her away." The thief scratched his chin. "Something truly does not like the lot of you. Good thing I got rid of those bracelets." He didn't see Yevele's glare, nor see her mouth the words: *but not Milo and Naile's bracelets*.

"Can you get her out? I could boost you up." Ingrge pointed to the silver latch on the cage.

"Doesn't look locked, but that doesn't mean it's not spell-locked." The thief was thoroughly engrossed in the room and didn't hear the "throoming" coming down the steps again. "I can defeat magic contraptions, you know. I managed Keth's bracelet, your bracelets and—" The elf clapped his hand over Berthold's mouth. Yevele extinguished the candle.

The unseen sentry stopped again at the front door, moved on in pattern outside of this one and the next. Then the "throoming" circled the room once more and went back up the steps. Yevele relit the candle.

The thief was sweating. "I . . . yeah, I think I can get her out. But should I?"

Ingrge looked puzzled by the question.

"No need alerting someone. Maybe opening the cages will set off some sort of alarm. And, besides, we need to free the wizard. Maybe the little dragon will get in the way, could be a problem. You said she's bonded to Naile. Well, she's not bonded to us."

"He could be right." Yevele was chewing on the words, as if she found it distasteful to agree with the thief. "We've been through the upper levels, Ingrge. Maybe we should find the way down. Maybe we should find the wizard, then get all of us, and Alfreeta, out of here."

Ingrge knew the little dragon could understand them, but he explained it all again in his lyrical tongue, adding that Naile was safe and guarding a caravan, that they all would be reunited soon. He didn't add that hopefully they would all be back to their respective homes, he to Florida; Naile to New York. Which would leave Naile and Alfreeta farther apart than ever.

Forty-two steps, Ingrge thought. He forced his mind to remember it was fifty-seven to the sea. But what was his handle?

"We will be back for you," the elf finished, shaking off his scant thoughts of home. Then he extinguished the light and led them to another door.

"Let me check that," Berthold said. But the thief wasn't fast enough.

Ingrge turned the knob and opened the door, hoping to find a staircase that would lead to the depths of the tower. Instead, he found a scythe-like blade slice down and cut off his arm.

NINETEEN

Tattoos and Visions

It was midafternoon before the bodies of the merchants and the guards, and the one villager who'd been killed had been buried in the town cemetery. The dead bandits were buried in a mass grave north of Hart.

A few horses had been rounded up, but not enough to pull all of the wagons, and neither were there any available in town. One of the cheesemaker's guards had ridden south with the coins from the shoe-maker's wagon and other contributions in the hopes of purchasing more horses. If and when enough horses arrived, the caravan would be turning around and going back to the city.

The two surviving Glothorio priests said prayers for the dead and consecrated the ground, not asking for a single coin for their efforts. They now sat on one of Ludlow Jade's blankets, in the shadow of their battered wagon. Naile and Milo knelt in the grass, the dozen pouches that had been taken from the bandits emptied, and the coins stacked up in precise rows.

"Forty-eight gold coins," Milo pronounced. "One hundred and

eleven silvers and two half-coppers. I figure that should be enough to buy some of your magic."

The two priests quietly regarded him for several moments before replying. The tallest was the one who'd been in charge, and only one tattoo remained, this a foreign-looking alphabet on his neck. The younger priest, a man Milo guessed to be in his late teens, had tattoos dotting his head and his left forearm. All the others had been used up between the battle with the undead and with the archers.

"More than enough," the tall priest decided. He was the one who earlier told Milo that divining magic was his specialty and that questions and mysteries swirled around the two men. He was also the one who'd declined to help until they had gathered enough coins to meet the price his god demanded for their spells.

"What do you wish to know. . . ."

"Milo Jagon."

"And Naile Fangtooth."

The priest nodded to each. "Pity that I had not learned your names before this juncture. "I am Brother Beauregaard, and this is Brother Reed." The young priest smiled. "Now, what is it you wish me to divine?"

"Where to begin?" Naile rocked back and tipped his face to the sky. "We need a lot of information. We need—"

"I'll ask the questions," Milo cut in. "I got the money after all." He sat cross-legged, his elbows on his knees. His chainmail shirt was laying next to him. He'd taken it off when he helped bury the bodies, finding it heavy and unnecessary.

He told them everything Berthold had revealed, about the wizard held in Quag Keep, about how they were magically summoned to this world. He'd considered holding some of that back, not wanting anyone to know they weren't "from around here." But he decided to put his trust in the Coin Gatherers, and hoped spilling everything would get them more accurate information.

Brother Beauregaard leaned forward and took four gold coins off the stack, and three silvers. He closed his eyes and drew his chin down to touch his breastbone. At the same time, he held his arms high and began moving his fingers. To Milo he looked like the conductor of some symphony, signaling the brass and the woodwinds to join in. The priest cocked his head now, as if he was indeed listening to some great opus, then he grimaced, and the tattoo on his neck detached itself and hovered in the space between he and Milo. There was a red welt where the tattoo had been, and Milo realized it must be painful for the priests to use this magic. But the welt disappeared, leaving the flesh unblemished and ready to receive another tattoo.

Around them the air grew hazy and motes of gray and silver lights winked on and off where the tattoo floated. It unwound itself, looking like a ribbon now, and it wove its way among the motes.

"Something wards what you seek," Brother Beauregaard said. He brought one arm down and tugged at the cord at the V neck of his robe. There were more tattoos on his chest, and as he gestured two of them pulled free to join the floating ribbon. Milo thought the undead battle had all but stripped the priest of his magic. Was the man's entire body covered with the arcane marks? Then the priest's hand stretched out to the coin pile and took several more gold pieces. "Magic has a price," he said by way of explanation.

Milo didn't care, he was caught up in the spell that had grown to fill the air between him and the priest. The two additional tattoos stretched and soon looked like ribbons, too. They tied and untied themselves, cavorted like wriggling worms. Then in a flash they were gone. In their place hung the haggard-looking face of an old, old man.

His skin looked so deeply wrinkled it might well have been tree bark, and it was practically that color. But it was tinged gray, as if the man was unhealthy. Heavy dark circles ringed the eyes, adding to the worn appearance. The eyes were shiny, though, not looking at all like they belonged to an old man. And they were a dark purple flecked with slivers of amber.

There were no eyebrows, just bony ridges where eyebrows should be. And he had a high forehead that sloped back. A thick mass of silvery hair spilled down over slumped shoulders, straight until near the ends, which curled and undulated in a nonexistent wind. The figure had a beard and a mustache, both a few shades darker than the hair, all of it unkempt and dotted with the husks of insects and with specks of dirt. His mouth, difficult to see for all the hair, was small, and the lips cracked.

"I am Jalafar-rula," the image said. "Jalafar-rula of Stonehenge. And I called you here." His voice was weak, yet it had a sense of power about it. "It is I who summoned you to this land."

"Jalafar-rula is indeed a great wizard," Brother Reed supplied. "I have read of him. He is old. Very. So old I thought him certainly dead."

Brother Beauregard nudged the young priest.

"Sorry." Brother Reed bent his head and folded his hands in his lap. "I did not mean to interrupt."

The image of the wizard glowed a little brighter. "I sent for you, Milo Jagon and Naile Fangtooth. You and more than a dozen others. Pulled you from Earth and brought you here."

"Why?" asked Naile, shifting a little to directly face the image. "Why us? Why bring anyone here? And . . . just where is *here?*"

It was long minutes before the image answered. "I foresaw my capture, Naile Fangtooth, and so I created nearly two dozen miniature warriors, thieves, and sorcerer figures—in the event my capture truly came about. Miniatures, of the kind you use to represent characters in your game."

"Our game?" The disbelief was thick in Milo's voice. "You summoned us because we're gamers?"

"I needed the miniatures to be discovered by those you call 'gamers.' Each person grasping one of the miniatures would be pulled here. Part of an elaborate calling spell capable of breaching dimensions." The wizard seemed quite pleased with himself, and a bit of the fatigue vanished from his face. "I needed your kind because you have such rich imaginations. You crave fantasy. You dream of knights and dragons. And, deep down, many of you believe that magic really exists."

"Not in our world," Milo said. "Here maybe, but—"

Brother Reed reached over and pulled more coins from the stacks as Brother Beauregaard added another tattoo to keep the enchantment going.

"Yes, in your world." Jalafar-rula's eyes seemed to grow larger and brighter. "A very long time ago the pulse of magic was strong and fast on Earth. Stronger there than it is here."

"Stonehenge. You said you are Jalafar-rula of Stonehenge." Naile seemed in awe of the image and the magic that birthed it. "Stonehenge in England."

"The same. I had it built when your world was quite a bit younger, and I was younger, too." The image sighed, shoulders slumping more and head lowering until he looked more than a bit like a turtle with his face protruding from a shell. "But there's not much of Stonehenge left, just rocks and ruins. Not much left of me, either. Not in Pobe's clutches in any event."

"So what happened to the magic? On Earth?" Naile pressed.

"Magic ran like rivers through the ground. You could breathe it in the air."

"But what happened?" This from Milo. He was growing impatient, and fearing that the wizard would not get his tale told before all of the coins disappeared.

"Pobe happened. Called the Dark One or the Darkness by my brethren and the powers of this place. He is a creature of this world who grew more powerful and learned from the wizards of this realm that there were layers of dimensions. Earth is one. Not able to take over this land, at least not completely because the wizards here were in good number, he still found a way to touch your world. Nestled safely in the arcane richness of this place, not draining a drop of the magic here." Jalafar-rula's expression showed that there were things he was not telling. "He and his minions began siphoning the magic from your world. Pobe feeds on magic. He needs it to survive."

Small images began to build around Jalafar-rula's head . . . Stonehenge as an immense castle; Stonehenge now in ruins; horses pulling buggies down narrow English streets; Model Ts coming out of early factories; skyscrapers in New York; cars streaming over the Golden

Andre Norton and Jean Rabe

Gate Bridge in California; people looking up at the arch in St. Louis; the opera house in Sydney; a sprawling shopping mall in Minneapolis filled with shoppers; the space shuttle blasting off; and satellites orbiting Earth.

"As technology improved, Pobe's work became easier. People from your cities stopped believing in magic. Technology was easier for them to grasp. People didn't need magic any longer. Factories manufactured televisions and microwaves . . . electricity and variety shows filled the gap. And now, there is little magic left. Oh, there are some pockets here and there. Milo, you unknowingly live in such a pocket on Earth. Your quaint, quaint town. The battlemaid Yevele is near another. But Pobe has nearly drained your world dry. And soon he will turn to another and another, living off their layers. He cannot drain this world, Naile Fangtooth, Milo Jagon. That would be the death of him. But yours . . . what will your world be like if it has no magic at all? Not a breath of it?"

Milo stared speechless at the wizard, and he watched the planes and the other images fade out.

"Why didn't the wizards here stop him?" Naile raised his voice.

"To get near him is to risk death. He feeds on magic and can drain us dry if he chooses."

"So you needed someone other than a wizard. And someone not from this world because likely the people here are either too afraid of this 'Dark One' or don't believe you or just don't have the guts to take him on. Or they don't know anything about Earth and these layers, and so it's not their problem." Naile shook his head. "You needed outsiders, huh?"

"So I brought you here to stop Pobe and to save your world and rekindle its magical spark. Your world is in jeopardy. Your responsibility to aid it. I had intended to meet with you personally, traveling to your world, but Pobe lured me back to this one and into a trap and caught me with my defenses down. I had to rely on my agents and the miniatures. And when you came here, I still tried to reach out to you, but my magic wasn't strong enough. Pobe siphons me, too, just to keep me from escaping. I only was able to contact . . ."

Return to Quag Keep

"Berthold of the Green," Milo said.

"Yes. And I talk to you now only because of these kind and powerful priests of the Coin Gatherer. I have been bodily imprisoned in the depths of Quag Keep for . . ."

The priest's spell wavered, and he added another tattoo. Brother Reed leaned forward and took more coins from Milo's stack. Milo likened their operation to a video game. To keep playing, he had to put more tokens in the slot.

". . . many long months."

"Pobe, this villain, he means to kill you?" Naile asked.

Jalafar-rula shook his head. "He needs me." The wizard paused. "I am a conduit."

"And he's siphoning Earth through you." Milo leaned farther forward. "He's using you to steal the magic."

"Not precisely. He has a device, something of great power that lets him leach the magic from your world. But he needs me to keep the link open."

"So he has to keep you alive."

A nod.

"So, if you died, Earth would be spared?"

"Milo Jagon, I am not so altruistic as to kill myself to save your magic. I am a good soul, but I will not sacrifice myself to that end. Too important. Too many things left to do."

"So it's up to us," Milo stated. "We have to take care of this Pobe for you."

"For your own future," Jalafar-rula corrected. "Which is why I summoned you . . . gamers . . . here. Consider this your grandest game yet. One worthy of true adventurous spirits."

"And if we fail?" Naile was on his knees, eye-to-eye with the wizard. "So what happens with magic gone? It's like you said, people don't believe in magic on Earth anyway."

The old, old face looked pained. "Naile Fangtooth, without any magic at all, Earth will lose its spark. Imagination will stagnate, and the Dark One's minions will be loosed to feast on the remains."

"And that means we have to rescue you," Milo cut it. "Doesn't it?

Andre Norton and Jean Rabe

We can't stop this 'Dark One' without your help. We can't find this 'siphoning device' without you."

Another nod.

"So we have to get to Quag Keep." Milo looked to Naile. "We have to get to the tower and explain all of this to Yevele and Ingrge."

"And Berthold of the Green."

"But Quag Keep is a long way from here, Naile. It could take us weeks."

The image of Jalafar-rula of Stonehenge wavered, then winked out. The priest shook his head and blinked, then slumped, the spell obviously taking a lot out of him. His eyes had a faraway look, and were pale, like water running over stones.

"I sympathize with your plight, Milo, Naile." The priest's voice was halting, his breathing labored. Brother Reed helped steady him. "We can help. Together we can cast a spell that would send you straight to Jalafar-rula of Stonehenge."

Milo brightened and jumped to his feet. "Great! You could send us right to this wizard?"

"Yes," Brother Reed said. "We have such magic."

"But it will cost you," the elder priest added. "More coins than you have left."

Milo looked down at the smattering of silver pieces remaining at his feet.

TWENTY

Breath of Life

Ingrge fell forward into the room, the swinging scythe passing above his prone body. Torchlight from the main room spilled in to show that blood streamed from what remained of his right arm. He was conscious, and he was doing everything he could to keep from screaming in pain.

Berthold watched the timing of the scythe, then leapt between the swings and vaulted to Ingrge's side. Yevele was on his heels, narrowly avoiding the blade, though it sliced her cloak. She made a move toward Ingrge's head, but slipped on the blood and fell, her sword and chainmail shirt clanking as the metal hit stone.

"Quiet," Berthold warned. He rolled Ingrge onto his back and tugged a dagger free. Then he pried open the elf's clenched teeth and shoved the pommel in. "Bite down on this, Ingrge. Try to keep quiet. Please, please try to keep quiet." He glanced at Yevele, intending to ask her for help.

But she was up and at the door, yanking the scythe blade free of the mechanism above the door frame, and making more noise in the process. "Should've thought," she said. "Ingrge and I should've been more careful. Every time in the game that you get ahead of yourself, get careless, something bad happens. Except in the game you're only losing paper characters. You can always get new ones, sometimes better ones depending on how the dice rolls. No great loss, paper."

"But Ingrge's not paper," Berthold pointed out sharply. "And we could lose him." It was as close as he'd come to directly telling her _I told you so._

She leaned her head out into the hall, then, satisfied nothing was outside, she slipped away.

"What do you think you're doing?" Berthold fumed. He was about to call her back inside. Ingrge had broken into a cold sweat and was going white, the blood spurted faster from his stump, and Berthold's attempt to stop the bleeding with his cloak was doing nothing. The elf was dying.

A "throom" sounded from above.

Yevele returned a moment later, holding a torch she'd retrieved from the main room. She slammed the door forcibly behind her. "The troll's coming. It is a troll for certain. Saw its big green foot on the top stair. Hopefully it didn't hear me fall, and more, I hope it wasn't taught to count the torches." She slipped in the blood again, but this time kept her footing, kneeling in the growing pool and nodding to Berthold.

The "throoming" was growing louder, it was true that the sentry was coming down the stairs and making his circuit of the main room again.

Berthold held Ingrge's mouth closed on the pommel and Yevele thrust the torch against the stump, attempting to cauterize the wound. The torch gave off no heat, yet it burned the elf, and he thrashed. The stench of burning flesh was strong, and they looked to the door, thinking the sentry would smell it, too, and come to investigate, and that they should have waited just a moment, but the "throoming" went past the door, just as Berthold lay on top of the elf to keep him from writhing. The thief feared Ingrge would either hurt himself or make noise that would bring the troll down upon them all.

Suddenly, mercifully, Ingrge went unconscious, and Yevele and

Berthold sagged back to catch their breath. Neither said a word, both intent on those heavy footsteps that were pausing somewhere for a moment then continuing on. When the "throoming" finally retreated up the stairs, Berthold tugged his tunic up to wipe the sweat off his own face.

Yevele shrugged her cloak off and began tearing it into strips. The first piece she rolled into a pad, which she carefully knotted onto the end of the elf's stump with another longer strip. Ingrge had lost his arm just above the elbow. She threw a piece of her cloak over the lost limb so she wouldn't have to look at it.

Moving around to Ingrge's shoulders, she settled there and pulled him up so she was cradling him, dabbing at his face with a strip of her cloak, whispering that everything would be all right, even though her voice made it clear she was uncertain.

It was almost tender, and it was the most sympathetic Berthold had seen the battlemaid. He nearly made a comment about her having a heart after all, but wisely stopped himself and looked around the room. It was lit by the torch that lay on the stone floor a few feet from Ingrge, still not consuming itself nor giving off smoke.

Its far wall was curved, following the outline of the tower. Against it were curved bookshelves that reached up to a ceiling nearly fifteen feet high. The books gave off no scent, which surprised the thief. He'd expected to smell old paper and leather, and rotting wood as the shelves were old and had wormholes. He retrieved the torch and went to the nearest shelf. None of the spines had titles, but he knew from studying medieval times that books were not labeled like they are now. Tucking the torch under one arm, he pulled down a thick book and carefully kept it away from the magical flame. There was a thick layer of dust on the top of it, and he noticed the same on the other books nearby and on the wood. No one had been in here for a while. Berthold flapped open the cover to find a title and saw that it was written in a form of Old English that was difficult to read, though not impossible. But it would take a while.

"Like trying to read *Beowulf* in the original script," he muttered.

"We don't have time for you to look at books," Yevele said. She still cradled Ingrge, slightly rocking him. "We need to get him out of here."

"To take him where? This room's as good a place as any." Berthold selected another book and thumbed through it. And then another. "I thought maybe these books might tell us about the Keep. Maybe show a map or something. Let us get down below. Tell us about whoever used to live here."

Yevele's eyes flashed with fire. "Aren't you listening to me? We have to help Ingrge. That's our first priority."

Berthold whirled to face her. "I'd love to help Ingrge. He's a fine fellow—in this world and probably back in his own. But I've done all I can for him right now. And there's nothing more that you can do either. In the game, at least in the game we played, we always took a priest or a wise woman with us. So that when some monster tried to eat our face, she'd heal us. Or we'd carry potions in our pockets. Heavy duty, magical Pepto Bismol that would make everything all better again."

"We *had* a priest with us," she answered softly. "His name was . . . *is* . . . Deav Dyne. He went to the swamp with Gulth."

"Who?"

"Gulth. Doesn't matter. At least they're safe. But we have to help Ingrge."

"There's no hospital here, Yevele. No priests. No potions. We can't help Ingrge." He replaced the book and rubbed his chin. "Or maybe we can. Maybe the best thing we can do is find out how to get below this tower and free the wizard. Maybe the wizard can do something. I certainly don't have a better idea than that. All I know is I'm losing touch with Kentucky. It's getting harder and harder to remember things. That scares me. It we lose touch entirely, what's all this for?"

Yevele brushed a thin strand of hair off the elf's forehead. "*If* we can find the way below. *If* we can find the wizard. All of that might be too late for Ingrge. And does the wizard even exist, or did you dream him up on a night filled with too much wine?"

"I don't know anymore, Yevele. I don't know for certain what's real and what's a dream. Maybe I'm Berthold of the Green only dreaming that I'm really Bertrum Wiggins, patrolman from Bowling Green, Kentucky." Berthold looked at another book, then gave up. "But the tower's real." He turned to face the wall behind Ingrge, seeing shelves containing rolled parchments and jars filled with things he didn't want to think about.

"So what do you want to do, Yevele?" His stomach growled at that instant, and he selected another book. "I'm hungry. Forgot it's been a while since we ate. You hungry? What do you want to do, Yevele?"

"I've an idea." She eased herself away from Ingrge and returned to the door, listening carefully for any sound from the troll. "I could slay it, the troll, I'm certain of it. They're strong and vicious, but not especially bright."

"Fine, so you want to kill a troll. I don't see how that would help the elf."

"But I might not be able to kill it quickly, and it could make quite a bit of noise first. It might alert other things in the tower. Maybe more trolls. Maybe too many trolls. When we were here before, we saw odd beasts and had a few nasty fights."

"So you don't want to kill the troll."

"No. Not yet." She carefully opened the door and looked out into the main room. Then she opened it all the way, came back to Ingrge and picked him up. The gesture looked effortless for her, and she carried him out of the room and into the one housing the menagerie.

Berthold followed, magical torch in one hand, a book tucked under his arm, careful to close both doors behind her. "So you've moved him," he said. "Not an especially wise thing to do in his condition. Just might make him bleed some more. And from the looks of the floor back there, you can see he's already lost a lot of blood. Too, too much blood."

She carefully laid him in front of a row of cages, using the last of her cloak for a scant pillow. Then she pointed to Alfreeta. "You said you thought you could get her out of there."

"I also said I thought there might be some sort of glyph or such, something that might trigger a magical alarm. Alert all those trolls that might be walking the halls."

"Or maybe there isn't any alarm. Free her." Yevele made it clear that it wasn't a request.

Berthold shrugged, decided not to argue. "So be it," he whispered. "If an alarm sounds, we probably won't have to worry about finding our way down below the tower. And we won't have to worry about finding something to eat. I suspect—"

The "throoming" started again. But this time it was louder, and there was a longer interval between steps. Yevele and Berthold looked at each other, and Yevele crept to the door and put her ear to the crack. The "throoming" made the same circuit of the room, but when it stopped in front of the menagerie's door, it was accompanied by a wuffling sound, something sniffing at the crack. Yevele stepped to the side, her hand clenched around the pommel of her sword.

"Rruf?" It was a loud sound and it made the door vibrate a little. "Rruff nerug." Then the "throoming" resumed, stopping at the next door, making another circle of the main room, at last going up the stairs. Yevele risked a peek out, catching a glimpse of the creature disappearing into the shadows above.

She closed the door and closed her eyes, let out the breath she'd been holding. "It's a giant," she said softly. "With big, hairy legs. And it was dragging a big club. There wasn't a giant when we were here before."

"Not that you saw, anyway." Berthold wiped at the sweat on his face again. "I think I've lost three pounds since coming in here, Yevele. All this nervous sweat."

"I could take the giant, with your help," she said.

He turned his attention to the cage holding Alfreeta. She was at the front, wings moving, though there wasn't enough room for her to flap them and fly. Her eyes blinked furiously, and her tongue darted in and out, touching the bars. Berthold knew she should be making some noise, but there was only silence.

"The occupant of the tower, he mustn't want to hear the ruckus from these creatures. They should be seen and kept in cages, but not heard." He was on his tiptoes, hands above his head and fingers running over the latch. "Yeah, it's got some sort of enchantment on it, but I think I can break it."

Berthold leaned back on his heels and retrieved his leather pouch, opening it and studying the picks inside. "This one and this one." He pulled two out and replaced the pouch. Then he stood on his tiptoes again and started to work on the lock. "Not quite tall enough," he said to himself. Then he felt himself being lifted, Yevele's hands on his hips and holding him higher.

He nearly dropped the picks in surprise and embarrassment. "That's not at all necessary, Yevele. I can. . . ."

"Just open the cage, thief."

He glared at her, and her face softened.

"Just open the cage, please, Berthold."

"Fine." Berthold could see the mechanism better from his higher vantage, and from the light of the torch which flickered nearby on the floor. There were tiny symbols on the latch that he hadn't noticed before, and these he scratched at with the thinnest pick. He likened it to criminals who filed the serial numbers off guns so the guns couldn't be traced. But it was hard to file everything off, and most often the numbers could still be lifted. But in this case he only wanted to ruin a couple of the symbols. That should prevent the magic from working . . . whatever the magic was supposed to do. He didn't know just how he knew that, like the elf knowing about the constellations and the Celestial Dance.

"Hurry," Yevele urged. "I'm strong, but you're dead weight."

"I'd prefer a word other than dead." Berthold continued to scratch away at the symbols until he was satisfied that he'd defaced enough. Then he used the other pick to worry inside a tiny keyhole. He listened for the "click," but then realized no sound would come. All the cages had been magically silenced. "That ought to do it. I hope."

Berthold closed his eyes, slowly released a deep breath, turned the latch up, and opened the cage door. His face was instantly battered by small claws and wings as Alfreeta flew out. Away from the cage he could hear the miniature dragon. She was making a purring sound, not wholly unlike a cat, and her wings "shushed" as they carried her farther away from the cage. Yevele lowered him roughly to the floor and watched Alfreeta land on Ingrge's chest.

The elf didn't stir.

"We haven't a priest with us," she said. "Or pockets full of potions. But I know there's magic in that small, gentle beast."

Berthold stared in fascination. Alfreeta was dragon-like, but clearly not a dragon. Her scales were oval and glistening, looking like purple tinted mother-of-pearl stones one might set into jewelry. The scales were lighter around her middle, darkest along her neck and the underside of her snout. Her head was the shape of a bull terrier's, though her lips looked leathery, as did her ever-flicking tongue. Her nostrils were heart-shaped and glistened with moisture. Her ears were small and set tight against her head, elegantly pointed, and the ridge that ran from just above her almond-shaped eyes to the tip of her tail was covered in needle-like spikes that moved in the still air as if they were supple like blades of grass.

As Alfreeta beat her wings, the elf started breathing in time with them, his chest rising and falling regularly and with more force now. Her tongue was lapping at his face, somehow coaxing a little color to it. His head moved back and forth fitfully though, revealing his pain was intense.

"I'm glad he's not awake," she said. Yevele took the torch off the floor and stuck the end through the bars in Alfreeta's vacated cage. Higher, the torch lit the room better. "No way to ease his pain. No pocketful of potions." She sat near the elf, cross-legged, arms stiff behind her and leaning against them.

Berthold paced in front of a row of cages, the animals inside intently watching them, hope in some of their eyes, fear from the rabbit with the horn on its head. "He'll wake up sometime, Yevele. And then he'll have to deal with the pain." *Or he'll never wake up.* He didn't have to say those words, they both knew that was a possibility, despite the ministrations of Alfreeta.

"Do you think he can hear us?" Yevele wondered aloud. "Worrying over him, over us?"

Return to Quag Keep

Berthold dropped next to her and opened the book he'd brought with him. He'd hoped it was something about this tower or about wizards. "A play. I've found a play, I think. Wonderful. Or a story about a play. Hard to make out all the words, this language is so old."

"Read to him," Yevele said. "For a while. Please."

Berthold took a mouthful from his waterskin, there was little water left, and he started:

The elf maid strolled across the stage, sea-green gown swishing softly behind her, love letter held against her heart. A small ginger dog dutifully followed her. 'It will be a grand wedding, mother. Can you see me in a dress of ivory lace? I will wear flowers in my hair, Jully's favorite — white lilacs. And a string of pink pearls around my . . .' she paused dramatically and gracefully settled herself at a desk near the edge of the stage, and with a flourish reached for a quill and began penning a note.

'Dearest Jully,' she said, as she tipped her face to the audience, batted her eyelashes, and smiled wistfully. 'I received your last letter, so beautiful it made me weep. I think of you every day, and I pray to my grandmother's divine spirit that we will be together soon. Forever.'

As she continued, a matronly elf glided up to stand behind her daughter, looked sadly down at the people seated in the front row of the audience, and then rested her hands on the girl's shoulders. 'You've met this man only once dear, sweet Irisal,' she said.

'Once was all it required. I knew from the first moment that I loved him. And with each letter Jully writes to me I grow to love him more and more and more.' The young elf continued scratching at the parchment.

'He might be wed, Irisal.'

'No. Not possible.'

'He might have another love.'

'No. Not my Jully.'

'He might . . .'

'No.'

'Then why doesn't he come to see you, Irisal? For the past six months all he's done is send you letters — affixed to the neck of this dirty, smelly mongrel.'

The dog hung its head low, looking horribly offended. An elderly man watching from the second row made a sorrowful 'awwing' sound.

Irisal pushed away from the desk, stood, and with a sweeping motion placed the back of her hand against her forehead. 'My darling Jully Willowstream is a very busy man, mother. He is deep in the Quillar's Woods at this very moment, working against those foul Bandits of the Dark Pass and all of the other vile forces of evil. He is risking his life, mother, so you and I and all of the Autumn Elf Clan will be free and safe.'

She waited for the smattering of applause to die down, then she grabbed up the note she'd been writing, carefully rolled it, and stuck it in a small tube dangling from the mutt's neck. 'Good dog, return to your brave master at once!'

The dog gave a yip and then leapt off the stage, bolting down the center aisle, stopping to jump into the lap of young girl. He licked her cheek, then began a lightning-swift course that took him zig-zagging around the chairs in the back row and had half the audience on its feet clapping. A heartbeat later the dog was out of sight.

Behind the stage, the playwright paced.

'Hear that applause?'

The playwright looked up at the stagehand and grinned weakly. 'At least they liked the trick with the dog. Distracts them from the scenery change.' The playwright was still wringing his hands, but the tempo of his motions had slowed considerably.

The stagehand offered him a broad smile. 'Dogs are indeed your forte, Sir. I know you are at your best when you write what you know. And I believe you've done that quite admirably.'

'Good advice,' the playwright returned. 'You know, there's an empty seat in the back row, just in front of that big elm. I think I'll go watch my play for a while. And maybe I'll stop worrying so much.' Then he slipped around the far edge of the stage and made his way into the audience.

Berthold closed the book. "Oh, that's just bad," he said. "Like the books you find in the supermarket. Ugh. I could write better than that. A lovesick elf." He looked to Yevele, leaning back on her arms, she'd fallen asleep. The exhaustion was etched deep on her face. Ingrge slept, chest still rising and falling in time with Alfreeta's wings. "Couldn't I have plucked a more useful book to read? A romance? Really."

The little dragon turned her head, wide eyes meeting his.

"Really," he whispered. "Really! What a wonderful book. Yevele, me, the elf, you, Alfreeta. . . . We're all in a play of sorts, aren't we? Just like in the game, all of us assuming roles and playing a part in a grand adventure." He turned to the very back of the book, where there was a blank page, and he carefully ripped it out. Then he skittered over to Ingrge's other side, where the stump was bandaged. "Good thing Yevele's sleeping, she might take exception to this."

Next, he pulled out one of his thieves' picks, touched it to the bloody cloth, and using the blood as if it were ink, and the pick as if it were a quill, he started to write a letter.

'To Naile Fangtooth:'

"I know you're not a dog, Alfreeta, and that this isn't a love letter, and that it might not work quite like in that book. . . . But it's worth a try."

He worked at the note for some time, as writing with blood and a pick wasn't particularly easy or fast. When he was done with his note, he blew on it, rolled it up and wrapped it in a strip of cloth from his own cloak, trying to make sure it would stay dry. Then he removed his belt, cut it in half with a dagger, and made a collar out of it. The miniature dragon watched him the entire time, and when he was finished she flitted over to him, hovering just above the ground. He put the collar on her, attached the note, then went to the door and listened.

"You can find Naile, can't you Alfreeta? Just like Lassie could always somehow find Timmy. Even when he fell down into a well."

There was no "throoming," and so Berthold opened the door just a bit. Safe. He opened it wider and tiptoed into the main hall, and to the door that led outside. Berthold looked to the stairs, held his breath, and opened the latch. It was lighter outside, as if the day was moving toward dawn. A few hours had passed since they came in here.

"No wonder I'm so tired," he whispered. "Haven't slept in nearly two days." Slightly louder: "Go find your friend, little dragon. Bring the cavalry around the bend." *If the cavalry is still alive,* he thought. *If they're not dead because I didn't remove their bracelets and something came to eat their faces.* He considered, just for a moment, fleeing the tower and making his way through the forest, finding some small city where he could practice his thieving trade and live reasonably happily ever after.

"Is it possible I've only dreamed that I'm Bertrum Wiggins?"

He watched Alfreeta disappear from view, then he closed the door, returned to the menagerie room and slid a cage behind this door for a false sense of security. Then he stretched out on the stone floor next to Ingrge.

He pictured a shiny black Corvette, leather upholstery and a six-speaker sound system. Then he drifted off to sleep, just as the "throoming" came by again.

TWENTY-ONE

Ludlow Jade's Sacrifice

Milo continued to stare down at the smattering of silver pieces at his feet. He looked at the two rings he wore, and tried futilely to take them off and use them for payment. He had tried dozens of times before to remove them, not to use them as money, but because he didn't like being forced to wear something, particularly enchanted jewelry. Next he tried to tug free the copper bracelet with all the gem dice.

"Look, I'd give you all this stuff," Milo grumbled, "if I could take it off. See . . . won't budge. Can't you give us a break?"

"I believe you think wrongly of us," Brother Beauregaard said. "You think us a greedy order, exacting coins in return for our aid. But we do so out of necessity, Milo Jagon." The Glothorio priest sat on one of Ludlow Jade's blankets, locking eyes with Milo.

"I haven't more coins," Milo said flatly. "And I don't see how I can get you more. I'm working as a guard to pay off a debt. I'm not earning a wage."

"Then, sadly, we cannot help you," Brother Beauregaard said. "Our tattoos, they are costly, the dyes and enchantments that go into them. Ours is not so charitable an order, Milo Jagon. We cannot afford to be, if we wish to flourish. If we cast spells with our tattoos for just anyone, for any cause, we would surely become insolvent. Our order would fold, and our work would be only a memory."

"I don't suppose you'd take a rain check?" Naile asked.

Brother Beauregaard raised an eyebrow.

"How about you send us there, to the wizard," Naile tried again. "And we'll pay you later. Promise. Scout's honor and all of that. The wizard's bound to have hundreds of gold coins, right?"

Brother Beauregaard shook his head. "That is not how . . ."

". . . you operate," Milo finished. "Yeah, I understand. We pay up front, right. We give you coins, you cast your spell."

Brother Beauregaard and Brother Reed nodded in unison.

"Come to us again, when you've enough to pay," Brother Beauregaard said. "Then we can help you."

"Fine," Milo said. "Fine. Fine. Fine." He stood and stretched and tried to cast off his growing anger and frustration. "Look, thanks for what you did. For contacting the wizard for us. I wasn't sure Berthold's story had any truth to it. So thanks for that."

"Would've liked to have found out where Yevele is," Naile said.

"And Ingrge. Maybe even see how Deav Dyne and Gulth are doing, if they made it to the swamp."

"And Alfreeta," Naile said. "Find out where she is. Alf. . . ." The berserker put his back to Milo's and looked up. He thought he saw something in the sky. A bird?

"Come to us again, when you've enough to pay," Brother Beauregaard repeated. "We understand the urgency of your self-imposed mission. Perhaps whatever god you worship will lead you to the coins necessary for our enchantment. Perhaps—"

Milo shook his head. "I think we'll be walking to Quag Keep." He looked at his boots and pictured the blisters on his feet. "I think—"

"I think that Brother Beauregaard and Brother Reed will be casting that spell and sending you to the wizard Jalafar-rula." Ludlow Jade came around the corner of the wagon, hands in his pockets and shuffling. He pulled a pouch from his pocket and dropped it in front of the Glothorio priests. "I trust that will pay for the enchantment."

Naile cupped his hand over his eyes and squinted. Something was coming closer and tugging at his mind. Something familiar, still too distant to be sure. "Alfreeta?"

Brother Beauregaard opened the pouch, not taking his eyes off Ludlow Jade's until he spilled the contents on the blanket. A dozen gold coins gleamed so bright it looked as if they'd been newly minted. But the true valuables were three rings, all gold and set with gems.

"They belonged to my son, Zechial."

The elder priest picked up each ring and examined it, as if he were a jeweler. "Fine workmanship, Ludlow Jade. And sufficient to send one of them." He glanced between Milo and Naile. "Which one of you shall Brother Reed and I send to the wizard Jalafar-rula?"

"Both of them," Ludlow Jade said. "I was listening earlier, saw the wizard and heard his story. I still follow the Coin Gatherer, Brother Beauregaard, and so I know your magic is true and comes with a high price. Milo and Naile are not from here, and they've their home to save." He took off three of his own rings and dropped them on the rug. "Both of them, with your spell."

The wind picked up suddenly, sending the canvas on the wagon and all the men's cloaks flapping. The edges of the blanket ruffled. The Glothorio priests worked the leather lacings open on their robes to their waists, revealing the myriad of tattoos, most of them black, but a few dark blue and blood red. Nearly all of them were swirls, like an artist had painted them on with a thick brush. There were also a couple of symbols that looked like bird wings and deer antlers.

"I think it's Alfreeta up there," Naile said, still glancing aloft. But Milo wasn't listening to him.

Brother Beauregaard stretched his hand forward, grasping the rings and putting them in his own pocket. Then he held his hands in the air, Brother Reed copying the gesture and chanting in the tongue Milo had heard them speak before. This time there were no familiar words interspersed.

A bird-wing tattoo detached itself from Brother Reed, leaving behind a red mark that did not immediately fade. A similar tattoo floated away from the elder priest, and they twisted together in the air between the two priests. More tattoos began joining them, and in the space of a few moments, all the symbols were gone from the men's chests and arms. Only a few tattoos remained on Brother Reed's neck, and these eventually joined the rest in their mystical gyrations.

"Expensive indeed," Ludlow Jade said to Milo. "To leave them naked of their magic, and defenseless like this. No wonder the price for your spell is so lofty."

The symbols wove themselves in an intricate dance, then slowly moved away from the priests and expanded, touching Milo first, then Naile, who was excitedly gesturing to a small dragon-like creature diving toward him.

"It is Alfreeta," Naile said.

The symbols expanded further and completely engulfed the two men, and then Alfreeta, who flew to Naile's shoulder.

"I trust that you will pay me back, Milo," Ludlow Jade said. His face was all business. "You can find me back in the city when you are done rescuing the wizard and your world. You've quite a debt to me."

Milo tried to tell the merchant that he would reimburse him somehow, but his mouth wouldn't work and the words froze in his throat. Then he felt like he was being lifted, like he was floating with the symbols. They wrapped around his head, twisted down his body like a serpent. He felt Naile behind him, and something twitching against his shoulder. He felt the breeze, which was growing stronger still.

Though he closed his eyes he still saw the symbols twisting all around, listened to hear something like a purr. Alfreeta? He'd heard Naile speak the little dragon's name. Was Alfreeta here? Or was he dreaming it? Was he dreaming all of this? Was it possible he was sleeping in his second-floor efficiency? Dreaming that this was all an extension of the game? Was he dreaming that he was a warrior named Milo Jagon on a quest to find a wizard?

But no dream would be this vivid, Milo told himself. He had an imagination, but it wasn't this good. And though he considered his mind strong, it wasn't strong enough to conjured this . . . or to hold tight the details of home. Things about Wisconsin were getting fuzzy. He tried to raise his arm, curious to touch one of the writhing symbols. His muscles felt like lead, and his chest impossibly tight. Then the symbols stopped moving, and he was falling. The world turned blackest black, and his feet touched something solid.

"Milo Jagon." The voice came out of the darkness. "And Naile Fangtooth. It is my pleasure to make your acquaintance."

"Jalafar-rula?"

"Why yes, Milo. Jalafar-rula of Stonehenge. Now if you would be ever so kind as to get me out of here."

"So where . . . precisely . . . are we? Where is here?" Naile asked. He felt Alfreeta on his shoulder, her wings beating slightly, and her tail twitching, then wrapping loosely around his neck.

"You are with me," Jalafar-rula said. The wizard's voice was not near so commanding as they'd heard it in the Glothorio priest's spell. It was the voice of an old, old man, more of a whisper, thin, though they could tell he wasn't whispering. "You are in a very dark place. In a cell in Pobe's dungeon."

"I think we could've figured that out on our own, that we're in jail. Naile and I are making a habit of getting tossed in cells. A bad habit. At least this time we haven't been drinking first, and my head isn't pounding from a hangover—though maybe it would be better if it was. You'd think for the value of those rings the Glothorio priests could've sent us outside your cell." Milo sniffed. "Stinks in here. Not so bad as the last place, though. Dark as dark gets. Can't see anything. And my eyes are wide open."

"Pobe likes the dark," Jalafar-rula continued. "He is a part of it."

"Is he here?" Milo rested his hand on the pommel of his sword. "This Pobe?"

"No, for you would smell him. Sulfur and worse, he exudes. And you would hear him, rattling like a snake, slithering over the stones. I believe he has gone below, or perhaps he is elsewhere, conversing with his minions."

"Minions," Milo muttered. "Sulfur and worse. Locks you up in a place where you can't see anything. This Pobe sounds like a wonderful sort."

"You need to free me, Milo Jagon and Naile Fangtooth. That is why I summoned you here to this land."

"Have to find you first." This from Naile. "Keep talking, Jalafar-rula." He reached to his shoulder and scratched Alfreeta's stomach. Dismal as his surroundings were, the berserker was pleased he'd been reunited with his scaly friend. "What's this?" He felt something rolled in cloth at the little dragon's neck, noticing a collar that hadn't been there before. "Where have you been, Alfreeta? Where'd you fly off to? I missed you." He took the rolled cloth loose and felt the parchment inside. "Might be a spell scroll. Might be a map. Might be important." He stuck this in his belt, knowing he couldn't read in here without any light. Then he removed her collar. She lapped at his face. "Now let's find Jalafar-rula."

Milo felt Naile bump into him and heard Alfreeta hiss. "Let me get out of your way." Milo edged forward, fingers extended in front of him, and touching a damp wall. Something spongy was growing on it, and he shook his hand and wrinkled his nose. "Naile's a lawyer, Jalafar-rula."

"Of that, I am aware," the wizard replied.

"Lawyers are supposed to be good at getting people out of jail. He wasn't any help at the last place, though. Suspect he'll be just as useful here."

"Copyright infringements, remember Milo?" Suddenly Naile stopped and clenched his jaw. *What was the last case he'd been working on? What was the issue? Who was the client?* It was nearly painful to try to remember.

"A good lawyer," Jalafar-rula pronounced.

"Yeah? You really know that I'm an attorney, Jalafar-rula?" Naile waved his arm around in front of him, touching stone, then moving on. "From Brooklyn. You know that?"

"I know all about you. Graduated from a legal academy more than two of your years past. High in your class. More than a few lawyers are . . . gamers . . . as you call them. Quite the imaginations you legal types have. But, then, that's one of the reasons why I chose you."

"Then if you know all about us . . . what's Milo do . . . back in Wis-kaaaahn-sen?"

Milo spun about, smacking into a stone wall.

"Yon Milo is a counter man."

"Counter man?"

"That's enough," Milo warned. Unbidden, some of the memories of his home floated around in his head. He had the sense that the wizard had done something to stir those memories, perhaps making it urgent to get out of here and get back to his apartment.

"Ah, a counter man! A clerk? Milo's a salesman?"

"Salesman," the wizard said. "Yes. That'd be the term you use."

Milo tried to scrape the mossy stuff off his hands and face. "You don't need to say more, Jalafar-rula." He started feeling around the walls again, looking for a door to the cell.

"What's he sell?" Naile pressed.

"What I *used* to sell isn't important," Milo cut in. "What's important is rescuing Jalafar-rula and getting out of here. Finding a way out of this dungeon. Finding Yevele and Ingrge. Saving our world . . . if it really is in jeopardy. Getting home. Besides, my memories aren't as clear as they used to be."

"Mine neither," Naile admitted. "Been fading with each passing week. This morning I could barely recall my address."

"Like we're losing ourselves," Milo added. "I want to get back home."

"Back to Wis-kaaaahn-sen," Naile said. The berserker's fingers brushed a robe, floundered forward and felt the emaciated form of Jalafar-rula. "Got you." His fingers drifted up to touch the old man's face, gently running his thumbs across the wizard's features the way a blind man would examine someone to get a mental picture, then drifting down to feel the beard that stretched to the wizard's waist. "Yeah, I'd say you're the man we saw in the priests' magical picture."

Next, Naile felt for the wizard's hands, finding heavy iron shackles around his wrists, with chains that extended to a wall behind him. Naile crouched and touched the wizard's bare feet, shackles around his ankles, blisters and sores, and more chains. "Trussed you up real good, Jalafar-rula. Didn't want you going anywhere. He's starving you, isn't he? Pobe? You're all bones."

"To keep me weak. But Pobe will not let me die. He cannot afford to."

Naile tested the spot where the chains met the wall. "This could take a while."

"Can't seem to find a cell door," Milo said. "Stone all the way around. Don't feel any mortar between these bricks, either. Yet they're tight. Wonder how it all holds together."

"Magic built this place," Jalafar-rula said. His voice seemed to be a little stronger, perhaps because he was using it, or perhaps because he now had hope. "Magic is the mortar. The very weight of the Keep holds it together, too. I helped build this place. As I built Stonehenge." His voice sounded almost wistful. "So much magic your world had then."

"So you said." Naile continued to work on the chains. "Were there any wizards on Earth? Other than you?"

"I was but a visitor, friend Naile. But there were other people of magic native to your lands. For a time they were called witches. And the people of industry and Pobe's minions bred distrust around them."

"Burned the witches," Naile said.

"Hung them, and their familiars. Stoned them," Jalafar-rula said. "The last one killed in the land of the Scotts was in . . ." He paused, searching his vast memory. "In your year seventeen twenty-seven, I believe. Or very close to that date. Not so long ago for me. I would have tried to save her, but I was away at the time. I believe I was working in my laboratory on—"

"So if you built this Keep," Milo interrupted, "you should know where the cell doors are."

"Are you standing?"

Milo nodded, then realized the wizard couldn't see him. "Yes."

Return to Quag Keep

Then he stretched his arms above his head and started feeling higher along the walls.

"Then you should be looking low, Milo Jagon. Close to the floor is where the door be."

"Wonderful." Milo got down on his hands and knees and started searching, damp moss—he hoped it was moss anyway—seeping through his trousers and getting the skin beneath wet and slimy.

Naile continued to tug on the chains. "So what did Milo sell, Jalafar-rula? Cars? Real estate?"

"No, Milo performed a most valuable service and sold to the masses."

From somewhere in the darkness, Naile heard Milo make a growling sound.

"What to the masses? Sold what?"

"Garments," the wizard continued. "Colorful garments for those of all ages and sizes." Jalafar-rula couldn't see Naile raise an eyebrow. "Symbols on them—"

"T-shirts!" Milo sputtered. "All right, Naile? I sell . . . *I sold* . . . T-shirts. Cheap cotton ones that would shrink a whole size the first time you washed them." His anger nudged his memory, his blood pounding, the words came quick. "T-shirts. And more T-shirts. T-shirts with slogans on them. T-shirts with pictures of the lake. Green Bay Packer T-shirts. Lemon yellow ones with Brett Favre's smiling mug in the middle. Brewer T-shirts that hung on the rack forever because the team sucks and no one wants to be caught dead in them. Pink T-shirts with kittens on them for little girls. T-shirts that say 'my parents visited Wis-kaaaahn-sen, and all they bought me was this lousy T-shirt.' Oh, and my favorite, Frazetta's Death-Dealer printed on ash gray. I have three of them—free 'cause the design was done crooked and they wouldn't put them on display. Oh, and more than T-shirts. It's a little tourist trap I worked . . . work . . . in, sandwiched between a badly aging arcade, where half the games don't work right, and a restaurant that sells chocolate-blueberry coffee and has uncomfortable vinyl chairs. Less than a block from the lake, we pulled . . . pull . . . them in during the summer. Stocked shot glasses and toothpick holders with women in bikinis printed on them, plastic back scratchers, postcards—lots of postcards, chintzy jewelry, charms of water skiers and power boats, mugs with decals that are good for about a year before the dishwasher dissolves them, bean bag frogs. We have ballpoint pens in the shape of fishing poles, soap dishes that look like overturned turtles, flip-flops in case you forgot to pack a pair, sun-tan lotion—but not the kind that'll keep you from getting burned—it'll just make you feel greasy, bobble-headed cats and dogs to stick in your back window. But mostly we sold T-shirts. Cheap T-shirts all the way up to size triple-X." Milo sagged against the wall. "Satisfied, Mr. Copyright Infringement?"

"Sorry, Milo. I was just curious. Didn't mean to strike a nerve. And you don't need to be all sensitive about it."

"Well, I am," Milo admitted. His anger starting to fade, the memories were going with it. What was his phone number? "It was a lousy job. And if I ever get back home, I'm going to look for a better one. Should've looked for a different one last year. Oh, and bumper stickers. We had a shelf full of bumper stickers, some dating back nine or ten years—when bumper stickers were popular."

"Tell you what." Naile smiled. He felt one of the links near the wall open up. "If we get back, I'll get you a job at the firm."

"Doing what?"

Naile shrugged. "Filing, doing some leg-work. Bet it'll pay more than selling T-shirts and toothpick holders."

"You couldn't pay me enough to live in Brooklyn."

"Would you rather stay here?"

The three men were silent for a while, Milo searching for the cell door, Naile working on the wizard's ankle chains, Jalafar-rula resting his voice. Alfreeta made little chirping sounds of encouragement to Naile, her beating wings keeping him cool as he struggled with the links and finally managed to break one.

One foot free. Now the other. Naile started on another link against the wall.

"Found it," Milo said. "All the way at the bottom. Not quite two feet square. Yuck. What is this stuff? Never mind. I don't want to know. There. I feel some wood and . . . yuck. No latch on this side. Jalafar-rula, you'd herd pigs through something like this."

The wizard sighed. "I did not help build the dungeon for comfort. Had I known I would be staying in it, I would have done things a little differently."

"Pobe threaded you through this, huh? Chained you up?" Milo kicked hard at the door, managing to jam his knee in the process. "Strong wood."

"It's enchanted," Jalafar-rula said. "You likely cannot break it. We surely will need magic, or skills beyond our own. And, no, Pobe did not put me in here and chain me up. His minions did. They feed me, too, from time to time."

Milo suppressed a shudder. "And just what kind of minions does he have?"

"Trolls, mostly, a giant or two for effect," Jalafar-rula said. "Lots of smaller things that aren't too troubling. The smaller things herded me in here."

"Yeah, I didn't think a troll could fit through this little door. I don't know if I'll be able to fit through this door, let alone Naile."

"Pobe uses goblins, mostly, among all the smaller beasts. They're not much taller than two feet, and they can crawl through most things."

"And they're smelly." This from Naile. "King Kale dropped another goblin in the mud. And the moon gleamed high and pearly, pearly bright."

"So you've heard of King Kale," Jalafar-rula said.

"In a song."

"He was a friend of mine. King Kale and I shared many a bottle of wine in our younger days."

Naile put all of his strength behind this pull, bracing his legs against the stone. Another link snapped and both of the wizard's feet were free.

"Naile, you think Alfreeta could help with this door?"

"She's got her own kind of magic, and she's handy in a fight. But she's not strong. Sorry." Naile stood and felt for the chains holding

Jalafar-rula's wrists. He started tugging. "Did you have these chains installed, too, Jalafar-rula?"

"Why, yes. They were the strongest iron available at the time."

"Always buy the best for your dungeon," Naile said. His muscles bunched, and he felt the veins standing out in his thick neck. Alfreeta rubbed her face against his cheek, encouraging him. "Wouldn't want to make it easy for one of your prisoners to escape." A loud clank, and another link was snapped.

Milo continued to pound on the door with his feet. "Hope this noise doesn't bring anyone . . . or anything . . . down here."

"I really don't think you can break that open," Jalafar-rula mentioned again. "I tried to make sure the doors were impregnable. It is too bad you did not appear on the outside of my cell. It would have made things far easier."

"So how do we get out of here, Jalafar-rula, if we can't physically break the door down?" Milo kicked at it one more time. "I keep thinking about what I've got smeared all over my clothes and armor. God, but I reek. Naile, I never imagined this in the game."

"What?"

"The smells. Oh, I always thought about what a world like this would look like and sound like, what the food and ale would taste like. Our game master was always pretty vivid in his descriptions of those things, but he never got to the smells. If I ever get home, I'm gonna open his eyes. Dungeons stink. Stink. Stink. And stink some more. The people stink, none of 'em taking baths often enough. Their clothes stink. The —"

"Milo, we get your point. How about I help you kick at that door? I'm strong."

"It won't work, I say." Jalafar-rula rubbed his wrists, still shackled, then reached out to touch the berserker. "Thank you, Naile Fangtooth. It is good to move around again. I'd prayed that you would find me here."

"Just too bad we didn't end up on the outside of this cell."

"Perhaps we should take a look at our surroundings. My magic fails me at the moment, but if I could borrow a little of your friend's energy."

"Alfreeta's?"

The little dragon gave a cooing sound.

"She says all right. She says she'd like to help."

Alfreeta uncurled her tail from Naile's neck and flitted away.

"I think she must be able to see in this darkness."

"Aye, I think you be right," the wizard replied. "She's with me now. On my shoulder. Little girl, I need some of your strength. Just to borrow it, you'll gain it back. There. That's it." Then Jalafar-rula started speaking in a soft sing-song voice, the words similar to those which the Glothorio priest had spoken. But there were subtle differences, more slurring and changes in pitch.

When he was finished, an egg-shaped olive colored flame appeared inches above the wizard's open palm. It cast a ghoulish light in the cell, but it allowed them to see their surroundings—though it tinged everything green.

The moss that covered all the walls quivered, as if it were a living thing. Something dark and viscous dripped from the ceiling to pool on the floor near the small door. There were moldy piles every few feet, a few of these quivering like the moss. The same moss was smeared all over Milo's leggings.

"If I'd had lunch, I'd be losing it right about now," Milo said. "This is worse than the jail in the city." He looked at his arms and chest, smeared with something gray and oily.

"It was not meant to be a pleasant place, I told you." The wizard's face looked haunted, the cheeks sunken and eyes hollow-looking, worse than the Glothorio priests' spell portrayed him. His hair was spotted with pieces of moss, and the corners of his mouth were crusted, as if he drooled as some old, old men do. However, his eyes were bright, looking large, black and pupilless in the olive light. They seemed to measure Naile and Milo, weighing them in his arcane mind and pronouncing them . . . "More than adequate, you turned out to be."

Andre Norton and Jean Rabe

"But not adequate enough to get this door open," Milo returned. "Maybe you can take some of Alfreeta's energy and blow it off its hinges."

"Wait." Naile pulled the parchment from his belt and stepped next to the wizard. He unrolled it and held it near the light. "Smells like dried blood, this scroll."

"Aye, you are correct, that note is written in blood."

"It is a note. I thought it might be something special, like a map. Hey, Milo. It's addressed to me."

"A love letter?" Milo had returned his attention to the door.

" 'Dear Naile Fangtooth: I hope your dragon-creature Freida . . .' He wrote Frieda. Her name's Alfreeta."

"Just read."

"Aye, you should read, Naile, this light might not last much longer."

" '. . . safely finds you. We have made our way to Quag Keep.' They're here, Yevele and Berthold. Somewhere here."

"Read," Milo and the wizard ordered practically in unison.

" 'There are trolls in this place, and at least one giant that Yevele caught a look at. But perhaps worse are the traps. Ingrge lost an arm to one, and he is in dire condition.' " Naile looked to Milo, who returned his concerned expression. " 'We are holed up in a room full of small, strange beasts. This is where we found your Frieda.' Alfreeta. 'We intend to explore this place further, once Ingrge is stable—or dies. The wizard could be our only hope. Him—and you. If this note finds you, come to Quag Keep as fast as you can.' It's signed Berthold of the Green. So they really are somewhere in this Keep. We're all together here."

"Well, you are here with me in any event. They are here elsewhere. So together you are, just not all in the same place. But let's see if we can rectify that. Little Alfreeta, I know you haven't the power to break through that door, and I know you can't get us all out of here. But can you find Berthold again?"

The little dragon chittered and cooed.

"She said 'yes,' " Naile translated.

"Then can you go to Berthold and bring him and Yevele here?"

Alfreeta cooed long and high-pitched, then she flew from the wizard's shoulder and to the small door. She shimmered, her scales looking molten and her wings transparent. Then like a ghost, she passed through the door and disappeared.

"Hope she really can bring the cavalry," Milo said.

"I hope you are right."

The olive flame that flickered above the wizard's hand dimmed and sputtered. A heartbeat later it winked out.

"Good," Milo pronounced. "I'd rather not see this place. It's too depressing."

TWENTY-TWO

Going Down

Ingrge leaned back against the cage, the horned rabbit in his lap. His cloak was wrapped around him, with the remainder of Yevele's cloak behind his head against the wire bars. Berthold held the waterskin to the elf's lips and watched him take a few sips.

"I'm going to leave this with you. There's not much in it, but it's better than nothing. Wait." The thief pulled himself up to Alfreeta's vacant cage and brought out her water bowl. "Here's some more. Looks clean enough." He set the bowl next to the elf.

"We're not leaving him, Berthold."

"Yevele," the elf's eyes were narrow and his expression was stern. "As much as I would like to go with you and see if Berthold's wizard exists, I can't. Leave me here."

"No, Ingrge."

"I'm a liability, Yevele. And you know it. I'm useless at the moment. I'd be worse than useless in a fight."

"Yes, I know it. Of course you're a liability. A bowman who can't fire a bow. You're right-handed, so you can't even use your sword to any advantage. But leaving you here—"

"Is the only thing that you can do. You want to help me? Then be right for yourselves. Find the wizard."

She nodded slowly. "Yes, I know. I don't like the idea, but it is the right thing to do."

"Leaving the elf here?" Berthold asked before he thought.

"Yes, Berthold, leaving Ingrge here." She spoke very slowly and knelt next to the elf, rested his thin blade across his lap, and placed his left hand on the crosspiece. "But I needed it to be his decision. Completely. And I wanted him to convince me. Ingrge, we will be back for you, if the fates allow. You know that there are horrible things in this tower, and who knows what stands in our way. I do not believe the odds favor us."

Berthold shook his head and padded to the door, set his ear at the crack. "Can you paint a more dismal picture of our chance for success?"

"I am a realist, Berthold of the Green."

He snorted. "Realists shouldn't play fantasy role-playing games. They take the fun out of everything." Satisfied there wasn't a troll or a giant outside, Berthold carefully and slowly opened the door. "Join me?"

Yevele touched Ingrge's cheek, and their eyes met for a moment. Then she was fast after Berthold, and—equally carefully and slowly—she closed the door behind them.

After they'd been gone a few moments, Ingrge stared at the bank of cages opposite him, the magical torch lodged in the wires of Alfreeta's empty cage showing all the curious and sad faces watching him. He closed his eyes and tried futilely to shut out the pain. He wondered if Yevele and Berthold found the wizard, and thereby found a way home, would his Earth-self also be missing an arm?

"Forty-two steps to the beach," he whispered. "Sand between my toes. How many steps to the sea?"

Then Ingrge slipped into unconsciousness again.

Berthold and Yevele had made two circuits of the main room, using their hands against the walls, pushing and prodding the stones, hoping there might be a section that would swing open and reveal a way below.

Berthold put his hands out to his sides and made an exaggerated shrug, clearly not knowing what to try next. Yevele frowned at him and made another pass, this time pushing harder on any stone that looked slightly darker than the others.

The thief watched her again, then began to circle in the opposite direction, pausing almost at once as he spied the snake-like threads in the carpet follow him.

"I wonder." He leaned over the carpet, and the writhing threads congregated under him. He brought a hand near the nap, and some of the threads rose and tried to strike at him.

"Interesting."

"We must hurry, Berthold, to find a way below," Yevele said. "Soon another troll . . . or worse . . . will come down the stairs." She stood next to him, watching the threads. "Yes, it is interesting." Then she bent and grabbed the edge of the carpet and flipped it back. The threads hissed at her, but she was so quick they could not bite her. "Very interesting."

A wooden trapdoor was set into the floor, under where the center of the carpet had rested.

"Oh, that's just too easy," he said, "hiding a trapdoor like that. Under the carpet is the first place someone would look."

Yevele made a move for the pull-ring on the door, but she stopped herself and gestured to Berthold. "Look it over. Might be something dangerous about it . . . being so easy to find and all."

"Easy to find? I don't know about that." The thief crept forward and looked closely, tracing his fingertips around the edge of the door and looking for small symbols, like were on the cages. "Safe," he decided. She stepped back from him and looked up the stairs, cocked her head and listened. Satisfied no sentries were coming, she gestured again. "Fine, I'll open it." He did, and fusty air wafted up and made his eyes water. "You know, those trolls'll notice the rug messed up. No way we can pull it back just right."

"Doesn't matter," she said. "They can't fit through here."

"Maybe they don't need to. Maybe there's something just as bad downstairs." He took a deep breath, held it, then started down what looked like a rickety spiral staircase.

She was on her feet and ready to elbow him aside. "I'll go first."

Berthold shook his head. "You're the best swordsman . . . swordswoman . . . I've seen. I watched you in that fight with the skeletons, when Ingrge brought me to the caravan. You're quick and deadly. But you're not sneaky. I dare say you're a bit clumsy." He flinched, waiting for her reaction to the last statement. But she just stood there, and so he continued. "You're not quiet. Not in that armor. So let me see what's down here. If I don't come back in a few minutes, you'll know something got me. And you'll know that you better come back with Milo and Naile before going any further."

Then he was gone, silent like a cat down the spiral stairs, another of the magical torches tucked under his arm. The stairway was strong, and though it *looked* terribly old and weathered and rickety, Berthold suspected the stairs could support a lot of weight. So a troll couldn't fit down here, or a giant. But what else could? What else heavy and threatening? He shuddered at the thought, and kept going. It was a long way down.

He guessed he was thirty, thirty-five feet below ground when he moved off the last step. Looking up, he could see Yevele peering down at him, her face partially obscured by the rungs of the stairs. He motioned, not sure if she could see him, then he looked around.

The chamber seemed identical in size to the main room above, and even with the torch he couldn't quite make out the features of the ceiling. He thought he saw something moving, maybe bats, maybe something bigger. He thought he smelled guano. Berthold had been in some of the caves in Kentucky—bats lived in all of them. Lost River Cave, right in Bowling Green, was his favorite, with the largest cave opening in the eastern United States. He'd taken a boat tour along the underground river a few years ago, sailing right under the city through that cave. And he'd went with a high school group once to Mammoth Cave, Kentucky's gem—the largest known cave in the world, with more than three hundred mapped miles of caverns and tunnels. This was just like a cave, he thought, smelled like one, felt damp like one. He tried to remember his other cave trips, but the experiences were elusive. What else was he forgetting about his real life? he wondered. Was his real self slipping away?

The floor and walls were worked stone, the bricks just like those on the tower's exterior, but they looked much older. He walked away from the stairs and held out the torch. The stones were definitely worn, like running water had worried at them, and they were moist, blotches of a quivering moss stuck to the ones toward the floor. As Berthold followed the wall, he spotted a section of flowstone, similar to what he'd found in Kentucky caves—a type of onyx created by mineral-laced water flowing slowly over rock. Mounds of the moss were along the edges of the wall, and there were smaller patches closer to the stairs. There was another trapdoor, though he could clearly see only the edge of it. Moss and guano were spattered thick on it, and so he guessed the door hadn't been opened in quite some time. Still, he was curious where it led.

He saw small bones, too, probably from rats, and pieces of leather and canvas. In some places the floor was thoroughly clean and shiny, and after a moment he realized this was a path that went from the stairs to a shadowy part of the room.

He held the torch closer to the shadows and saw a tunnel that twisted away into darkness, and he shuddered again at the thought of exploring down there by himself.

Quite the tale I'll have to tell the guys at the stationhouse, he thought. *If I ever get back to the stationhouse. Not that they'd believe me in the first place. Who'd believe any of this? Well, let's see where this goes.* He started into the tunnel, then spun back when he heard a clanking sound—Yevele rapidly coming down the steps, her sword's scabbard thwacking against the rungs.

"Quiet!" he said in a stage whisper. "You'll bring all the trolls down on us."

"Already happening. Company," she said before she reached the bottom. "The giant's coming for another looksee. Couldn't move the rug in time so he's going to know that—"

"Nerragh!" A voice boomed down the spiral stairs.

". . . a couple of trespassers have crawled down into the basement."

"Let's move." Torch in one hand, dagger in the other, Berthold hurried along the tunnel, staying close to the wall. Yevele's chainmail shirt made "chinking" sounds as she ran behind him.

"Nerraghhhhhh!"

No doubt it was a word, Berthold guessed. It was louder this time, shouted in anger and repeated twice more. Perhaps it was a curse word, the giant upset that it had been lax and let uninvited guests inside. Or maybe it was an alarm, it certainly could work as that. Behind them, he heard the flutter of wings, the shout having disturbed whatever had been clinging to the ceiling.

"Bats, I hope it's bats. They're harmless," he said to himself.

A moment later proved him right, as a stream of bats shot down the tunnel and disappeared in the darkness ahead. A few of the bats were disconcertingly large, and Berthold was happy the tunnel was tall and therefore kept them a good distance away.

"Where are we going?"

Berthold followed the tunnel around a corner and skidded to a stop. There was a chamber ahead, practically identical to the one they'd just come from, but there was no matching spiral staircase. From the flutter of wings, he knew the bats were at the ceiling, disturbing other bats previously hanging there. The air smelled hurtfully strong of guano, and he gagged.

"There," he pointed. The light from the torch barely stretched to an alcove. "See, a path leads straight to it."

Yevele grabbed his shoulder and pointed. His intended route consisted of a path with less guano on it than on the rest of the floor, and footprints were visible along it. They were large, troll or giant-sized.

"They can't possibly fit down that spiral staircase," Berthold said. "You said there's no way that —"

A "throoming" sound echoed somewhere behind them.

"Maybe it's a skinny giant," Yevele said, the sarcasm thick in her voice. "Or maybe it just sucks in its stomach and squeezes through the hole." Then she pointed to another path, and another, not used as often as the first, judging by the thickness of the guano. She started down the nearest of those, tugging Berthold with him. "Hurry."

"Nerraghhhhhh!"

The path led to another alcove where Yevele thrust Berthold in, then followed. Here the walls were covered with the quivering moss, as was a moldy wooden door she pushed open and stepped behind. "Hurry."

Berthold considered a retort, as she certainly didn't need to order him around so. But he kept quiet, as the "throoming" grew louder. She closed the door behind them, all but a crack, and he gave the torch to Yevele, praying that she kept it far enough back that light wouldn't spill out. A part of him demanded that he shut the door all the way, put his back to it, and pray with every bit of his will. But the larger part was curious—bad enough curious that he hadn't looked down that second trap door. He just had to see what was making the "throoming" noise.

The creature was carrying one of the smokeless torches, and so Berthold could easily—and unfortunately, he thought—see it. Yevele had called it a troll, but it wasn't what he thought a troll should look like—not close to the miniatures used in the game, or the pictures in the monster books, and nothing like his game master had described. So it might not be a troll at all. But whatever it was, it was hideous.

"Nerraghhhhh!"

It stood easily nine feet tall, with broad shoulders that, judging by the gouges, Berthold suspected had been scraped on the edges of the trapdoor opening when he squeezed through. The arms were long, like an ape's, with overlarge hands ending in gnarled fingers hanging down to its knees. All of its joints were exaggerated or ballooned, and the rest of its arms and legs were almost skeletal, the scaly, drab green-gray skin pulled so tight across the bones it looked rubbery and painful. It wore no clothes, and so Berthold could see that its ribs protruded above a sunken stomach. Clumps of calluses were scattered everywhere, especially on its joints, and were likely the result of the creature rubbing against walls and doorframes as it patrolled the place. The beast's head was its most horrific feature. Long and thin, with a crooked upturned pug nose that was black and wet. The left side of its face looked as if it had melted, the corner of its mouth hanging down below its chin, and a thick rope of drool spilling from it. The left eye was twice the size of the right, yellowed, and set where its cheek should be. The right eye was active, though, a scabby, wrinkled lid blinking as the monstrosity searched the chamber.

Each footstep was heavy, making the "throoming" sound they were used to. Some of the bats stirred against the ceiling high overhead. For a moment, Berthold thought the footsteps were echoing. But they weren't evenly repeated.

"Nerraghhhhhh!"

"There's another one coming," Yevele said. "Best to deal with them one at a time." She flung open the door, sword leading. "Yo, ugly," she called to the troll.

Berthold's heart rose into his throat as the misshapen monster dropped its torch and charged the battlemaid. "No. No. No." He stood in the doorway, aimed his dagger and threw. "What are you doing, Yevele?"

The dagger sunk into the troll's chest, but it didn't slow the beast, only seemed to annoy it. As Berthold tugged two more daggers free and prepared to throw them, Yevele moved in, driving her sword forward like it was a lance and running it all the way through the troll's stomach up to the pommel. Thick, black blood gushed over her hand as she pulled the blade free.

The troll howled, and the "throoming" of the second approaching beast grew louder. Yevele skewered the troll again, leaping back to avoid its long arms, "whooping" when it fell to its knees and then fell forward.

Overhead, the bats started flying, disturbed by the noise of the fight and torch that flickered on the ground.

"I told you I could kill one!" Then she rushed toward the tunnel they'd come through, where the second troll now stood. This one was larger, its face intact. A deeper green, it had a long twig-like nose, but its arms were shorter and muscular. It dropped its torch and roared, then it reached for her. She deftly dropped beneath its flailing arms and shoved her sword up, catching it just under the rib cage. She stood, in the same motion lifting the beast onto its toes, and kicked hard at its left knee. It roared again as she slammed her head into its stomach, tugging her sword free, and danced back.

"Neraggggggghhh!"

Berthold watched her, mouth open, daggers ready to throw. Yevele made his help unnecessary, however, as she swept her sword in a wide arc, slicing deep into its abdomen and killing it. "One at a time, they're manageable." She looked around for something to clean the blood off her sword. Finally she settled on wiping the blade on the fallen beast's hide, then sheathing it, grabbing up the discarded torches and bringing them to Berthold. She shook her sword hand, trying to get some of the blood off it, then she glanced at the ceiling, which was too far away to see. But she saw some of the bats dip low.

"We shouldn't just leave those bodies there, should we?"

"Probably not. I'm worried about Ingrge. What if a troll or a giant starts looking around upstairs, too? Finds Ingrge? Maybe we should go back up." She studied the thief's face, expecting him to say something. "But maybe we should keep going. Find your wizard, and help Ingrge that way. If he's still alive." Yevele let a breath hiss out between her teeth and set the torches down outside the alcove. "It's pretty dark over there. You get the feet."

It took more than a few minutes to drag the big bodies to the far part of the chamber. There were no alcoves there, and the guano and other decaying matter was deep. Berthold saw hundreds of small, broken bones that had been picked shiny-clean. The bats were settling down again.

"Don't think anything comes over here," Yevele said. "Not anymore anyway. Though it looks like plenty of bats congregate just above here. I think the trolls'll be able to rot in peace."

"Rot?" Berthold pulled out his longest dagger and started stabbing the first troll Yevele had killed. It was so dark here, he couldn't tell if the thing had started breathing again.

Andre Norton and Jean Rabe

"What are you doing, thief?"

"Making sure it stays dead. And I thought you'd stopped calling me thief."

"Sorry. Berthold."

He started stabbing the other one. "In the game, they regenerated, remember? That's what makes trolls so tough. And you had to burn them. Otherwise they could regrow arms and legs, grow a whole new troll from just a toenail. You'd turn your back, thinking you'd killed them, and they'd come up right behind you and try to eat your face." He looked back to their alcove and the torches laying on the floor.

"Don't do it, Bert."

"One of those torches burned Ingrge's arm, should do just fine on—"

"They're not healing, Bert. They're dead. Dead, I say. And this isn't the game. This is real. Things don't work like they do in the game. These things aren't going to get back up."

"Yeah, well, these things might not be trolls anyway."

"They're trolls. I don't know how I know that. . . ."

"Yeah, but you just know. Fine."

Berthold wanted to leave the chamber anyway, the stench of the guano and the trolls so strong he tasted bile in his mouth. His stomach was roiling, and he was glad he hadn't eaten in some time. His head was aching, too, from the smells and lack of food, pounding over his right eye like a migraine in the making.

In the alcove once more, he laid one of the torches on the ground, kept one for himself, and handed one to Yevele. He kicked at the discarded torch, burning his foot and cursing to discover he was unable to put the flame out.

"We'll leave it," she said. Then she gestured him forward and let him get a few yards ahead before "chinking" along behind him. "If a monster finds it, well . . . I'm not afraid of a good fight."

"That makes one of us," Berthold whispered.

TWENTY-THREE

Shadows and Other Dark, Moving Things

The tunnel continued to slope down until it turned at a sharp angle, doubling back on itself twice before going deeper. Here and there were interruptions, insets in the walls, like something that might be found in an old church or mausoleum. Some of the niches were outlined in fanciful stones and contained clay bowls filled with ashes and bone chips, engraved brass labels identifying whose remains were inside, while other niches sheltered elaborately painted ceramic jars that looked quite valuable.

Berthold stopped at one of these to hold the torch close, his curiosity finally getting the best of him. Horses and centaurs raced around the outside of a jar as big as a pickle barrel . . . literally raced . . . the images in constant motion. When he held his ear to the jar, he could hear men shouting in a tongue he didn't understand—a dozen or more different voices—and horses whinnying and stomping, the wind blowing. He could smell the dirt being churned up by their hooves. Yevele was just tall enough, standing on her tiptoes, to see inside.

"Well?"

"Well what?"

"What's in there?"

"Eyeballs," she said, continuing to look. "Different sizes, different colors. All of them so fresh and shiny, like they've just been plucked. A few have the muscles still attached. And a large bloodshot one is rolling around and looking at me." She seemed oddly unaffected by the contents.

"Lovely."

"Want a boost so you can see?"

He shook his head. "Let's not peek in any more of those things."

However, they did just that at the very next one. It was a low, wide jar, and whatever decorations that had been painted on it were long worn away. The niche it sat in had flowstone along one side, and Berthold was quick to explain to Yevele how it formed. She seemed uninterested in that, but the contents of the jar were another matter.

"We shouldn't," she interrupted him. But she stood directly in front of it and kept staring, making it difficult for him to squeeze in for a close look. The light from her torch made the jewels inside sparkle. "Emeralds. One as big as a date."

"And rubies as big as grapes," Berthold said. "You're right, we shouldn't." But he didn't move away either, instead managing to wedge himself in until he was so close the colors reflected against his face. "Just why shouldn't we?"

"Because we're on an urgent mission, to find this wizard of yours and to get Ingrge out of here. To see what we can do to get home. To get back to Milo and Naile." She put her hand in the jar and stirred the gems. "Pearls, too. Sapphires, some beautiful dark purple stone. Oh, that's just gorgeous. In a dozen years I'd not earn enough at the museum to buy that one." She was looking at a plum-sized rosy-colored stone cut in the shape of a heart.

Berthold leaned all the way over the jar. "We might not be able to get home, Yevele. You realize that, don't you?"

"I'm the realist, remember?"

"And so these gems could come in handy."

"Wonder why they'd leave all these gems in a jar, open like this, where anyone could get to them? You'd think they'd be locked away and guarded."

Berthold shook his head. "Not just anyone can get to them. First you have to sneak by the gargoyles outside, find the trapdoor under the carpet, get past the trolls and the giant, and then—"

"Enough." She thrust her fingers in deeper and pulled out a handful. "Just in case we don't get out of this crazy world. This could buy me better armor, maybe an enchanted sword, a magnificent war horse." Yevele put the gems in a small pouch at her side, and seeing there was room for more, started picking through what she thought were the better ones, making sure she took the heart-shaped rose stone.

"I'm not sure quite how I know this," Berthold pointed. "But those dark purple ones are worth the most." He picked out the best ones and thrust them in a pocket, careful to leave some for Yevele. He had four pockets between his tunic and leggings, and he filled all of them to capacity. Then he searched through the bottom of the jar and found pearl necklaces and rings.

They hastened now to divide the pieces of jewelry, wearing as much as they could. In the end, she had several necklaces draped around her neck and a ring on each grimy finger. He'd taken a few necklaces also and three rings that fit him. There were still gems in the jar, and Yevele clearly didn't want to leave them there. She tugged the waterskin off her belt, upended it and drank it all.

"Was thirsty anyway," she said. Then she started squeezing the smallest gems through the opening in the skin. She looked to Berthold's waist, but he'd given his waterskin to Ingrge.

"Just like in the game," he said. "Looting the castle."

"But this isn't a game," she stared at him as if he had suddenly taken on the guise of a man she'd never seen before. She finally blinked and shook off the image. "Now, let's find this wizard, shall we?"

They traveled in silence for more than an hour, occasionally pausing, looking into jars in niches, studying a piece of statuary, or poking at a carving of a creature they'd not seen before. They passed through several empty chambers, empty save for the bats that clung to the ceilings. And in these places they took their time as they carefully prodded stone walls, wondering if there were swiveling walls or hidden passages, and wondering if there was an end to this place.

"So what do you do in Canberra? At the museum?" Berthold was tired of the quiet.

"I'm a curator." She swallowed hard. There wasn't much she remembered about her treasured museum, and now she forced herself to picture some of the displays, the intricately painted soldiers representing a moment captured in time from some important battle. Holding onto the image was giving her a headache.

"Yeah, I got that. But what's that mean? Curator?"

"I oversee particular exhibits. Anzac and the battle of Gallipoli are my specialties. I studied it all in college, took a summer tour of World War I battlefields, corresponded with some scholars. The museum is known for its miniature exhibits." She frowned, trying hard to picture her college, the trip to Germany and France on the tour. Couldn't picture it. "Incredible miniatures," she said, shaking her head.

"Like the miniatures in the game?"

"I suppose. They're a little bigger, some of the soldiers as tall as my hand. They're painted better than most gamers paint their figures. We paid professional artists to do it. And the scenery is incredibly detailed. Most tourists go to Sydney or Brisbane, but our museum gets them to take a side-trip to Canberra. Folks from all over the world take tours." She clenched her fist, feeling her fingers grow numb. *Remember!* she scolded herself. *Remember as if your life depended on it!* "Most of the displays are behind big glass windows, the museum board doesn't want to risk anyone stealing anything. They're amazing, Berthold. If we get out of this, you'll have to come see them. Miniature pieces of war."

"You like war, don't you? Battles and fighting?" He sucked in his lower lip, instantly regretting he'd asked such a thing. He hadn't meant the question quite as it had come out.

She shook her head. "No. I think it's a hellish thing, actually. But I believe it should be studied, maybe so we don't repeat the same mistakes." *Remember. Remember. Remember.* "And then there's all the arguments over which country turned the tide in a particular war, which commander was the smartest. Political things to fill up history books. They're still arguing over whether an Aussie or a Canadian killed the Red Baron."

"Really?" Berthold had started the conversation, so he pretended to be interested.

"And there should be no argument there at all. An Aussie gunner did shoot him down."

"Oh." He scratched his head, scowling to feel something sticky there. Guano. He tried to pick it out. "So it's your interest in war that got you into role-playing games?"

She let out a soft laugh, musical and pleasing. She was smiling, and Berthold thought for a moment that she actually looked very pretty when she smiled. She clenched her fist tighter, felt her throat go dry. Her head was pounding harder as she searched her memory. "No. Reading did that, drew me to the game. Jack Vance, Tolkien. And my Uncle Wes. He played the game a lot, and finally talked me into giving it a whirl. Great fun. I got hooked and started playing in three different games a month. Went to the Cons at the Uni once in a while." She paused and brushed her hair off her shoulders, let out a deep breath and relaxed her hand. "I bet they miss me. I play the only cleric in two of the campaigns. I was their healing battery."

"Then how'd you end up like you are here? A woman-warrior?"

Another smile, this one reaching her eyes. She breathed deep, proud that she was recalling more pieces of home. Her head continued to throb. "In the third campaign, I'm the main fighter. So when the special miniatures came in the mail that day, Wes handed me the battlemaid. The figure was amazing, as well sculpted, if not better, than the World War I soldiers in the museum." She shook her head. "Very amazing. It brought me here."

Berthold held a finger to his lips and peered down the tunnel. It opened into another chamber, but the torchlight didn't reach far enough for him too see all of it. "Thought I heard something down that way."

They were quiet for a few minutes, hearing each other's breathing, hearing the drip of water from a spot on the tunnel ceiling almost directly above, hearing the whisper of air moving around them.

"Nothing," Berthold pronounced, leaning against the tunnel wall. "So . . . you like it here, don't you? I don't mean anything by it, just curious. Lord, but I was never so curious back in Kentucky."

She forced herself to relax and worked a kink out of her neck. Her headache had started to recede. "I could live here," she admitted after a moment. "I miss cold water out of the tap, hot bubble baths, watching soccer matches on Saturday afternoons. I miss restaurants. *Really* good restaurants, raspberry tea, and bowling. And I miss some of my friends, and Uncle Wes. He's not really my uncle, everyone just calls him that. Most, I think, I miss soft beds and softer pillows. But, yes, I could live here."

He tipped his chin, inviting her to continue.

She let the memories of Canberra slip away, the pounding in her head becoming muted. "I feel really alive here. I know it's dangerous, trolls and dragons and all sorts of beasts. I know the food isn't the best. I'm so hungry right now I could choke down a pig. But this is all so exciting, Berthold. I'm strong, stronger than I ever could be back home. I killed skeletons, trolls. And I'm not afraid. Maybe, just maybe, I could have taken on one of those little dragons." She let more of the memories slip, felt the pressure in her temples abate.

"So you'd choose to stay here. If we can find a way home, you'd stay here, wouldn't you?"

She shook her head. Her eyes were wide and intense, but the turn of her mouth made her expression rueful. "I don't belong here. I should be working on the exhibits in the museum in Canberra. But, then, we might never find our way home, and it might never be an issue." She seemed to brighten just a bit at that thought. "And you?"

Berthold made a sputtering sound. "I don't belong here, either. And I'd kill to find a Mickey D's right now or a White Castle. Best of it, I've got a shiny black Corvette waiting for me in Bowling Green." He jiggled a tunic pocket. "And I'm going to pay cash. Buy me a house with a garage, too. I'll need someplace nice to keep my car. Some caving gear, so next time I go I won't have to rent the stuff. Trouble is, it's getting hard for me to remember what my place looked like, what options I picked out on the car." He sighed and shook his head. "What're you gonna do with your loot if we get home? Go on some nice vacation and—"

This time Yevele put her finger to her lips and nodded toward the chamber ahead. Berthold moved away from the wall and crept down the tunnel, holding the torch well in front of him. "Definitely heard something that time. Funny noise, like a kid squeezing a squeaky toy. Lots of squeaky toys."

The chamber ahead was the size of a basketball court, impossible to tell from here if it was made of the same stones as the rest of the complex. Berthold could see that on the walls where his light reached, there was a carpet of thick, black moss. It quivered more than the greenish moss elsewhere. The floor was covered with the same, and held no trace of guano.

"Ugh, but I don't want to walk on that stuff."

Yevele nudged him. "No choice. Not if we want to keep looking for your wizard."

"Yeah, I know." He stepped into the chamber and felt something squish beneath his foot. He nearly lost his balance. "Yevele . . ."

"What?" She nudged him again.

The squeaking grew instantly louder, like an obscenely off-key chorus. Sparks of yellow appeared in the black writhing mass. Eyes.

"Yevele, this stuff isn't moss."

Then the squirming black carpet flowed toward them.

TWENTY-FOUR

Rats and Other Vermin

"Rats!" Berthold shouted, though he knew the word and the warning unnecessary. "Lots of rats!"

There were hundreds, perhaps a thousand, a moving, breathing, hissing black mass that poured down the walls and streamed across the floor like a wave crashing against them. More came from behind them, racing down the tunnel and clawing their way up Yevele's legs.

Berthold was being swarmed, too. Rats nipped and scratched at him, climbing his legs and chest, chittering around his neck. He dropped his torch when one bit at the back of his hand, and when it hit the floor, the magical flame burned the rats around it. He started stomping on them, the sickening crunch of their bodies beneath his feet making him nauseous. He stabbed at the ones on his leg, his other hand plucking them off his tunic and squeezing them, throwing the dead and dying ones onto the torch.

The smell of the burning rats, and the rats themselves, was too much. Berthold couldn't breathe. He was gagging, his chest tight. Growing light-headed, he started swaying. The rats climbed up on his shoulders, started nipping on his face. One was on top of his head, scratching at him.

"Gonna die," he managed. "No one will know."

"No! I won't die here!" Yevele redoubled her efforts. She ignored the rats clinging to her and concentrated on the approaching wave, using the torch to burn the ones coming close. At the same time, she used her sword to skewer the ones around her feet. Her motions were frantic, but effective, and within moments dozens lay dead around her. She started using the edge of her sword to scrape the rats off her, then she rammed her back against the wall, crushing the ones that had been hanging there.

Out of the corner of his eye, Berthold saw her, fighting magnificently against the black mass. She shamed him and inspired him, and he held the little breath he sucked in, scraping at the rats on him, copying her and slamming himself against the cavern wall again and again until the rats dropped off and he could barely stand.

"Won't die here," he admonished himself. He started throwing his daggers, aiming at the largest rats that he could see. Most of the rats were the size he'd expect to find in a high school biology class, but there were some that he was certain could eat his neighbor's prized Chihuahua. He managed to hit two of the big ones with his first two throws, then he clamped his teeth together when their death shrieks cut through the wall of chittering sound.

"Not natural," he said, though he suspected Yevele couldn't hear him over the rats. "Something . . . someone . . . set them on us." Not any of the trolls upstairs. The two trolls Yevele had killed didn't seem smart enough to direct anything. He wanted to puzzle it out, but he couldn't allow himself to be distracted, not now that he was gaining a measure of an upper hand. His hands and face stung from where he'd been bit, and his eyes were watering fiercely from the strong smells. He blinked to clear them and stomped faster, threw more daggers, then crouched and started stabbing at the smaller ones on the floor.

"Winning," he announced, finding his strength returning through sheer force of will. "At least I think we're winning."

"No more coming down the tunnel," Yevele announced. "But

there's so many left." Then she let out a piercing war cry and leapt away from the wall, driving her heels into the rats scurrying across the floor, burning them with her torch, waving the blade above her head until it whistled.

Berthold continued to smash the ones nearest him, and to hurl daggers at large ones deep in the pack. At the same time, he watched her. She was vicious and powerful, raging and self-assured, driven and unstoppable, graceful and beautiful. Yevele was the sum of all of those things and more, and she belonged in this world, Berthold knew. She was alive here, she'd said it herself. More alive than she could possibly be in the halls of a military museum. This warrior the curator had become suited her. They'd make it through this chamber, and the next and the next, he was certain. Because of her. They'd find the wizard—if he was here to be found—because this persona that had been thrust upon her when she touched that miniature didn't know how to quit.

And if they found a way to get home, Berthold thought he might have to convince her not to take it.

"Winning!" he yelled again, this time with much more voice and enthusiasm. Indeed, they clearly were. Rats still streamed toward them from the darkest part of the chamber, but they were coming in fewer numbers now. There were still some overly large ones, of the size one might find in a New York City alley, but they were staying back. And then suddenly they were changing.

"Omigod," Berthold breathed.

A dozen of the largest rats reared back on their haunches, their eyes glowing dully yellow and their fangs bared. Snapping and popping sounds were heard amid the chittering, these coming as the rats grew larger, their limbs elongating and turning into human arms and legs. Berthold stared slack-jawed at the closest one. Three feet tall and growing still, its snout was receding into an all-too-human looking face, and its ears were shrinking against its head, all of its fur melting away to be replaced by the pale flesh and raggedy clothes of a beggar.

Half of the large rats had completely transformed into men, and somehow their claws had turned into curvy-bladed daggers. They were an ugly lot, with warts and scars, matted hair and teeth that remained rodent-like. Their lips constantly worked, like their rat-brothers', and their shoulders were hunched and their backs curved. The others had not completely shifted their forms, adopting bodies that were half-man, half-rat. Some kept their rat paws and sported long wicked-looking claws. Others had arms and daggers, but their rear legs remained muscular and hairy, and their snouts long and sprouting whiskers. Their hair and fur were a mix of colors now, mostly black. But some were dark brown, and the older ones among them displayed a smattering of gray.

"Were-rats!" Again Berthold realized he again had announced something unnecessary.

"Yes, they are," Yevele returned. She'd managed to rout a swarm of normal rats and was charging toward the closest aberration. "Let's pray they're like the trolls!"

What? Berthold mouthed.

"Easier to kill than the ones in the game."

He continued to stamp the rats nearest him. At the same time, he hurled a dagger at one of the half-rat, half-man things. Berthold gasped when the creature caught the dagger by the pommel and hurled it back. The thief ducked just in time, and the dagger hit the stone behind him.

"They bleed!" Yevele hollered.

Berthold understood. In the game you had to have special weapons to battle were-kind, blades that had been dipped in silver under the light of a full moon, or ones crafted by wizards and enspelled to slay abominations. So you didn't have to burn trolls here, and you didn't need anything special to slay a were-beast. Yevele dropped the one in front of her and went to the next, sword singing through the air and slicing the rat-head off one of the creatures.

Berthold scared away the small rats around his feet by practically dancing over the top of them. Closing the distance to a man who was as small as himself, Berthold threw a dagger, then pulled the last one from a sheath on his leg, crouched and waited. The man snarled and chittered, and his lips curled up showing brown and yellow jagged teeth. Spittle flew from his mouth as he lunged.

Feinting to his right, Berthold slashed with the dagger as the were-rat hurtled past. He cut the creature deep on the side, a rib bone gleaming dully in the torchlight. The were-rat didn't cry out, but Berthold could tell the thing was hurting. It held its arm against its side as it came around again, this time it was swiping at him with a dagger. It was like a dance, the thief reckoned, one darting in, the other spinning away. But the thief was the better dance partner, more nimble and not bleeding from a deep wound. He would have liked to fatigue the creature, continuing the dance until he easily had the upper hand. But there were too many were-rats for that luxury.

Yevele slew another one as Berthold lashed out with a round-house kick that nailed the were-rat in the stomach. The impact sent the creature back a few feet, Berthold following and kicking again, this time tripping the were-rat and dropping him. Without pause, the thief jabbed his dagger in the were-rat's stomach, then jabbed him in the neck. It threw back its head and shrieked, its arms flailing use-lessly and dropping its own dagger, which Berthold was quick to claim.

He glanced back at the battlemaid and saw her shear the arm off the next one she faced. But it didn't deter the wounded were-rat. Seemingly oblivious to the pain and the blood that pumped from its shoulder, it lunged at her, dagger leading in its remaining hand. She stepped aside and then came up behind it. With one swing aimed hard at its waist, she cut the creature in two, then paused to assess the chamber.

She'd killed four of them and was spattered with their blood. Eight remained, two of them squaring off against Berthold now, four of them advancing on her, one of those running. A pair held back and watched. She tightened the grip on her sword and decided to let them come to her; no use charging toward them and putting more distance between her and the thief.

"Stick together," she said. "Berthold, work toward me!"

The two watching were preoccupied now, one directing what was left of the carpet of rats to stop their flight and again swarm toward her. The other's mouth was moving, but with the squeaking of the rats and the pounding of her heart, she couldn't hear what he was saying. He turned his head, looking behind him and talking to someone behind him. Then she swore she could hear music, like someone was singing slightly off-key.

"Stick together? Stick together, woman? Die together!" It was the first time one of the were-rats spoke. He was the tallest of the lot, at roughly five and a half feet, with a shaved head and tiny eyes and teeth. "Die woman!"

"Not by you. And not today." Yevele lurched forward, the tip of her sword aimed at his heart. But he anticipated her move and ducked. Had Yevele followed through, she would have missed him. But she slipped in a pool of blood and fell, her sword slicing down as she went and cutting him from throat to waist. He crumpled on top of her, and she pushed him off, getting to her knees just as his three fellows reached her.

One was young, in his teens, she guessed, his human face so smooth, with no hint of wrinkles around his hard eyes. She brought her blade up to parry his dagger, then she jammed the torch against his knee. The instant he recoiled, she slashed the abdomen of the were-rat to her left and used the torch like a club on the leg of the one to her right. She swung it so hard against him that the bone and the torch both broke. Its fire continued to burn though, igniting the fur of the rats swarming around her.

"Yevele?"

"I'm all right," she returned, risking a glance around the were-rat with the broken leg. "You?"

"Great. Just great." Berthold was working toward her, tiny step by tiny step. Small and agile, he devoted most of his energy to crouching, turning, and jumping to avoid his opponents' daggers and claws. He looked a little comical, but his moves were effective. "But I think I'd rather fight one of those trolls. Bigger, but they don't smell near so bad."

"I agree, Berthold. The trolls —" She rammed her sword up to the hilt in the chest of the young were-rat, almost sorry to kill someone of so few years. "Singing. I do hear singing."

She stomped on the small rats squirming around her feet, and with her free hand plucked one that had managed to climb up to her waist.

> Down in the garden where the red roses grow
> Oh my, I long to go
> Pluck me like a flower, cuddle me an hour
> Lovie let me learn that Red Rose Rag.

"Berthold, do you hear that?" Yevele was trying to listen, while at the same time fight the two were-rats that were stabbing at her. So far her chainmail shirt had protected her, but they'd sliced up her leggings and cut her in several places. Now they were trying to come at her from opposite sides. "None of that," she hissed, raising her sword and spinning behind her, slicing the head off one. "Only one left."

Plus the two that had hung back in the shadows. It looked like the one had given up directing the rats, which she and Berthold were continuing to stomp on. The fellow in front of her was losing his confidence and was working to keep away from her swinging sword. He started chittering and shrinking.

"A rat! Run like the rat you are!" she hollered. Indeed he was doing just that, turning into a plump, big city alley-sized rat and racing toward the shadows. "Run, you slimy. . . ."

"Yevele! Listen, there is music. You're right. Someone is singing. And it's nothing medieval. Almost familiar."

> Red leaves are falling in a rosy romance
> Bees hum, come, now's your chance;
> Don't go huntin' possums, mingle with the blossoms
> In that flowery, bowery dance.

TWENTY-FIVE

Fisk's Dance

"Where's the music coming from?" Yevele peered into the shadows, where the two cagey were-rats still stood. It seemed as if someone else was standing behind them, but the shadows were thick, and so she couldn't be certain. The one who'd run from her, was the third shape his? Had he turned back into a man? No, she decided a heartbeat later. The form was wrong. A little too tall, shoulders straight, and a little too thin. Maybe it was nothing, just her imagination.

She decided not to worry about it, and to instead tackle the two Bertrum hadn't yet managed to slay. But she hadn't taken more than a couple of steps toward the thief when that third figure came forward, just so the edge of the torchlight could touch him.

"Fisk?" For an instant she was almost happy to see him, though she was puzzled why he would be here. Then she saw that smile. It was evil, matching the dark glimmer in his eyes. A shiver raced down her spine as he continued to sing.

Andre Norton and Jean Rabe

Pick a pinky petal for your papa's pride.
Beg a burning blossom for your budding bride.
Woo me with that wonderful wiggle wag

Certainly not a medieval song, she thought, but she couldn't place it. And certainly he was not the man she thought he was, not the helpful fellow who'd told her where to find Naile and Milo in the city jail and who helped them find work with Ludlow Jade and the caravan. An evil man.

"What are you doing here, Fisk?" A look to Berthold told her the thief was holding his own and had managed to wound one of his foes.

Fisk's pale face and hands looked disembodied, standing out so starkly against the shadows and his black clothes. There weren't any tattoos on his head, and so she suspected he was not a Glothorio priest at all. What was he? A good man wouldn't masquerade as a priest. How many people had he duped?

"What have you done to us, Fisk?"

He reached into the folds of his robe and drew a wavy-bladed dagger in his left hand and a short sword in his right. Both dripped a gray-green ooze that Yevele instinctively knew was poison.

"What are you doing here?" she repeated.

"Ah, sweet Yevele, you are always a woman to me."

She frowned, not understanding what he meant now.

"I suspect you could do worse than throw shadows at me, but perhaps you could wound me even with your eyes. The great poet William Joel penned words similar to that. They apply to you, don't you think?"

"Fisk! What's going on?"

"I'm here to kill you, sweet Yevele. You and Berthold, the elf when I find him. Is he with you, the elf? Or did you lose him somewhere in the woods?" He searched her eyes, looking for a hint. "So you won't let your expression betray you, sweet Yevele. A fine companion you are, not giving up your friends." He crouched, ready for her approach, but she stopped a few yards short of him, obviously wanting to lure him away from the two were-rats.

"I killed your friend Wymarc, sweet Yevele." His voice was flat and showed no emotion. "Pity to silence such a singularly beautiful voice. But he taught me a few songs before I let him bleed out in the alley. Would you like to hear my rendition of the boy and the pipes? And I will kill Milo and . . . oh, I've forgotten the name of the hulking mountain. They still have their bracelets, and they are somewhere below."

"Why?" she demanded hoarsely. "We've done nothing to you, Fisk. I thought you were helping us!"

"I am being helpful." He smiled, as one offering encouragement. "I helped you out of the city, so it would be easier to fulfil my contract."

"The undead! They were your doing?"

He bowed theatrically. "And the bandits. But you and Berthold and the elf had already left the caravan, so you knew nothing of my carefully planned bandit raid. It was suitably bloody, but unfulfilling. You left Milo and the hulking man at my mercy. And you managed to break your bracelets." He made a tsk-tsking sound and waved the short sword scoldingly. "And without the bracelets, it was much more difficult to find you."

"So how did you find us?" Berthold shouted to Fisk. The thief finally dropped the wounded were-rat, and now faced only one.

Fisk glanced to the thief. "By accident, curious Berthold. I came here to speak with my Master, who waits below. And by chance I heard you and Yevele traipsing through this maze, discussing some far-off realm. Canberra? I think that's what you called the place. Is that on the other side of the Windhold Mountains? Or is it just beyond the Northern Wastes?"

Yevele spit at him as he moved closer and closer. Fisk was no longer paying any attention to the thief. "I don't know what your game is, Fisk. But I'll not play!"

Something dark flashed in Fisk's eyes and the flesh of his face rippled. Yevele stared as hair as fair and fine as a baby's started sprouting on his cheeks and chin, flowing like water up to cover his bald head and down his neck. She rushed forward, drew her sword back over her shoulder, and brought it down hard at an angle, expecting to cleave through Fisk's neck. Instead, the blade whistled through the dank air. He'd spun around and came at her from her left side, wavy-bladed dagger slicing through several links of her chainmail shirt. He made a tsk-tsking sound again, as if he was scolding himself for not drawing blood, then he leapt back just in time. Yevele had turned, bringing her sword around and slicing through the air where Fisk had stood.

"Quite the warrior you are, sweet Yevele. You almost scare me." He continued to change, his nose elongating into a rat snout, wiry whiskers appearing. His eyes became shiny like oil, no white showing. The baby-fine hair was turning just as black, thickening until no trace of skin could be seen. His nose quivered.

Yevele cursed herself for being caught up in his transformation. "Vile little man!" She dug the nails of her free hand into her palm, the pain helping her concentrate. She stepped in and slashed at Fisk, cutting through his robes and tangling the blade in the fabric for a moment before yanking it free.

Then the robes fell from him, as his body seemed to shrink. He was a foot shorter than Fisk, the man, had been, and yet he retained a vaguely man-like form, human arms and legs that were covered with fur, human hands with long curving nails. A hairless pink tail undulated behind him.

She'd witnessed Naile transform into a boar, and wondered if he was capable of adopting a form half-man, half-beast like Fisk. Naile's metamorphosis had always been a little disconcerting, but it didn't bother her as much as Fisk's. Naile had only become an animal when things were dire and he let a blood-rage course through him. There was nothing evil in that, and he always managed to best some foe they were facing in the process. She considered everything about Fisk vile.

"Why do you want to kill us?"

Fisk sneered, needle-like rat-teeth gleaming white in the torchlight. "For my Master. To fulfil my promise to him." His voice sounded small and hollow now, like the winter wind finding its way through a rotted log. "Pobe wishes you dead by my hand. I do not care to disappoint him."

"Why?" she persisted. "Why?"

She sidestepped the swipe of his short sword and brought her blade up to parry his dagger. He'd left an opening, but she didn't take it, not wanting to kill him just yet. She needed information. "Who is Pobe, and what have we done to incur his wrath?"

Fisk grinned wide, and his black tongue darted out to lick his lips. "Pobe is the darkness, sweet Yevele. He is magic. He is the mortar of this Keep." He rose up on the ball of his right foot and twirled, dagger out and clinking against the chainmail over her abdomen. "And he wants you dead because—" He cackled and let her question go unanswered as he twirled again and skittered back, retreating from the torchlight and disappearing in the shadows.

"Why?" she screamed. "What have we done to him?"

The two were-rats who'd been standing back rushed toward her now. She took one more look at Berthold, who appeared to have the upper hand on his winded opponent, then she charged to meet them, mindless of the shadows that could conceal a swarm of rats. She pulled her sword back and sucked in a deep breath.

"Why, Fisssssssssk?" Her scream was long and her swing was fueled by anger, and the lead were-rat paid dearly for it. The sword sliced deep into his side, then she struck him again, blinking furiously when his blood spattered her face. He howled as he fell forward, and she drove the heel of her boot down on the back of his neck, snapping it. "Fisk! Talk to me! Now!"

The second were-rat hesitated, which proved his undoing. She brought her leg up, kicking him in the stomach and setting him off-balance. She kicked him again, and he dropped his dagger.

"You can't win," he said, trembling but making no effort to run. "Fisk will kill you and feast on your . . ." She grabbed the pommel of her sword in both hands and angled the blade down, raising it above her head and driving it into his chest.

"It is I who will win," she said. "Can you hear me, Fisk Lockwood? I will find you and—"

"The Master wants you dead simply because you live." Fisk crept out of the shadows, looking a little more like a man, with his bald head gleaming in the torchlight, but with rat fur covering the rest of him. "You must die because your presence poses a threat to his plans. Because though you don't know how strong and important you are, you could well find out. He can't afford to let that happen." His face became that of a rat's again in the passing of a few heartbeats. "Come dance with me again, sweet Yevele. You are always a woman to me." His voice was hollow once more and sent another shiver down her back.

"All right, Fisk. I'll dance." Yevele moved toward the dropped torch and rocked forward on the balls of her feet. Behind her, she heard the clang of weapons parrying, the thief continuing to fight the remaining were-rat.

Fisk glided toward her, the hair on his arms receding and then growing back, his face shifting from rat to man, then back again, and all the while his tail wagging slowly. The constant transformation made her dizzy, as he continued to move, rising up on one foot and performing something like an arabesque. In that instant she thought he looked like the king rat from the Nutcracker ballet.

"A perverse King Rat," she spat.

"What did you call me, sweet, sweet Yevele?" His eyes were switching now, from the larger round man-eyes to the solid, black tiny eyes of a rat.

"I call you dead, Fisk. We've just begun and already I tire of this dance."

"Already?" He licked his lips and nodded. "Very well, then. But to your death, not mine." He threw his dagger, and as she turned to avoid it, he slipped close and looked up at her. His breath was fetid and hot on her face, and she grimaced. "Your death." He made a move to drive his short sword in, but the blade was pulled away.

"Didn't you hear the lady?" Berthold was suddenly there. He pulled Fisk's arm down, in the same motion bringing up his leg and cracking it against Fisk's hand. The were-rat's short sword clattered against the stone floor. "She doesn't want you as a dance partner. You're a little too short for her."

Yevele locked eyes with Fisk then and pressed her sword to his stomach. "I normally prefer a fair fight," she said, as she shoved the sword in. "But I've not the time for such chivalry now. Nor, in this instance, the desire."

Fisk fell as she pulled the sword out, the rat fur melting like butter and leaving behind a naked, pale-skinned man. She looked around for his discarded robes and cleaned the blood from her face and weapon on them, tried futilely to wipe the blood off her chainmail.

"Are you all right, Berthold?"

The thief was retrieving some of his scattered daggers.

"Berthold?"

"No, I'm not all right. Scratched all over." His face, neck, and the backs of his hands were crisscrossed with tiny scratches from the rats that had swarmed over him. "Aching. I'm thirsty and very hungry and tired. No, I'm not close to right. But I'm alive, and they're not. So we won." He took a few deep breaths, leaned over and put his hands on his knees. "No more fights, Yevele. I feel like I've maybe got a dozen hit points left."

She offered him a crooked smile. "It's not a game, remember?"

He rested a moment more, clearly favoring his side as he straightened his tunic. "Can't find four of them. My best daggers." He pointed to empty dagger sheaths. "Lost 'em in the bellies of those New York City-sized rats." He padded toward Fisk and kicked the body. Then he picked up the wavy-bladed dagger and sniffed the oozy stuff that dripped from it. "Nasty stuff." He dropped the dagger and pointed toward the darkest part of the cavern. Then he scooped up the torch on the floor. "Let's get out of here, eh?"

Yevele took a last glance around the chamber and walked by Berthold, snatching the torch from him as she passed. He started to protest, but she cut him off with a glare.

"As you said, you're not all right. And I've never felt better. Follow me." The torchlight held the shadows back, revealing a wide doorway and another sloping hallway with more niches and jars.

Berthold tugged up his tunic and inspected an ugly mark on his side. One of the were-rats had bitten him there, the indentations from the teeth still seeping blood, all of it looking swollen and infected.

Andre Norton and Jean Rabe

"It's not a game," he whispered. "Don't let it be like the game, please God." When a character got bit by a were-creature in the game, there was a chance the lycanthropy was passed along, like a cold or flu bug. He prodded the wound and winced. His skin was feverish there. There was no guarantee the disease would be transmitted that way, just a chance, he reminded himself. He might not turn into one of those were-rats. "This isn't a game." The trolls were different here, they didn't come back from the dead like in the game, didn't have to be burned. "I'm all right," he told himself. "I've never felt better."

The chamber was growing dark, as Yevele had taken the torch farther away, and the broken torch somewhere behind him finally went out. He hurried to catch up to the battlemaid.

"I've never felt better either," he lied again.

They walked side by side, not stopping this time to look inside any vases or jars, glancing occasionally at sections of the wall where flowstone obscured the bricks, speeding up after the tunnel twisted back on itself and then angled down more steeply.

"Something in the air ahead. Can't see it too well," Yevele said.

"My eyes are a little better." Berthold put a hand on her shoulder, getting her to stop. His narrowed eyes peered into the shadows ahead. He stomped his foot and shook his head. "The cavalry won't be coming, Yevele."

The battlemaid looked at him curiously and tried to see what he'd noticed.

"That little dragon, she didn't find Naile and Milo. She didn't even leave the Keep. Wonder how she got down here ahead of us?"

A heartbeat later, Alfreeta flew into view, her transparent wings shimmering in the torchlight, her tongue flitting across her lips and her wide eyes sparkling. The little dragon looked anxious, and she glanced behind her and retreated down the tunnel, motioning with her head and tail.

"She obviously wants us to follow her," Yevele said. She hesitated only a moment before doing just that.

Return to Quag Keep

"Just like Lassie," Berthold muttered, prodding the wound under his tunic. "Timmy's fallen down into the well and we need to go pull him out."

Behind them, in the dark chamber littered with the corpses of rats and were-rats, Fisk stirred. He rolled onto his back and stared up at the blackness, willing himself to be part rat again. He pressed his hands against the wound Yevele had given him and spat a gob of blood out of his mouth.

He laid there for quite some time, until he felt the slice in his belly closing up and his breath coming even and stronger.

"Damn the woman," he hissed. Fisk was unaccustomed to feeling such pain. "And damn the little thief who walks in her shadow." He heard faint chittering, his surviving rat brothers returning and offering him succor.

For more than an hour, he remained still, feeling the welcome weight of the rats on his legs and chest, taking some of their strength and continuing to heal. Finally he rose, his head transforming wholly into that of a rat, his eyes now able to cut through the black and find the chamber walls. He fixed his gaze on the passage that led up into the higher levels of Quag Keep and followed that, a small wave of his rat-brothers scurrying behind him.

"I leave her to Pobe," he told the rats. "She travels toward him now. And when she meets him . . . she will wish that she had died to my poison." He began whistling the woman tune penned by the poet Joel.

TWENTY-SIX

Into the Labyrinth

Alfreeta led them down and down. Berthold guessed they were a hundred or more feet below the surface, though he had no way to truly know. He had passed the point of thinking there was an end to the Keep, and wondered if they were caught in some magical trap that would force them to walk through this maze until they dropped.

Alfreeta took them through several small chambers, one of which looked like a shrine to a foul god and had disturbing images on the walls that made them dizzy. Then they were at a wide, steep stairway, the first they'd seen since the spiral staircase beneath the carpet.

The steps were made of a different stone than the rest of the place, the edges sharp and showing no trace of wear. So it was perhaps of more recent construction, Berthold pointed out. The walls had less of the quivering moss on them, and there was no trace of flowstone. There were two smokeless torches halfway down the stairs, and Berthold snatched one.

"If we could take anything back with us," Berthold mused, "I think I'd grab as many of these as I could carry. Sell 'em to one of those big campsites down by Paducah or Lexington or Louisville. Make a small fortune. Repel mosquitoes and—"

"Cells," Yevele announced, as she left the last step and disappeared around the corner. "Some sort of prison down here."

"More like a corner of hell," Berthold said. He waved his free hand in front of his nose. "Stinks worse than the were-rats. Than the trolls. Stinks worse than anything. And it's so dark down here, even with the torches."

"Almost as if the walls drink in the light." Yevele stared down at small doors set in a line along the bottom. "Lots of things have died in here, Berthold. And from the smell of this place, it does not seem that any of the corpses were ever removed."

Alfreeta led them through a half-dozen prison corridors, then down another flight of stairs. The smell did not let up. If anything, it worsened, and even the battlemaid was having a difficult time continuing, coughing, then gasping now and then.

"A lot more of that slime on the walls down here, Yevele. I don't like this place at all. We need to go back. In fact—"

"Shhh. I hear something."

"You hear my empty stomach loudly protesting this horrid place." She cut him a cross look.

"Yevele?" The word sounded weak and came from behind one of the doors along the floor. "Yevele? Is that you?"

She crouched in front of a small wooden door. A heavy brass lock hung from a moss-covered latch. "Naile?"

"Milo! Yevele's here. Alfreeta brought our cavalry after all."

"I guess Timmy really did fall down into the well." Berthold laid his torch near the corridor wall, careful not to let the flames touch the slime and moss and thereby possibly add to the stench of the place. Then he reached for his pouch of picks and tools. "Let me have a look at that."

Yevele was quick to move out of the way, glancing right and left and listening to make sure nothing that passed for a guard was approaching. "Get them out of there, Berthold. Hurry. I do not like this place."

Return to Quag Keep

The thief sighed and sat cross-legged in front of the cell. "Yes, ma'am." After a moment: "Quite a bit of magic in this lock and in this door. It's hard to explain, but I can feel a sort of energy surrounding this. It's going to take some time."

The battlemaid started tapping her foot as Berthold started worrying at the lock. At the same time, he worried over the deep bite mark on his side. He couldn't risk looking at the wound right now—not with Yevele so close. But he felt where it was beneath his tunic and prodded it with his fingers again. It was sore, and he could feel the heat from it even through the material. He scratched it just a little, then forced himself to stop.

"Naile." Berthold kept his voice low. "We fought were-creatures. They were men who could turn into rats." He could hear Naile breathing behind the door, but the big man didn't say anything. He decided to risk a question. "Naile, do you know how you became a were-boar?"

Naile snorted and gave a sad laugh. "Yeah, I picked up a miniature during a role-playing game, and I got sent here."

"No, I mean—"

"I've a false memory, Berthold, of being born to were-boar parents. Why?"

Berthold's hands were shaking as he manipulated the lock. "There were just so many of them, the rat-men. Fisk Lockwood was one of them. Remember him? That Glothorio priest? Well, he's not a priest. In fact, he led them. I wondered how there could be so many."

"We found out Fisk was bad news, too. After you left for the Keep, he sent some bandits on us, got Ludlow Jade's son killed. Jalafar-rula says Pobe—"

"Who's Jalafar-rula?" This came from Yevele, who was standing over Berthold. "And Pobe. Who's he? Fisk mentioned a Pobe."

"Jalafar-rula is the wizard Berthold wanted us to rescue."

Berthold fumbled faster. "He's in there with you?"

Naile proceeded to explain about the Glothorio priests' vision and their spell that sent him and Milo directly to Jalafar-rula's cell. Yevele in turn regaled them with the tale of how she, Berthold, and

Ingrge reached Quag Keep and found Alfreeta, and about the battle with the trolls and were-rats. She left out the part about finding a big jar filled with gems and baubles, though it was obvious they would see the latter hanging around her and Berthold's necks . . . provided the thief could open the lock.

"So Ingrge's hurt bad?" Naile's voice was filled with concern.

"Very," she returned. "I don't know if he's still alive."

"We'll find out," Naile said. "As soon as Berthold gets us out of this dump."

She nudged him with her knee. "Hurry."

For the first time Berthold looked truly angry, and he jabbed her in the leg with his elbow. "Give me some room, Yevele. And I *am* hurrying. The lock's magic. The door's magic. And if I kill myself on either because I hurried, your friends will never get out of there. They'll rot just like the other prisoners who are stinking up this place. And you'll be left to your lonesome in this hell-hole."

She backed up and looked down at him, her raised eyebrow showing her surprise at his reaction. *Sorry,* she mouthed.

He returned to work on the lock. "Hot in here," he mumbled. "He felt beads of sweat forming on his forehead and trailing down into his eyes. He didn't bother to wipe them off. His hands were sweaty, which made his task even more difficult, and he finally wiped his palms on his leggings. The material was practically shredded in places, from the rats that had swarmed him. Even the smallest cuts were itching. The bite mark on his side was itching fiercely. "Hot as Bowling Green in the middle of August."

Alfreeta perched on his shoulders, beating her wings, the movement of the air cooling him a little. She stayed that way for a long time, not seeming to tire, swiveling her head nearly all the way around to watch Yevele, who had started to pace behind Berthold.

"Can you stand still, Yevele?" Berthold was terse. "All that clicking from your heels is distracting. If you have to pace, do it somewhere else. And quit making that huffing sound. You being impatient isn't making this go faster."

She stopped a few feet away and found a relatively clean spot of wall to lean against. *Sorry,* she mouthed again. *Sorry. Sorry.*

Alfreeta wrinkled her nose, offering the battlemaid a sympathetic expression. Then she hovered above Berthold's shoulder, shimmered, and flew through the door to visit with Naile.

The thief settled back to work a kink out of his neck, took a deep breath. After a few more minutes he tugged on the padlock. It came unhinged, and he removed it from the latch. "Not so fast," he warned Yevele, who was instantly behind him again. "There are tiny runes all over the wood here. See?" He pointed with his finger. "Hold the torch for me so I can see better. Not too close. It's hot as all blazes in here." He registered that she wasn't sweating, then he wiped his hands on his shredded leggings again and started picking minute pieces of brass inlay out of the wood, in much the same manner a dentist would work plaque off a tooth.

Much later, or so it seemed, the thief rolled his shoulders, scooted back from the door. He got to his feet, stretched, and refused to utter the groan that was building in his throat. Replacing his picks and tools, he stuck the pouch in his belt. "Should open," he told her.

He didn't utter a word of protest when Yevele caught his arm. "Open?"

"Should be," he said, but he made no move to prove it.

She gave the door a solid kick. Moments later, Naile, Milo, Jalafarrula and Alfreeta were standing in the corridor. The old wizard beamed, his fatigued expression vanishing and his eyes brightening.

"I chose well," he said. "My magic reached out to your world and brought you here. Yevele, you are a fine lady." He bowed to her and held her hand, the chain that still hung from his wrist clanking against the floor. "Susan, right?"

She nodded. "Of Canberra. I . . . I . . . live in a small house near the Uni."

"Yevele suits you better," he said. "And Bertrum of Bowling Green. . . ."

"I prefer Berthold of the Green here."

"And of course Milo and Naile. Much easier to see you here in this light. Good people all. I chose you well." Alfreeta flicked her tongue and beat her wings, taking her above Naile's shoulder. "Yes, yes, and Alfreeta, too." The hint of a smile played at the thin corners of his pale lips. "Somehow I knew you would reach me, free me. And now together we must—"

"Go find Ingrge," Naile said. He was talking to the wizard, but was studying Yevele, who was apparently returning the intensity of his look. "Can't let the elf get caught by some troll or something."

"Not yet." Milo was scrutinizing the thief, eyes dropping to the necklaces. "Can you get those off him?" He pointed to the chains on Jalafar-rula's ankles and wrists. "Naile got him loose from the wall. Can you finish it?"

The thief let out an exaggerated sigh and produced his picks again, setting to work on the shackles.

"What do you mean not yet?" Naile still watched Yevele. "Not go after Ingrge yet?"

"We're too close to stop, and you know it. We're too far below the ground, from what Berthold says. Too close to whatever Pobe is using to siphon magic from our world." Milo tried to explain more about the Glothorio priests' spell that brought Jalafar-rula's image to them, and about the wizard's story. "We have a larger concern than just our friend, the elf."

When the shackles were off his wrist, the wizard finished the story. "Ancient Earth had so much magic," he began. "More than this world, more than many of the worlds I've had the honor to visit. Magic flowed like the rivers and streams and was accessible to everyone who had the imagination to play with it. Just not everyone on Earth believed in the magic, and that made it easy for someone to slip in and to siphon the arcane energies away."

"So the magic on Earth is gone?" Yevele finally glanced away from Naile.

The wizard shook his head. "Not entirely. Come here, Alfreeta, let me borrow a bit of more of your arcane energy." The little dragon obliged, and a heartbeat later an ephemeral globe hovered at the wizard's eye level in the prison hallway. The continents glowed green, the water blue, and there were motes of gold twinkling like stars. The globe grew larger, as wide as the hallway now and slowly spinning.

"That's Wisconsin," Milo said. He touched his finger to one of the gold spots.

"Your home, Milo, where you live as the young man named Martin Jefferson. The magic that remains is strongest there, near the lake. The pieces of gold represent reserves where the magic remains." Jalafar-rula pointed to other states. "Illinois, this particular spot is near . . . I believe they call it Chicago. And here."

"Kentucky," Berthold supplied. He released the shackle from the wizard's right ankle and started on the left. "But then I always thought Kentucky was a magical place. All the caves and pastures."

"And here," Jalafar-rula continued.

"That would be New York, where I'm from." Naile was standing next to Yevele now, their shoulders brushing. "And it looks like there's a little spot in Connecticut, Nebraska, Oklahoma. And down there in Florida, too."

"Where Ingrge's from," Yevele said. She drew a line up to North Carolina. "Wymarc came from some place around there. And there's Australia." The globe had turned and she stretched a finger out, caressing the gold spot close to where Canberra was. "Uncle Wes." As she watched, the gold light flickered, then winked out. "Oh!"

At the same time a gold spot in Canada dimmed. The wizard's face looked longer and his expression doleful.

"Pobe grows ever more powerful by draining your world. When he's taken every last sip of magic, imagination will stagnate. Even the "gamers," as you call them, the science-fiction fans with their plastic pointed ears, the Tolkien scholars with their reams of manuscripts and maps of a non-existent Middle Earth . . . all of them . . . will lose their spark when the magic dies."

"We'll all become Mundanes," Milo translated.

"What is left of my beautiful Stonehenge will crumble to dust.

Easter Island, no trace. The memory of Atlantis will fade. And yon legends of King Arthur and more will all be forgotten. Eventually, Earth will dry up and cease to exist."

Silence reigned in the hallway, until Berthold removed the final shackle.

"So the elf will have to wait," Berthold agreed. "Earth comes first. It's just like I told all of you when I caught up to that caravan. We help the wizard, then we can save our planet and go home. While we can still remember we've homes to go to."

"So how do we find this Pobe?" Yevele asked.

Jalafar-rula watched another mote of gold light disappear, then he dismissed his globe. "Hopefully we won't find him. Pobe is powerful and could well be beyond all of us. All we need find is the device he uses to drain the magic. A safer plan, and just as effective."

"So how do we find that?" she pressed.

"Yon warrior Milo will show us the way."

They all looked to Milo, who stood where the globe had been. "I haven't a clue. I don't know what the wizard is talking about."

Jalafar-rula shuffled toward him, placed a pale hand on his shoulder. "You're the only one who can find the device, Milo Jagon. It is up to you." The wizard dropped his hand to Milo's and touched the ring on his thumb. "This will show us. You must have a little faith."

Milo stared at the ring. It was dull green and had thin red lines and small red dots on it. Similar to the ring on his other thumb, but that one lacked any of the lines. He'd tried to take them off when he first arrived, tried more times than he could count. And like the bracelets still affixed to his and Naile's wrists, they wouldn't budge.

"Alfreeta?" The little dragon landed on the wizard's arm, and he drew more of her magic. In response, the red lines writhed like snakes, then turned white, the dots disappeared, and the dull green stone grew black and glossy.

Milo felt himself being tugged toward the far end of the corridor. "What's happening?"

"Milo, your ring will lead us to the most powerful source of magic in Quag Keep. And that undoubtedly will be the device Pobe uses to drain your world. Let it pull you, Milo, before the device chances to siphon your ring, too. If we cannot find that device, I'm afraid there'll soon be nothing worthwhile left of Earth. And after Earth, can this place and other worlds be far behind?"

Jalafar-rula shuffled after Milo, an old man's gait, but a determined one. Yevele moved to the wizard's side and draped his arm around her shoulder. And Naile, Alfreeta happily perched by his neck, walked directly behind, holding a torch Yevele passed him.

"I thank you," Jalafar-rula said to the battlemaid. "I've been in that dungeon for quite some time and I'm afraid I'm a bit stiff. You are a strong, strong woman."

Berthold watched them all before slowly following a few yards behind, torch in one hand. He picked up the hem of his tunic, just high enough so he could see the bite mark on his side. It was red with a fever, but it looked to be healing. And at each place where a tooth had pierced him, small tufts of soft black hair sprouted.

"This isn't a game," he said. "And this isn't *like* the game." His throat was dry and tight, and his stomach felt like a rock had settled in the bottom of it.

TWENTY-SEVEN

Dark Reflections

They traveled deeper still, Jalafar-rula explaining that Quag Keep extended much deeper below the ground than it rose above it, and that the lowest, darkest levels were the most recent construction, having been excavated in the past thirty or forty years. The air was almost sweet here, compared to the air that hung heavy in the prison corridors and where they'd encountered the were-rats. It stirred, as if it was blowing in fresh from somewhere, but they saw no cracks in the walls, and had no clue where it was coming from.

In the first chamber they discovered an oval pool ringed by smooth green stones, the water looking dark blue under the light of the torches. Milo started to walk past it, but Yevele called for a stop.

"Wizard, you know of this?" She nodded to the pool and extricated herself from his arm. She knelt at the edge of the pool and looked at her haggard reflection.

"A source of water," he said. "Safe to drink. Nothing more, nothing magical, if that's what you mean." He awkwardly got to his knees next to her. "But in being nothing more, it be everything at the moment. Sometimes the most simplest of things be the most precious and valuable." He dipped his cupped hands in and drank.

Satisfied it was safe, she took off her helmet and used it as a cup, hungrily drinking the water and splashing it on her face and neck, upending the helmet over her and closing her eyes. The water was clear and sparkling as summer rain, removed from the pool, and it made the chainmail links of her shirt gleam. She continued to upend her helmet, her auburn hair plastered now against the sides of her head and her leggings dark with the water. She reached to her water-skin, intending to fill it up, then remembering it already was full — of gems. So she drank deeply again, and Naile joined her, carefully laying the torch behind him in the event water could put it out.

"So thirsty," Naile admitted. "To take something like water for granted." He drank and drank, saying how sweet and cool the water was, even though it had a metallic taste from the minerals in the rocks. Softly: "I missed you, Yevele, worried about you."

Milo drank his fill, too, but Berthold held back, sipping only a little, rubbing water on his face and hands, and again prodding the wound on his side. "I know caves," he said. "This water shouldn't be polluted or anything, but I'd go easy on it. Not that any of you will listen to me. In the game nobody pays attention to the thief."

They ignored him, drinking more, Naile splashing himself with the water, finally sticking his head under it, then flinging his shoulders back and shaking, spraying everyone and causing the torch behind him to sputter. He took off his tunic and borrowed Yevele's helmet, letting the cool water run down his broad chest. Alfreeta glided away from him, hovering over the center of the pool and using her tail to splash herself.

"My parents tried to get me to go into environmental law," he told the battlemaid. He was struggling with the memory, though he tried to sound confident. He thought perhaps talking about his New York self might keep his mind clear. "But I wasn't interested in the environment. Told them there wasn't enough money in it. Should've listened to them. Keeping water clean and drinkable, now that's something important. Protecting copyrights? Who am I helping there? Composers and mystery writers. John Williams and Mary Higgins Clark." He upended the helmet over his head again.

Milo drank a little more and closely watched Naile and the battle-maid. Was there really something between the two of them? Or was it just interested, curious looks that they passed back and forth? Did he have a chance with her? He got up and walked toward her, extended his hand. She accepted it, and he helped her up.

"Ring's still pulling me, Yevele," he said. "We're exhausted, all of us, but the water's helped. So we should probably get going, while this magic's still working. While we're still awake. You still feeling strong enough to help Jalafar-rula?"

She nodded and smiled at him.

Milo had one torch, Naile the other.

"I want you playing rear guard," Milo told the berserker. "Just in case something creeps up behind us. You've the best chance of noticing." *And I want you farther away from Yevele,* he added to himself. Then Milo took the lead, the battlemaid right behind him, still helping Jalafar-rula. She left her helmet at the edge of the pool, and let her hair hang loose around her shoulders. Milo glanced back at her every once in a while, not seeing Naile scowling at him.

The thief walked in front of Naile, wanting nothing more than to slip around behind him, lag behind and inspect the bite mark. He'd poured water on it when he was certain the others weren't looking, and that helped quench the fever. But it was feeling warm again, even through the material.

"Not like the game," Berthold said. "Don't let it be like the game. Not like it at all."

"What did you say?" Naile thought the thief had been talking to him.

"I said we don't smell gamey anymore. The water worked a proverbial wonder."

They advanced in relative silence for several minutes, then abruptly the precise stone blocks of the corridor stopped and natural unworked stone began, as if they'd entered a cave.

"Quag caverns," Jalafar-rula announced. "As old as the beginning of this world." He stepped away from Yevele to run his age-spotted hands along a length of dark granite. The wizard had regained more of his strength and was walking at a steady pace. "We built the Keep directly above these caverns, building up and up first, as that seemed to be what wizards should do, live in a great, high place from the top of which we could watch over everything. Then we built the black wall around it all."

"I remember," Naile said. "The first time we came to Quag Keep we passed through a black stone wall."

"But it wasn't there when we came through the forest this time," Yevele said.

"That must have been some months ago you saw the wall. Pobe, during one of his visits to the dungeon, told me his minions had taken it down and the enchanted stone was being used elsewhere. The wall was hardly necessary to keep people out anyway." The wizard stopped where a section of the wall warped outward, looking smooth and rounded like a natural column. "The reputation of Quag Keep did that. Only the bravest and most foolish of adventurers came here."

"Like us." This from Naile, who was rubbing some dried blood off Yevele's face that the water hadn't caught.

"You were meant to come here, Naile Fangtooth."

"But are we meant to get back out?" Naile held the torch high, trying to get a better look at the place. Something glinted off the walls and caught his attention. "Now that's interesting." He stepped toward the closest wall, on the other side of the column from Jalafar-rula. "Yevele!"

Milo had been heading across the cavern, lured by the magical pull of the ring. But he stopped and looked back. Yevele, Naile, Berthold, and Jalafar-rula were studying something, Alfreeta hovering above and flicking her tail like someone might crook a finger, beckoning.

"I thought we were in a hurry," Milo said, as he backtracked and stared along with the rest of them. It wasn't like he could keep going on his own, he needed his companions. "All right. It is interesting. Now let's keep going."

There were crystals sprouting from the granite, not the kind of crystals that were part of the granite itself, but crystalline shards and spires, chunks and protrusions, some of which were as long as antelope horns. Under the torch they acted like prisms, throwing rose, green, and delicate blue fragments of light along the rock wall and the floor and across their faces. When Naile held the torch farther away, the light shards shrank, but somehow became more intense.

"I don't recall these being here," Jalafar-rula mused. "Well, not this big, in any event. They were small, warts on a witch's nose. There were always crystals in this cavern, and in the one below. But the size of warts they were, I tell you." He looked to Milo. "There's only one more cavern beneath this. If the ring is still pulling you, that is where we are headed. It figures that Pobe would go to the depths of the cavern, probably thinking an old man like me couldn't find his way there . . . even if he were free of that prison. But these crystals." The wizard's brow furrowed, not so much in puzzlement, but in concern.

"Wonder if you can pull them out?" Berthold wrapped his fingers around a spire and tugged at it, like he'd tug a dagger from one of his sheaths. It didn't budge, but he felt it move, quivering like the moss had in the levels above. He held onto it and brought his ear close. "Can you hear that?"

The others shook their heads.

"I've elven blood, you know," the thief continued. "Makes my senses sharp." He put his ear to the crystal. "It's humming. If Ingrge were here, I bet he could hear it." He took his hand off the crystal, and the noise stopped. So he touched his finger to the shard again. "Humming. And it feels warm." He was certain he could pull it free if he were rested.

"Natural stones do feel warm." This came from Yevele, who was copying Berthold and trying to tug one free. "I think I hear it." She ran her fingers along the edge of a small piece that gleamed like a diamond. "It's how my mom taught me to tell a real stone from paste. Said if a guy gives you a real stone, he's serious. If he gives you a piece of paste, he's just. . . . If you hold a piece, say jade, it warms up against your skin, more than a hunk of green plastic would."

Berthold moved on to another crystal. "I know all of that, and not just because I'm a thief. But these crystals are . . . I don't know . . . oddly warm. This one's almost hot. It hums, too." The thief was smiling now, the sound coming from the crystal pleasant and relaxing. "Here." He motioned for Milo to bring his torch closer, and he touched a crystal with each hand. "Almost like music."

"Berthold . . . they do move a little. At least, I think they do."

"Quivering, Yevele, just like the moss on the walls." The thief pulled back from the wall to acknowledge the battlemaid. "I think so, anyway. Vibrating just a teense like a tuning fork." He looked closer, seeing his eyes reflected in one of the longer crystals. They looked darker than usual, sparkling, yet at the same time bloodshot with fatigue.

"Breathing," Yevele said.

"Breathing?" Berthold considered this possibility. "You mean the crystals are breathing? Like they're alive?"

Jalafar-rula's eyes grew wide, and he inhaled sharply.

"Wizard, you think they could be alive, these crystals? Like they might be creatures?" Berthold had edged farther down the wall, where the light barely reached him. His side was itching fiercely. The crystals were providing a needed distraction, but not quite enough of one. He turned so the others couldn't see him, and he reached a hand beneath his tunic. All signs of that bite mark were gone, though not the other scratches and bites he'd received from the normal rats. But there was no longer a trace of the injury from the were-rat, just the small tufts of hair that felt baby-fine. He pulled the tunic back down as the light came closer. Milo was coming his way.

"More crystals over here," Milo called to the others. "They're all along this wall. They look like quartz. No, they look more like diamonds, too clear for quartz."

Milo pushed at a thick, stubby crystal, feeling its warmth. He held the torch almost directly on it and watched the colors swirl against the wall. Primarily green from this one, blue from the next one.

"Can you hear them?"

Milo studied Berthold. The thief was moving back and forth between crystals that were set roughly level with his ears.

Return to Quag Keep

"Yeah, I do hear them. A little. Sounds like a kazoo stuck on the same note. But I think we've spent too much time listening to them already. We've let ourselves get distracted." He extended his hand with the ring, still feeling the pull. "Time to go." He looked to the others, seeing them still playing with the crystals—all but Jalafar-rula, who was behind them, staring at the ones higher up on the walls, brow knitted and lips working. "Wizard!"

Jalafar-rula scratched at his forehead. "Yon Milo is correct. We must leave now." The wizard was moving quickly for his age, motioning for Milo. "We should get away from the crystals."

"Away from them?" Berthold leaned closer to the one in front of him, put his ear on it. "But I think they're trying to talk to us."

The wizard gestured furiously now, getting Milo to follow him, taking the light away from Berthold. "They be talking, but not to us. They be alive all right. I'm certain you are correct, Berthold of the Green. These be creatures."

Naile was the last one to step away from the wall, the torch he was holding making their light shards dance almost hypnotically. He noticed there was a rhythm to the way the colors moved, the ones to his right showing rose, then the color flowing across the wall before it changed to green, then blue. It looked like one of the light shows he'd seen in a Manhattan dance club. But there was no loud, annoying music to accompany the color shifts.

"Yeah, I think you're right," Naile said finally. "I don't know why, but I think they're communicating with each other, or maybe with something else."

"Or maybe someone," Milo posed.

"Pobe," Jalafar-rula said. "They be talking to Pobe."

There were more crystals along the far wall they passed by, these higher up, the colors changing faster than the shifts the other crystals displayed. Some of these crystals were artful, one looking like a faceted mushroom growing from the granite, another resembling flower buds clustered together, a large one looking like a turnip, another akin to the curving beak of a tropical bird. Most were like the spirals they'd seen earlier, though larger and more colorful, only a few were clear here. There was no reason why the crystals should sprout from a granite wall, nor from the chert walls the next corridor was made of.

"None of these rocks make sense. Granite next to chert. Here's some slate. Look." Berthold was pointing to a section of wall. "I've been in plenty of caves. When I was in Kentucky, especially. These combinations of rocks don't make sense. And the crystals. They just don't—" He let the others get ahead of him and he grabbed his side. It felt like he'd been bitten again, over and over. His hand clawed at the spot, pulling up his tunic and feeling that the baby-fine hair had thickened and spread. "Don't let it be like the game. Please. Please, don't let it be like the game. Let this all be a very bad dream."

"Berthold, move!" Naile was calling to him.

"Fine. I'm fine," Berthold returned, hurrying and noticing an entire section of the wall where it met the ceiling seemed to be made of the crystals. The colors pulsed softly, violet added to the mix now. "Magic," he decided. "Magic grew the crystals and formed these caves. Magic, I say!"

Naile heard him, and waved him to catch up. "Of course it's magic. Wizards built this place. Probably everything about it is magic."

Berthold instinctively knew the crystals were valuable, a type of gemstone not seen on Earth and likely not seen here except in these ancient caverns. He pictured them faceted and set into rings, pictured how many coins he'd gather from merchants wanting them. And if they were creatures, perhaps wizards would pay for the crystals with wagonloads of potions and elixirs. They could enchant a magical sword for Yevele. Wait! What was he thinking! For Yevele? Magical daggers for himself.

"Berthold!" Naile motioned for him again. "Don't want to leave you behind. Milo says it's always a bad idea to split the party."

Berthold took another look at the crystals and hurried along. He could come back later, with a large sack—several sacks—and take as many of the crystals as he could haul away. It would be better then, as he wouldn't have to share the crystals with the others. And he could come back here again and again, filling up sacks and selling them across the country, amassing a fortune.

"Better to keep them all for myself," he whispered, as he caught up to Naile. "Lord, what am I thinking? I'm not a greedy soul." A pause: "But I need them more than the others do. I need the wealth."

Alfreeta was again perched on Naile's shoulder, her head crooked around and wide eyes staring at him.

Berthold raised his upper lip in a sneer and narrowed his eyes in return.

The little dragon shuddered and wrapped her tail around Naile's throat.

When the entourage was clear of the cavern, and the last of their footfalls faded to nothingness, the place was once again bathed in soothing blackness and solitude. The crystals waited, holding their breath and making sure none of the trespassers were returning. Then they created their own light.

Pale olive green, warm rose, golden yellow, and sky blue pulsed from the various shaped crystalline creatures. Had Ingrge been here to see them, he would have believed it a recreation of the night sky's Celestial Dance. There was a pattern to the way the colors appeared, how long each hue stretched between crystals and how bright they were. It was a language that was at the same time simpler and more complicated than ones spoken by the men of this world, and it was more beautiful. It carried through the walls the crystals were wedged in, like a tremor that follows a quake.

The words continued to shimmer through the rocks in the great caverns beneath Quag Keep for some time, searching for someone who would listen, finally finding just that. "They come," the crystals reported. "The otherworldly trespassers come to you."

TWENTY-EIGHT

Realm of the Shadow Fey

"This is it? As far as this place goes?" Milo stood at the entrance to a cavern so massive the light from his torch couldn't stretch to the walls or the ceiling. "This is the last of it? Even though the last of it is huge?"

The wizard nodded behind him and again took himself away from Yevele.

"The ring stopped pulling me the moment I stepped foot in here." Milo stared at the ring on his thumb. The lines were narrower than before, almost impossible to make out.

"It's still pulling," Jalafar-rula said. "If it's black, it's still pulling. You just have to be more perceptive." He was much stronger now, and he raised an arm above his head to stretch. "But you be right, Milo Jagon. This be the last bit of the great Quag caverns. It has been a long time since I've set foot down here. I'd forgotten how impressive it is. And how far from the surface. Quite the climb for an old man like me."

"Quite the climb for a young one," Milo added. "My legs hurt worse than when I went out for track in high school." He brightened at the memory from home, then instantly scowled. There was nothing else from high school he remembered, and he was losing track of the inventory of the T-shirt shop. What sizes did it carry? "What does it matter, the sizes. What does any of it matter?"

"Pardon?" Jalafar-rula gave him a curious glance.

"And I just realized when we're done down here . . . with whatever it is we need to do . . . we'll have to climb all the way back up. Wish those Glothorio priests would have given us a round-trip ticket with that spell they cast. Ludlow Jade paid enough for it." He bent and with his free hand rubbed the muscles in his thighs. "I feel horrible." He brought his hand up to his stomach.

Yevele gently took the torch from his hand and went to the closest wall. "Granite and chert, like the other chamber. No crystals. Wish we could see this better. Searching this cavern is going to take a while." She leaned against the wall and held her stomach, too. "Can't see it all."

"I can be of some help to you." Jalafar-rula held out his arm like a falconer would, and Alfreeta obliged him by perching near his elbow. "I hate to keep taking your magic, little one, but mine is slow to return. Don't have enough of it back yet for what I need. Just a wee piece from you, all right?" The little dragon gave a nod, then swiveled her head around so she could keep an eye on Berthold.

Jalafar-rula closed his eyes and raised a hand to stroke Alfreeta's scaled belly. "I could have done this earlier," he said. "But we were not close enough to our goal. No use wasting magic, ye understand." His wrinkled eyelids fluttered as if he was deep in a dream, and Alfreeta gave a small whimper as he pulled more magic from her.

Then his eyes snapped open and a green egg-shaped flame hovered in front of him, growing as large as a boulder before settling on the ground in front of him and illuminating more of the cavern.

"Like Kentucky." Berthold turned, trying to take as much of it in as possible. "Just like some of the caves I've been in."

The ceiling of the cavern stretched up nearly sixty feet in the center, sloping down to the walls. There were stalactites and stalagmites every few yards, some stretching the height of two tall men. Crystals were embedded in some of them, thin like icicles, thick and curving like tusks, and all of them glowing green in the light of Jalafar-rula's magical flame. Everything in the cavern had a green tint to it, just as his lesser spell had given a green tent to the cell Milo and Naile and he had been in.

Here, the green cast made everything look eerie and alien, and it made their faces seem worn, their expressions defeated.

"So tired," Naile admitted. "And this cavern is so — "

"Like Mammoth Cave," Berthold said. "I remember a few things about the place. Hard to think . . . Mammoth Cave is maybe the biggest cave in the world . . . our world. It has chambers in it like this one, but they have paths on the floor where the rock has been smoothed from so many people walking on them. But this cave, this is as close to untouched as you'd find one."

The thief went down on one knee and let his fingertips brush the floor. "See, there are some sharp places here, and here. Not many people have walked across this stone. No electric lights installed for the viewing pleasure of the tourists. No guard rails to keep you out of the tunnels. Perfect for a cave."

Milo snorted. "Glad someone likes this place."

"I can feel the air stir," the thief continued. "More than in the chamber above. See the cracks in the floor over there? Air is coming through them. Must be some tunnels running just beneath this that wind their way up and bring air in from outside. It's cool air. Smell it?"

Then Berthold lost interest in the air and the cracks in the floor and moved to the nearest cluster of crystals. His back to the others, he pulled a dagger out of a sheath and stuck the tip at the point where the crystal met the stone. Pretending to study something in front of him, he worried the blade in, careful not to shatter the crystal. After a moment, he'd managed to work it out. It was roughly the length of his hand, warm and trembling against his palm. He was certain it was worth more than any of the gems he and Yevele had taken from the treasure jar. Thankful he'd lost two of his daggers, he put the crystal into an empty sheath. And started work on another.

"I'm not feeling so well, either." This came from Naile, who was

Andre Norton and Jean Rabe

bent over, hands on his knees. "Sick to my stomach. Must be something about this cavern. Some type of foul magic or a curse. Maybe we triggered some sort of spell. Ugh. This is awful."

Berthold freed another crystal, this one looking like an icicle, and fitting almost perfectly in another empty sheath. "I don't think we triggered anything. I think it's all that water you drank. I warned you." He surveyed his companions. Even the wizard looked a little nauseous. "I told you not to drink too much of that water."

"Poisoned?" Naile was gagging up some of the water, one hand on a knee, the other clutching at his stomach.

"Not at all," Berthold continued. He was acting a little smug, but figured he had that right. "But I know caves, and with some exception—in our world and in this one. The water in caves is full of minerals, and certainly bacteria. You're not used to drinking it, and it isn't agreeing with you."

Yevele was leaning against a cavern wall, her face pale. The wizard was near her, not faring as bad, but then he'd not drunk so much as she had. Milo straightened, his lips pulled tight in a grimace. He joined Yevele against the wall.

"So how long are we going to feel like this?" Milo directed his question across the yards to Berthold.

"How am I supposed to know?"

"You know so much about caves, or so you say." Milo turned away from Yevele and spat up as much of the water as he could manage. He dropped the torch he'd been carrying, not needing it with the wizard's magical light. "You're the cave expert, Berthold. How long is this going to last?"

"I know enough about caves not to drink the water in them. I'm no doctor. I've no idea how long you're going to be sick. I think. . . ." Berthold looked up. Part of the ceiling overhead was shadowed, but he thought he saw something moving. "Not bats. No guano. Haven't seen any bats since we found the three of you in that prison."

"No. There are no bats in these caverns. Never have been as far as I know." Jalafar-rula held Alfreeta in front of him. He made a cooing sound to her and closed his eyes. She whimpered again as he drained more of her magic. "Just a little, my friend. You need to help this old, old man feel better." In a few heartbeats his color had returned, and Alfreeta seemed unhurt, though tired. He stood straight and looked to Yevele and Milo, then turned and shook his head to note how badly Naile felt. "Would that I could help you. All of you. The magic I know to cure ailments is . . . personal. And would that I had thought about not drinking so much of that water."

"Great. So you have no Tums or Pepto Bismol to share with us," Naile grumbled. "Well, at least one of us is feeling better."

The wizard cocked his head, not understanding.

"Never mind," Naile continued. "I can tough this out. I'm a were-creature, right? A berserker. No stomach-bug is going to take me out." He groaned when he stood, then he glared at Milo, who was standing close to Yevele. "Isn't that ring leading you somewhere, counter man?"

Milo glared back. Then he dropped his gaze to the ring and concentrated on it.

Berthold was still looking toward the ceiling. "If there are no bats in here, Jalafar-rula, what might there be? What would keep the bats away from such a cavern?" He knew he wasn't imagining things. Something was moving up there. "What would live here?"

"Oh, all manner of things, I suspect. Pobe likes trolls."

"Can they fly?"

"Why no, Berthold of the Green. Whatever would make you think a troll could fly?"

"Because this isn't like the game, old man. Not exactly. Because you don't have to burn trolls in this world. And because something is flying up there."

Jalafar-rula rubbed his chin and looked to the green flames. With a gesture, the fire grew brighter and taller, illuminating much more of the cavern. Along the ceiling shadows cavorted, but not caused by the flickering green flames. They were lithe, having the shape of women, and sporting lacy gray butterfly wings from their backs.

Some had wings on their ankles and on the tops of their heads. One that he saw had scalloped wings beneath her arms. None looked taller than two feet, and all of them looked two-dimensional.

"Shadow fey," the wizard pronounced. "You be seeing some of this world's most ancient and treasured souls, friends. I feared they had all left this place when Pobe grew strong. They are generally peaceable, sometimes curious. But they do not like the type of creatures Pobe surrounds himself with."

"You mean trolls."

"Correct, Berthold of the Green. The shadow fey do not stomach the presence of such abominations. In the wilds, trolls hunt the shadow fey and consider them a delicacy. So take heart in knowing that there be no trolls here. For the fair shadow fey and the grotesque trolls are like—"

"Oil and water," Berthold supplied.

The wizard nodded and watched the fey ballet that moved from the ceiling of the massive chamber to the curving fall opposite Milo and Yevele. They looked small and fragile farther away, like insects caught in a beam of starlight. A few slid onto the floor and came near Berthold. But they darted away when he tried to touch one.

"I think I'm feeling a little better." Naile was pacing in a tight circle, oblivious to the creatures cavorting across the granite and chert. "Now it only feels like I've been punched in the stomach a couple of times." He took a few deep breaths, then glared at Milo again. "Well, what about that ring?"

Milo glanced away from the fey and again studied the ring. "Too many distractions," he whispered. "The crystals, the tiny dancing shadow-women. We need to find the . . . there! I feel something." His thumb tingled, and he realized it had been tingling for some time and that he'd been dismissing it as part of his malady.

Stomach still churning, he pushed himself away from the wall and followed the pull of the ring. Milo's course took him through a line of stalactites and stalagmites that reminded him of a row of teeth. The tingling grew stronger when he passed around a rocky outcropping where the light from the green flames couldn't quite reach.

"Wish I hadn't dropped that torch. Could go back and get it, but —" Louder: "Jalafar-rula! Can you move that green bonfire? Can you bring it over here?"

"Glad to help, Milo Jagon." The wizard took a little more of Alfreeta's energy, then with a finger wave sent the green flame rolling toward Milo. The fire made the crystals in the stalactites and stalagmites glow and sent shards of green light up toward the dancing shadow fey.

"This is beautiful," Yevele said. "Wish I felt better and could fully appreciate it."

Berthold was also watching the dance between the light shards and the fey creatures. "Nothing like this in the caves in Kentucky. Something like this . . . well, it would bring in a lot more tourists. Imagine the money the parks departments would make. It would take in an awful lot of money."

The cavern floor sloped down steeply around a curve in the wall. But it was rough enough. Milo didn't need to worry about his footing. A few of the crystals protruded from the floor ahead, and as the huge green flame moved behind him, the light shards they cast danced wildly. Shadow fey slid down the wall and toward the shards, cavorting with them while staying a safe distance from Milo's feet. He glanced at them as he continued to follow the gentle tug of the magic.

"Yevele! Come see this."

That gentle pull had taken him to something amazing. In an alcove that stretched to the ceiling, mushroom-shaped crystals of blue and green were so thick he could see very little of the granite they grew from. Their colors pulsed in time with his heart. Even from several yards away, Milo could hear a soft hum coming from the crystals. Beyond this alcove other crystals were scattered sporadically in the wall, these looking like icicles, fingers stretching out. The shadow fey darted among them. On the floor beneath the icicle crystals was a mound of treasure.

"A dragon's horde," Milo said. His voice was filled with awe. "Yevele!"

The green flame moved closer, as did Yevele and Naile, Alfreeta again on the berserker's shoulder. Berthold and Jalafar-rula stood at a distance taking it all in, the thief's eyes wide and unblinking and assessing which pieces were the most valuable.

Coins were spilled across the floor, of various shapes and with different faces pressed on them. They were all gold, though they were all tinted green in the wizard's light. There were gems scattered in the mix, though the exact colors were difficult to tell because of the green flame, and there were necklaces and bracelets, too, some long strands of pearls, others heavy gold links. A scepter sat on top, gold and festooned with dark stones, looking heavy enough to be wielded as a weapon.

"The scepter . . . could that be what we're looking for?" Milo kneeled at the edge of the treasure sprawl and stretched to reach the scepter. His ring had stopped tugging him, and so he guessed whatever it was he needed was in the mass of wealth. "It is heavy." He set it back down and remained hunched over as another nauseous wave struck.

Jalafar-rula shook his head. "I don't think so. If I remember correctly, yon scepter once belonged to King Kale."

"And King Kale dropped another goblin in the mud," Naile said.

"You need to find something not made by man, Milo Jagon. That would be what Pobe uses to pull the magic. Something beautiful that made itself."

Milo raised an eyebrow and started sifting through the coins and gems. In a heartbeat Berthold was at his side, slipping small stones into his boot, not caring that the crystals pressing between the leather and his leg were uncomfortable. Naile took off his tunic and ripped a strip off it from the bottom. He was fashioning a crude sack, intending to use the strip to tie it closed.

Berthold started to do the same, then yanked his tunic back down, not wanting the others to see the patch of rat hair growing on his side.

"Might as well gather up some of this wealth," Naile told Milo. "At least while we're looking for something that made itself. No use letting all this stuff just lay here. If we don't get out of this realm, all this gold could be handy." He spread out his makeshift bag and started putting necklaces and gems in it, along with some of the larger and heavier coins. "Yevele, don't you want some of this?"

She shook her head. She was already loaded down with gems. But then a long pearl necklace caught her eye and she moved forward. She had room around her neck for a few more baubles. And there was nothing yet on her wrists.

"This is like the game," Naile said. "You enter the castle, defeat the monsters, and then collect the treasure. But this is a horde my game master never would have given us. He always held back and kept us from getting rich." Naile laughed. "He said that I made enough money as an attorney, I didn't need to make money in the game." Then the berserker doubled over and clutched his stomach. "Damnable water."

"I don't want this to be like the game," Berthold muttered. "I don't. . . ." He spotted a dagger with a bejeweled handle, the blade made of something mirror-bright. "Now that's for me." Next to it was a scabbard of polished ebonwood and inlaid with gold or brass—too difficult to tell with the green flames. "This is nothing that made itself." He strapped the scabbard to his belt and tested the feel of the dagger. "Balance is perfect." Then he sheathed it and returned to picking through the treasure pile.

Milo wasn't gathering treasure, though he was pointing out some choice pieces to Naile, and he tossed a gold and jade bracelet to Yevele. He was looking for something unusual that might be Pobe's device. "Why would this fellow Pobe keep something so valuable and important to him in the middle of his treasure pile? Wouldn't he keep it separate? I would. I wouldn't want any trespassers to pick it up."

"Not just anyone could find their way here, Milo," Berthold lectured. He'd said something similar to Yevele when they stood before the jar of gems. "I'd say anything in these caverns is safe from looters."

Milo shook his head. "Maybe." The edges of the coins bit into the palms of his hands as he knelt on the middle of the pile. He glanced over his shoulder at Jalafar-rula, the wizard standing next to the flames as if he was cold and needed the fire's warmth. The old man's hair seemed to be the color of olives, and the lines on his face looked deeper in the eerie light. But the eyes were bright, and they met Milo's. The wizard looked hopeful.

"You have to have some idea what I'm looking for," Milo said. "Can't you cast some spell and conjure up an image of this device?"

Jalafar-rula dropped his gaze to the treasure. "I think I'll know what it is when I see it. Keep looking."

Milo gave an exasperated sigh. He saw one of the shadow fey melt from the wall like butter and move over the top of the coins. It was a slight female form with wings on her feet, and she circled his hand. It was the closest one of them had gotten to him.

"Can you hear me?" Milo asked.

The shadow fey circled faster.

Was that an answer? he wondered.

"Creature, do you know what we search for? Something that drains magic? Something that made itself?"

She darted away from him and up the wall, and Milo shook his head and cursed himself for trying to talk to a piece of shadow. But a heartbeat later she returned and circled his hand again, then she moved away more slowly, making sure she had his attention this time. She was leading him away from the mound of treasure, farther from the green bonfire and toward another alcove filled with crystals.

Milo followed her, nearly stepping on Berthold's fingers as he tromped across the coins and down the other side of the treasure pile.

"Wizard, come take a look at this." Naile had found something beneath a bowl of pearls. "Do you think this is what we're looking for?"

Milo didn't turn back, he kept after the shadow fey, hand pressed to his aching stomach as he went. The crystals in this alcove looked darker, partly because they were farther from Jalafar-rula's bonfire, and partly because they looked to be made of a different type of stone. Smoky like quartz, these were shaped roughly like elm leaves, with the ones toward the bottom of the alcove larger. The colors around their edges moved, glowing golden and orange. Though there was a patch of crystals that showed no light.

Behind him, Milo heard his fellows discussing some metal sculptures, heard Jalafar-rula say "they did not make themselves."

Farther away, where Berthold had noticed cracks in the cavern floor, something stirred. The shadows darkened there to a blackest black, and something oozed from one of the cracks. It looked like a pool of oil, and it shimmered darkly, pulsing in time with the crystals near it.

"They come," the icicle-shaped crystals told the ooze. "They are here."

"The trespassers pick from your treasure," reported the crystals shaped like mushrooms. "The wizard Jalafar-rula with them."

The black ooze rippled in anger and amusement.

TWENTY-NINE

The End of the Game

"Unusual, and no doubt magical," Jalafar-rula pronounced the metal sculpture Naile held high.

The thing was made of brass and silver, having the tail of a fish, the torso and arms of a man, and the head of a lion. It was pitted in places, from coins rubbing against it, but it was nonetheless impressive looking.

"Magical, huh?" Naile asked. "Any idea what it does?"

The wizard shook his head. "So many of these bits of treasure are familiar to me, Naile Fangtooth, as years past I used to travel these chambers—before my bones got so old and other things started to interest me. Perhaps it turns into a ship or summons forth a sea beast. Whatever guess you have would be as good as mine." He steepled his fingers under his chin. "Not what we are looking for. If my memory serves, what we seek is made of crystals."

"And it made itself," Naile said. "Made of crystals and made itself."

Milo heard that, and the grumble in his throat matched the grumble of his stomach. "I think Jalafar-rula knows exactly what we're

Andre Norton and Jean Rabe

looking for. I think wizards just feel a need to be mysterious." He kept his musings soft, sharing them with the shadow fey woman who continued to swirl around on the crystal alcove. "Made of crystals and made itself."

Milo scratched at his head. "Fey woman. . . ." The small shadow stopped dancing, hovering now on the wall directly in front of him. "You're alive, so these crystals could be alive, too, huh? Growing? Making themselves? Someone mentioned them breathing, Yevele, I think."

The shadow fey woman swam in circles against the crystals on the walls, and Milo took that for a yes.

"The crystals humming, blinking like the lights on a department store Christmas tree. They really are talking, aren't they?"

Another circle.

"Are they talking to you?"

The shadow fey remained immobile, save for her fluttering two-dimensional wings.

"To someone else?"

She circled twice more.

"To Jalafar-rula?"

She stopped moving.

Milo tugged his fingers through his hair. "This is like talking to my old boss, like pulling teeth to get a good answer. At least you're not as ugly, and you don't have three chins. At least I remember that much about the shop." He stared at her and then swallowed hard. Suddenly his stomach churned, the sensation not entirely due to all the water he'd drunk. "Are the crystals talking to this fellow Pobe?"

She circled rapidly, beating her wings so fast Milo thought he could feel a breeze from them. Then she climbed toward the ceiling overhead, where she disappeared in the shadows. On the wall in front of him, the crystals hummed softly and continued to blink gold, orange, and yellow.

Was it his imagination, or were the crystals blinking faster?

―――――

"Keep looking, Naile Fangtooth. That which you seek must be near. My divinations told me as much before Pobe lured me into his clutches and locked me away." The old wizard was wringing his hands. "You must be close. I think you should be able to feel the device."

Yevele was putting another strand of pearls around her neck. "Damn me, paying attention to this treasure."

"You're human is all," Berthold offered.

"What do you mean, feel it?" Yevele dropped an armband she'd intended to put on. She picked it back up and fastened it above her elbow. "How would you feel it?"

Jalafar-rula pursed his pale lips. "A device that pulls magical energies to it would . . . feel like something," he tried to explain. "It would not be a static thing, battlemaid. You should feel it. Whether it be warmth or—"

"Could you hear it?" Naile interrupted. "Because I think I hear something. Other than these humming crystals."

"Feel it, hear it," Milo mumbled several yards away. He was on his hands and knees now, face inches from the part of the alcove where the crystals were the thickest, and where the fewest of them gave off light. There was something here that clawed at his curiosity, something that didn't sit quite right with him. "Feel what?"

He held his hand against the crystals, feeling the ones sparking gold and yellow vibrate. He put his ear to them. They were humming, louder than they had been. But not the dull, smoky crystals. No sound came from them, no vibrations. Milo tugged at one of them, and it broke off easily. Then he pulled at another and another, breaking them away like dry twigs. Something glowed behind them, a soft rosy hue. He worked faster and meant to call out to his companions, but they were chattering about various objects they were uncovering.

Jalafar-rula was pulling more arcane energy from Alfreeta to make the green bonfire brighter to aid in their search. More of the light was reaching Milo's alcove now, making it easier for him to work.

"Should call for them," Milo said. "But not yet." Besides, Milo thought, this might not be it. This might just be more of the crystals.

Some of the brighter crystals around the hole he was making blinked faster, and Milo blinked, too. He could have sworn they were moving. Slightly, turning just a bit, certainly not moving like he could move or like the shadow fey could move.

Pobe oozed closer, spreading out over the floor and studying Jalafar-rula bathed in the eerie light. Pobe preferred the darkness, welcome and smothering and mysterious. The wizard's light bothered him, and so he sent a ripple outward through the cavern's floor. It was the first spell he'd ever perfected, learned shortly after he gained awareness in this very cavern beneath Quag Keep. A part of Pobe felt obligated to Jalafar-rula, for the old wizard was one of those who helped give him life from the malignant runoff of their own enchantments. But that part of Pobe was small, and the sense of obligation was overwhelmed by the need for power and magic.

The green flames dimmed a little at Pobe's coaxing, and he oozed closer still.

Jalafar-rula and his otherworld assistants were so caught up in their search through the treasure that they didn't notice the flames lowering and the light dimming. And only one of them heard the "shushing" sound Pobe made as he flowed across the stone, and he wasn't being taken seriously.

"I really thought I heard something," Naile said. He turned his head toward the flames and listened more closely.

Berthold scooped up handfuls of coins and let them fall, the clinking drowning out whatever Naile had been paying attention to.

"I hear the sound of a dozen Corvettes," Berthold said. "A garage big enough for all of them." The thief was on his hands and knees, rooting through the pile of riches. He swiveled to look up at Jalafar-rula. "We are going to get back home, aren't we? We find whatever device you're looking for, and then you'll use some of your magic to bop us back to Earth."

The old wizard finally noticed his light had faded and he drew more energy from Alfreeta to power it. The little dragon whimpered, but didn't protest. Then the wizard smelled something sulfurous, and he drew more energy still.

"He comes," the crystals hummed. Though Jalafar-rula and the others did not understand their language, they could hear the pleasant musical sound intensify. "Pobe comes."

"He's here," Jalafar-rula warned.

"Who?" this from Yevele, who was standing now and drawing her sword, sensing the old wizard's unease.

"Pobe," the wizard returned. "Can you not smell him?"

"I smell something as foul as the pit," Naile said. "And I still hear something."

"You hear Pobe." Jalafar-rula drew still more energy from Al-freeta, feeling the magic fill his old body. "And you smell his stench."

Drained, the little dragon glided to Naile's feet. The berserker was standing, too. He held the scepter as if it were a mace. His nostrils quivered, and his eyes constantly moved, looking at eye-level for what he expected to be a man.

"I had hoped we would be here and gone before the Darkness came," Jalafar-rula continued. "Found what I needed."

"The Darkness?" Berthold had finally stood up, too, the bejeweled dagger in his hand.

"Pobe. You should know that Pobe is also the Darkness." Softer: "And the darkest part of a wizard's soul."

Jalafar-rula pointed to a spot beyond the olive-green bonfire.

"It looks like an oil slick," Berthold said. "Wait a minute."

The pool of black shimmered and sent a ripple away from it. The ripple coursed through the stone, as if the granite of the floor were liquid, and the ripple stretched to the magical fire. The light dimmed again and the cavern trembled.

Then Pobe grew still, his surface a black mirror that reflected the flashing crystals in the nearest stalactites and stalagmites. The flashes grew brighter then arced to Pobe. Miniature lightning bolts of rose, green, and blue crackled along the black pool's edges.

"We are doomed," Jalafar-rula said, "lest we find Pobe's device. He'll not harm us if we hold it. Look quickly." This he directed to

Berthold and Naile. He gestured with a hand to Yevele. "Stand with me, battlemaid, and together we will try to keep the Darkness at bay."

Milo was only halfway paying attention to what was going on with his companions. He'd widened the hole by breaking away more crystals and discovered a large niche. He thought perhaps these smoky crystals had grown over the niche to hide and protect what was inside.

He reached his hands in and gently slid the crystal out. The light had dimmed from Jalafar-rula's fire, but the crystal itself was lighted, and so Milo could make out all the incredible detail. The base was as large as a serving platter and made of a single clear stone. Along the outside other crystals grew in blocks, a formation vaguely familiar to him. There were more crystals placed along the tops of these blocks, making "T" shapes and Pi symbols, and there was a miniature castle in the middle.

The crystal was smooth, yet faceted, looking like a solid diamond that had been carved into this image.

"It made itself," Milo whispered. He thought it possible—given everything he'd seen since coming to this realm. He'd spotted a few of the crystals on the wall near him moving almost barely. So why couldn't they have shaped themselves into something so exquisite?

Was this the device the villain Pobe was using to siphon Earth's magic? The device Jalafar-rula had bid them search for?

There was magic in it, Milo didn't need a wizard to tell him that. The crystal felt like no other crystal—like nothing else—he'd touched before. Warm, like natural stone, but warmer than he'd expected it to be. It wasn't hurtfully hot, but it wasn't comfortable to the touch. And the surface of it tingled, like some of the other crystals had. But this . . . tingling . . . was different. It felt electric, like the air charged by lightning during a summer storm. And it felt powerful.

The thing took his breath away, in its simple beauty and with the strength he felt running beneath his fingertips. Milo was mesmerized by it, and in a faceted section he saw himself—shattered. There was

Return to Quag Keep

Milo the warrior, muscular and newly dressed in the chainmail shirt and wool cloak Ludlow Jade had provided, and there was Martin Jefferson, smaller and with a shock of unkempt mud-brown hair and wire-rim glasses—and wearing a crookedly printed Death Dealer T-shirt.

He blinked and turned the crystal so he couldn't see himself. Is this what Pobe uses? he wondered. "Is this what Jalafar-rula says we should be looking for?" Still he kept staring at the facets, sometimes seeing his eyes reflected, sometimes seeing sparks of light, sometimes seeing shadows pass over it, the shadow fey scampering around on the walls.

Milo inhaled sharply. "Stonehenge." That's what was familiar about the image. The row of crystal blocks around the outside of the sculpture resembled pictures he'd seen of Stonehenge. Except the pieces didn't look as ruined as the real thing. And in the center was a castle. Had the castle once existed? Had this been Jalafar-rula's castle?

He forced himself to look away, wrapped his fingers around the edge of the base and stood. He slowly walked toward the others, careful to keep his eyes from resting on the crystal and becoming hypnotized again. Milo didn't notice that the walls of the cavern were drawing in, and that the great cavern was slowly getting smaller.

"Jalafar-rula!" Milo had to call the wizard's name twice more before the wizard turned. "Is this it?"

The wizard spun around, mouth open, eyes wide. "The device!" There was urgency and fire in his old voice. "Flee with it, Milo Jagon! Run from this cavern. Up with you. Don't stop! And whatever you do, Milo Jagon, do not drop that precious device!"

"We'll hold off this dark thing!" Yevele called. "Hurry, Milo!"

Milo cradled the crystal device to his chest and started running, up the sloping floor and around an outcropping, through the row of stalactites and stalagmites that he thought resembled teeth. He saw the pool of black, with its colorful lightning bolts. It was growing thicker, and he sensed the incredible magic flowing in the thing. It started oozing toward him, but Yevele and Naile intervened. Naile slammed the scepter down onto the pool, and colorful sparks flew.

Andre Norton and Jean Rabe

Jalafar-rula was weaving his fingers in the air, forming a gold and silver globe that he hurled at the Darkness. Pobe howled when the globe hit. It was a mournful, high-pitched cry that caused rocks and stone dust to rain down from the ceiling.

"Careful with that device, Milo!" Jalafar-rula called.

"Fool," Pobe rumbled. "A mere man should not have such a thing. You will die, man, then your friends."

"All of us will die," Milo returned. "Every single one of us." Then he was nearly to the entrance of the cavern. He whirled, seeing his friends fighting the viscous pool of black. The wizard's green fire was fading, and shadows and shadow fey were claiming the cavern. "Won't be able to see." He looked around for the torch he'd dropped, not finding it, and knowing the light from the device he held wouldn't be enough to show him the way. Milo knew the other chambers would be as black as pitch, and he'd have to feel his way out of here. And then what of Yevele and Naile and Berthold?

And what of Jalafar-rula?

"Why must I protect this?" Milo stopped, his feet rooted to the cavern floor. "Why not destroy it?"

Somehow Jalafar-rula heard him. "It is precious and priceless, Milo Jagon. You must take care with it. You must save it for. . . ." Then the wizard was casting another globe at Pobe.

The Darkness had started to ooze up Yevele's boots.

"And why is it shaped like Stonehenge?" Milo risked another glance at it and saw his warrior-self reflected back.

Overhead, the shadow fey spun nervously. The cavern continued to shrink. Rocks and stone dust filtered down like a constant rain, and the granite started to groan.

"The cavern's getting smaller!" This came from Naile, who was frantically pounding on the black pool. The scepter was breaking, and he tossed it away, stomping on the pool now. "Get out of here, Milo!"

"Why does Jalafar-rula want this?" Then Milo was racing back toward his companions, gaze darting to the edge of the treasure mound. He couldn't see all of it from his vantage point, but he could see Alfreeta sitting on a bed of coins. The little dragon was exhausted. "Because Jalafar-rula drained her. Just as Pobe is draining our world."

Milo looked to the wizard. "You'd use this, too, wouldn't you?" Milo was shouting to be heard above the protesting stone and the battle shouts of his companions. "You'd drain our world just like Pobe is! Maybe you *were* draining our world, Jalafar-rula! Maybe Pobe stole this from you."

Milo raised the crystal sculpture above his head, and Jalafar-rula screamed.

"No! it is precious, Milo Jagon. I did not bring you here to destroy it!"

"You brought us here to save you, and to help you get this back." Milo didn't know if he'd guessed correctly. It was possible Jalafar-rula was on their side. But he didn't like the looks of Alfreeta, and it troubled him that the wizard could drain magical energies . . . could do just what the wizard claimed Pobe was doing.

"Save that device!" Jalafar-rula cried. The wizard backed away from Pobe, leaving Yevele and Naile to contend with the malevolent pool, and heading toward Milo.

The Darkness had oozed up to Yevele's waist, and pain was etched on her face. Naile was covered with the blackness, too.

"It is precious, Milo Jagon. You must protect it. You must give it to me."

"Oh, now I know you shouldn't have it," Milo answered. He slammed the crystal down hard on the granite floor, watching as it shattered into a thousand pieces, shards of light fragmenting.

The cavern started shaking, as if it was caught in the throes of an earthquake. The shadow fey fled the place, swimming across the face of the jarring granite to chambers higher up.

Pobe screamed in anger, a hollow, haunting voice that bounced off the trembling walls. Then he was retreating, too, sliding into a crack that was growing in the wall.

Jalafar-rula's eyes were daggers aimed at Milo. "You have no idea what you have done!" Spittle flew from the wizard's cracked lips. "You are the basest of men, Milo Jagon. You have denied me power, and now you have denied yourself life!" The wizard gestured to the ceiling, chunks of which were raining down.

Yevele and Naile were scrambling away from the growing crack and calling to Berthold, who'd with one hand snatched up the makeshift sack Naile had filled with treasure, and with the other grabbed Alfreeta by the tail. The three were racing toward Milo, who was grinding the shards of crystal sculpture beneath his boot heels.

"We won't make it!" Berthold called to them.

Milo narrowly dodged a melon-sized rock that dropped from the ceiling and watched as smaller stones pelted Naile. Cracks were widening in the floor, and it was difficult to stand. He looked to the tunnel that they'd traveled to reach this cavern. Already it had been filled in with rocks.

"I should kill you!" Jalafar-rula shouted. "Kill all of you for this affront!"

The old wizard shook his fist at Milo then whirled his fingers. For a moment Milo thought the wizard would cast some foul spell at him, but the magic had a different purpose. Jalafar-rula shimmered and turned liquid, looking like Pobe, though gray instead. He oozed into one of the spreading cracks on the floor.

"There's no way out of here," Milo said. The quartet stood together now. Alfreeta was again on Naile's shoulder, tail wrapped around his thick neck. "Not unless we can turn into ooze and escape with Pobe and Jalafar-rula."

Yevele defiantly shook her head. "I'd not run with the likes of them, Milo. I'll die here with you!" Her face was angles and planes, beautiful in its determination. Her eyes sparkled in the scant light. "We'll all die together!"

"It has been an honor, Yevele—" Milo's words were cut off as the cavern shook more fiercely. Falling rocks pummeled him and drove him down. As he fell, the ring on his left thumb, the featureless one that he'd never discovered a use for, shattered.

And in its breaking, a burst of magic was released.

Epilogue

Milo's head throbbed, and he held it with both hands. He was stretched out on the sand, the coarse grains well entrenched in the links of his armor and rubbing against his neck and the backs of his arms. The sand was damp and cold, and the wind that blew across him birthed goosebumps.

He propped himself up and stared in disbelief. He was at the edge of a lake, gray in the early morning light and cut through with flecks of white on the waves. A few gulls were dipping to the surface, feeding. On the shore, a few yards away, a pair of Canadian geese returned his stare.

"Where are we?" Yevele was near him, sitting cross-legged and holding her head in her hands. Her hands were bleeding, from fending off the falling rocks, and there was a gash on her forehead.

"Yes, indeed," Naile cut in. "Where in the name of all that's holy are we?" The big man was a little farther up on the beach, standing and rubbing at his right shoulder. He, too, was a mass of cuts from the rocks in the cave-in. Berthold was sitting in Naile's shadow, arms clutched around the makeshift sack that still bulged with loot.

"Lake Geneva," Milo said, as he forced himself to his feet. A wave of dizziness threatened to send him back down. "Wisconsin." His memories rushed back, crowding his thoughts and making him shiver.

"Wisconsin?" Yevele looked at him incredulously. "Wisconsin? What happened to the cavern and the wizard and Quag Keep?"

Milo looked at his left hand, where a gold band still clung to his thumb. The stone was missing. He held his hand up. "The magic in this ring. It took us home. Maybe it could have taken us home all along. Just like Dorothy's ruby slippers."

"Why Wisconsin?" Naile made a growling sound from deep in his throat. "Why not Brooklyn?" He looked at Berthold and then Yevele. "Why not Kentucky or Australia? Why Wisconsin?"

Milo shrugged. "I don't know. I . . . I think because there's still magic here. It was the brightest spot on Jalafar-rula's globe. The magic that's left on Earth is strongest here." He held his hands in front of his face, let his fingers run down the chainmail shirt. Then he smiled. He much preferred Milo Jagon's body to Martin Jefferson's.

They'd all somehow kept the bodies the magic had given them. They were all their heroic selves . . . save Berthold who looked small and sneaky.

"Wisconsin," Naile grumbled. "Wis-kaaaahn-sen."

"The magic's strong here," Milo repeated. "You know the game started here. That role-playing game we all played, the one that caused us to pick up those little miniatures and that ultimately sent us to Quag Keep. The guy who created the game, supposedly he doesn't live too far from here. Gary something or other."

"Wisconsin," Naile repeated. "Wis-kaaaahn-sen. Wis-kaaaahn-sen. Friggin' Wis-kaaaahn-sen." He rubbed his stomach and looked across the lake, watching a gull dip low, then fly off. "Kind of pretty here, I have to admit. And kind of cold."

"It is fall, after all," Milo said.

"Do they have food around here?"

Yevele and Berthold seconded that notion.

"Yeah, up the street from here." Milo gestured up the beach, where parked cars lined a street, only a few of them had Illinois plates. "There's a little T-shirt shop. And next to it is a diner. Chocolate-blueberry coffee. Hamburgers. Their pancakes are pretty good." He started walking that way. "I think we'll stand out a bit. But most of the tourists are gone for the season. Shouldn't have any trouble getting a table."

They followed him, Berthold clutching the bag tightly with one hand, sheathing his dagger and scratching his side where the fur had spread.

Yevele caught up to Milo and touched his shoulder. "You know, Milo Jagon . . . Martin Jefferson . . . if there is some magic in this little town of yours, maybe we should go look for it."

Milo grinned wide. "A wonderful idea. I figure we'll need magic to get back to that world."

Berthold groaned. "Why would you ever want to go back there?"

"For Ingrge," Yevele answered.

"And Deav Dyne and Gulth. Have to go get them," Milo said. "Can't leave them there. So we have to find the magic here and figure out how to use it."

"After some pancakes," Naile said. "After a very big plate of them."

Ingrge drank the last of the water from Alfreeta's bowl. It had been three days since he'd lost his arm, and the pain was still strong, but he was managing it better and knew now that he was going to live. No one had come to check on the animals in the menagerie in all that time, but he discovered the food and water bowls inside the cages refilled themselves, and the cages cleaned themselves.

His course took him around the room, stopping at each bank of cages. He yanked on the doors of each one, as he'd done the day before. He wanted some of the food and water, but more—he wanted to free the unusual animals inside.

"I can't help you," he said. "I can't help myself." He made another circuit, tugging repeatedly on the cage with the horned rabbit. Then he slammed his heel against the floor and stormed to the door.

The elf kept his ear to the crack for several minutes, hearing nothing. He hadn't heard the trolls or the giant yesterday, either. They'd stopped their regular patrol the evening before that. It was that night that he'd felt the floor rumble and watched the animals panic. The rumbling went on for some time, like an earthquake. Then it stopped abruptly, no aftershocks like he'd heard accompanied quakes.

Ingrge thought he'd heard at least one of the trolls leave that evening, after everything had settled. Maybe a second one left shortly thereafter—he'd been dozing and wasn't certain. But he knew he'd heard nothing since. Twice he'd opened the door and looked out into the main room, seeing only an empty room with the big carpet pulled back to reveal a trapdoor.

Yesterday, he guessed it was in the evening, he crept out and looked down the hole in the floor. It didn't go very far. There were a few feet of spiral stairs and then a solid mass of dirt and rocks. He looked up the staircase that led to the higher levels of Quag Keep. He, Yevele, Milo, Naile, Wymarc, Gulth, and Deav Dyne had ventured there long months before. This time he knew that Yevele and Berthold had gone down. And he knew they wouldn't be coming back up—at least not this way.

So Ingrge returned to the menagerie room and waited, praying there'd been another way out of Quag Keep's basement and that they would be coming back for him. But there'd been no sound, save that of his feet sliding across the floor and opening and closing the door to the menagerie room.

"Gone," he told the horned rabbit. "Dead. Yevele and Berthold aren't going to come back. I'm kidding myself that they got out of there. But I'm going to get out of here. And maybe I'll return to Quag Keep. Just for you." He thought the animals had a spark of intelligence and just might understand him. The rabbit especially intently watched him. "I'm going to look for Ludlow Jade's caravan. Maybe I'll find it back in the city. I'll find Milo and Naile somewhere . . .

they leave quite the impression, and someone will have seen them. Maybe I'll talk them into coming back here and helping me break these cages. Get all of you out of here. Maybe all of us find a way to dig below and . . ." He let the thought hang for a moment. "We should find Yevele and Berthold and bury them."

He took a last look into each cage, a last listen at the door, then he went back into the main room and out the Quag Keep door. The sun was setting, brushing the stone of the Keep with an orange tint. Ingrge didn't bother hiding from the gargoyles. Their heads continued to turn, and he was certain one looked directly at him as he cut across the dead grass that separated Quag Keep from the woods.

He was deep in those woods by evening, looking up through breaks in the canopy at the riot of stars that winked overhead.

"Forty-two steps to the beach," he said. "I forgot how many more to the ocean. Bound to be an ocean around here somewhere. Maybe Milo and Naile and I can find it. Because I don't think we'll ever find our way back home."

In late fall the swamp was not as steamy as Gulth would have preferred. But it was warmer than the lands to the north, and there was no sign of any hated city. The air was different here, moist and filled with the scents the lizardman loved best—the wet loam beneath his clawed feet, flowers that grew on vines draped from the acacia trees, the plants themselves . . . some of which he steered Deav Dyne around, warning him they were dangerous. There was a faint cloying odor of something that had recently died and had started to rot, and the smell of dampness everywhere. With each step, the earth tried to pull at his feet, the vines caught around his ankles. It was as if the swamp was telling him to stay.

And that's what the lizardman intended to do.

He'd regained some of his color, and most of his scales were once again the shade of the ferns that grew in profusion along the bank of the river they paralleled. Deav Dyne walked behind Gulth, struggling through the undergrowth, but not complaining.

It had taken them more than three weeks to reach these lands. There had been other marshes farther north, but they were smaller and there'd been no sign of other lizardmen. Deav Dyne had asked lots of questions in some of the southern villages, and people there said Gulth's kind could be found here.

"I am feeling better, priest . . . Deav Dyne."

"You look much better, Gulth. And it does me well to know you will be all right."

The lizardman stopped, relishing the feel of mud that was seeping between his claws. "You did not have to come with me, but I was grateful for your company. Where will you go now?"

The priest tipped his face up, smiling to feel the warmth of the sun. "With you for just a little while longer. Until we find your people. Then I'll go back to the city."

"To find Yevele."

"And Milo and Naile and Wymarc. And maybe the four of us will find our way back home."

"And where is home for you, Deav Dyne?"

"Bremen."

"Where's that?"

"Germany."

"A long way from Toledo."

"A longer way from here." Deav Dyne gave a single nod. "I run a little hobby shop there, and I sell at the conventions in Hanover. I sell games, Gulth. Board games, war games, card games . . . role-playing games. And miniatures." He laughed, and Gulth joined him. "I sold miniatures. Right up until the day I got a special package in the mail containing the one that looks like I do here."

Gulth put a clawed hand on the priest's arm. "You could have picked up this figure instead." He pointed to himself.

"If we find a way home, Gulth, I can come back here and look for you. Get you home, too."

The lizardman shook his head. "I've forgotten the name of my aunt, the one who let us play the game in her house. Can't see her face. Can't remember the names of my friends who played the game with me. And I like this well enough, priest . . . Deav Dyne. I like this place just fine."

They walked deeper into the swamp, finding a footprint here and there that likely belonged to another lizardman.

Neither of them knew they were being followed, had been tracked by the bracelets still on their wrists. The man moved silently and at a constant pace, trying to close the distance. They weren't terribly far ahead now, he knew, as he saw their footprints in the mud and places where leaves had been pressed against the loam. A twig broke here, bark scraped there.

"Ah, Danny Boy, the pipes, the pipes are calling for you."

Fisk Lockwood hated the swamp with all of his being. It was warm and the insects were thick. It was difficult terrain to cross, not a single merchant trail cutting through the morass to make the going easier. But he promised Pobe he would slay the people who'd come unbidden to this realm. In all cases but slaying the bard Wymarc and the bard before that, he'd failed. His bandits and undead could not best the other-worlders. And deep in the bowels of Quag Keep he'd not been able to kill the warrior-woman and the little thief.

He'd not heard from Pobe in some time, but that didn't negate the promise he'd made to the ooze. Fisk assumed Pobe was angry with him, and he hoped that killing the priest and the lizardman might bring him a measure of acceptance.

They were so close, his targets, and so unsuspecting. He drew a long knife from the folds of his tunic. The lizardman first, Fisk decided, as Gulth was larger and would prove the bigger threat. The priest would fall easy after that.

"The Master will forgive me then," Fisk whispered. "I will—" His free hand went to his throat, which was constricted. The assassin tried to suck air into lungs that were instantly on fire. "The pipes, the pipes."

Fisk gasped and dropped the knife, ripped his tunic open, thinking the fabric too tight. Foam flecked at his lips, and the muscles of his face twitched. He dropped to his knees, then fell on his side, struggling and spotting a vine that had wrapped around one of his ankles. A moment more and his struggles ceased; his body was paralyzed.

Poison. Fisk knew poison, and he'd used something similar on the blade he slew Wymarc with.

Attached to the vine was a large red flower that looked to be growing on an exposed, knobby root. Splinters of bones were scattered around its stalk. The flower's petals opened wide, showing a maw ringed by tiny teeth. The vine pulled him closer.

Fisk hated the swamp.

One month to the day after leaving the city, Gulth was welcomed into a clan of lizardmen. They didn't know he'd only worn their skin for less than a year, and that he didn't really come from the city to the north like he told them. They didn't know that he really came from Toledo, Ohio, where he used to play a game around his aunt's table.

Deav Dyne returned to the city, weary but satisfied that he'd helped his scaly friend. He found no trace of his companions, and he learned that Ludlow Jade's caravan had disbanded. The priest searched for word of Yevele, Milo, Naile, Ingrge, and Wymarc for weeks before finally giving up. He hadn't a coin in his pocket, but he had faith he would make it in this world. The dice-shaped gems on the bracelet on his wrist were valuable. Certainly in this city he could find someone able to take it off.